GENTLEMEN DON'T LIKE AN INDEPENDENT WOMAN.

"I beg to differ. Gentlemen especially like an independent woman," Beau asserted firmly.

Jemima bristled at his smug tone. "Only in such case as they seek to prey upon her. Without visible support of family or husband, a woman becomes an object only of seduction for gentlemen."

"Do you read minds as well as characters?"

"One does not need divining arts when gentlemen provide daily example for all to see."

"What—forgive my lack of edification—should a gentleman seek of an independent woman?" he inquired with all politeness.

"Her society for conversation, ideas, a shared appreciation of like minds." Jemima paused as the music stopped. "A waltz."

"Then I have been very fortunate in my judgment of you tonight. We are waltzing and the conversation is stimulating." Beau paused as if in some thought. "May I call upon you tomorrow?"

"I don't think that would be prudent."

"When tonight were we prudent?"

BOOK YOUR PLACE ON OUR WEBSITE AND MAKE THE READING CONNECTION!

We've created a customized website just for our very special readers, where you can get the inside scoop on everything that's going on with Zebra, Pinnacle and Kensington books.

When you come online, you'll have the exciting opportunity to:

- View covers of upcoming books

- Read sample chapters

- Learn about our future publishing schedule (listed by publication month *and author*)

- Find out when your favorite authors will be visiting a city near you

- Search for and order backlist books from our online catalog

- Check out author bios and background information

- Send e-mail to your favorite authors

- Meet the Kensington staff online

- Join us in weekly chats with authors, readers and other guests

- Get writing guidelines

- AND MUCH MORE!

Visit our website at http://www.kensingtonbooks.com

NOTORIOUS

Laura Parker

ZEBRA BOOKS
KENSINGTON PUBLISHING CORP.
http://www.kensingtonbooks.com

Chapter One

The tale of the wedding-that-never-was took up the whole of the week's news in Chapel Hill. None of the inhabitants had actually witnessed the event for it had occurred in town, London to be precise. Yet there seemed not a soul in all the village who did not claim certain knowledge of it. The butcher boy had the news direct from Lady Chitwood's chambermaid, who heard it from Cook, who happened upon her mistress exclaiming over the matter to her husband at breakfast, the details of which had been sent to her in a post from her London cousin's wife. Sir Robert Neville had left Miss Hortense Thornslip of Chapel Hill waiting at the altar!

Unassuming as it might seem to passersby, Chapel Hill was not simply a sleepy hamlet of bucolic beauty and very little else. It was a veritable beehive in the production of one invariably sweet commodity for which nearly every inhabitant had an insatiable craving: gossip.

In the immutable way of country society, their exchanges revealed a decided partiality for the titled. In this instance,

Sir Robert. After all, 'twas no secret or shame that a younger son must marry for fortune. Therefore the blame for the debacle must be placed at the door of the jilted bride. Had Miss Thornslip been more prudent in advertising her generous dowry portion, then its promise might not have caused Sir Robert to pursue her nor bolt when it had been gambled away by her father, Squire Thornslip. Or so the reasoning went.

In all Chapel Hill there were but a few souls in sympathy with Miss Hortense. One of them was Miss Jemima MacKinnon of Haversham House. Clever and rich, owing to an inheritance from her Scots grandfather, Jemima was perfectly at ease in her spinsterhood and generally wore the title as lightly as morning does the dew. Just now, however, the news of Miss Thornslip's humiliation obscured her serene disposition as she hurried home with a quickened pace and a heart beating with affront for the dear maligned girl.

Unfortunately on this cold January afternoon, it was Miss Jemima whom Mrs. Hollingsworth, the physician's wife and an inveterate magpie, halted in the lane to spread her latest bit of scandal meat.

"Have you heard about our poor Miss Thornslip?" Mrs. Hollingsworth said in lament. She felt it was only good manners when cutting up another's character to make a show of pity. "They say she's shut herself away and none can persuade her to come out."

"Perhaps she finds a stout door the only respite from gossip," Jemima answered coolly.

Mrs. Hollingsworth blinked twice. As a rule, Miss MacKinnon was a pleasant enough if reserved young lady. Today, however, behind the oval lenses of her spectacles, the serious dark gaze of the mistress of Haversham House suggested that she did not care to be the recipient of gossip.

Yet the matron of six, a veteran of many skirmishes with resistant will, plowed on.

"Discretion is best, to be sure. The lack of it is a common failing I believe. In point of fact, I have it from a reliable source 'twas the *indiscrete* gambling habits of Miss Thornslip's own father that are to blame for the daughter's present misery."

Jemima smiled slightly. "How odd. I'd have thought it was the disgraceful behavior of her betrothed that caused her inconsolable state. Of course, sweet soul of charity that she is, Miss Hortense may have set in motion these disastrous events for the sole purpose of fortifying the countryside's talebearers and gossipmongers with a very tasty dish upon which to dine."

Before Mrs. Hollingsworth could gather breath, Jemima continued. "You must excuse me. I do not wish to be late for my Ladies Social hour." So saying, she continued on her way, her steps as quick as they were deliberate.

The older woman's expelled breath of surprise formed a chill mist. She was not clever. The subtleties of sarcasm and irony were lost on her. Yet when spoken to in a manner beyond her understanding, she became suspicious that she was being made fun of. On most occasions she was correct.

"If that is how you feel, well, I most certainly do not understand," she said a bit tardily, for her audience was now beyond hearing.

"That's what comes from educating a female," Mrs. Hollingsworth murmured to herself as she hurried toward her own home. The only accounting for such discourtesy must be the streak of Bluestocking in Miss Jemima. It was said she had formed a small circle of like-minded spinsters and twice a month they met for discussions of such unfeminine things as books and politics.

"Education coarsens a lady's mind," Mrs. Hollingsworth

said in explanation of the incident to her neighbor Mrs. Dodge the very moment she reached her gatepost.

"It goes against nature, all that reading and thinking," concurred Mrs. Dodge, who shared a love of gossip. "Too much freedom and twenty thousand a year, in her own keeping. I shouldn't wonder Sir Robert hadn't better bend his interests on Miss Jemima, for all she is become a spinster."

Mrs. Hollingsworth brightened as her memory stirred. "But of course! How remiss of me not to remember." She leaned toward her companion with a gleam in her eye to match the spite in her tone. "Have you forgotten? Miss Jemima was herself thrown over by a suitor when she was not more than seventeen. Quite shocking it was, at the time. Being as she is a lady, one did not quite know what to make of the rumor that . . ."

Chapter Two

Unaware of the new round of tongue-wagging she'd left in her wake, Jemima continued on her way home. By now her disposition had turned from sadness and compassion to outright cross!

How easy it was for the smug housewives of Chapel Hill to lob stones at defenseless maidens. No doubt it salved the envious hearts to pick over the remains of pretty Miss Thornslip's misfortune. Left at the altar! Could any humiliation be more public or complete?

To her surprise Jemima felt tears scald her eyes as she considered all the humiliations great and small that were being heaped on Miss Thornslip. Better than most, she understood the injuries being inflicted and those still to come. For once she had been condemned to the same fate.

There'd been no rescue from the shame. No one to challenge the spiteful tongues. Certainly no knight in shining armor to come to the defense of the reputation of a jilted bride.

"She will steep in her mortification until she turns bitter," Jemima murmured to the wind, "and becomes the very thing gossip would cast her as, a female unworthy of marriage."

At the end of the lane, Jemima paused in the shadow of a bare-limbed willow to remove her spectacles and dash a hand across her eyes to wipe away the damp proof of her anger. It was a curse to be born a female with a brain, to understand so completely the farce that was perpetuated upon females that the only fully respectable rank for a girl above the age of seventeen was that of "Mrs."

Her own reputation had just survived. The inheritance of a substantial fortune demanded an outward show of respect from all who knew her. That respect had not stilled rumors nor erased her desire to be forever burrowed away far from the hurly-burly of London after one disastrous Season. Retiring from any thought of a social life, she had turned her considerable intellectual faculties to study and become quite a scholar of social convention. All of which furthered her dissatisfaction with the duplicities of society and, in particular, given her a very jaundiced view of the devious ways of gentlemen.

Remounting her spectacles upon her nose, Jemima marched into her home, that thought still uppermost in her mind.

If the maid noticed the cross look on her mistress's face when she entered or the butler heard Miss Haversham whisper an oath more worthy of a coachman as he took her cloak and bonnet, they each kept their own counsel. Such occurrences were rare but not altogether singular. After all, the mistress would read the mail even when it plainly contained an announcement of imminent wedlock. Worse yet were the Sundays when marriage banns were read at church. On those occasions Haversham House bolted down the furniture and switched to the second-best china until the tempest of their mistress's distemper passed.

Half an hour later Jemima paused outside her bedroom

door to shake a wrinkle from her plain muslin gown. She did *not* glance at her image in the hall mirror. At six and twenty years, she was neither old nor ugly though her spectacles did make her seem bookish. In fact, she had once been termed quite fetching when she dressed her black hair and wore elegant gowns. These days she did not care for fashion or her looks. Both had betrayed her at a tender age and she had determined then never again to become ensnared in the lure of her own charms. With both her temper and her wits under control, she descended the stairs with a complacent smile to play the congenial hostess to her Ladies Club.

When tea and cakes had been served all round, Jemima graciously accepted her guests' exclamations of delight. There were the usual *oohs* and *aahs* caused by the unseasonable appearance of cucumber sandwiches, of which in all the neighborhood only Haversham House with its many greenhouses could boast. Slivers of plum pudding, the last of the holiday fare, made them giggle like schoolroom misses. That is until served tiny strawberries and clotted cream, a purchase from Fortnum and Mason, the London grocers. Pink with rapture, they rejoiced for five minutes together over the generosity of their hostess.

Jemima, firm of smile, refused to be drawn into the discussion. They were, to her mind, all too easily made to feel they should prostrate themselves in gratitude whenever shown the slightest deference. *As if they do not deserve to be,* she thought. Yet she refrained from chiding those who by virtue of their dependency upon the charity of others could not indulge fine thoughts about themselves.

One must make acquaintances among the flock into which one has been shepherded, she reminded herself. Her flock consisted of the three excessively respectable but poor spinsters in the village.

There was Miss Amelia Valentine, her cousin. Thin of blood and wan of disposition, she had recently been fired from her post as a governess, "Owing to the sudden onset of a nervous condition," she'd said. Jemima suspected there was more to that story for Amelia had failed to obtain the usual letter of recommendation from her former employer. Without it, she was all but unemployable. Calling it a favor, Jemima had offered Amelia a small cottage that had stood vacant on her property. For poverty, no matter how genteel, is a slow death.

Next to Amelia sat Miss Henrietta Smythe, the vicar's gregarious daughter whose chief contribution to the company was a mind as well educated as Jemima's. Twoscore and more, Henrietta could be counted on to provide what news of genuine importance there came to the vicar's door and to pronounce a tart-tongued opinion on each issue.

Years before, her suitor had gone away to fight in the American colonies and not returned. "My Tom preferred death in the colonial swamps to life with me. I think that sets the cap on my character," she once stated with a chuckle. Yet the rumor persisted that "her Tom" had succumbed not to an enemy's musket but to the smile of a colonialist lass. In any case, he was long lost to Henrietta.

Miss Ianthe Strickland made up the fourth of the party. The youngest of the group at just twenty, she most often kept her eyes on the carpet and had not an unkind word for anyone. The buttercup curls that occasionally escaped her old-fashioned bonnet and her slender hands, chapped by manual labor, hinted at the possibility that beneath her drab exterior lay a quite dazzling creature. One could not be certain because the poor girl lived all but hidden beneath the heavy thumb of her ailing mama. A meaner, more suspicious and spiteful creature than Mrs. Strickland nature could not have created.

"I can't think what spinsters should find to prattle about

so frequently,'' Henrietta admitted her mother saying when she begged favor to join Jemima's little gathering. "Better they should be about charitable works or assisting in a married relative's nursery. Mark my words, no good ever came of idle hands and minds.''

"She provides the example,'' Jemima had murmured to herself.

Confined to her bed by gout and dyspepsia, Mrs. Strickland still managed to acquire and dispense more gossip than anyone else in the village.

"Poor Miss Thornslip,'' Amelia opined after a short interval, touching upon the subject no one else had dared mention.

"If only we could do something to comfort her,'' echoed Ianthe.

"Yes. If only.'' Jemima sighed inwardly. In the beginning she'd had high hopes for her group as a motivator for social change—if not outright emancipation—for single ladies within their own tiny hamlet. So far, they had done little more than deplore the ills of the world and then go back to participating in them.

"I was much astonished to hear Squire Thornslip wagered his daughter's dowry in a gaming hell the night before the betrothal,'' Ianthe murmured into the silence.

Three heads swung abruptly toward her, causing Ianthe to blush strawberry pink.

"How do you know this?'' demanded Henrietta.

"Mama said . . .'' Ianthe's voice trailed off, but it was enough. Mrs. Strickland might be the worst proselytizer of gossip, but her main facts were seldom incorrect.

"Why have you not shared this with us before times?'' Henrietta demanded.

Ianthe wilted like a rose too long in the sunshine. "No one has asked my opinion before.''

"What else can you tell us?'' Jemima demanded.

"That Sir Robert has left London . . .''

"And?" three voices said in unison.

Realizing that more was expected of her, Ianthe only shrank into the squabs of the settee with a shake of her head.

"You're a veritable fountain of facts, today. Do not dry to a trickle at this point," Henrietta encouraged with a chuckle.

Ianthe bent her head so low that her companions found themselves staring at the crown of her worn bonnet. "Mama says Sir Robert left for Bath because it was he who won Squire Strickland's bet on the eve of the marriage."

"Ah!" Jemima shot to her feet, cup and saucer in hand. "Is it my fancy alone or does someone else see the deviousness revealed in this news?"

"What sort of deviousness?"

Amelia looked all at sea, but Henrietta smiled broadly. "Upon my soul, I do see a pattern. Perhaps Sir Robert no longer needed a bride once he had fleeced the father."

Indignation flooded Jemima. "Oh, but that is so like society to cast rumor in a guise to protect the true villain. Someone should unmask the rogue. Why not we?"

"We?" Amelia echoed all abashed. "Who would listen to us?"

"No one." Jemima sat down with a sigh. "We are invisible. Spinsters put upon the shelf to be used or disposed of as easily as a jar of jam."

"Oh, but it was a perfect thought, wasn't it?" Ianthe ventured when Jemima's harsh declaration had silenced the others. "To think our little party might seek to rectify a wrong. Quite like knights of old!"

"Oh, yes!" Indignation animated Henrietta's usually bland expression. "How I should like, just once, to serve an inconstant suitor his just desserts!"

The fervent light of hope flickering in the expressions of her companions emboldened Jemima. "What if a letter containing the damning facts were sent for publication to a London newspaper?"

"But who would sign it?" questioned Ianthe.

"No one." Jemima set her tea aside and began in earnest to set forth the plot that was hatching within her mind. "Daily we are privy to every sort of confidence. There is no harm in us knowing its foibles because society believes spinsters hold no position of importance. Yet we are positioned best to see the world as it really is. Who better to dissect truth from rumor and fashion it into a noose with which to hang the guilty?"

Amelia shuddered. "I do not think I approve of . . ."

"Fustian!" Henrietta answered. "We shall speak only the truth. Should the guilty be held to account for themselves, it will be by those whom they have done the harm."

"Will *we* not be held to account for disabusing gossip?" whispered Ianthe.

"There's scant chance of that." The avid gaze of Mrs. Hollingsworth was still fresh in Jemima's mind. "Even so, our efforts must remain secret."

"Secret? But everyone in the village knows us," answered Ianthe.

Henrietta nodded. "Our social hour is remarked upon by all."

"So then, no one will think to question our new true purpose."

"Oh my!" Amelia's hands flew up to cover her cheeks. "I don't think I can be party to . . . well, I shouldn't—no, I mustn't."

"Too late," Henrietta declared flatly. "We need a name. All secret societies have names."

"Let me just think . . . ah, yes!" Jemima's lips curved into a mischievous smile. "Henceforth we shall be known as the L-A-D-I-E-S Club."

"Why do you spell it?" Amelia's tone was querulous.

"Ah, that is the delicious part. Each letter shall stand

for a word that best describes our purpose: *L*adies *A*gainst *D*eceivers *I*nfesting *E*legant *S*ociety.''

And so it was done. Each of the ladies present swore a hastily worded oath to hold each of them to the secret.

''Revenge upon deceivers!'' Jemima finished in a ringing indictment of the masculine sex.

Chapter Three

When the others had made their good-byes, Jemima went up to her room where she composed a letter containing the facts of the Neville-Thornslip affaire, as she saw them. Sober reflection and quotations from classical and biblical sources annotated each fact. Yet when she was done, she could but pronounce her effort as little more than just the sort of tedious sermonizing she most deplored.

Certainly no gentleman of the *ton* would sit for a feminine homily on the rewards of the virtuous life. Rather they would despise and ridicule . . .

"Ridicule!" Spoken aloud, the word took instant root in her thoughts. When men set out to ruin one another, they most often chose ridicule as their method.

Not a sermon but *satire* was the answer.

The best satire by far was the work of caricaturists who by mere pen strokes captured perfectly the absurdities and hypocrisies of the day.

Abandoning her writing table she called for her maid to

help her find every *Gazette, Courier,* and *Morning Post*
within the walls of Haversham House. She scoured the pages
seeking puns and cartoons. She studied each one closely,
murmuring an occasional "aha" and "but, of course."

Finally she turned back to her desk and reached for quill
and ink. Where to begin? She lightly tapped the tip of the
feather upon her full lower lip as her thoughts raced to and
fro. Her sketch must not depict Sir Robert by name or no
paper would run it. It must give life to the lie and yet not
baldly reveal it.

Two candles gutted on the desk beside her as she sketched
and scratched and crumpled paper, seeking inspiration from
the black lines of her quill. It had been twelve years since
she had been acquitted an accomplished artist by the art
teacher her father had hired. But as she worked the method
of drawing line and shadow slowly came back to her.

Finally, when she sat awash in pages of discarded effort,
she sighed in weary satisfaction. The sketch was complete.

It depicted a gentleman with pound notes flying from his
pockets as he chased after the departing Bath Express coach.
Beneath his feet lay a trampled wedding bonnet. Behind
him stood an old ram shorn of his fleece with a startled look
on his face. At the very rear of the picture, the bride stood
in the open church door weeping.

Jemima smiled in satisfaction. The proportions might have
been more accurate, but the thoughts behind them could not
be more to the point. Only the deaf would lack rumor to fill
in the names.

As she turned to pick up the newspapers she had earlier
scattered, her gaze fell upon an altogether different sort of
sketch. It was political in nature, a representation, not lampoon. She reached for the spectacles she had abandoned in
her fatigue to be sure. Yes, that beautiful countenance and
silver white hair could belong to only one gentleman.

She touched the inky image with near reverence. Her

friends thought she disdained all men. That was not true. There was one gentleman for whom she held the greatest regard. His name was Lord Bellaire.

Though she could not boast a true association with him, she had never forgotten their introduction at Almacks. At seven and twenty years, he was already a favorite among the progressive Whig Party and that rarest of beings, an honest politician. To the lament of numerous mothers with eligible daughters, he was already spoken for, affianced to the single loveliest lady in a decade, the boast often went, the Incomparable Miss Fiona Aisling.

But that night owing perhaps to some rare alignment of the stars she, Jemima, white-faced with fright upon her first occasion within the walls of the revered hall, had caught his eye. He had, with all the room watching, walked the long distance from one side of the dance floor to the other and asked her aunt to introduce them that he might ask for a dance.

She had stood one dance with him. A simple quadrille, it did not require much in the way of conversation, but she remembered ever after every word he spoke. Even now she recalled the dance as the shining moment of her Season. The subsequent attentions of suitors of her own and then her engagement somehow became, in her mind, entangled in that meeting. She was certain she would not have had even one suitor had he not chosen to honor with his attention the painfully shy creature she had once been. His notice had set her on the sometimes-precarious path to matrimony. The difference was, Lord Bellaire had married his Incomparable while she . . .

Jemima shook her head to dislodge the snare of memory. She was long done with self-pity. And yet, to this day, Lord Bellaire was for her a veritable paragon of manly virtues. Sadly, it did not spare him tragedy. The loss of his wife to childbed fever was said to have marked him for life. No lady had again gained his favor. Rumor said it was because no one else could ever compare favorably to his Incomparable wife. Rather than blemish her memory with a lesser alliance, he was content to remain a bachelor. If only all men would aspire to his untarnished character.

Yet they did not. London teemed with gentlemen like Sir Robert. And it was the duty of the fearless to call him into account.

"What shall I call myself?" It had come to her as she toiled over her lampoon that she could not send in her cartoon anonymously. She must have a *nom de plume*, something clever and yet simple. Something . . .

She noticed again the ruined paper at her feet and began to smile. She would call herself Foolscap, after the document upon which she recorded her scorn. Christian name? It must be simple, strong, manly. Jonathan!

"Sir Jonathan Foolscap," she repeated under her breath. Who better than one of their own to hold up to public ridicule the desecrators of the very society of which they were a part? Now there was only the question of how to deliver Foolscap's drawing without having its contents rebound upon herself and her LADIES. Who could she trust with their secret? Who could be counted on to play the game yet never divulge her part in it?

"Of course! Julien!" Having pulled a leaf of stationery from her box, she began very deliberately to write the letter that would accompany her sketch.

"Dear Cousin Julien . . ."

Chapter Four

Unable to still his curiosity over the source of the violence being done inside, Richard Langley opened the door to the library at Cochraine House and stuck his head into the breach. A book, seeming to sprout wings as its covers spread apart during flight, flew past his left ear and smashed with a decided *thwack* on the far wall of the hallway behind him.

" 'Pon honor, Cousin! You nearly brained me. What cause all the thunder and rumble?"

Lord Bellaire stood at the far end of the parlor, a study in thunderous rage. "That calf-witted brother of mine!"

"*Ah.*" Slight of frame with a head of red-gold curls, Richard debated the merits of self-protection in a hasty retreat.

As a rule, his cousin Beauregard—the name a lamentable lapse of judgment on his parents' part—could be counted on as a cool head in any crisis. Cucumber, he'd been nicknamed in public school. Behind his back, of course. One did not mock this man. The few who dared address him as anything other than Lord Bellaire knew he preferred the truncated version of his Christian name: Beau. As for Beauregard? Well, it just wasn't spoken. Ever.

A bit of a wag and curious by temperament, Richard could not imagine the events that had led to the spectacle of Cousin Beau's present consternation. The temptation to learn what could put so powerful a self-command in full fury was too good to pass up. Besides, he had a boon to ask of the family patriarch. He shut the door and approached.

"What has Cousin Guy done to reduce you to mangling your precious books?"

Startled by the suggestion that he might be out of control, Lord Bellaire glanced in surprise at the text in his hand. As it was one of his favorites, Euclid's *Elements,* he set the leather-bound volume on a nearby table and gave it a brief pat, as if begging its pardon, before speaking.

"The young fool's been sent home to rusticate for the rest of the term!" The grim lines of temper gathered again, straining the corners of his eyes and fine mouth. "For consorting with a strumpet. What the devil do they teach at Cambridge these days?"

"Couldn't say," Richard answered calmly. "Oxford man, myself."

Beau scowled but did not respond to the jibe. "I suppose I should thank the gods that she is not with child."

"Well, then!" Richard, who could boast a thorough knowledge of schoolboy antics with lightskirts, was unalarmed by the news. "One might consider the peccadillo the price of Guy's higher education. You will pay her off, of course."

"*She* isn't the problem." Beau's face darkened. " 'Tis Guy. Fancies himself in love! Stood where you are now and dared mention marriage!"

"Oh, *lord!*" The mention of marriage was all it took for

Richard to decide that he required the fortification of a glass of the Madeira that sat idle by Bellaire's book.

Richard offered to pour his host a glass but got a sharp motion that indicated no. As he helped himself, he said, "What do you plan to do about it—er, him?"

"You needn't concern yourself. The family name will not be dragged through scandal mud for as long as I am its head."

"Bother! I had rather hoped for a right to-do." Richard winked. "A gentleman must have his diversions, you know."

"Look elsewhere."

Richard downed half the contents of his glass. To judge by his older brother's harsh expression, Cousin Guy was in for a bad time. Perhaps intercession by a relative might save the boy's bacon.

"You will be lenient with the lad? You were young once. At least, one may suppose so." Richard chuckled. "Though, damme, if I can remember you as anything but a graybeard."

"It suits me." Beauregard *Eve*-lyn—the parental lapse was quite extensive—Somerset, the present viscount of Bellaire, smiled for the first time.

Beau had begun to gray before entering Harrow. By the time he entered Cambridge, he was as silver as men trice his age. Now at the age of six-and-thirty, his full head of silver hair gleamed with pewter highlights. All who knew him, the ladies in particular, were quick to remark on how the premature silvering did not make him appear elderly. Instead, it emphasized his glacial blue eyes and robust physique. It also gave him an authority beyond his years in the House of Lords, as did his extensive knowledge of the ancient and modern world. But it was his singular status that made him a much sought-after dinner guest in highest society. Nature may abhor a vacuum, but that is nothing to the abomination with which society ladies regard an unattached monied title.

At the moment, his advantages were weighing heavily on Beau's mind for his younger brother blamed his birthright as the eldest as the source of his older brother's obstinate nature.

"Everyone fears you. But that can't last forever. One day soon you shall meet your match. And when you are defeated, I shall stand and applaud the loudest," Guy had said before he stormed out of his brother's presence. Of all the impertinent—.

"Impertinent? I?"

Beau blinked and realized that he must have spoke his last thought aloud for his redheaded cousin was smiling at him with more interest than he desired. "Enough of my troubles, Richard. What brings you out before two of the clock?"

Richard thought quickly. Curiosity was a poor answer, and he quickly surmised the main reason, the need of a loan, must needs wait upon a more opportune occasion. Seeking a diversion, his roving eye spied the morning's newspaper, and he snatched it up. "You have seen it, I take it. The work of the newest caricaturist?"

Beau frowned. "I make it a rule to ignore political satirists."

"This one's different. He skewers the *ton*. Styles himself by the pen stroke Foolscap." Richard turned the pages until he found what he was looking for and held it up. "Here now."

Beau inspected the cartoon from a distance, as though he thought he might catch something fatal if he came too near. "I do not see the fascination."

"The decamping groom, 'tis Lord Neville's younger son!" He smacked the cartoon with his hand for emphasis. "Have you not heard the full accounting? The night before his leg-shackling, Robert Neville sat down to a friendly game with his soon-to-be father-in-law, a country squire by the name of Thornslip.''

"What novelty in that?"

" 'Odds truth, you would spike a man's wheel just to see him tumble." Richard caught himself and continued. " 'Tis said Neville persuaded Thornslip, down to his last farthing, to wager his daughter's dowry with the observation that what matter if he lose the blunt to his new son then or on the morrow?''

"I take it the Neville offspring won the wager."

"Precisely. And before the break of dawn he decamped for Bath, leaving the bride without a groom. Lord Neville fobbed off his son's actions by saying Thornslip's to blame. That no one could reasonably expect his son to marry beneath him when there was no dowry. After all someone else at table might as easily have won the sum."

"And this tale of folly and ruin forms the bulk of your day's entertainment?"

"Always were a high stickler," Richard murmured in exasperation. A man who held himself above the lure of gossip seemed a sour sort of person. Still, he knew on what side his bread might most easily be buttered. " 'Twas badly done, I give you that. But what an old fool Thornslip is."

Beau lowered his gaze to the cartoon. In all other aspects the sketch was an ordinary rendering, no more than proficient. Yet the illustrator had caught the injury and humiliation in the girl's face with unexpected compassion and skill. It moved him and that disturbed him.

He reached out and casually turned the paper over. "Perhaps Foolscap's poison pen will be sufficient to defend the bride's honor."

" 'Pond honor, I doubt it." Richard shrugged. "Once connected with scandal, a lady's reputation inevitably suffers a permanent decline."

Reminded of the cup of scandal broth brewing beneath

his own roof, Beau's expression hardened. "I blame the poets for filling the young with senseless romantic notions."

"You are thinking of Guy," Richard suggested in the hope he might hear more details of his younger cousin's peccadillo.

"Guy does not read well enough to be influenced by poets or philosophers. That is why Cambridge is displeased with him. I hesitate to say it, but he is a *born* dreamer."

"So then allow him to make his own mistakes. I wager in five years' time he will be wedded to a lady who will make for him an unobjectionable bride and he will be as miserable as any other husband."

"One would think you had experience on your side," Beau said coolly.

Richard coughed discretely to cover the beginnings of laughter and poured a second cup of Madeira. "Forgive me if I do not share your view that marrying young is the duty of every gentleman. Not all of us have had the good fortune to find and wed our ideal."

Beau's expression stiffened, but he did not answer the remark.

After a moment Richard said, "Sorry, old fellow. Didn't mean to dredge up misfortune. Your lady wife was all that any of her sex could aspire to."

"Just so," Beau answered softly, but there was nothing of fond remembrance in his expression. Rather it seemed to Richard a bleak countenance, devoid of all hope and promise of future joy.

"As for Guy, he will muddle through, I dare swear. Many a misalliance passes for marriage *à la mode* these days."

Beau's brows lowered over his bright gaze. "That is precisely what I do *not* wish for my brother. An ill-alliance would ruin him."

"Just so." Annoyed with himself to have stirred his cousin's ire, Richard decided retreat was in order. "Well, then, I shall be on the tottle. Join me for dinner at Waiter's."

Beau shook his head. "I've parliamentary matters that must take precedence."

"Have a king to topple, what?"

Beau frowned. "Another time, Cousin."

Thus dismissed, Richard set down his glass and made a mocking curtsey to his cousin. "Adieu, Cousin." When he had turned his back he added, "Marplot!"

No doubt Lord Bellaire was the only Whig in the country who was not entirely thrilled that a bill calling for a Regency government had been recently introduced into Parliament. Out of power since the death of Charles Fox four years before, the Whigs took delight in the prospect of a Regency regime, for it would mean the fall of the Tory government. True, the debate had gone on for too long while more pressing matters like the war with France lay idle. Barring a financial miracle, there would soon be no money in the Treasury to continue it. Then too, there were other more politically ambiguous goals in jeopardy. Since the Regency debate began, the king was showing a remarkable ability to recover his senses for longer periods. If it continued, his convalescence would throw the mechanism of government into confusion yet again.

Since these thoughts occupied his mind, a man with little political interest or ambition, Richard would have been amazed to learn that none of this occupied his cousin's thoughts at the moment.

No, Lord Bellaire was deep in his own reflection of thoughts both personal and private.

"Guy must not follow in my footsteps!" Beau said to no one but himself.

Their father was right in warning his eldest son against the false hopes of the newly fashionable Romantic Ideal that had sprung into rage along with other radical ideas like those

that led to the French Revolution. He had added that if
his elder son and heir did not learn to curb his too vivid
imagination, it would well bring him to ruin.

A bitter chuckle escaped Beau. Not quite ruin, perhaps,
but to expectations he had since learned no mortal lady could
live up to. That failure had cost him his belief in love.

Poor Fiona. It wasn't her fault that her red-gold curls,
soft sighs and sly glances had made him think of the clever
resourceful women in the *Decameron,* who through love
and loyalty and sometime stealth won the love of even
reluctant suitors. Alas, Fiona turned out to be something
less and something worse, a bore.

She did not love him or even understand him. As if confid-
ing in a sister, she innocently informed him on their wedding
night that she had accepted his advances only in obedience
to her father. But that now that the wedding was over, she
was quite looking forward to the many social advantages
that marriage would now give her. She laid out before him
her hopes for entertaining and socializing that, if pursued,
would leave him little time for reading, not to mention true
politics. Then, to his shock, she insisted that they sleep apart,
"Until I have steeled myself for the inevitable."

"The inevitable!" Beau murmured and reached for the
Madeira his cousin had abandoned. As a rule he did not
drink before two o'clock. Today it seemed an arbitrary rule
with no foundation in need.

In the end, he could not blame Fiona for his disappointment in her. She had never advertised herself to be other
than she was, a pretty frivolous girl of little understanding
and less inclination to puzzle over anything more taxing
than the daily on-dits her like-minded friends found so delicious. She was all and nothing but what society had made
her. Had he recognized this at once, instead of pressing on
her all the ardor of his youthful infatuation, they might now
be as other couples, quiet companions who shared the simple

joy of each other's company at decently spaced-out intervals. The perfect life.

"Perfect life!" He tossed down a large swallow of Madeira. Within the first month he lost all illusions of a perfect love, shackled to a pretty but vacant creature who neither shared nor cared to the most important things in his life: his work, his curiosity of the world, nor his sexual appetite.

There was no one in whom he could confide his misery. Friends thought him the luckiest of men who called the Incomparable of the Season his own. Even now he could not bring himself to accept the insidious disloyal feeling that crept over him in quiet reflective moments like this. *Relief.* Relief that she was no longer a part of his life.

Within eighteen months of their marriage Fiona lay dead and he had only their child, a girl, to remember her by.

Beau frowned. He missed Emma but could not in good conscience say he had done wrong by sending his infant daughter to live with his sister-in-law, Susanna. What could he, a man without a wife, do with a newborn? Better that Susanna take and rear her with her brood. That Emma preferred after eight years to remain with Susanna's family rather than come to London to live with him was a testament to his right thinking. The pangs of regret that he felt each time he thought of her, so silent and resolute as she waved good-bye to him at the end of the winter holiday, was the enduring cost of the burden of his mistake.

So then, he had made a mistake and paid the price, but not with the whole of his life. Therefore he could not in good conscience show to the world any emotion but sorrow at his loss. He owed Fiona's memory that much.

He picked up the gazette. Foolscap had it aright. Ladies were no less noble or virtuous than the expectations of the gentlemen in their lives caused them to be. Perhaps Neville's younger son had been mercenary in his courtship of the gentry's daughter. Squire Strickland had been no less so, dangling his child under the nose of Sir Robert in hopes his wealth could gain her a title and lift his grandchildren into the nobility. Miss Strickland was merely a pawn in the affairs of men, as Fiona had been.

Annoyed to have found his thoughts once again circling the same drain, Beau crumpled the paper and heaved it into the fireplace. He knew what was wrong with him. It wasn't only Guy's imbroglio. A dalliance was what he needed, free of the constraints of maudlin protestations of everlasting devotion.

A smile of lust filled his handsome face. He kept no mistress, but he did know an obliging lady or two, married of course and strictly in command of her favors. Perhaps the lady he had in mind could direct him to a like-minded lady to whom he could introduce Guy. Nothing cooled a lad's ardor for one woman like the ministrations of another. He would see to it that his brother did not make the mistake he had. Love was a game for those who did not expect certainty or constancy or duration.

When he had refilled his glass, he lifted it and said, "To Foolscap!"

Chapter Five

With the arrival of May, Jemima spent every spare moment in her garden. Dressed in an old gown with her hair tucked beneath a straw bonnet, she busied herself staking rosebushes while honeybees hummed in her ears. Beyond her manicured garden, butterflies skimmed the buttercups and dropworth blooms that speckled the long green grasses of the untended areas. Farther on, the fields lay thick with oilseed rape. In a few weeks, their bright yellow flowers would garland the meadows backed by silver birches that had begun leafing out.

Yet the glory of the unusually warm day could not long distract her from thoughts of what had become in five short months, a positive obsession. The composition of clever verse and illustrated caricature that embodied the wit of Jonathan Foolscap had overtaken every other facet of her life.

Uppermost in her mind this morning was what to do about her alter ego. To her astonishment, Foolscap had become a *cause célèbre* among the *ton.* Gossip direct from London trumpeted the news that the fellow who tossed barbs at their profligate ways and poked holes in the fabric of their elite society delighted the *ton.* Moreover, they had embraced him as one of their own. Who but an insider would have access to their secrets and worst proclivities, or so went the thinking.

According to sources who happily passed on the gossip from person to person like a spring rash, substantial bets were being laid in gentlemen's clubs as well as gaming houses as to the identity of the wag. Some claimed certain knowledge of the identity of the elusive fellow but vowed they were sworn to secrecy over the matter. Every gentleman with a pretense to skill with a pen or sketch pad was suddenly receiving invitations to dine from intrepid society hostesses who hoped to unmask the provocateur before the third remove.

Cousin Julien assured her in one terse missive that the LADIES were in no danger of discovery. Jemima wasn't as certain. The mania for Foolscap had even reached the lazy still water of Chapel Hill. No less that Henrietta's own father, a quiet academic, felt moved to speak of Foolscap from the vaulted position of his pulpit.

"... Not since the heyday of Hogarth and Rowlandson has anyone dared turn so sharp and unflinching a glance on the malpractices of society ... a righteous pen to strike down the pretensions of society that would hold itself up as our betters."

Jemima still blushed to think of it. Today she had only her roses to match her rosy hue. Notoriety was not her purpose. More important than notoriety was the success their efforts achieved. From the first volley, Foolscap had scored a victory over vice!

The week following Foolscap's debut in the London *Gazette,* Ianthe made a rare detour from the strict schedule of her mama's making to pass by Jemima's door with the news. "The tide has turned in Miss Thornslip's favor. Mama says Cook told her she overheard the butcher telling Mrs. Hollingsworth that he always suspected there was something havey-cavey about Sir Robert." She leaned forward as if afraid the walls would hear her. "He left debts in town whenever he came calling upon Miss Thornslip. Debts Squire Thornslip felt obliged to pay. Mother says it's very bad form to so impose, before the nuptials."

Pleased by this report, Jemima had gone direct to Henrietta who confirmed and expanded on the matter.

"Only today Papa received a letter from his patroness, Lady Ashford, who resides in Bath during the winter months. She informed him that the very day after Foolscap's cartoon was published Sir Robert was caught cheating at cards. He has fled to the Continent to avoid being called out."

"Can it be so easy to rout a rogue?" Jemima had asked in bemusement at their success.

"If 'tis so," Henrietta had answered, "I should like to serve a few other Ganders the scandal sauce they first ladled on innocent Geese."

And so the LADIES proceeded to discover who next deserved a sharp jab with the point of Foolscap's quill. By correspondence with family and friends, along with an inordinate interest in the heretofore shunned practice of rumormongering, the LADIES soon learned a good deal about the many ways that foolish or unwary young women could tumble into scandal.

There was the case of the lady's maid dismissed as a thief and bound over by her employer for trial and deportation. On the errand of bringing the Good Word to a sinner, Henrietta's private word with the gaoled maid brought to light another story altogether. The supposed stolen bauble had gone no farther than the shop of a moneylender in a nearby town— left there against the loan of sufficient money with which to pay "my lady's gaming debts."

The very next Foolscap cartoon depicted a titled family at dinner. In the first panel each member was surreptitiously stealing from his or her companion. One lifted a coin, another a watch fob, a third a piece of jewelry. The lady of the household was secretly passing a purloined piece into the hand of a waiting footman. The second panel showed a footman in disguise sneaking into a shop above which hung a sign with three globes, the mark of a moneylender. The caption read, ''True Charity Begins at Home.''

The sketch saved the maid from deportation for the family did not want to pursue the matter by an open trial. Henrietta found the girl another position in a far away county, yet not so far away as Australia.

The most recent success was the case of the lost locket. Lost on an evening at Vauxhall Gardens, a heartless cockscomb had found and added the love locket to his watch fob, claiming it to be a favor won from a newly married lady after an evening of passionate embraces. It took only a cartoon of a Fop in full sartorial regalia on hands and knees under a bush to extract a locket and the caption, ''How Low Will a Fellow Go?'' to put into question the rogue's supposed triumph over virtue. Within a sennight, the abashed gentleman had returned the locket and retired to the country.

''So then why do I feel this dissatisfaction?'' Jemima murmured to herself.

The answer, which she knew only too well, added little credit to her character. She missed being present at the hour of reckoning. Secondhand reports of success gave limited satisfaction, like hearing of a delicious meal one could not eat. Just once she should like the gratification of witnessing the results of her ladies club's hard work.

''Impossible, of course.'' She paused to polish away the pollen that clung to her spectacles. She would never return to London and Chapel Hill was at a sufficient remove that not even a new pair of spectacles would grant her the view she desired.

That regret uppermost in her mind, she turned back toward her house and noticed a young woman coming up the drive. Though it was warm enough, the stranger wore a long heavy cloak and a bonnet more fit for winter winds than the fresh breeze of spring. Jemima saw her reach for the latch but instead of lifting it, the girl leaned against the gatepost as if too weary to go on.

"Do you require assistance?" Jemima called, but the girl did not respond. Instead, she collapsed in a heap before the wrought-iron gates.

Jemima hurried to her side. When she had managed to turn the senseless girl over, she saw her lids flutters and then a sea blue gaze looked up at her out of a face that was at once doll-like in its beauty and yet a bit too vivid for convention.

"Oh, miss, do not leave me here!" Her voice trailed off as her lids threatened to close. "I swear I mean no harm! Swear it." So saying she swooned fully.

"She's with child?" Jemima stood in her salon with the village doctor, Dr. Wesley, who had been sent for. The unconscious girl had been brought inside by the footman and groom and now lay in a small room off the kitchen of her home.

"I hesitate to discuss the subject with a lady. But as you are alone . . ." The pause gave full credit to the fact that Jemima lived without the protection of a male relation or even the companionship of a married female. "Allowances will be made for your generosity. You took in a stranger before your realized the full consequence of her situation. 'Tis fortunate you were not exposed to disease." Again his pause spoke volumes of rebuke. "I can only recommend that she be sent quickly on her way."

"I see no need for haste," Jemima answered calmly. "As you say, her condition is not contagious."

He blinked. "You cannot be thinking of taking the creature in?"

"Creature? Dear Dr. Wesley, you make her seem a demon. She was not discovered dancing naked with a witch's coven at Midsummer's Eve."

"You may make light of the situation, Miss Jemima. Others will not."

The doctor who had eased the young woman's passage into the world stared at her. She was once quite pretty. Now in her severe gown minus any attempt at style or elegance and her black hair scraped back so tight it must hurt to blink behind her thick unattractive spectacles, she had, alas, become long before her time a frump of an old maid. But none of that would matter once the gossip began. "You can be certain the villagers will not accept the presence of an unmarried woman in her condition in Chapel Hill."

Jemima made an impatient sound. "For all we know, she may have a husband . . . somewhere."

Dr. Wesley tucked in his chin to gaze at her over the top of his pince-nez. "A woman with a husband does not turn up on a stranger's doorstep without a word to say for herself."

Annoyance at the doctor rippled through Jemima for having pointed out the very weakness in her defense. "Would she say nothing for herself?"

"Not even a name."

"Perhaps she is afraid of revealing herself for fear of something or someone."

"More likely she fears being found out to be what she is."

Wanting to negate his opinion of the stranger she answered, "She speaks well. By the quality look of her bonnet and gown, she lived until recently quite comfortably."

"Well she might." The doctor pulled at his chin, as if pondering what he would say next. "Yet ladies of quality do not advertise their misfortunes."

"You believe her to be a lightskirt," Jemima said forthrightly.

Her reckless use of the word to denote mistresses, which even married ladies pretended to be in ignorance of, did not improve the doctor's opinion of Miss MacKinnon's judgment. "You are the most accomplished lady of my acquaintance, Miss Jemima. But accomplishments and learning will not spare you the hard opinion of your neighbors should you to attempt to install this person under your roof."

"I've endured hard opinion before," Jemima answered in challenge.

The doctor harrumphed. "I think only of your well-being, Miss Jemima, only that."

Seeing how uncomfortable she had made him, Jemima unbent. "I do care for *your* good opinion, Doctor Wesley."

The doctor cast a speculative eye on her. "I hope you do and will do nothing further to bring condemnation upon your own head. You may depend on it; her secret is her shame."

Jemima took this nugget of information to nuncheon with her and chewed over its implications as thoroughly as she did her cold plate of thin slices of lamb, beets and onions. By the time she set her napkin aside, she thought she had answers for the doctor's accusations. The girl may have worked closely with members of the aristocracy, possibly the assistant of a modiste or in a haberdashery. That would explain her clothing as cast-offs of her profession.

Of course there were other possibilities. She might be a lady's companion . . . or an actress. The doctor was not the only one to notice her unreliable aristocratic tone. She might have been instructed in how to speak as an aristocrat for the stage. Not that the reasoning did the girl any credit. Actresses were considered no better than—.

Jemima's own thoughts stopped her. No better than she should be! Damnation of the girl and her virtue in one phrase.

Yet a poor girl, even a very pretty one, would not have had many opportunities to better herself and still she had tried. Had she not, by bettering her speech and manner, sought to rise from whatever poverty she had surely come? What if poverty had forced her to a situation of her undoing? Her condition pointed out only too accurately who was to blame. A man, of course, more likely, a gentleman.

The more Jemima thought about it, the more convinced she became that the girl was a victim of her own naïveté and recklessness. Foolish, lacking proper moral education, she would have no one to protect her. London gentlemen would see her only as an opportunity for vice. The girl may have tumbled into sin, but she clearly did not go into that ditch alone. It was the duty of the LADIES—no, her duty— to learn the name of the fellow who had accompanied her fall. He would need bear some share in the responsibility for her.

"Don't bestir yourself over the likes of me, my lady." The girl shook her head against the pillow, her blond sausage curls springing back from the crunching. "I ain't—am not worth—. I cannot. I—I—I —." Her effort at speech ended on a hiccup of nerves.

"You must conserve your strength in your . . . your condition." Jemima had come prepared to hear a sordid tale of debauchery, but she wasn't a tartar. The instant she again saw the girl's pretty face, her stern feelings dissolved. She turned to the maid who had accompanied her. "Bring the girl tea and broth with a teaspoon of sherry."

"Two."

Jemima turned to find the girl again looking up at her with wide eyes so blue she instantly thought of the pansies in her morning room. "I am partial to sherry," she whispered and pinkened. "If your ladyship pleases."

Jemima nodded. "Very well. I suppose a little sherry, for medicinal purposes won't be amiss. Bring a small glass and the decanter, Mary."

"Yes, ma'am." Jemima's maid frowned but went to do as she was bid.

"Now then, we will begin with your name."

"Prudence. My-my friends call me Pru."

"Very nice. Now, Pru, please tell me how you have come to be in your present situation."

"Oh I couldn't, madam." The girl turned her head away as if in shame, but Jemima sensed that with very little encouragement she would say more.

"You may call me Miss Jemima. I am unmarried."

Sure enough, Pru turn back toward her. "You seem the kindest of beings, Miss Jemima. But you show me too much interest. Being an unmarried lady, you would not wish to hear my poor tale."

Jemima told herself it was the way the girl spoke the words *my poor tale* and not the word *unmarried* that tweaked an acerbic streak in her that might have served her in good stead as head mistress of a nunnery. "I understand enough. One may suppose by your reluctance to speak of it that there is no patriarch to your proposed dynasty." The girl's brows lifted in confusion at the loftily worded speech. "You have no husband."

Pru's thick golden lashes swept down over her lovely eyes. "I was to have . . . until . . . ." Two crystal tears escaped the flaxen thicket. "Oh, do not ask me to speak of him!"

"So then, you were seduced?"

"Forced, my lad—Miss Jemima."

''By the man you thought would marry you?''

Pru's eyes opened. ''Oh no! My gentleman was the loveliest kindest gentleman you ever could meet. So respectful, he was. No. He would have married me. Said as much.'' Her rosebud mouth formed a knot of anger. ''It was the other, his brother.''

''His brother?'' Jemima could not keep the surprise out of her voice.

''He wanted to ruin us—me. To make his brother abandon me. He—oh, my lady—he succeeded!''

The fit of weeping into which the girl fell faintly repelled Jemima. She was a firm believer in the principle that women should not use the weaker wiles of their sex to gain sympathy. But the girl's wretched sounds of despair quite tested her will to remain apart from her emotions in the matter. Grateful rescue came in the form of the maid bearing a tray.

''There, now, here's your sherry.'' Jemima poured a short portion herself. ''Drink a little of it and then you must tell me everything.''

Pru's weeping ended as abruptly as it had begun, the appearance of sherry making an effective dam to the flow, Jemima noted.

When the girl had drunk a few sips and Jemima had sent the curious maid on her way, she repeated her request to hear the whole of the girl's story.

''Oh my lady, I couldn't—''

''Rubbish! You can and you will if you mean to remain beneath my roof.''

''*Arrh* right!'' Pru answered crossly. ''His lordship's name is Bellaire.''

Jemima wondered if she had suddenly gone deaf. No, she had heard the words. Perhaps it was the girl's slip into untutored English that confused her. It was not possible she could have heard the girl aright. Not in the least possible.

Pru was looking up at her hostess with a puzzled expression. "Did ye not hear me, milady?"

"That cannot be true! It is not possible." Jemima said the words very quickly for she was not so shocked that she did not realize something must be said.

Pru cocked her head to one side, a calculated look of interest now in her blue eyes. "Why? Do you know him, Miss Jemima?"

"No. Only by reputation." Jemima had to pause to draw breath into lungs flattened by the blow. Bellaire? Surely there were other members of the family. It could not be Beauregard Bellaire. "But it is the sort of reputation that makes such a claim as yours seem impossible."

"Not so impossible." Pru smiled up at her with a glowing look and the smile said more than the glance. "Even the finest of gents gets a bit frisky now and then, taken by their natures. If you take my meaning."

Jemima thought she did, all too well. But then to consider the possibility that the only true gentleman of her slim acquaintance would be capable of the bold and calculated cruelty was enough to make her reject it again.

She recalled then doctor's opinion that Pru was an interloper, an actress, and a commoner. " I suppose you would not be familiar with the nobility. Perhaps you confused one gentleman with another or were tricked by a roué into believing . . ."

"His hair is silver, shiny as me mum's pewter teapot." Pru's expression was a self-satisfied smirk. "I'd know him in the dark!"

"While it is true he is silver-haired," Jemima said slowly while frantically seeking an alternate explanation. "Yet you may have seen—"

"If you don't believe me, Miss Jemima, you have only to wait until the babe is born. See if he don't bear the exact same coloring."

Jemima did not bother to deny this impossibility. "Yet you said you were in love with another."

"I was—am. His younger brother." Pru's expression crumbled, her pretty face dissolving into tears once more. "It's so awful, m'lady. He sent me a letter. Told me to come round at a certain time to see him. Only it was the earl waiting. He—he took me upstairs. He—he has ways, milady. And then he took me love and used it against me!"

Jemima took a step back, repelled by the implied violence of the violation.

"I could do naught. Me shame was so great I could not defend meself." Tears rolled off her chin, spotting her covers like raindrops. "Only that weren't the worst o' it. Comes a rap on his lordship's door and he goes to answer it."

Pru looked up at Jemima through wet lashes, her pretense at noble tones abandoned. "He weren't wearin' a stitch, Miss Jemima. His lordship flings open the door and ain't it me own love standing there. Oh, Miss! The ugly look what come over my lovely boy when he spied me in his brother's bed! The accusation! If he'd took and murdered me where I lay I could only 'a been more'n glad."

Her words should have been effective. They sounded sincere enough, forced out by extreme emotion rather than by design. But Jemima could not quite believe it. "Why? Why would Lord Bellaire do that?"

Pru gave her a jaded look. "I ain't a lady, Miss Jemima. I ain't the sort toffs marry. But me Guy would have. He told me so. Gave me this!" Pru reached under her pillow and withdrew something and held it out to Jemima. It was a signet ring. The crest unmistakable! Refutation seemed impossible.

The space it took Jemima to reach for the ring, her idol cracked, crumbled and fell. In the ruins took root immediately a rage more powerful than reason.

* * *

"I don't know, Miss Jemima." Henrietta had listened to Jemima's much-edited version of the Pru's story, minus the name of the gentlemen involved, over tea. "You may never be certain with that sort."

"You mean because she is a commoner." Jemima's shock had boiled down to a thick ugly molasses of vehemence overnight. "I would expect more compassion from a vicar's daughter."

"You don't know her sort. I do." Henrietta smiled tolerantly. "I have always admired your courage and willingness to believe in the best in people. Surely our sex is too often downtrodden by the very virtuous standards to which we are all held. But there are other sorts of women, Jemima. Women as rapacious and deceptive as their libertine brothers."

"You think she lies?"

"I don't know as I mean that." Henrietta sighed. "But perhaps the gentleman sought by his actions, however misguided, to discredit a false woman."

"When is rape an acceptable means to any end?"

Henrietta shook her head. "I cannot say. Yet I believe in this instance we need more experienced counsel. Allow me to take the matter to my father—"

"No!" Caught between revulsion and shame, Jemima had the strangest desire to protect the very man she had come in the space of twelve hours to despise most in the world. "No, we must answer for this ourselves. There is the child to be considered. It must be done right by, provided for. To that end the LADIES will take the matter in hand."

"We? You mean Foolscap." Henrietta sighed. "I am not sure, but this is beyond his reach. The matter, as you say, is not public knowledge. The girl, being who she is, will not make a sympathetic victim. As for the babe. God forgive me but a by-blow is born every minute in London slums and there's none to think much of it. Foolscap relies on public opinion to work his revenge. I don't see how it can be managed in this instance.''

Jemima lifted her chin. ''Then we shall have to find another means.''

Henrietta gazed at her friend a long time before saying, ''You have often mentioned Lord Bellaire as your ideal in gentlemen. Are you certain you wish to destroy a gentleman on the word of a—a stranger?''

Jemima stiffened. ''I will do no harm. If he is destroyed, it will be by his own action.''

''Accusation,'' Henrietta amended. ''You have no proof.''

''Then I shall have to get it.''

Chapter Six

"Julien, you came!"

Julien St. Ives glanced at Jemima, one raven black brow sketched high upon his forehead. "You sent for me in a manner I rather thought required instant response." He swirled his many-caped Garrick coat from his shoulders with perfected flair and landed it in the outstretched arms of the maid without even a glance in her direction. "Am I correct?"

"You are." Jemima smiled.

"Then send for coffee and brandy, and we shall hash out your dilemma in a trice."

She took his arm as he neared her. "Did I draw you from some pleasing vice, Julien?"

"But of course. The chorus at the Savoy was in need of a satyr for its Midsummer night revels."

" 'Tis but May."

He smiled a satyr's smile. "Practice makes perfect, Puss."

Refusing to be drawn in by his suggestive tone, Jemima turned him toward the drawing room.

Her cousin was half again her age, leaning hard upon forty. Neither a streak of silver nor a sliver of paunch betrayed that fact. His was not a handsome face, yet women seldom noticed. The combination of deeply arched black brows above hooded eyes, so piercing one suspected he saw more than other mortals, and a mobile mouth equally at ease expressing contempt or passion made him both a daunting and dashing figure. A brief stint in his youth as a hussar had marked a lightning-strike scar on his left cheek. That wicked wound advertised the truth of his character, that he was a bold dangerous gentleman, in both love and war. Which was all more the remarkable when one considered that no lady had ever managed to lure him to the altar.

She never quite believed the shocking tales Julien sometimes told her of the debaucheries in which he freely admitted indulging. Perhaps that is because she had been half in love with him since her swaddling days. For reasons neither of them understood, or ever questioned, he was the closest thing she had to a confidant and she the closest thing he had to a friend. And it all began after her disastrous London Season.

Humiliated to have been jilted in so public a manner, she had returned home and shut herself up in her room. Within a sennight, Julien had arrived without invitation and, finding her locked in, summarily breached her door by use of an axe. He then proceeded to cajole and hector her out of her blue devils with the most shocking suggestions. She had only to say the word and he would call out her errant groom and skewer him in a duel. Or better yet, he would accost the fool in a public street and beat the coward within an inch of his life. Most shockingly, he would hire a poxed whore to infect him. At least she should give him leave to ferret out the wastrel's every dirty secret and publish a broadsheet of the miscreant's misdeeds.

It was this last thought that stayed with her weeks after he had drawn laughter from her and hastened back to his own debauchery since he could not convince her to return with him to London.

Jemima frowned as she stepped over the threshold of the warm room. Nothing had ever induced her to think of returning to London, until now. And to do it, she would need Julien's help. For he alone knew the identity of Foolscap.

"What is it? Has Jonathan been discovered? Are you to be run out of the village on a rail?"

"Nothing quite so dramatic." Jemima folded her hands together in what she hoped was a demur fashion. After having considered over their meal how much she should tell Julien of her scheme, she thought it best to say as little as possible, in case she discovered she could not go through with it.

"I have need of introduction into the London Season."

Jonathan reared back in his chair. "You don't say? What has it been, eight years that I have teased and hectored to persuade this event? And only now you are intent upon a return?" He leaned forward quickly and placed a hand quite shockingly upon her knee. "Who is he, Puss?"

"It's not a *he* precisely—"

"But in the main 'tis always a man," he finished with a dollop of humor in his voice.

"It is a Foolscap errand I wish to run. To do it, I must go to London."

"When have Foolscap's sketches failed to turn the tide in your favor?"

"It is not enough. An anonymous humiliation will not serve in this instance. It must be done in public, in a moment when the villain will least expect it. The humiliation must be as complete a ruination as it . . ."

"Yes? But you lose steam in the very syllable in which I become interested. Who was ruined? Not you, surely?"

"No, of course not."

Julien leaned back in his chair, mild amusement tugging

at his mouth. "Of course not, she says. As if a dalliance with a charming rogue isn't exactly what she needs most."

Jemima's mouth primed. "You will not draw me out on this matter. I have said all I intend to. Will you help me?"

She saw him yawn and reach for his pocket watch and knew she had blundered. Julien loved nothing so much as devilment. He would not help her if she played the prim maid. "I need lessons in how to become notorious."

"A pity." He let his black gaze slide down her from brow to waist. "One's hearing begins to wane with the passing years."

He was daring her to repeat herself. She did, though it took almost more breath than she had left. "I wish to seduce someone. A lord."

Julien took his time in inspecting his timepiece before he dropped it back into its pocket. Yet when he looked up, the light in his gaze told her she had reengaged his attention. "Say again, dearest Cousin?"

With Julian's gaze upon her, Jemima found she could not. She lowered her lashes. "You heard correctly." She lifted her head. "Will you help me, Julien?"

"Puss, you do not know what you suggest. Your reputation—"

"I have no reputation."

"So say you." His voice was curiously mild, but the speculation in his gaze was vivid. "It is one thing to be falsely accused. No matter how wild or vile the rumor, you may comfort yourself with the truth, that you are innocent. But to deliberately cast away your honor, what then will you use to soothe your conscience if your scheme should come amiss?"

"That I lost it in a good and worthy cause."

Julien sighed. "There speaks the last of the innocent martyrs."

"So then you will not help me." Jemima's sigh was a

twin companion of her cousin's. "I suppose it was too much to ask of a relation. I must find someone else."

"I did not say no." Julien began to toy with the large black pearl clutched in the talons of a falcon that formed his stickpin. It was a tip of the hat to his family crest, which bore upon it the same such bird. "Better me than another roué. For, 'tis true, you are dearer to me than any other human who strides this earth. But I will exact a payment for my services."

"When have you not?" Jemima was not fond of paying her cousin's haberdashery bills but as she was a genteel lady of means and he was a minor aristocrat with pockets often to let, they found a mutual benefit in their collusion. "What it is this time, fifty pounds, a hundred?"

"Nothing so base as pounds and shillings, Puss. I require only your obedience."

"My obedience. Why?"

"Because you will not tell me who the fellow is. I must be certain that I have the reins in hand should it be you are about to come to real harm."

"I intend no harm to myself, I assure you."

"So then you intend to harm another."

Jemima bristled in annoyance at his quizzing. "I wish to expose a villain who does not deserve the distinction of a gentleman."

"If you will not tell me his name, at least tell me his crime."

Jemima braced herself for the telling. "He seduced and abandoned a young woman."

"And?"

"Is that not sufficient?"

"Surely you are not expecting me to disclaim the practice out of hand."

Jemima blushed. "This was more than seduction. It was a humiliation, done explicitly to ruin the girl's chance for marriage to another. Now she is with child and he has threatened to have her whipped from the door."

"She appealed to her seducer, you say, and not her lover?"

"The lover turned her out when he learned of the other man."

"He seems a fickle sort. If he truly loved her, why did he not act in her defense?"

"You ask a great number of questions, Julien."

"You seek to embroil me in your plot. I should like to know if it will be at rapier tip I must defend your honor."

"I believe the girl."

"Women deceive as much as men. Do not make that face to me. I am in a position to know things I hope you never learn."

"Perhaps there are some few women—" Julien's snort of derision made her want to rap his knuckles. "Some few unnatural creatures who would trade their bodies for coin. But when love leads the cause—"

"Men and women are equals as fools. It is a lesson you should learn."

"Woman are defenseless—"

"Sometimes—"

"Always. They are at the mercy of the men in their lives: fathers, brothers, lovers—"

"Cousins," Julien stuck in sweetly.

Jemima lifted her chin. "Women are the first to be thought ill of by the men who would deceive them and the first to be deceived. If you had but heard her. Seen how heartsick—"

"When a sorrowful tune is played upon the heartstrings, you may certain it is the purse strings that the player truly wishes to pluck. Did she not ask you for shelter, money?"

"When a lady's heart—"

"You truly believe she stumbled in at your door, finding it by chance the most moneyed door in all Chapel Hill?"

"You will see the worst in everyone."

"You are too naive by half. Is it coincidence that you should be convinced by her theatrics to take up the very battle she claims to be abandoning?" Julien yawned and sat back, crossing his legs. "This is a trap, Jemima. One set for you."

"You have been a villain too long."

"You might think on that when you ask me to aid you." He smiled at her surprised expression. "Come, Puss. I will not abandon you, as I see you are determined. At the very least, I will wager you that you learn your lesson by the summer's end."

"I will take your wager for I do not intend for my heart to enter into the matter."

"Then I will certainty lay claim to your purse strings. I will wager you one thousand pounds that by Michaelmas you will have learned that woman can be as devious in love as in revenge."

"One thou—"

"—sand pounds," Julien finished for her in unabashed amusement. "Do you care to have your theory thoroughly exercised and learn an expensive lesson most girls have knowledge of while still in swaddling?"

"You are a very wicked man. But I shall take your wager if only to prove to you my opinion of the inherent honesty of women."

He smiled then and all the angels in heaven must have looked away not to be tempted by it. "You would be notorious? That I provide. In your dress, in your manner, in your every breath, if you agree to do and act as I say, without question."

"In my dress?" Doubt had crept into her thoughts.

"Most particularly, your dress." He reached out and whipped her spectacles from her face before she could prevent it, and then folded them and tucked them into his pocket. "You know nothing of fashion and less of the art of seduction. You must allow me to lead you in both."

"And by following your lead in this manner, you are certain I will succeed?" The hauteur in her voice could not stop the blood from rushing into her cheeks, and she knew by his faint laugh that she had given herself away. "Very well."

"Now again, about this gentleman you wish to—"

"Vanquish," Jemima inserted before he could think of another way to embarrass her.

"An interesting choice of word, Puss. You propose to render helpless your enemy, to have him surrender utterly to you?"

"I—I propose only to ruin him." Prevarication was not her strong suit.

He tilted his head to one side, watching her. "There is no surer way for a woman to lead a man into disaster than for her to make him love her."

The thought of Beau Bellaire making love to her sent a sudden uncomfortable warmth spreading through Jemima, as though she sat too close to the hearth. "I doubt seduction is my suit, Julien."

"But this is delicious!" He sat forward suddenly, inspired by his own thoughts. "Between my wit and your yet-to-be-discovered charms, we shall raise a fever in the London Season the likes of which it has seldom felt. Have we a bargain, Puss?"

"It would seem an unholy bargain," Jemima answered primly, but she could not keep the beginnings of a smile under strict control.

His smile deepened into something much more dangerous. "All heaven would have no part in it."

"Nevertheless"—Jemima offered him her hand—"The bargain is struck."

Chapter Seven

"This was a mistake. A mistake."

It wasn't the first time Jemima had spoken those words since coming to London. But it was the first time she was completely assured of their accuracy. The carriage that carried her through the London streets seemed like nothing so much as a tumbrel rolling through the streets of Paris, taking her to her execution. As daunting as must have been the sight of the guillotine, her destination finally came into view—the London Opera House.

"I cannot stand it a moment longer!" she said between teeth she kept clenched to stop their chattering. The carriage ride had dislodged more than a few hairpins and all of her courage. "Take me home!"

"I suppose this is your idea of feminine wiles." Julien's bored tone cut across her nerves like a diamond dragged over glass. "Allow me to adjust your thinking. Nothing so off-puts a gentleman as a lady repeatedly denying her wish to be in his company."

Jemima turned a shockingly pale face to her companion. "I cannot do this, Julien."

"Certainly you can. You sit in a carriage as well as if it were an everyday occurrence. Nothing more is required at the moment."

"You know very well what I mean. I do not wish to attend the opera."

"Do you not care for Mozart? Neither do I. But I suspect the *Fleidermaus* will be our quarry's preferred entertainment for the evening. If I am wrong, you must tell me."

"No, you are not wrong." Julien had not been able to coax from her the name of her quarry, only that he was a single gentleman of great stature in society. Lord Bellaire was known to be a patron the arts, opera in particular. It was simply luck that Julien had suggested it as their first outing. But what if Bellaire was not there?

Since reaching London there had been multiple fittings for her new wardrobe, a quite entertaining and enjoyable experience once she got over her shock at the revealing sheerness of fashionable frocks. The lady's maid Julien had found her was a wonder with a comb and hairpins. Tonight she looked like someone other than her drab self. She felt elegant, almost a beauty. But none of that mattered now that she realized that when half of an hour had passed, she might be facing Lord Bellaire without the slightest assurety that she could pull off her design. Make him fall in love with her? A Bluestocking, over-the-hill, spinster. Was she mad?

"Give that to me." Julien extracted from Jemima's too-tight grip the ivory fan he had earlier presented to her. "Your nerves put at risk the work of a Chinese artist of extraordinary skill who spent a good many hours carving this item into its present flirtatious shape."

"I am sorry." Jemima's voice sounded hollow.

"And give me those." He took her glasses, pocketed them, and sat back. "You shan't be needing them tonight."

"But without them, I shan't recognize a soul. Oh dear!"

Julien glanced at her, his brows lifting in irony. "You shall not be sick. I forbid it. Jemima, if you retch, I will slap you."

Jemima swallowed convulsively twice and then made a little tight shake of denial with her head.

"Good, then perhaps you will tell me what you intend to do tonight? Providing your libertine is present."

"I—I . . ." Jemima ran out of steam. She hadn't imagined a first move in her game of ruin. She had only thought about the coup de grâce.

"If you require a spark for your tinder"—a smile of amusement flickered in Julien's face—"be certain to address him by his first name."

"What?"

"He is accustomed to deference, Puss. If you wish to make an impression, you will speak to him in public as his equal, better yet, his mistress."

Jemima again felt the stifling heat of queasiness rising. "What if I am snubbed? What if he should rebuff me in public? How then shall I ever recover?"

Exasperated by her mewling tones, Julien abandoned his indolent posture and sat forward, taking her by the shoulders in a surprisingly firm grip. "You are female. Have you no understanding of the power your sex wields? Banish the mouse and become the feline, Puss. You need be armed only with your best smile, bright eyes, and an audacity to match your fervor for revenge. You do remember your desire for revenge, don't you?"

"Yes." But it was a feeble yes and Jemima knew it.

She saw Julien's dark eyes glitter in the darkness, and then, to her shock, he leaned forward and kissed her on the lips. It was quick and hard but held in it enough of a sting of intimacy to shock.

"Julien!" Jemima backed away, her heart pounding, her ears stinging, and her face burning with embarrassment.

Julien released her with a smile that had very little to do with his thoughts. Jemima's eyes were now dark with a fury that both pleased and disturbed him. And because he was the sort to notice the small things, he detected in her glance a hint of an emotion he had not been certain his country-mouse cousin was capable of feeling. That thought lit a spark of interest in his jaded soul.

"If you but glance in your fellow's direction with such a look upon your face, you may be certain you will inflame more than his interest."

Appalled by the suggestion, Jemima shook her head. "I do not understand the nature of men."

Julien's elliptical smile flattened. "We are simple creatures. Never suspect there is more behind a man's eyes than what he is viewing. Believe me, you are vision enough for any man. Unless you believe it's breeches he fancies. Now that would require a very different approach, one with which I am only passingly familiar."

Though she did not understand his comment, Jemima smiled. "You are a thoroughgoing rogue. In truth, I have never understood why you ever offered your friendship to me, the grayest mouse of a cousin."

"Neither do I," Julien drawled and looked out the window as the carriage came to a halt. "Or perhaps, I've always seen possibilities of that mouse roaring to life one day and I wish to be present when you do so."

Jemima stared at him, head cocked to one side. "I believe you mean that."

He gave her a strange look, one that made her heart seem to stutter and then the enigmatic glance was gone. He gave her a little shove toward the door that the footman was attempting to open. "We are arrived, Puss."

When she moved forward to exit, he leaned in to whisper

in her ear, "Don't tempt me again, Cousin. We are different enough creatures for disaster to be the only consequence of a dalliance between us." He laughed at the alarmed expression she turned to him. "Had you not thought of that? Kissing cousins! We could legally wed." He gave a slight shiver. "Odious word, marriage. Now come along and taunt someone far more likely to respond acceptably to your charms."

As a rule, Beau enjoyed the opera. Tonight he felt betrayed by the very gaiety of the people surrounding him. It was May. London teemed with the Season in high gear as the last of country society swept into town for the annual Presentations at St. James, to be followed by the yearly exhibition at the Royal Academy of Art, and in quick succession the Derby and then Ascot. The laughter and voices of the opera patrons reflected the tide of rising expectations among the populace. In March the war news began to improve. Wellington routed the French Armee du Portugal. Only this week news had arrived that French Marshall Soult was defeated. The Regency, in place since February, seemed to have possibilities of being effective, even if the Regent had suddenly remembered he was royalty and that the Tories, rather than his friends the Whigs, might best keep him in power.

Beau's mouth firmed in irritation at the reminder of the reason he attended the opera late and alone. Recent word had gotten about that the Regent would soon be giving a ball at Carlton House to celebrate his new status. The prince's tastes were notoriously extravagant. The ball would cost a fortune the nation could ill-afford. Yet it might prove a stroke of political suavity. Even the Regent's detractors were beginning to talk less of finances and more about who would be invited and who wouldn't for the prince let it be known that he would follow the Hanoverian court custom. All members of Parliament would be invited, but women lower in rank than the daughter of an earl would be excluded.

This announcement was the cause of a tiff this very evening that had left him annoyed with the entire feminine sex. Lady Sarah Godsford, a discrete widow with whom he had spent several pleasant evenings in recent weeks, wanted him to ask that an exception be made so that she might accompany him to the Regent's ball.

"I've chosen my gown!" she'd cried in complaint. "Three seamstresses have worked night and day for a week."

Beau murmured a curse. That bit of logic was supposed to make him apply every cent of political currency at his command to do her bidding! His refusal to even consider her plea had cost him her companionship—in and out of bed—for the evening and perhaps ever after.

"That is why I keep no mistress, pay few bills, and seldom make references to a future time," he'd told Lord Dougherty whom he met on the way into the opera house and offered to share his box.

Lord Dougherty, as rotund as an apple in his evening coat of scarlet, was all sympathy. "Deserved the set-down. A woman, if she believes she has the upper hand, will torment the patience of a saint." He then proceeded at nauseating length to recall several such imbroglios in which he claimed he was the offended party.

To distract himself from his verbose partner, Beau lifted his lorgnette and began to search the house for familiar faces, a common practice among audiences. Unlike them, he was more interested in ferreting out unsuspected alliances among his political friends and foes than in observing whom dallied licentiously with whom. Nothing revealed a political scheme at work so much as a opera box full of convivial adversaries.

Tonight nothing of enlightenment passed before his view. He noted and, briefly lowering his quizzing glass, nodded

at the occasional acquaintance, but the second act was fully
underway and so conversation among the spectators was
loud enough to drown out all but the soprano.

Finally, he caught sight of Julien St. Ives in the box across
from him. The world of the *ton* was small, for all its habitués
considered it to be the center of the universe. Few strangers
went long unnamed or their places in it unassigned. He did
not know St. Ives personally but disliked on principle the
man's well-known reputation for dalliance and libertine habits. A cad was the proper term for his kind. Yet he'd been
recently informed that St. Ives might be of use to him in
matters most delicate. It was said if a mistress had the ear
of a member of the court, St. Ives had the ear of the mistress.
The idea of manipulating bedroom matters for political gain
put a bitter taste in Beau's mouth. He would find another
means.

Beau's gaze swept quickly on past St. Ives but moved no
farther than the lady who sat beside him before his interest
was again arrested.

This face was new to him and his perusal lingered in
curiosity. She wore a gown of sea green laced scandalously
low across her bosom but he had seen pretty provocative
dresses before. She wore her black hair dressed with Grecian
bands of pearls terminating in a tassel by one ear. This
fashion, too, he had seen before. The stage lights rendered
her profile softly yet sharply, like a Gainsborough painting
where personality was to be found in the precise curve of
cheek and determined jut of chin. Novel enough, this particular composition of line and shadow, yet her prettiness, too,
was nothing singular.

He was about to pass on when she suddenly turned his
way. The collision of their gazes sent a unpleasant shock
through his gut. Never before had he seen quite such a
murderous expression on a beautiful face.

Her brows were arched in challenge and her mouth firmed

in irritation. The direct look in her gaze had nothing to do
with coquetry. It was filled with dislike—no, more like spite.
The scorn in her expression was a like blow. Before he
could absorb it completely, she lifted her fan and snapped
it open, eclipsing her face from his sight.

He jerked his lorgnette away from his eyes, all but reeling
with the effect of her snub. Quite unexpectedly, he felt the
damnable nuisance of a flush creeping up from under his
collar and reached up to adjust his neckcloth. Who the devil
was this lady to stare at him—a stranger—with such disdain?

"Is he here?" Having heard her *snap* open his expensive
fan, Julien leaned forward in his seat, his gaze surveying
the boxes opposite. "Is he watching?'

"What—?" Jemima could hardly find voice for her heaving feelings. The chandeliers and mirrored walls made a
colorful blur of candlelight and beautiful gowns from which,
without the aid of her spectacles for her nearsighted gaze,
she thought she would never extract a single face. But she
was wrong. It was impossible to miss the signature sheen
of the silver-haired man in the box directly across from hers.
Bellaire was here! And more, he was staring directly at her!
As if he knew! "Yes, he is."

"Perfect. Then let us entertain him."

Julien reached out and brushed the back of his hand against
Jemima's cheek. Startled, she jerked away, but he merely
trailed his thumb over her lips before letting his hand fall
away from her face onto her bare shoulder.

"Why did you do that?" she asked in a tight voice of
annoyance.

He leaned in close, caught her nearest hand in his free
one and murmured, "It is not enough to attract a nibble.
One must set the hook." He shifted his chair closer until
his knee touched hers.

"*Ju*-lien," she whispered furiously as she shifted away.

Satisfied to have brought a quick blush into her too-pale face, Julien leaned back and away from her. "Now he will wonder at the nature of our bond."

Jemima wasn't at all certain she wanted Lord Bellaire or anyone else to wonder at their bond, particularly now when at the heart of it lay Jonathan Foolscap. But she was not so green that she did not understand that that was not the sort of bond Julien had in mind. She had asked to be made notorious. She was beginning to understand how it was to be accomplished.

The next hour passed in interminable singing and shouting of the performers and the occasional requisite applause of an audience much more interested in the opera remaining as background to their own pursuits.

Twice Jemima looked across the hall to find Lord Bellaire's gaze on her. To be precise, she felt it. Each time it seemed as if he were physically reaching out and touching her. Each time the effect was the same: The hair lifted on her neck and the tingling of her skin made her shiver.

After the second such reaction, she kept her gaze on the stage though the effort to focus made her eyes tear and her head begin to ache. Better, she thought gloomily, than to match gazes with a man who turned her insides to jelly.

Lord! But she had not learned a thing in the intervening nine years. She had only to glimpse him in the dark and all the foolish impulsive feelings of a green girl frightened ghost white by the trepidation of Almacks came back to her. Worse, she was besotted all over again by his attention.

He had been so easy to spy among the glittering throng. The candlelight gathered, shaped, and then reshaped gleams and shadows in his silver hair with his every movement. He looked still so strong and handsome. She wasn't accustomed to handsome men. Julien didn't count because she had grown to love him as a cousin long before she understood his fascination for women. Once Lord Bellaire had been her first and only standard for gentlemanly conduct. Now she knew him to be a sham.

That disillusionment soured her stomach. She rose abruptly. "I feel unwell."

Julien shot her a glance that said "coward," but he rose readily from his chair. "We've accomplished enough for one evening. Where would you care to sup?"

Food was the very last thing on Jemima's mind, but a fortifying glass of wine seemed a good idea.

Unfortunately they could not escape the third act crush. It was the custom of the *haute ton* to arrive at the end of the first act and then beat a hasty retreat at the beginning of the third that they might avoid the very crush they created by all arriving and leaving at the same time.

They were standing in line for their carriage when a portly stranger approached with a leering glance that took in Jemima's entire being. "St. Ives, old fellow!"

St. Ives raised a brow in inquiry at being so baldly addressed and then smiled a smile that Jemima recognized as malice. "Dougherty. I've been expecting you." He glanced at Jemima. "Puss, this is Lord Dougherty. We were speaking of him before. Lamb was the subject, I believe."

"Charmed, I'm sure," Dougherty said and smiled a little too warmly at her bosom. "Will you not introduce us, St. Ives?"

"No, I don't think I will," Julien answered with a spiteful glance. "Do make the marquis a curtsy, Puss. We would not miss the opportunity to give him a better view of your—charms."

Furious that Julien had precisely pointed out her discomfort with the large gentleman's perusal of her bosom, Jemima could not make herself smile though she extended her hand to Dougherty. "My lord."

"Your servant," Dougherty returned, reddening a bit as

her cool voice reached his ears. Yet as he bent over her hand, she noticed his gaze delved greedily into the shadow of her cleavage as though it had fingers attached.

But Jemima suddenly had other concerns. As Dougherty bent over her hand, he revealed Bellaire who stood a little way behind him.

Their gazes met before she could avoid it. Bellaire said nothing, merely stood at a distance that could not be mistaken for friendly.

Jemima held herself still, not daring to draw breath, aware only of his penetrating gaze on her. She felt violated by that insolent stare. She had not meant to draw his attention just yet. But it seemed as if he had been seeking her out, all too aware of her half-formed plot. Did anyone in the press of people notice how he stared at her? Of course they must. The din that passed for conversation in the lobby would not obscure the attention of those whose main intention in attending a public performance was to collect fodder for the morning's gossip. But she could not tear her gaze away as long as he watched her. After a moment, he looked away.

It was all she could do not to collapse when freed from the hauteur in his intense gaze. She slipped her hand free of Dougherty's moist grip and stepped back. In another second she suspected he would have drooled on her. Steeling herself against the urge to shiver in distaste, she looked up at her companion. "I am ready to leave, Julien."

"Would you fly away so soon?" The pudgy lord looked as disappointed as a boy told that there was no more pudding.

"I am feeling the chill," she said with a deliberate glance in Bellaire's direction.

"I don't doubt." The sphinx-like Lord Bellaire had stepped in closer. Impaling her with his gaze, he continued. "Your gown would fit easily into a gentleman's pocket."

The contempt in his tone was enough to send a sensible person fleeing. Instead she remembered who he was and what he had done and how much pain and sorrow he had caused the innocent young woman who cowered in shame even now in her house far from London. "I assure you, that is all about me that would fit a gentleman easily."

The moment the words were out, Jemima knew she had said something so shocking that there was no recovery. The glittering gaze of Dougherty and the jerk of surprise in Bellaire were not needed to confirm it

"Julien," she said a little desperately and took her cousin's arm.

"Gentlemen." Julien smiled a satyr's smile as he bowed his adieu. "Come, Puss, we've others to entertain. The night is young."

With as much dignity as she could muster before the cluster of shocked and titillated male expressions ringing her, Jemima turned, lifted the hem of her diaphanous gown in two fingers of her right hand and walked away with head high.

This must be how Marie Antoinette felt, Jemima thought as her measured steps carried her away all too slowly from the carriage wreck of her hopes. She was undone, thoroughly disgraced before the man she thought she might humble. She would now bury herself in Chapel Hill and never, ever allow herself to again think of this night. To have made such a complete fool of herself! To have thrown away her dignity without regard for how she might fail! She should feel the need to stretch herself on the carpet and weep for shame!

"Bravo, Puss. You've caught your fish on the first cast of your lure."

"What?" Jemima's distracted thoughts came together on the note of alarm that she had been found out.

"Tell me I am wrong. You have met and bested your quarry tonight."

Jemima bit her lip. So much for her hopes that Julien

would not learn about Bellaire until the moment of revelation to the rest of the world. "You have found me out."

"Well done. Though you might have spared yourself the worry that it would be difficult. A nicely grilled lamb chop strung about your neck was all that was required to draw him in."

"I beg your pardon?"

"Dougherty." Julien smiled. "You have whetted his appetite and may be certain you shall soon hear from him."

"Oh." Julien thought it was the portly gentleman not Bellaire she sought to ensnare.

"You give me too much credit." Jemima could not keep the relief out of her tone. Julien had not guessed! Her secret, for the moment, was safe!

The shock of it all loomed so great in her mind that all at once she felt the inexplicable urge to laugh. That the trill that escaped her lips sounded more like mirth than hysteria could be credited only to the acoustics of the room.

"Damme!" cried Dougherty in admiration as St. Ives led his lady away. "If she hasn't just set me up for the hunt."

"I should watch myself there," Beau cautioned slowly. "Know her, do you?"

"No." Beau paused as her laughter floated back to him. "But she has St. Ives as her protector."

"More the better, dear boy. Her association with St. Ives is likely to have taught her a few tricks even you and I do not know. And I've never heard it said that St. Ives was the jealous sort. Rather he tires so quickly of the same dish that the novelty for his ladies never has time to wane."

Beau did not answer this. He was watching the lady and St. Ives depart. From his observation of the way the gentleman's arm hovered about her shoulders, he doubted St. Ives would easily give her up. In fact, the fascination seemed this once to be more on his side than hers. He was certain he detected, however faintly, dissatisfaction on the lady's part to be so closely guarded.

"I wonder that *she* may not first tire of him."

Dougherty frowned. "You were a bit harsh. Not at all your style."

"No. Definitely not my style." He was the courtliest of gentlemen, and yet he had just spoken to her, a stranger, with a contempt he would not have addressed to a bawd in the street.

It must be that he had found grounding for his anger with her insolent behavior in the theater. But Beau knew at once that that was not true. From the moment he spied her in her box, he was struck through by the raw and urgent desire to bed her!

The violence of his reaction surprised him, even now. The overwhelming urge to rut seldom plagued him. His appetites were easily surfeited. Yet in all their time together, Sarah Godsford had never produced in him the carnal appetite St. Ives's lady had with a single glance. Even now he felt the inexplicable yearning to chase after her, to snatch her up, and carry her away to a place where he could learn in private the mystery that she presented.

For a few long moments he was lost in reflection of the erotic power she had held over him. Despite her shiny mane of black hair and lushly curving figure, she didn't have the look of a doxy, much less the sound of one. She was a lady, he'd wager everything in his pocket on that. And yet, her provocation seemed to have a specific purpose. She had set out deliberately to provoke him! The stirring in his breeches did not wholly account for his certainty of that fact. But it did add spice to his curiosity to discover if he was right. To do that meant he must see this temptress again.

He thought of Salome and her seven devilish veils, though

the temptress of this night appeared to have left three, perhaps four, at home.

"Where to now?" Dougherty asked when they reached
the street.

"Home," Beau pronounced and climbed into his carriage
without a backward glance at his companion. He had matters
to arrange before morning, matters that would now certainly
include Julien St. Ives.

Chapter Eight

By the time he had consumed his second cup of coffee and stood in relative peace as his man arranged his cravat, Lord Bellaire had attained equilibrium concerning the matters of the night before. Never before in his life had he insulted a lady. There must be a reason, a good logical reason that would ease his conscience. He'd found the wee hours a poor choice for wrestling with social triviality. Now in the light of a bright clear morning he saw that the events had been greatly exaggerated in his mind. Once overset by the peevish behavior of one lady, he had been spoiling for any excuse to exercise his temper on another. The sight of St. Ives's ladyfriend had merely provided him with grounding for his disordered feelings.

Yes, now that he had had time to give the matter the reasonable attention of his formidable mental faculties, he would see his error. Even be amused by the workings of a mind, even one as strong as his, in the grip of sexual frustration. No excuses were needed to explain his very natural response to the prospect of a pleasant evening thwarted. No, he did not blame himself—who would? It was nature taking its course in a manner that, to be sure, showed him to no great advantage but certainly did not label him a cad. The very thought of such a possibility made him wince.

"Sorry, my lord," the valet said, looking aghast as his employer winced in apparent distress.

"Nothing you've done. Carry on." Beau lifted his chin to give his man a better angle to finish his work.

No, he did not blame himself for even an instant of the night before. The matter was best discarded as an aberration of his nature.

"All done, sir."

Beau turned to appraise himself in the small looking glass that hung above his porcelain washbasin. Satisfied that he had achieved the newly fashionable waterfall effect, he smiled. It was not the sort of style he would wear to the House of Lords, but it would do very nicely for a tour of the annual exhibition at the Royal Academy of Art.

He was expected as were all officials of taste and culture to make an appearance there to view the new works of those artists fortunate enough to be supported by the academy. That he very often found the offerings stilted and indistinguishable enough to have been done by any of the group represented did not seem to bother most. Not that he was an expert on art. But he suspected more than a few of those refused by the academy had something more interesting to offer.

His mood improved directly when a footman brought him a small package that had just been delivered by messenger from a Bond Street haberdashery. He didn't recall having made a purchase. When he had unwrapped it, he understood why. Inside the tissue lay a pair of gloves of very fine leather. They were dress gloves, the kind a gentleman night wear to a formal dinner . . . or a ball at Carlton House.

''Sarah,'' he murmured with a smile when he saw the strongly scented card contained the single letter *S*. This was her form of apology. And well done! No, he had nothing to chastise himself with on this very fine spring morning. He descended the steps of his Mayfair home and entered his carriage with a smile of absolute smugness.

He was rolling along the street before he thought again of St. Ives's lady. To be precise, he recalled the lush swell of her cleavage in her gown. He was not a connoisseur of women, interested in comparing and contrasting their individual features, rating one against the other. But in this case he had been aware of her from the moment he laid eyes on her. Later, when he could see for himself the sheen of her black hair and the direct gaze of her light eyes, lust took control of his head. Quite extraordinary when he thought of it. Pretty young ladies weren't his style. He did not care for the high-strung nor those who accepted admiration as their due and measured one gentleman's attentions against another's in order to improve her advantages. He suspected St. Ives's woman was the worst sort of coquette, constantly seeking admiration. She was the sort whom men dealt with plainly. If she complained it must be for show.

Of course his memory would toss up for his perusal the site of her sitting so quietly in her box, scarcely aware of the glances and murmurs surrounding her. It had seemed to him that she, of all the audience, was actually listening to the opera. Except for twice, when their gazes met across the haze of the candle-smoked interior, she had seemed unaware of even herself. Was she new to experience? She did not seem a green country girl. Her figure was too mature, her features refined by those few years that change a girl into a woman. Perhaps she was a widow who had come to town to circulate in the hope of matching another match. Thanks to St. Ives he could not even inquire about her for he did not know her name.

Beau's expression soured. She had made an error in choosing St. Ives as her introduction to society. Someone should tell her so. Not that it was any business of his. In fact, Dougherty seemed more than willing to do the job of pursuing the lady in question. Yet, she was in need of the assistance of a disinterested party; someone she would realize had no personal interest in the matter beyond the courteous nod to a Town newcomer.

Beau lifted his watch, attached to his waistcoat by a fine gold chain and dangling a single exquisite fob. He supposed he could run the errand and still not be very late for the exhibition. He could be expansive. After all, Sarah had apologized. Yes, he could do likewise. Then his day would be perfect.

He rapped on the carriage roof and called to his driver. "Find out the location of Sir St. Ives's residence and take me there."

"Lord Bellaire," Julien's man pronounced in an awed voice that had nothing to do with the scene upon which he had entered. "He's asking if ye be at home, sir."

"So soon?" Julien sat up a little straighter in the chair in which he had been lounging, one leg flung over the arm. "This should be entertaining," he said to the young woman kneeling on the rug before him.

Smiling broadly, she had been about to minister to that part of his anatomy that seemed ever in need of a womanly touch. Regretfully, he waved her away toward the servant's entrance.

When he had rearranged his breeches in a more presentable fashion he smiled and nodded to his servant. "Send him in."

"Morning, St. Ives." Beau gave the room a quick curious glance before he continued. His host wore a vivid Paisley silk dressing gown and matching fez, the tassel of which swung jauntily by his left ear. It was a fashion of an earlier era, one more suited for a pasha visiting his harem, but then the decadent exotica suited St. Ives. Why that thought should irk him, Beau did not pause to ponder. He only knew that his dislike had grown stronger since the night before.

"I hope I have not interrupted you."

"Nothing that cannot be taken in—ah, hand later." The chill dislike in his guest's voice had warmed Julien's sense of humor. Though he did not rise, he gave voice to an almost toady welcome. "I am honored, beyond the ordinary. Yet perplexed. What brings the great Lord Bellaire to my humble door?"

Now that the question was spoken aloud, Beau could only think that the answer was not reason enough to cover his spur-of-the-moment decision to call. Still, he pressed on. "I had hoped you would convey my apologies to your lady."

"Apologies? What have you done to her?"

"I? Nothing." Painful recognition of his position did not help Beau's kindling temper. "I refer to last evening. Dougherty was in his cups. No doubt that accounts for it."

"It." Julien smiled and stood up with great flourish. "So then you are here on Lord Dougherty's account."

"Not precisely." Beau felt his face stiffening. "Perhaps I, too, was—abrupt. And presumptuous."

"Most entertaining. I assure you I was not offended."

Beau scowled at St. Ives, certain he was being made fun of, a thing he disliked in particular. "I refer to my manner of addressing your lady. Please convey my regrets to her."

"Would you care to do so yourself?"

"She's here?" At the sound of feminine laughter sounding suddenly in the house, Beau could not stop himself and glanced upward toward the second floor.

"She is not here." Julien met Beau's eye with a wink. "I would not mind the arrangement, but society would have so much to say on the subject, even if we are related. My cousin is a stickler for that kind of thing. Detests gossip above all things.''

"You are cousins?"

Julien gave him a knowing look. "You thought her my paramour."

"I did not know what to think."

"You might wish to sound more sincere when you speak to her. She has taken a house in Belgrave Square. I warn you, she is less and more than she seems. You will not easily cozen her with evasions."

Beau considered the riddle but decided not to ask Julien to refine upon it. He wanted, he suddenly realized, to discover the answer himself. "So then, you will tell your lady cousin that I sincerely regret the lost opportunity to be made known to her."

"But you are known to her. As she is to you."

"I cannot believe that is so." The image of her sitting in her box, profile as sweetly neat as any in his recollection, was brand new to his memory. "I would not have forgotten her."

"My own mother introduced you. It was long ago. The year you wed. Puss was but a green girl of seventeen. Tiresome things, these country-bred misses trotted into town every May like spring lambs to be sold in the marriage market then slaughtered on the altar of matrimony."

"That description is more vivid than kind."

"Do you think so? I doubt my cousin would agree with you. One Season was enough to convince her that she could not afford a second airing. But then you will place her when I say she paid a dear price for her ignorant innocence. 'Incomparable Whore' was the unkindest appellation pinned on her."

Beau thought a moment. The Season he was to be wed he could think of nothing and only of Fiona. No other lady no matter how lovely would have held even a passing fascination for him. By that fact alone, he accounted himself to be desperately and completely in love.

"There was a scandal about her marriage," Julien prompted when it seemed his guest would woolgather at length. "Or I should say lack thereof."

Beau knew when he was being made to dance for his supper. St. Ives was enjoying himself far too much. "The only scandal I recall the summer I wed was of a incautious jilt who recklessly tossed away a promising marriage for a night in the arms of a libertine. She was, I believe, unmasked at her own wedding."

St. Ives inclined his head.

"That was she?" Beau flung back his thoughts. Incautious he had thought her the night before. The gossip of nine years earlier labeled her a false jade, a heartless seductress and worse.

"She was called out at the altar as a false baggage by her to-be husband and heard it confirmed by her lover's own word who so fortuitously happened to be among the guests. I'm told he was quite eager to tell those gathered of their tryst the evening before."

"Blackguard," Beau murmured in disapproval.

"Quite." Julien steepled his fingers beneath his chin. "The shock of it all cracked her father's heart. He was dead within a fortnight. Her mother, unimaginative woman that my aunt was, could not conceive of life without her husband and went into a decline that allowed her within the year to join him under the turf. Good riddance to the pair, I said. For they did not stand by their child." Julien yawned. "You may understand that their child does not share my point of view. Children have become so tiresomely well bred. Conceived that she was to blame for her parents' death, she has dared not show her face in London these last nine years."

Beau wondered again if they could be speaking of the

lady whom he had watched so carefully from his box the night before. A beauty, yes. But she did not shine with the sharp edge of desire nor exude the easy charm of an unrepentant flirt. The glance he had first encountered was vehement but not sultry in the least. She seemed, anger aside, almost puritanical in her dislike. St. Ives had just said as much. And yet, he did recall the scandal. Not even a wedding sojourn to Italy shielded him from it. Fiona was the most dutiful correspondent of her flock of letter gossips so that the news had reached him in some detail within a sennight of the incident. To think that a girl of seventeen could so callously take a lover on her wedding eve? It made no sense.

Beau winced. *Who can ever know the mind of a female,* he reminded himself. Fiona's attitude toward him had come as a complete and utter shock. And from that he learned never to trust his feelings where another of her sex was concerned.

"What, if I may ask, after all this while brings her to town?"

"Me." Julien smiled sweetly. "I have conceived the notion that it is a pity to see all that beauty expire unadmired in a village. You will agree with me that she is a prize to be won."

"I will agree that she is striking. But if rumor be true—"

"You are a student of the vice?"

"I detest gossip. But have learned one can seldom escape it entirely."

"Too true. So then, why not embrace it?"

Beau frowned. "Embracing a lie does not make it true."

"Tell my cousin that."

"You would so counsel your own cousin to accept what gossip would make of her circumstance?" Beau could not contain his abhorrence.

"Do you suppose that if she behaves as if butter will not

melt in her mouth, she will be treated as other than rumor once stamped her? I instruct in a more pleasant truth. It can be a delightful thing to be shorn of virtue, and the results are often a great deal more entertaining.''

Beau had never liked St. Ives. Now he found himself feeling a personal revulsion for the man. ''You are no friend to her.''

''But then friendship is not my aim.''

Beau did not pretend to misunderstand. ''You should be gelded.''

St. Ives laughed. ''You are not the first to suggest it. You are welcome to try. But I warn you, I am deadly in a duel.''

''Does she know of your design?''

''Which is?''

''To drag her into the hell of your debauched life.''

''Ah, no. And I will thank you not to tell her so.''

''I doubt I should have the chance as I do not intend to have anything more to do with either of you.''

''Good. Then I wish you a good day while I will be about the business that has brought my cousin to Town. She is not so fond of Town life. I would keep her company lest she flee before I tire of her.''

Shocked more than he could express, Beau gave his host the briefest of nods and turned to the door. He reached it before he could find suitable words for a final volley and turned back. ''Perhaps the occasion will arise when we cross paths again. Look to yourself.''

''I always do.'' So saying St. Ives reached down and squeezed the swelling where his breeches covered his groin.

Beau shut the door with a bang.

''And that should be enough to make her Beau knight brighten up his armor!''

St. Ives's laughter could be heard all the way to the basement kitchen where the cook, a good Irish Catholic, crossed herself and then made the sign of the evil eye.

Chapter Nine

Beau was taken aback to find the very woman he was castigating himself for calling on standing only a few feet away when he entered the Royal Academy of Art. St. Ives had jogged his scant memory of a Jemima MacKinnon. She was the niece of Lady Hermione St. Ives, an old friend of his father. He vaguely recalled asking a pretty girl, gray-faced with fright, to dance at Almacks. He would have forgotten her but for the uproar at the end of the season when she was rejected at the altar. It was a scandal that took the fancy of the whole of London.

Confirmation of her identity had taken only a quick side trip to his club, where he found as expected a reference to the MacKinnon on-dit written into the wagering book just below the inscription of his own marriage. The wagers were so heavily in his favor, he noted not for the first time, that there had been no takers on the opposing side of his marriage being a happy one. Annoyance rippled through him. So much for wagering being a good prognosticator of the outcome.

But with MacKinnon there was more compelling information. The ledger contained various bets as to whether the jilted bride would throw herself into the Thames, be stowed away forever in an Italian nunnery or, most heavily wagered upon, succumb to the life of a Cyprian for which it seemed her lascivious tastes best suited her. So that was she! The intervening nine years must have seen her delivered abroad, though by the looks of her the previous evening it was more likely a brothel than a nunnery to which she withdrew.

Armed with the name he sought he had gone round to Belgrave Square and had his driver inquire as to her residence. When he had sent up his card, her maid said she was not at home. He had taken it to mean she was not "at home" to him. He doubted St. Ives was ever given such a response.

But here she was at the Royal Exhibition, gazing wondrously at a pastoral scene on a canvas seemingly large enough to step into. The sight of her was balm for his injured pride.

She stood appraising the painting far longer than he would have done and so he took the opportunity to study her. He was not the sort of man to notice what a lady wore, unless it was designed deliberately to draw male notice. But he could not help but compare the scandal of a frock of last evening to what she wore today. Her high-necked tunic dress of natural cambric muslin with a fluted ruff was more suited to an ingenue than a spinster. A white chip hat tied round the crown with a lilac satin ribbon, the only concession to color, covered her hair. The other thing he noticed was that neither St. Ives nor anyone else was with her.

After a moment she stepped back and turned to face him. The moment she did, he stepped from the shadow of the entrance into her sight. Though the distance of the gallery separated them, he knew she must see him for she stared right at him. Taken aback a second time by her direct invitation, he reached up to doff his beaver top hat in salute. Even as he did so, she turned and moved in noiseless kid slippers toward the next gallery. If she had seen his acknowledgment, she gave no indication of it.

Or had she? As he moved to follow her, he noted that the gallery toward which she headed was less crowded than the main hall.

Beau smiled to himself. Of course! She would be discrete. She was, after all, St. Ives's protégée. He might be a thoroughgoing rogue, but he was an elegant one and would require no less of the women who accompanied him in public. She was no doubt extensively educated in all the art and artifice of her position. Then the reason she was alone fell neatly into place. A kept woman must be on constant lookout for her next protector before her present one grew tired of her. She must be here in the hope that a likely gentleman might come along.

How pleasant to find that she had the presence of mind to lead him toward an assignation he had thought he would not want. But seeing her now, so unexpectedly, and in such unexceptional surroundings, piqued his curiosity as to how she would eventually receive him. Would she do it with a glance from beneath lowered lids, with a small knowing smile or perhaps a word spoken so low it could but be meant for him alone?

The idea of a clandestine meeting with her seemed at once so agreeable that he did not ponder why he should be disapproving of it all the same. So that when he followed her through several succeeding rooms and she refused to catch his eye, he decided to take action. Perhaps she preferred a more coming sort of gentleman. If that were so, she would not find him lacking in initiative.

He almost lost her when she turned into a small alcove. But he felt his pulse quicken. What a hussy! She was leading him into a very private place. What delicious things did she have in mind? His imagination was quickly gaining control of his being so that he walked full into a gentleman approaching him without the slightest inkling that he was about to do so.

The collision was uneventful, but it gave him the presence of mind not to fling himself headlong into a situation from which he did not at all know what to expect.

He adjusted his hat and frock coat and then strolled more slowly toward the corner around which she had disappeared.

He found her in a narrow corridor, empty but for a galley docent who stood with his back to the hall. As he slowed his walk even more, so as not to seem too eager, he saw her reach into the reticule and remove from it a pair of spectacles, which after a surreptitious glance about, she perched on her nose. Then she walked up to a set of small frames on the opposite wall and began examining them carefully.

He paused to observe this new facet. She needed spectacles to view something a foot in front of her face? He was certain she had not worn them at any time during the opera the night before. Why would she wish to hide the fact she needed spectacles? But, of course, she was vain. Pretty women often were. Possibly she hid the defect with hauteur and affected not to see a person . . . she could not recognize!

That realization deflated the soufflé of his ego. Perhaps she had not recognized him after all. Perhaps she had not been gazing boldly at him the night before. He must test his theory. But how?

He hung back until she was done with her study and had slipped the offending spectacles back in her reticule. When she turned back toward him, he pretended that he was just turning the corner around which he had been spying on her.

She passed him without so much as a glance. His jaw dropped. Confound it! He might not be an Elgin Marble but he liked to think he cut a distinctive figure in public. There was his height and most particularly his hair—

He reached up and whipped off his top hat. Smiling rue-fully, he turned to follow her, assured this time he would not fail to capture her eye, even if he had to pin himself to the wall for exhibition. For reasons he was not entirely certain of, he was enjoying himself quite a lot.

He found her in another large gallery before another enor-mous canvas.

It was an excessively ornate version of the *Rape of the Sabine Women*. The soldiers were steely eyed and stout-limbed, their chargers dancing on rear legs. Hooves charged the sky with an illusionary vigor to match their riders' lust. The virgins themselves were scantily clad and of such abun-dant flesh that they appeared to be fashioned of pink marsh-mallow crème. They did not seem so much hoisted onto the backs of the ravishers' steeds as tethered there by their captors' strong embraces lest they float away like so many newfangled hot-air balloons.

This time he did not wait for her to move away but came right up to her. When after a few seconds she did not acknowledge his presence, he said, "If you do not speak, I must consider it a direct cut. I have learned, you see, that we are known to each other." That made her look up. He smiled and nodded. "Your aunt, Lady St. Ives, introduced us at Almacks."

Jemima had not seen him! She had not even suspected that she was being followed. But when she looked up, she could not mistake the gentleman standing beside her for any other than the hateful Lord Bellaire. Now he had recalled who she was! That he was smiling at her seemed impossible, unless it was to disguise his next attack.

She had not been able to sleep a wink after their encounter at the opera. Memory hectored her until five of the clock with endless images of the many ways she had embarrassed herself and for it gained nothing in return. The morning had brought a missive from Henrietta about her cousin Amelia, who was keeping watch over Pru. The girl had recovered quickly from her ordeal. Remarkably so. It seemed she was tired of being housebound and decided to stroll through the village. Amelia's warning that her belly, growing larger with every day, would not draw the sort of attention she would like fell on deaf ears. The outing had proved just short of disastrous, with none of the merchants willing to wait on Pru. The women of the village had shut their windows and doors as she passed. Amelia, who accompanied Pru, found it a strain and worried that a further escapade might bring worse consequences. The girl needed to be removed from Chapel Hill, and soon!

That meant that Lord Bellaire must be brought quickly to account for his misdeed. And pay for Pru's child's upkeep. Yet after the opera, Jemima wondered if her plan to accomplish all that was a good one, after all. He did not seem the sort of man to be easily brought low. In his gaze was the power of a formidable enemy.

To distract herself from her dilemma, she had come to the exhibit. Now the very person she hoped to avoid all thought of had found her.

"I meant no slight," she began coolly. "Yet my oversight could have afforded you the opportunity to forego acknowledging our association in public."

The manner of her phrasing surprised him. "Did you think I would prefer a more private association?"

Jemima did not trust the cordial expression on his face. "I am not in a position to say, as I know you not at all."

Before he could stop himself, Beau's gaze shifted from her face to her bosom, primly covered this day in vertical rows of tucks. Yet it took no effort at all to recall to his manly mind the very different display she had offered the world the night before. He wasn't the sort of man to rise in his breeches at the sight of any and every pretty face. His passion was as self-disciplined as the rest of his life. Yet being in Miss Jemima MacKinnon's company disturbed the very essence of his orderly restraint.

Grasping for a neutral topic, he glanced up beyond her. "Are you fond of Gainsborough?"

"I do not know. I have never seen his work before."

"Yet you stand before his work brooding. It can only mean that you like or seriously mislike the work."

Jemima turned back to the portrait of the lady whose serene painted eyes seemed to gaze back at her. "I like the look of the lady's expression, as if she had found the secret to happiness and was content."

"You see so much? What else do you see?"

"That she must be beyond the cares of the ordinary sort. She is confident, in her self and in her place. No hard knocks disturb her life."

Jemima remembered the part she had come to London to play, that of coquette. Yet she could not marshal the need to be civil to a man who had so fractured her belief in his goodness. She turned and regarded him coldly. "A pity we all cannot share the joy of an unshadowed life."

Beau accepted the full thrust of her indignant stare. Though he could not begin to fathom the reason for it, he knew he had been summarily dismissed. "I beg your pardon. I have disturbed you. Deeply. Go on with your meditation. I will look for something to keep me less equitably occupied." He inclined his head. "Good day, Miss Jemima."

Jemima stiffened at the brazen use of her name. She had not given him permission, and he knew it. But just when relief replaced her nervousness, she realized that if he left now she might never again get the opportunity to regain his favor. She wanted his favor. No, she needed it if her plan were to proceed.

"My lord," she said stiffly and curtsied so slight as to be just short of insult. "I prefer caricature myself."

"Do you indeed? Then perhaps the new fellow Foolscap is more to your style."

Jemima drew a quickly breath. Was it design or chance that had made him mention Foolscap? "As a matter of fact, he is."

"I should not be astonished. It is, I am well aware, one of the favorite pastimes of pretty women to be at collecting and examining examples of the faults of others. One would think they should be wary of attracting the same censure."

"I am supposed to say that I agree with your superior point of view. But it has been my experience that gossip has no particular affinity for the well favored. To the contrary, I find gossip to be the very aqua vitae of the *ton*. You seem an elegantly mannered flock, but it is mere camouflage to hide a rapacious appetite for scandal and mischief and a capacity for any cruelty that serves up an opportunity to be entertained by the misery of others."

Jemima paused to gather breath after that lengthy speech. As her companion seemed in no hurry to answer her but only tilted his head in inquiry, she found she had more to say when she had regained her wind. "As it happens Foolscap's sole purpose is to poke holes in the fabric of fashionable society. He debunks rumor not encourages it."

"Do you think so?" Beau smiled. He could not think of three ladies who could have answered him as well. She was no peahen, squawking with nothing to say. "I find his work self-congratulatory. I suspect his is the labor of an old roué who is perhaps feeling the cold breath of mortality on his back."

"Old roué?" The very idea injured Jemima's perception of herself as a vigorous defender of womanhood. "I should think Foolscap in the pink of life to be so engaged in defending blameless souls who have been wrongly accused."

Beau noted the slight tremor in her voice as she said

blameless. She was quite agitated over the subject, something he did not expect. And so he pressed her. "You are convinced the fellow is a reformed rake? Let me guess. You would cast him as a knight-errant to ignorant and silly girls who have no better use for themselves than to land in the scandal broth. He must, in the way of all tragedians, be atoning for his own guilty past. That is a fantasy fit only for schoolroom misses and lending library romantics who wish their heroes to be golden-locked and unbearded." He lifted an eyebrow in challenge, thinking he had set her up for a lively retort.

Instead she turned and walked away.

"Wait!" He did not say the word especially loudly or with vigor, yet it sailed through the large open room like a ship before a gale. Several visitors turned in question. He did not care, only that Lady Jemima kept walking away.

He just stepped in front of her before she exited the building. "I beg your pardon though I must say I do not understand the manner in which I have grieved you."

Jemima gave him a hard glance. "You would make sport of me because I am female, unchaperoned, and once scandal's plaything.'

"That is not true." He hoped he sounded convincing because it was true he was thinking those very things. "But I should advise you as an old acquaintance not to place much hope in erasing from society's mind your former misfortune if you continue to allow yourself to be squired about by a disreputable companion."

Jemima looked as if she had been struck. "You dare— dare to instruct me in the model ways of virtue!" She just bit back the accusation that had brought her to town. Oh but how she would have liked to have cut up his consequence by speaking aloud his calumny for all the academy visitors to hear. But it would spoil her plan, spoil it completely. And so she settled for defense of her cousin.

"Cousin Julien is the kindest, most generous soul in the world. You cannot and never will know the friend and good counsel he has been to me. I do not like to think what would have become of me if not for him. You can say nothing to me that is against him. Nothing!"

"I beg pardon." Beau's natural arrogance came to his defense even as his manners supplied the correct words. "I would not wish to say or do anything that would give grievance to you."

Jemima did not overlook the censure in his tone despite the unobjectionable phrases he used. "You may think as little of me as you like," she said in a tight voice. "I am aware that my reputation has materially lessened my chances of maintaining the polite company of gentlemen of any consideration in the world."

"Is this your desire?"

"Thankfully, no. I am well enough situated not to require the guardianship of any man, certainly not a husband."

"Indeed. I did not know."

"And now you do, for all the good it will do you." She stared at him a moment longer, at what seemed to be a genuine desire to be forgiven reflected in his now open expression, but she didn't trust it or him. "Good day, Lord Bellaire."

"Good day, Miss MacKinnon."

As he stared after her, Beau could not keep from smiling. Though their conversation had never risen above conversational tones, he felt as much exhilaration as if they had been roaring at each other in full throat.

So heated a defense of St. Ives came from deep feeling. Clearly she adored her wicked relative. The affection might not erroneously be called love. Perhaps that is because she did not know what her rogue of a cousin intended for her. Yet he did.

Beau set his jaw, thinking again of the way St. Ives had

flaunted his despicable design, as if he were issuing a challenge. If that had been his purpose, Beau thought darkly, then he had chosen his confidant unwisely.

Society thought of him as a patient tolerant man, a voice of reason, a scholarly politician who never ventured forth with an opinion that he had not first thoroughly investigated. If not exactly cautious, he was levelheaded, prudent, not given to spontaneous action.

So then had any person been privy to the rough disorderly thoughts running through his head at this moment, he or she would have been mightily amazed. There were unconnected thoughts of besting a rival, doing down a rabid dog, saving Lady Virtue from the Pillagers of Sabine. Luckily he did not give them much creed until they congealed into a single clear aim.

Now, more than ever, he wanted to spike St. Ives's wheel. To do that, he must gain Miss MacKinnon's favor and confidence. A thing that, at the moment, he could not conceive of being less likely to achieve.

Despite his own conclusion, Beau smiled. How she had glared at him, all fire and glory in her unusual eyes. Plum colored they were, so dark a blue with brown depths, he had never seen the like! Whoever said dark eyes hide the illumination of the soul had never gazed in the eyes of Miss Jemima MacKinnon.

Chapter Ten

Cousins Richard Langley and Guy Somerset sat to a game of whist, but it was only a prelude to the evening's main entertainment, a masquerade at the pleasure gardens. To that end they were dressed in elegant eveningwear. Beside each sat a headdress they would wear as disguise. Guy's choice was a black-and-white Harlequin's mask and hat with two pointed ends from which hung jingle bells. Langley had chosen a cock's head, with gold and white feathering and a bright red cockscomb of satin.

"My signature, don't you know," he'd said with an upward glance toward his own red head when he first walked in with it under his arm.

Now, two hours and two bottles of port later, Richard doubted he had ever been as green at nineteen as his cousin was proving to be. More handsome than his elder brother, Guy had the added advantage of bashful blue eyes and dark hair that remained untouched by a single thread of silver. Yet instead of running after the muslin set, like all young bucks are want to do, for the past month Guy had been seeking out less savory pastimes, gaming and betting and drinking, and doing none of it too well, to hear his older brother tell it. Twice in as many terms, the first midway through Lent and now a month into Easter term, Guy had been sent home after repeatedly being fined for not being in college by nine of the clock.

A more prudent fellow would have pulled in his horns a bit and mouthed the appropriate mea culpa to his brother. But not Guy. Being escorted home by the night watch had replaced being dragged back to college by "bulldog" proctors. He and his newly made London friends would amuse themselves by dousing passersby in a horse trough. Another time they were detained for tossing stones at night lanterns for sport. Disgusted and embarrassed by his brother's continuing peccadilloes—and fearful that Guy might soon come to disaster—Beau had recruited Richard to take his younger brother in hand, "Before I am forced to deal with him in a manner I shall later regret!"

Having witnessed Beau's temper a few months' earlier, and feeling that it was every young blood's right to raise a little hell, Richard had reluctantly agreed to at least try to steer Guy from the worst company. But if he were going to succeed he would need a little in the way of information on the matter standing between the brothers, which so far neither saw fit to mention in any detail.

"How's the family?" Richard inquired of his companion in pleasure for the evening.

"Couldn't say," Guy groused as he fanned a new hand of cards. "We ain't speaking."

"My little niece then?"

"I never see Emma. Beau says London is no place to rear a child. And as he is confined to London as long as Parliament is in session, well, the dear child must doubt she has even one parent to call her own."

" 'Tis common opinion that Cousin Beau is excessively fond of his daughter."

"He cares for little than his own consequence these days."

"That would explain why he makes such dull company."

Guy's brows shot up. "You do not approve of my brother?"

"Didn't say that, old boy. I share at least one of his interests. For instance, I'm thinking of placing a tidy bundle at the Derby. Don't suppose you know which of his prime bits Beau will be running?"

"I'd be the last to have Lord Bellaire's confidence." Guy shook his head so that a shaft of dark hair sprang forward onto his brow. "Doesn't hold my opinion fit for any subject. Yet he will lecture me every hour about his consequence and how my actions jeopardize it."

"He likes to hug the rail, keep his course inside the pack," Richard answered mildly. He had discovered that the cant of the racing set gave a dashing quality to his speaking. Even with plumb pockets gone flat, he had been reluctant to retreat from Tattersalls' stalls to take on this family duty. "Still, I hear he backed the wrong filly in this season's Parliamentary Session."

"As if I care a fig for politics. But I know Beau's musket is spiked by the news that the Regent is claiming full rights to the throne." Guy's tone was sheer malice. "Serves him right to be taken down a peg. Though I'd as lief do it myself."

Richard stroked his chin. Beau had already made him privy to the threat to lock his brother in the attic until he was twenty-and-five. Even so, Guy's unremitting rage against his brother made no sense, unless there were more to it than a woman.

"Holding a grudge overlong, ain't you?"

Guy's handsome face puckered with an expression suspiciously like that of a sulking boy. "I should think I may wish my brother at the devil seven times a day and no one's business if I do."

"Rushing your fences there. Beau's a prime bit. Mortality ain't his gate."

"More's the pity." Guy's chin sunk farther into his collar as he played a card. "Getting so a man can't walk the streets without hearing me brother's name."

Richard poured the last of the claret into Guy's glass. " 'Pears you and your brother have had a falling out. Is it the matter of Cambridge?"

Guy's sulk turned to anger. "It is not."

"Perchance a lady?"

Guy flushed up to his ears. "What have you heard? If Beau has making sport of my humiliation—"

"Hold on, dear boy." Richard set his hand of hand-painted tiles facedown and leaned toward his cousin. "I ain't heard nothing requiring you to play gull to your elder's wit. I was inquiring in the main to be sociable."

Guy grumbled and hunched his shoulders as though half-conscious of defending himself against a blow.

Richard picked up his cards thinking that though Guy was closer to him in age and temperament than his cousin Beau, his younger cousin had little to recommend him to the world beside a handsome profile and superb tailoring. To be besotted over the same comely wench five months together, well, that spoke of feelings too easily engaged and a sentiment too fondly refined upon. At Guy's age he had been in and out of love every week. But he did not mistake the inclination for genuine attachment.

As for unsavory friends, the attraction on their part was obvious. With five thousand per, Guy possessed a greater allowance than many younger sons. With his poor instincts for cards so evident, it seemed that relieving him of a bit of his blunt was practically a duty. When cousins played, the money remained in the family, so to speak.

Equally foxed and aggrieved, Guy played cards with all the attention one usually reserved of an overlong sermon. He was tethered at his brother's home with no hope of escape until Michaelmas, when he could return to Cambridge. But it was spoilt, the whole idea of college because his heart was broken, smashed to bits by the treachery of a man he must call brother. The anger roiling in his chest could not long be contained by any activity. Even in the most tranquil moments, there would steal over him an image he would never have thought imaginable!

His temples began to pound in anticipation of the memory. The lights blurred; the roaring in his ears increased. Mortified and humiliated beyond recovery, he was once more standing in the doorway to Beau's room, staring at his brother with his sweet Pru in bed beside him!

"What's this!" Richard cried in alarm as Guy suddenly swept everything from the table with a slash of his arm. Pence and pound notes went tumbling after claret bottles and silver plate, striking the floor in a discordant jumble of sound.

"You think I don't know why you're here? Beau has set you as his watchdog. He must show himself as superior in every way. Society thinks him a saint. But I know different. Treats me with a contempt he wouldn't show a cur." Hectic color climbed Guy's neck. "He would not scruple to stab a brother in the back! One day I shall pay him back in kind! Caesar shall then have his Bruce."

"Brutus," Richard corrected with a sigh. Melodrama was not Guy's forte. Drunken self-pity, even less so. But Guy was out of his chair and struggling with his domino. "What are you doing?"

"I'm going out. *You* can do to the devil! I will find a way to best Beau. Even if I must ruin myself to do him down."

Richard came to his feet as the specter of explaining to

his elder cousin how he'd lost Guy on their first outing rose in his mind. No, he'd have to do something.

"If this is about a woman," he began carefully, "why don't we find you another whor—light o' love. A better one, much handsomer than Cousin Beau's present companion."

"She's old," Guy said churlishly and he reached for his mask. "Must be thirty. Missing a tooth. And she dyes her hair. I heard it from Hamilton."

"Shouldn't put much store by Hamilton," Richard murmured, thinking that a man with a head of yellowing teeth so crooked they looked like a badly stacked log pile should not be commenting on the dental works of another. "But we stray. We must find you a Fashionable Impure, a real goer, nay, a Cyprian!"

For the first time in an hour, Guy focussed his foxed gaze fully on his cousin. "How'd we do that?"

"You, dear boy. You shall do it. You have the looks, the blunt and the—er, wit to recommend yourself to all the demimonde. Set yourself up with a mistress of the First Water and your brother will have to look upon you in a new and improved light."

"I don't know." Guy lounged back against the wall and folded his arms across his chest. "Have you ever been in love?"

Richard nodded, not trusting the kind of waggish doggerel that might emerge if he spoke.

Puffed up by injured pride, Guy's handsome face turned sulky. "Another woman, even a beautiful one. It wouldn't be the same."

"My point exactly. You don't *want* the same." Richard smiled encouragingly. "Imagine, a whole world of lovely ladies awaits. Lovely, luscious, amendable to all that your imagination can think to supply in the way of request."

"I don't know."

"You suppose that you are being unfaithful to your memory of love."

Guy blushed but did not reply.

"It would be of opposite effect. If, at the end of a short rigorous dalliance with a new mistress, you find you still cannot forget your lady love, then you can do ought but find and marry her."

Guy's expression brightened. "You agree then that I have that right?"

"Exactly." Or not, Richard thought as he glanced at the fallen wine bottles. Playing one brother's interests against the other's was thirsty work. "You owe the experiment to yourself, nay, to her. You should test the depth of your own feeling before you allow your heart to languish upon the funeral pyre of your lost lady. What if you should discover a wobble in the constancy of your feelings? Would that not mediate Cousin Beau's damnation? By the by, you've never said what the transgression was."

"And will not," Guy answered, putting a period, for now, to Richard's sorely teased curiosity.

"To be relieved of these torturous feelings. That would be heaven." He glanced again at his cousin. "You think a lady with such power exists?"

"I'd wager. . . ." Richard looked down at the two hundred pounds on his side of the table. "I will wager you double or nothing that the lady may be found this very evening, if you put your mind to it."

"So then, why do we tarry?"

Richard smiled and began to pocket his cash. The wager would be forgotten as easily as it was made, even if he had to use part of his winnings to bribe an opera dancer to look with special kindness upon his companion. "If I'd been born with half your looks, I'd own a harem," Richard said with a companionable clap on Guy's shoulders. "Shall we go and give the ladies a thrill?"

* * *

"This is ridiculous!"

Jemima turned from the glass and placed a hand on each hip. "I shall be thought a runaway from a biblical pageant."

"The play must be Sodom and Gomorrah, Puss." Julien's smile caught fire slowly as he walked deliberately about her, observing every angle. He was dressed in a Turkish robe with baggy trousers tucked into boots and an open shirt. "I am a pasha and must have my favorite little Blackamore Page beside me at all times."

"I do not look the part." Jemima reached up to stop the swing of the tassel that hung from her large softly draped turban, cocked rakishly over one eye.

"There you are wrong. You may not be Moorish or a boy, but your curves alone proclaim you a quite exotic creature."

Jemima glanced back over her shoulder. Sure enough in the mirror she saw reflected that the gathers of her red silk pantaloons emphasized a female derriere and narrow waist. The full-sleeved white silk shirt she insisted be worn under the heavily embroidered vest of vivid hues only accentuated the bosom her cousin had forbidden her to bind. "I shall be arrested for indecency."

"Not if you are cloaked until you've entered Vauxhall Gardens. Once inside a masquerader may be dressed as outlandishly as he or she likes."

Jemima glanced doubtfully at her silk-slippered feet. "Are the bells necessary?"

"For a lady, you are remarkably unfashionable. You are the page of a despot. You can not be too ornately dressed. Here, I've a gift for you." He produced a thin chain of gold links from his pocket. At one end was attached a thin circlet set with red stones.

Jemima backed up a step. "What is that for?"

"Your leash, Puss. Devil of a fellow that I am, I wish all to know how very fond I am of you. And therefore you must not be allowed to stray."

"I certainly will *not* wear a collar like a cow!" Jemima folded her arms across her bosom. "You may put that away, instanter!"

Julien turned his head to one side as he held the chain up to inspect it. " 'Tis real gold, the stones genuine rubies. A dainty thing. Try it. 'Tis mere affectation."

"You are a little too fond of your supposed power over me," Jemima said with some asperity. "I may be new to London ways, but I am not entirely lost to all sense of decorum. I will not try it on."

"A pity." Julien repocketed the item. "So then, we're off to sport with our prey."

Jemima smiled knowingly. "Such an evening would not seem to be his taste."

"I have taken care of that possibility. Sent him a particular invite."

Jemima jerked in surprise. "You did what?"

"He responded that he awaits our arrival."

"But you do not—You wrote to Dougherty?"

"The very one. You disapprove?"

"Very much so," Jemima answered. At least she would be spared meeting Lord Bellaire in her outlandish costume. Yet now she must deal with the odious Dougherty. "You presume too much, Cousin."

"At every opportunity. You asked for my help. But then you slip free this afternoon for a full two hours." He reached up to rub the polished curl that hung free of her turban. "I am most curious to know why you will not tell me of your assignation."

"Oh, but I did." Jemima slapped his hand away. "I went to view the exhibit at the Royal Academy of Art."

"Art." Julien allowed his gaze to wander below her neck. "I'd hoped you'd slipped off for a passionate dalliance."

Jemima gave him an imperious glance. "That should not be likely as we haven't even been introduced."

"A matter of formality I shall take care to remedy tonight. I am daily amazed by how very sheltered a life you've led. A romantic interlude with a stranger can be quite edifying." He caught her chin on the point of his forefinger, forcing her to look up at him. "If, perchance, you should find yourself in a delectable position which you do not wish to be removed from, you have but to signify it."

Jemima wanted to reply, *I should be only too glad to be rid of the company of a man like Dougherty*. However, she could not very well protest too much or Julien would be at her again with speculation about her real quarry. "Did you pass a pleasant day?"

He released her and half-turned away. "Quite pleasant, but for the intrusion of an unwanted guest."

"Who would that be?"

He glanced back at her. "Lord Bellaire."

Jemima did not hold his gaze long. "If he was not welcome, then I hope you sent him straight away."

"And spoil the chance to insult a high stickler? Never."

"What did he come to see you about?"

Julien smiled. "There is only one subject about which men will meet in private to declare their dishonorable intentions."

Jemima chewed this information carefully before she swallowed. "You mean a woman."

"A lady, though I doubt the distinction makes the gentleman's interest any less carnal. But then, I shouldn't be surprised to learn Lord Bellaire is anything but ordinary. He would call me out without even the benefit of having sampled the ware he defends."

Jemima frowned with the effort of trying to keep apace

of her cousin's announcements. "He challenged you? Over a lady's favors?"

"Why, Puss, what can you know of such matters?"

"You do not answer my question."

"You are curious, are you? His parting words were to look to myself when next we meet."

"What time did this occur?"

"Too damn early, Puss. I had not quite given up the pleasures of my bed."

Jemima bit her lip. So then, she and Lord Bellaire conversed after his visit with Julien. Is that why he had sought her out with questions about her connection to Julien? Was he meaning to call her cousin out for a duel and wondered how Julien's loss would, should he be bested, affect her?

She stared at Julien a moment longer, measuring him against recent memory of Lord Bellaire. They were similar in build and height. Yet one was all stiff formality, it seemed, but the other was a sensualist of decadent proclivities. Their tastes could not appear more dissimilar. Yet they had quarreled over a woman.

How like men to throw one woman over and then move onto the next with a passion that would seem to belie the former connection. Really, she did not understand men at all!

"What is the lady's name?"

Julien had been watching her with equal interest and so could surmise better than she might suspect the nature of her thoughts. "Believe me, it would do you no good to know." He swung a large enveloping cape about her shoulders that completely shielded her costume. "Come on. We shall be late."

As he turned away, Jemima put a hand on Julien's arm to stop him. "You will not fight him? You will not accept a challenge? Promise me."

Julien looked a long time into her upward gaze, his smile fading slowly. "Would you care if I were dead?"

"Of course."

"Of course." He lifted her hand from his arm and tucked it into the crook of his elbow, pressing her hand hard against his side.

They walked out into the night in a silence that lasted so long a time that Jemima began to wonder if she had insulted him, and how.

Chapter Eleven

Their earlier conversation was forgotten the moment Jemima and Julien crossed the bridge over the Thames. Divided from London proper by the river, Vauxhall Gardens glowed in the night like a forest alive with thousands of fireflies.

Julien commanded their driver to set them down as soon as they crossed for the avenue was blocked by dozens of chaises and traps and barouches, all carrying passengers to the masquerade balls. It would be an hour or more before some of them reached the main entrance, he told her.

Jemima noticed that, like her and Julien, the passengers were dressed in long shapeless capes with hoods to conceal both their costumes and exact identities. Paradoxically, many of the carriages bore the crest of the august personages they carried toward the evening's risqué entertainment.

Hundreds of gas lanterns lit the Grand Walk of the entrance lined by linden trees. A long covered colonnade ran the length of the walk to offer shelter at those times when a shower might threaten to spoil the outing. Tonight the sky was clear, its violet depths sequined with starlight veiled in the gossamer breath of the Milky Way.

Having never before visited a pleasure garden, Jemima was all astonishment behind the shelter of her mask. When they approached the first of several archways, she stopped to admire the transparency of a mythical scene that had been hung there. Backlit, it looked like a stage set. There were others in each of the succeeding archways. Somewhere beyond them in the night a band played. That was the place toward which the revelers hurried. Very quickly they were enveloped in the carnival atmosphere of the park. There were booths for buying trinkets, oranges on sticks, games of chance, and palm readers. Jugglers and fire-breathers vied for attention with large pavilions whose banners promised "Extraordinary Panoramas of the World," "Enactment of the Battle of Trafalgar," and "The Cascade."

Julien swept her past it all in a determined march until the sounds of cannon fire mingled with cries of delight and peals of laughter teased Jemima to the point she could stand it no more and dragged him to a halt.

"What is the Cascade? Oh, Julien, let's go back and look."

He glanced down at her with affectionate exasperation, for he alone among the crowd wore no mask. "Child, do you truly wish to view vulgar spectacles?"

"Oh, yes!"

Jemima soon found out what the Cascade was, as Julien led her toward an extravagantly painted backdrop of a mountain vista from which a real waterfall cascaded into an artificial lake. The crowd *oohed* and *aahed* its approval of the cleverly devised display while the more scientifically minded among them debated loudly the possible mechanics that recreates the "magic" of the exhibition.

A little distance away two gentlemen, one wearing the

head of a cock and the other a Harlequin, observed the crowd from a private supper box.

"I see nothing to tempt me," Guy mumbled and turned up his tankard of ale.

"You must be patient," Richard counseled. "I've spotted more than a few prime goers. You have but to—what's *this?*"

Guy cocked his head toward his friend, his bells jingling gaily. "What do you see?"

Richard lifted his lorgnette, reserved for notable viewing, from his eyes and smiled. "St. Ives. With a prime bit to harness."

Guy borrowed his companion's lorgnette and held it up to look in the direction he was shown. After a moment, he lowered it. "Dash it all, Rich! He's got a boy with him."

Richard shook his head. "Not a boy, Guy. A female dressed as a boy. Don't you know what that means?"

"I—, no."

"To be in the company of St. Ives she must be a Cyprian of the demimonde."

"Are you certain?"

"With those glorious hips? If I be mistaken, may my grandsires reach out of the grave to geld me!"

Guy snatched off his Harlequin mask in order to have a better look. Sure enough, this time he noticed the flare of young female hips beneath the silk trousers and, more intriguing, the thrust of breasts. He lowered the glass. "I say. He's a *she.*"

Richard grinned. "Which means she's exactly what you need."

"But she's with St. Ives," Guy said thickly. "I've no title to compare to his."

Richard shot his cousin an impatient glance. "Pounds and pence are not the coin of this realm tonight. Have you no sense of adventure? This is a masquerade. A dustman may dance with a countess. So even a younger son may caper with a duchess of a whore.''

Guy's smile seesawed on his face. ''You think her a whore?''

Richard lifted his eyes heavenward. Had Beau taught his brother naught of the delights of the female sex? No wonder the poor fool thought himself in love with the first one he'd bedded. ''She may be a genuine duchess. No matter.'' Grinning, he laid a conspiratorial arm about his cousin's shoulders. ''Tonight she comes costumed, a very provocative costume, to be the partner of the man who can win her affection. She's *yours* to win!''

''Mine.'' The idea took slow shape in Guy's inebriated senses, but as slow as the gain was, it became all the stronger when it arrived at maturity. ''By Jove! A duchess whore! That would show up Beau's Harriet!''

''I believe we've covered that point with sufficiency,'' Richard said, steering his charge away from the front of the booth where they could be overheard by nearby onlookers. ''You must keep names out of the evening's entertainment. We are here not as gentlemen but as strangers with no account to our actions. Discretion, Guy! For God's sake, do not abandon it with all else.''

Guy nodded, looking for all the world with dark hair hanging in his eyes like a drunken cherub. ''I know what's 'o clock.'' He smiled. ''How do I get her?''

''All in good time.'' Richard pointed him in the direction of the exit and out toward the wooden dance floor that had been laid in preparation of the late evening's frolic. ''We shall wait here until we see them again. And then— Where's your mask? Here, put it on. Now then, you shall wait until she comes here and then ask her dance. Make it a waltz. If she accepts, she's yours.''

A few minutes later, Julien helped Jemima slip off her cloak inside another private box erected to resemble an

Arabian mosque. "You must help yourself to a little supper or you will not be able to keep the pace of the dance floor."

In amazement, Jemima looked out onto the platform at the front of the box where beef pastries, broiled pheasant, and a sundry of pastries and fruit glacés filled a table.

"Julien! It is wonderful."

He smiled slightly. "You are so easily pleased, Puss. Come and drink a cup of Vauxhall Punch."

Jemima took the silver cup he handed her and sipped it. "It's delicious. What's in it?"

"Fairy dust and angel tears and a clipping from Satan's tail."

"Will you never be serious?"

"Not with you, Puss. It would utterly destroy the charm of our unnatural relationship."

"Unnat—?"

Jemima bit off the question as Julien leaned in close, the dark smile on his face far from reassuring. "Remember that I do not cherish our cousinly relationship as you do."

With that enigmatic thought to keep her company, Jemima turned away and again sipped her punch. She knew his reputation, his supposedly sinister character. Yet she couldn't quite believe that he meant her to take anything he said seriously.

Within half an hour, an orchestra replaced the band and at last struck up its first tune for dancing.

Julien rose from his chair and offered her his hand. "We will dance."

Jemima came a little unsteadily to her feet. The effects of the punch rose through her in waves of pleasant sensation. "I have not been foxed since. . . ."

"Yes? Since when, Jemima?"

Jemima shook her head. She might be halfway in her cups, but she had not had nearly enough drink to divulge that secret. To stop her wayward thoughts, she grasped his hand tightly. "Yes, let's dance until we are part of the very night!"

Masked at last, Julien led her out onto the floor. Within moments, they were part of the dozens of swirling couples who had rushed into the open area. Though she felt herself to be the most unusually dressed woman there, she soon spied others able to vie for the title. There were Marie Antoinettes and Cleopatras, even a Virgin Queen, although the low cut of the woman's bodice would not have been permitted in a royal court. After a full turn about the floor, she noticed one daring beauty who had cut holes in her bodice so that two of the pink love knots covering her bodice were, upon closer inspection, revealed to be her own nipples.

For the most part, the gentlemen simply wore dominoes over their evening clothes and small black masks. They seemed as eager as the ladies to thread a measure on the boards. Soon the crush of partners led to numerous collisions and trod-upon shoes. On all sides, laughter oiled the mechanism of courtesy and good manners.

But very soon she noticed the bystanders, mostly gentlemen, who watched the crowd as if it were a parade, or a market. As she passed on Julien's arm, she heard one exclaim in drunken roar, "Damme! There's a fair Hyacinth, full-cheeked for Greek embraces."

"Have you knowledge of that particular arse?" inquired an equally drunken companion.

"Nay, only a longing for such fierce embraces as I should ever remember."

Though she turned scarlet behind her mask, Jemima said nothing, and if Julien heard them, he did not mention it.

A very little later she brushed up against a couple wearing identical nun's habits. The taller of the two revealed himself to be male when he brushed hard against Jemima and whispered, "I smell the scent of a bitch in heat!"

Jemima jerked away, stumbling against Julien's chest as she did so.

He steadied her with a firm grip. "What is the matter?"

She couldn't look at him, couldn't bear to see her shock turn to humor in his derisive gaze. "Nothing."

"You wished to be notorious."

Jemima set her jaw. He would remind her at every moment of her supposed folly. No wonder she detested London and all its society stood for. No noble cause was deemed sacred when ridicule and contempt could shrivel it. Even the caprice of a masquerade held in its heart darker corners.

Julien swung her about, his arms tightening on her to draw her closer than was strictly necessary for a quadrille. As he did so, Jemima felt him bend to her until his lips were against her ear. The warmth of his breath quite amazed her. It was very like an embrace and yet she could not credit it for they were, after all, in public.

"You have nothing to fear," he whispered and drew her a fraction closer so that she could feel the strength of his longer, harder body. After a moment he added, "If anyone so much as touches you, I will kill him."

Jemima shivered. He had not said it as a warning or a pledge but as a matter of fact. She leaned back a little from him so she could see his face. "I'd never want murder for my sake on your hands, Julien."

He gave her an odd look and then lifted his head as his gaze suddenly focused on a distant sight. "Then you'd better distract me with your dancing, Puss. For I am feeling quite put out."

It took Jemima only a second to realize that he was talking about something other than her concerns. She turned her head to follow his stare. But, unlike the fireworks and Cascade, her poor vision rendered the crowd as so many blurred faces, none distinct. "Who do you see?"

"Our favorite high stickler."

"Lord Bellaire?"

"Clever girl."

Alarmed, Jemima stepped out of his embrace. "I don't feel well. It must be the punch. Take me back to our box."

He glanced down at her, a faint smile dancing in his gaze. "Coward."

As he started to move in the direction where he had been staring, Jemima grabbed his arm. "Julien, don't. You promised."

He shook off her touch, his expression now so blank it disconcerted her. "I said nothing of the kind. Rather I welcome a wrinkle of interest in what was otherwise a bore of an evening."

Jemima let him go, because she had felt a warning in his voice that was not in his words. And because he'd called her a bore. She was woman enough to feel the sting of his words but wise enough to wonder why after all this time, he should want to back her off. What had she done . . . ?

The other woman. Of course!

Jemima swung around and started after her erstwhile companion. No doubt Lord Bellaire had brought with him the woman he and Julien were presently at odds over. What sort of woman could put two such different but interesting men at each other's throats? She did not know. But she wanted very badly to learn.

Julien quickly outpaced her crossing the dance floor. Then he turned into the dark shadows beyond the well-lit area and disappeared. Determined not to be left behind, Jemima plunged into the crowd ringing the dance floor after him.

The lanes were clogged with revelers who had long been imbibing and now wanted release from their inhibitions. As she passed them, faces and costumes blended and blurred through her nearsighted eyes into strings of brightly colored beads. One man in a domino looked exactly like another. It was soon obvious to her that she was lost and that Julien was gone.

She paused to reach into her trouser pocket for her spectacles, and then remembered she had left them behind in the box. Julien thought them the single most offensive thing about her and told her so often enough. Annoyed that she had allowed him so much control of her, she hurried on, feeling that the sight of two gentlemen quarreling would produce an exhibition unique enough to attract even her foreshortened vision.

In the process of scouring the gardens for potential trouble, she was forced to fend off more than one amorous carouser who tried to woo her with offers of wine or Vauxhall Punch. One wag, dressed at the King of Hearts, simply stepped in her path and put his hands on her vest over her breasts. "Guess who?" he crowed like a drunken soldier.

Instead of replying, she shoved him hard in chest. The push sent him careening backward before he tipped into the crowd, who laughed at his misfortune.

Annoyed and faintly apprehensive that Julien's promise of protection might have been more than gallantry, she turned away from her search and hurried back toward what she thought was the dance floor. Instead, she soon realized she had only stumbled into a deeper, quieter, darker part of the gardens.

When a hand reached out and caught her by the wrist, she nearly screeched in fright. She saw her assailant was a tall man whose hair gleamed dully in the moonlight.

"Lord Bellaire," she said stiffly, feeling equal surges of relief and anger. "How ungallant of you to try to frighten me."

"How do you know who I am?" His voice was devoid of humor, but she could not be certain it was not part of his expression. Despite the luster of his hair, the night was dark enough to conceal his features even without a mask.

Moments before she had known, without a doubt, who he was and had been comforted by the knowledge. But now, alone in the dark, the instinct for self-preservation made her hesitate. What if she was wrong about her security? He was after all a stranger. What if this gentleman who lurked in such a secluded spot was in hope of finding a woman alone and unprotected to press his attentions upon?

The very vulnerability of her situation pumped anger into her veins where fright was holding sway. He would not know her fear. She would not show it.

She stiffened in anticipation of resistance. "Do you propose to ravish me? I should warn you I will fight and scream and very likely make you wish you had chosen lesser prey."

His reaction was a short bark of dry laughter. "I assure you I seek no such thing. You are headed in the wrong direction."

"How do you know where I am headed?"

This time she heard his real amusement in his laughter. "Lady, you do yourself too little credit. You are dressed for a masquerade. Therefore you must be in search of the dance floor."

Not entirely mollified by that statement, she replied, "Then you will release me that I may find it."

He did not let go of her wrist. Instead he tugged on her arm to draw her closer. "If it is a dance you desire, dance with me."

Chapter Twelve

Beau had not been deliberately lurking in the shadows of the Pleasure Gardens nor had he meant to become a stalker of the lady in boy's garb.

Quite by accident he had noticed her on the dance floor. In that moment, backlit by the distant lights, the "boy" revealed the shape of a girl! His gaze had fixed upon her tantalizing silhouette of slim thighs beneath silk trousers. And when she turned in profile, the rounded cushion of her bottom could not be mistaken for male. Then her partner swung her into a quick turn and her vest flew open so that the light cast in silhouette the rounded contours of ripe young breasts beneath her shirt. The sight had stopped his breath. What beauty was this? He had to know.

So intent was he upon her that he had crossed half the dance floor before he recognized her partner. St. Ives! A narrow strip of velvet could not disguise that saturnine countenance. So then, this was Lady Jemima, tricked out like a boy to serve—what?—her cousin's pederastic tastes?

The revulsion Beau felt was not generalized. He was much too much a man of the world to condemn out of hand what he did not delight in. But the thought of the reserved lady he had spoken with of art just this morning, readily in the clutches of a man avowed to debauch her, brought out in him the long-forgotten gallant.

In that same moment her partner looked up across the floor and recognized him. Beau knew then that he might yet have the trouble of finding an excuse to call St. Ives out. But, perhaps, one had already been issued.

The cryptic invitation he'd received as he sat to supper two hours earlier had been the factor in his presence here now. It had read: *Join the Devil's Revels in Vauxhall Gardens.*

As a point of pride he never attended events at the Pleasure Gardens. Thought it the lazy pastime of those without the taste to appreciate the literary pageant of the theater, the elevating spirit of good music to be found in opera, or the refined inclination to exert one's mind in the pursuit of reading. Sarah, whose notes always came with such a sufficiency of perfume as to leave him sneezing for some minutes together, had given up urging him to don a domino and join in the frivolity of a masquerade. But this was the bold pen stroke of a gentleman's hand. He did not even need to wonder at the author. In large script were writ the initials *J S I.*

At first he was determined to ignore it. St. Ives was up to something. Not a political animal, he must have personal reasons for issuing the invite. But to what purpose?

The image of Jemima MacKinnon as she had been in the Royal Gallery soon supplied him with a reason. Perhaps she had told St. Ives of their afternoon meeting, informed her cousin of his dislike and the warning he'd made to her. So then, the invite must be a challenge. Perhaps St. Ives meant to flaunt his control of Lady Jemima. To show him how completely she was a creature under his nefarious influence. The very idea repelled and appalled him. She was none of his affair. If she succumbed to her cousin's vile embraces, he would console himself with the view that he had warned her.

So then, it was with some surprise that he found himself begging off an invitation to a late supper with Whig friends in order to take the bustling journey over the Thames.

No sooner did he arrive at Vauxhall Gardens than he began to regret his hasty action. St. Ives, a man who, for whim and daring, might choose his arrival as an excuse to issue a more direct challenge. He had never fought a duel, thought it unworthy of men of great wisdom and intellect. Yet there were times when circumstance would not yield to reason and courage was required. He was accounted a good shot. He hoped that would be enough. Still, it might not come to that if the lady herself could be persuaded to see her dear cousin for the snake-in-hiding he was. For that she needed a comparison. He did not believe he did himself too much credit by thinking himself a proper candidate.

Then he saw her.

One glimpse of her glorious figure and every high-flown ideal took flight from his thoughts as lust rushed in to replace them. Delicious delightful voluptuous designs crowded his mind as he watched her dance. Yes, this was Salome, garbed in fewer veils than before.

Then his gaze met St. Ives's and he knew each understood instantly that they shared a single thought.

That realization pricked Beau's most vulnerable spot and betrayed a sudden jealous fury that had been flaring beneath his glacial calm all day long. He wanted Lady Jemima, wanted her much as her cousin did. He had come here not as a protector. He was here as a rival!

He was not surprised when St. Ives abandoned the dance floor to approach him. He planted his feet in expectation that there might be a mill. But to his astonishment, St. Ives walked right past him as though he had not seen him.

Shaken not by fright but by the leftover verve of an expected fight, Beau stood his ground a moment longer. Like lava flowing under the polar ice cap of his self-possession, his jealousy fixed upon Jemima as she dashed heedlessly past him after St. Ives. Curious to know how she would behave when she found her cousin determined his decision to follow her and watch.

But her quarry disappeared long before she gave up the chase. She was seemingly unaware that certain areas of the gardens were preserved for privacy where every sort of mischief took place, some of it amorous but much of it dangerous to unchaperoned females. So he followed her meandering, providing a shadowy guardianship she was unaware of until the push of lust and the opportunity to be alone with her on the aptly named Lovers' Walk became too much temptation. He stepped out of hiding and took her wrist.

Now she stood before him, trembling a little. Was she afraid of him? Or for him? Was this a trap? How like St. Ives to use her to lure him into vulnerability.

The air lifted on Beau's arms as he swung suddenly about, staring into the darkness that had been at his back.

"What is wrong?"

"I thought I heard something, or someone." Beau's gaze came slowly back to hers after making a searching arc through the surrounding shrubbery. "Is there a reason I should look to my back?"

A cold sensation of dread snaked through Jemima as she recalled St. Ives's careless warning that he would kill anyone who harmed her. And then she recalled the look on her cousin's face when he spied Lord Bellaire in the crowd. She did think he intended some sort of mayhem. Which was why she had followed him. Now she was caught between desires. How to protect them from each other? By distraction!

She took a step toward him, wishing the night would yield to her better clues of his mood in his expression. "Did you not just offer me a dance?"

Beau smiled. Never before had he heard a cordial note in this lady's voice. "Indeed. Can you catch the beat from this distance?"

Surprisingly when she put her thoughts to it, Jemima realized she could hear the full flow of music floating above even the laughter and voices in the park as it curled back to earth in this solitary place at the back of the gardens. "It is a waltz, my lord."

"Yes, the very thing for a night of mystery and romance."

As he stepped up to her and slid his arm about her narrow waist, he realized his description of the night was apt. "Then dance with me, lady."

From the moment he touched her, Jemima lost all sense of reality. She had never waltzed with a gentleman before. Even in this modern day, the waltz was still considered a scandalous exercise, forbidden at court. The idea of partners holding each other in a prolonged embrace spoke of a degree of intimacy with a man no unmarried lady should allow and no married woman should admit to outside the marriage bed. Or so the thinking went.

Yet she had practiced the forbidden dance just last winter right after Amelia had returned home from her post as governess. Amelia admitted she had observed the dance in the home where she was employed, watching from the balcony above as her employers and their friends waltzed. With a little urging, she had shown Jemima how it was done.

But swirling around in her own parlor with a female cousin was a far cry from stepping into the arms of a virile gentleman. As Lord Bellaire moved into the first step, it naturally brought her into close contact with his chest and a shock not unlike a spark went through her.

Sensing her hesitation as unfamiliarity with the dance, Beau said easily, "The lesson is more easily accomplished if you lay your free hand on my shoulder."

He took a firmer grip on her right hand, his larger engulfing her smaller in a warmth that surprised her. "Shall we?"

Unsure of herself but curious to know how it was done, Jemima placed her left hand on the crest of his shoulder. For a moment it perched there like a bird on an unfamiliar limb. "I do not know the dance, my lord."

"It is a simple exercise that requires no great mastery. The dancer need only listen to the beat of his or her heart. It is the rhythm of life. One . . . two, three. One . . . two, three. Follow the music, and your heart."

They began once more to move together. The high ridge of his shoulder blocked out the night, but she no longer thought about anything beyond the circle of their embrace.

She was seventeen again, with ribbons in her hair, and a chaste white frock holding her hammering heart in her chest as she entered Almacks. If only she did not breathe too hard, perhaps no one would notice her tremulous fear that she would be the single wallflower left to occupy in mockery the velvet chairs reserved for the elderly and infirm. Her future might be cut short by a total snub, her happiness snapped as a bud before it could reach full flower. So little was required that night. A single dance with an awkward youth or an elderly gentleman thrice her age. Any sign of consequence shown would be enough to make a success of her first night.

Then Lord Bellaire appeared. Would she dance with him? She could not find the simple word *yes* within her power to speak. Yet she took the hand he extended and floated like a leaf blown after him onto the floor. Never forgotten. Never.

Now she was moving in his arms, gliding along as effortlessly as before in the wake of his powerful steps. The melody compelled rather than pushed or shoved them along. In delight and trepidation, she moved with him as easily as if they had done this a hundred times before.

Small things registered in her senses, the clean wool smell of his domino, the heat of his hands where one hugged her waist and the other grasped her hand, the tensing of his muscles as he moved. He was more real than the first time they danced and she was aware as she had not been then of the import of the pleasant tension between them. This time they were illicit partners compelled by a dark sky and seclusion to indulge in the forbidden dance.

"Lady, you are a natural."

His words floated to her across the darkness that made her more brave than she would otherwise have been. She leaned into him, the darkness releasing her of the consequence of looking upon his face. Yet she was more aware of him than she had ever been. The hard strength of muscle lying just behind the layers of clothing reminded her once again that she knew too little of men to understand precisely what drove them.

Then she remembered, there was another woman, a woman both he and St. Ives preferred to her company. The spell broke and she backed a little away.

"Where is your lady, my lord?"

"I came alone tonight."

"That will come as a disappointment to someone," she murmured under her breath. Yes, that was better, a reminder of who and what he was. "I would expect a gentleman of your consequence to find such common entertainment beneath you."

Beau smiled. "Are you proficient at reading character?"

"In the main, yes. A spinster seldom has much to occupy her time. She must find simple pleasures where she may."

"In the dissection of the characters of her acquaintances. That seems a mean way of paying back your society."

"What society do we spinsters so enjoy that we cannot afford to lose it?" Jemima demanded. "We are just so much furniture in the lives of our families. Dealt with as one does a poker or a dust broom, to be picked up and used and then set aside until needed again."

"That is harsh."

"The truth sometimes is."

"Then allow me to say I think you quite fond of the paradox you resent. You claim to be a put-upon-the-shelf spinster. Yet here you are, alone with a gentleman who is not a relation, dressed to provoke the interest of the most jaded roué. Waltzing under the stars in a secluded corner is not the realm of a spinster but of the Fashionable Impure."

Jemima bristled at his smug tone. "I should expect you would lend your observation to condescension. Gentlemen don't like an independent woman."

"I beg to differ. Gentlemen especially like an independent woman."

"Only in such case as they seek to prey upon her. Without the visible support of family or husband, a woman becomes an object only of seduction for gentlemen."

"Do you read minds as well as characters?"

Beau guided her into a deep turn before she continued. "One does not need divining arts when gentlemen provide daily examples for all to see."

She heard him murmur what seemed a derisive phrase, yet he was all politeness when he next spoke.

"What—forgive my lack of edification—should a gentleman seek of an independent woman?"

"Her society for conversation, ideas, a shared appreciation of like minds." Jemima paused as the music stopped. "A waltz."

"Then I have been very fortunate in my judgment of you tonight. We are waltzing and the conversation is stimulating." He paused as if in some thought. "May I call upon you tomorrow?"

"I don't think that would be prudent."

"When tonight were we prudent?"

Suddenly Jemima was aware that they were no longer dancing but standing within a shared embrace. "Then no."

"No?" She held her breath as he reached up and touched her face. "I have often wondered why women bother to come masked to a ball. Now I understand." His finger moved to her mouth and traced her upper lip with infinite care. "It brings a man's attention to her lips. I am enamoured of yours. I ache to taste them."

She saw his intention reflected in his eyes a scant instant before his lips lowered. Yet his mouth did not engulf hers. His lips met hers softly, lingering a moment, then lifted. The action so surprised her that she didn't turn away. So his lips descended again as his arms slid about her. This time he caressed only her lower lip, drawing the tender fullness between his teeth as he gently suckled it.

Though his touch was gentle, Jemima's body reacted with a violent response that sent hard shivers through her. Heat, sweet and liquid, burst forth within her, setting her heart hammering. Then the flick of his tongue made her gasp.

When he lifted his head, his eyes were wide with passion and wonder and challenge. He stared at her, daring her, it seemed, to deny what she felt and she knew he felt. Jemima could do neither. She had tasted passion and the result was devastation.

Instead, she drew together the shards of her shattered pride and said, "Have you satisfied your curiosity?"

"Not in the slightest, madam!" Yet he released her and gave her a little push. "We'd better see you back to your protector before we both regret where our feelings could so easily lead us.''

Jemima felt defeated but too shaken to contest her loss. She might have fought him, denied him, but then he knew as she did from her kiss, she would have surrendered to a pleasure they could not afford to share.

''Did you see that!'' Guy whispered rather loudly from a nearby hedgerow. ''Beau has taken my Cyprian!''

''I have eyes.'' Richard heaved a great sigh of disgust.

They had been in pursuit of the coquette in question for some little time, ever since they saw her leave the dance floor. It gave him a sharp turn to find her in the arms of the very gentleman the evening was planned to avoid.

He knew better than to dip his oar into family affairs. They were never certain, full of treacherous currents, and bound to end as most all family squabbles did, with the outsider accused of the problem he had stepped in to help solve.

He jerked Guy by the coat sleeve. ''Come away. We will think of else!''

''I will best him yet!'' This time Guy did not sound angry. There was something faintly dreadful in his tone.

Richard tried to shake off the sense of dread at the turn of the night's events. He should not have encouraged Guy to follow the lady in boy's clothing. But how could he know? Lord Bellaire at Vauxhall Gardens? The odds were more likely in favor of snow before dawn.

A little ways away, Julien St. Ives assessed the scene with a more clear understanding and only a little less emotional involvement. He had given Jemima to Bellaire. And succeeded. There was only the matter of her desire now. If she did not want a lover or if her expectations of Bellaire were not met, he would kill him for her. Or, perhaps, he might have to kill him for himself.

The sight of his cousin in another man's embrace had yielded an unexpected result. As the seconds passed, he found he was capable of an emotion he had always thought beneath him. He was jealous!

Chapter Thirteen

They came in baskets, dozens of flowers of every kind and shape. And with them notes from strangers bearing ardent expression of infatuation, desperate urges to please, indulgences for an interview, waggish invitations to debauched delights from roués who thought Jemima well schooled in the libertine activities. She could not imagine how they found her location. She had spoken to no one, given her name to none . . . but Lord Bellaire.

Jemima opened and discarded the cards, preferring the flowers to the sentiments. One card she kept. It had been attached to branches of peach blossom and pungent sweet William. The meaning was clear; peach blossom represented a Captivated Heart and sweet William stood for Gallantry. The words on the card were ordinary. "Your servant." The sender extraordinary. It was signed *Lord B.*

The declaration of her would-be lover was not extravagantly made. Lord Bellaire did not seem the sort of man to make grand displays easily. His actions were another matter altogether.

All through the night, even into her dreams, Jemima had relived every second of their meeting in Lovers' Walk. The memory of his touch and kiss, his tenderness and urgent desire had blended in her mind to become an undeniable and insistent ache deep inside her that was entirely new in her understanding of herself. Only in the morning light did she come to a clear realization of its meaning. It was ridiculously simple and quite, quite shameful.

She was still in love with Lord Bellaire!

Yet that could signify nothing, *they* could mean nothing to each other unless she was willing to settle for an affaire.

That lowering thought had quite cut up her calm so that she had shredded two handkerchiefs before noon.

She had done it! Had won the attentions of her quarry. But at what cost to herself?

She had walked about all morning, muttering invectives under her breath, certain his spell would wear off after a good breakfast and a bit of exercise. It was now two of the clock and she was more enthralled with each hour. At least she had been saved Julien's sneering face. Unaccountably quiet as they returned home in the early hours, he had sent round his regrets before breakfast. A previous engagement would keep him away for the day. Thus sparing her his insightful glances and burrowing comments about her prolonged absence from his side at the masquerade. She had more important things to mull over.

It had never occurred to her that she would need to plan how to handle the moment once she won Bellaire over. In fact, she had never—not really—expected to do it. She had only foreseen in the vaguest terms the moment when he might profess his feelings for her and then she would turn on him in public and denounce him for the deceiver and seducer he was. But a bouquet did not provide a forum for that. And her feelings were not cooperating.

For one wild moment she allowed herself to conceive a

future in which they were together. She had never really had a beau. She smiled. Her Beau. The man she had agreed to wed had been as much her parents' choice as any. A dutiful daughter did not need strong affection to marry where she was bid. Perhaps that had made his desertion and the surrounding lies all the more horrid.

The world thought her an adulteress on the eve of her wedding. The truth was, she was still a virgin.

But Lord Bellaire did not know that. And the manner in which he treated her the night before was not that of a potential husband. It was as a lover come to claim his new mistress.

"I am marked for a sheep. Why should I not be one?" Jemima wondered aloud in her solitude. That question would not leave her be. She was certainly of an age and independence where she might do as she wished. If she were to take a lover, why not Bellaire?

It was a heady daydream that unfolded inside her mind, one of heated embraces, long lingering kisses, hot melting glances . . . not necessarily in that order. To think it! She, a middle-aged spinster by some ways of reckoning, had aroused the interest of a lord thought by many to one day seek the office of Prime Minister.

If she encouraged it, he would offer her a slip on the shoulder. It was the way of gentlemen who did not prefer whoring. He would come to visit her, share intimate meals and lots of champagne, and, after some required dissembling, her bed.

You know how that will end, the sensible part of her answered. She had the growing evidence of it tucked away in her house. Though he might not know he had a child about to be born, she did. And she could not forgive him for the deed. The quest for vengeance had become personal the moment she learned Pru's history.

"This must be how he captures the confidence of unsuspecting young women. I should have thought of that. He makes himself unobjectionable, charming in the extreme, and so the lady lowers her guard against the machinations of a rake! How clever, how sinister, how positively vile!''

If it had been the sin of any other gentleman, she might have been able to separate her private feelings from her sense of outrage and injustice. But it wasn't any other man. It was Lord Bellaire, her knight-errant. But now her paragon was tarnished beyond repair. For the loss of that illusion, she would never forgive him. Never!

There was only one cure for her bedazzled senses. She must exorcise her demon infatuation. And she knew just how to accomplish it.

For the next hour Foolscap bent ''his'' satirical powers on blasting Lady Jemima's romantic illusions of a night in Vauxhall Gardens.

Foolscap was not the only person to note the revels of the night before at Vauxhall. Using the usual allusions to great personages by their initials, the gazettes published in the following days were full of accounts of the doings of Lord G——and Lady Q——, Sir K——and Miss D——. The common Mr. and Mrs. were omitted, as it was quite impossible to learn the names of persons of no consequence. And, being persons of no consequence, why would anyone care to know their names? But of the fashionable *ton,* there were many possibilities to choose from. And on this occasion, there was mention of a most telling curiosity, the name Lord B——B——. This appellation had never before appeared in connection with frivolities at a masquerade. It was enough to set tongues wagging as to the exact lord in question. In fact, by midafternoon of the third day, London roiled with speculation.

If only Lord B——B—— had been mentioned in the

singular this might have been a sunrise-sundown wonder. But in this instance the person in question was coupled with that of "Miss Hyacinth," a comely masquerader in boy's trousers, a thing more shocking than a too-sheer gown. An anonymous tipster who had also given the Fragrant Flower's address had identified her as Lord B——B——'s partner in a moonlight dance on Lovers' Walk. By teatime of the third day, Jemima had found her metier in London. She was now notorious!

So it was with some surprise that on that fourth day, Julien found her packing. He entered her home unannounced and when she could not be found below, he went straight up to her bedroom.

"What is this? You are doing laundry?" Her bed overflowed with underclothing in the midst of being packed. "I'd hoped to find you entertaining a certain gentleman."

Jemima gave him an unfriendly glance. "Go away, Julien."

"I shall, soon enough." He followed this speech by dropping onto an elegant little side chair before her fireplace.

He noted first with pride that she wore a fashionable traveling dress of lavender that make her skin look creamy and her dark hair shine with blue highlights. The only blight on the vision she presented was the spectacles perched on her nose. One day he would lose them for her. Then he noticed her maid, a newcomer with a perky manner and artful glances sent in his direction. *There* looked a bit of fun! Finally he spied a trunk standing open in the corner. "'Pon oath! You are packing enough for a month."

"I am leaving."

"Yes, one rather presumed the point. Has Lord Dougherty invited you to a wicked weekend at a country house? They can be delicious interludes for a tryst. Fewer prying eyes of the *ton* upon one's every move. Which party is it? I have several invitations myself."

"I'm going home."

"But you've not the house for a really fine country weekend." Julien smiled at the maid with one eyebrow lifted. "One must have many bedrooms, connecting entrances, parks, woods, gazebos. Oh, a dozen delightful corners for trysting."

Jemima ignored him as she continued to place her things in a portmanteau. "You have no idea what the last days have been like. My address has been published! Published, Julien! Like that of a common strumpet! So that now all the world beats a path to my door. I am roused day and night by callers, some of whom have tried to force their way in after I refused to be at home to them. It is intolerable! Last evening we had to call the Night Watch. People had gathered on the square to watch and comment on the procession of carriages past my door. It is insulting and entirely unsupportable!"

"It would seem I have missed a great deal," he answered mildly, for he had discovered a new interest in her undergarments. He did not remember the lace corset.

That reminded Jemima. "Just where have you been?"

"Reminding myself who and what I am." He sent the maid a sizzling glance that made her look away. After a long moment he said softly, "It does not do at my age to aspire to that which should not be."

Jemima paused in folding a petticoat. "Is something wrong?"

He smiled at her in lazy amusement. "The thing about a lady is, once a man's found one to his liking, he inevitably begins to feel he must make plans, contingencies, plot a future. Now with a whore—"

"Julien!" Jemima bent a glance on her maid that despite Julien's brilliant presence sent her scurrying from the room.

"Now with a whore," Julien continued as if there had been no pause, "a man knows what he's paying for and how much he's going to receive in return. Mistresses are different, of course. A man can get to feeling possessive about a mistress as well, especially one as pretty as . . ."

His gaze cut suddenly toward Jemima and the effect of it went through her like a bolt of lightning. "The liaison can become as dangerous as a marriage."

"I don't understand you," she answered primly, returning to her task.

"It's as well you do not."

His gaze caught and lingered on the sheer lace-edged chemise she held up. This he had chosen for her. She hastily bundled it up and put it down as his gentle laughter suffused the room.

"With whom did you slip off the other night?"

She knew the question would come, had not doubted it, but she still felt the urge to cower and dissemble. "I went in search of you and became lost in the crowds." There, that was the truth, if not all of it.

"The name of the gentleman who escorted you back to our box?" This time his unholy smile did make her cringe inside. "Did you think I did not notice him?"

"Then you know who it was."

"Lord Bellaire." Julien plucked an imaginary speck from the waterfall folds of his neckcloth. "He begins to be a well-rung bell in our conversations. Why do you suppose that is?"

Jemima shrugged yet put down the pair of stockings she was rolling and turned fully toward him. "Why don't you tell me?"

"I believe, Puss, that he is infatuated with you."

Jemima looked away. "How can that be when you said only a few days ago that you and he were at odds over another lady?"

He was silent so long curiosity finally overcame her reluctance and she looked back at him.

He was watching her with unnerving appraisal until his answer supplied the reason. "I've never admired Bellaire's taste in women. You are an exception, a delectable one."

Jemima spun away from him, trembling as she did so. "You are never to speak to me in that way ever again, Julien. Never!" She turned back to soften her remarks, but he was no longer looking at her. "Julien, you *are* dear to me. But I can no longer accept such outrageous teasing as innocent or benign. You must cease."

Julien looked up slowly from a perusal of his pocket watch until their gazes met. "You are like a spoiled child, Puss. You must have what you want, when you want it, and no more. You are willful and stubborn and a trifle too proud for your own good. You ask for sympathy and aid, yet you listen to no needs but your own."

He sounded hurt. Jemima was incredulous. What did it mean? She sensed something important in the strange expression on his face that was no longer sneering or amused but a combination of both and something more. Then she realized he looked very tired, almost haggard, as if in the past four days he had been drinking too much and sleeping not at all.

"What do you need of me?" she asked softly.

You dare ask me that! Anger flushed Julien's face. He wanted to leap from his chair and shake her silly, to force her to confront that which she preferred to ignore with the blinders of her oh-so-careful upbringing. But she was not ready, not nearly ready. And he was a patient man.

In the end he only said, "That you remember the reason you came to London and that you remain brave enough to face the consequences."

This time Jemima looked away in shame. "I thought I could do all that and more. I believe now that I've made a mistake."

"That is an everyday occurrence with you. Yet in this

instance you are wrong.'' He tossed her a newspaper he had brought in with him. ''Your newest Foolscap is the talk of town. I especially appreciate the vultures edging the dance floor. Though I can't approve of his company, Foolscap is being mentioned in the same breath with reformers like Hannah More and William Wilberforce. Contrarily, you should follow in the footsteps of Lady Melbourne and Lady Bessborough. Now there are two sophisticates of amorality! You've had a good beginning in the art. Your address has become the biggest boon to florists and perfumeries since the Regent returned from Brighton.''

''Don't forget the boon to the butchers,'' Jemima added, for she could not long stay angry with her cousin. ''A side of beef, a brace of fowl, and a dozen lobsters were delivered only this morning.''

''In that case, I invite myself to supper. Half past nine?''

''I did not accept them!'' Jemima sounded indignant at the very suggestion. ''It is not done.''

''Yet the hall below stinks of hothouse blooms,'' Julien observed in mild disappointment. ''Why not accept what at least could be put to some use?''

Jemima blushed. ''I could not eat a side of beef in a month!''

''Beside the point. You might have fed an orphanage. Ah, now you are sorry. You are a queer girl. A side of beef for your own use stamps you a courtesan. But if it is used to feed the wretched poor, then you then feel you might style yourself a Lady Bountiful. You should make up your mind what you want, Jemima, before age puts a cap on your plans and stamps you fit only to lead apes in Hell.''

''You are in a perverse mood. If you have come only to lob invective at me, you may show yourself out.''

''Is that how Lord Dougherty does it?''

Jemima smiled. There was one consolation in the vexation

of the last days. Julien still believed her target was Lord
Dougherty. "He has not yet seen the inside of my door."

"And the other?"

Jemima frowned as she found a run in her pink-clocked
stockings. "I am at home to no one. Except you, for the
present."

"Nicely done. Put me on my toes in anxiety that I shall
be struck from your list." He rose gracefully in a single
movement. "Come drive about with me. Your leaving can
wait a day."

"Thank you. No."

"No? You say that too often for a notorious lady. 'Perhaps' is a better term."

"Perhaps I shall keep that in mind."

A knock interrupted them followed by the reappearance
of Jemima's maid. "There's two gentlemen below, ma'am.
They wish to be known to you."

"Send them up!"

Jemima sent Julien a quelling glance before addressing
her maid. "Who are they?"

"A Mr. Langley and a Mr. Somerset."

"I do not know them."

"And will not if you persist in formalities," Julien rejoined.

"You seem to forget, Cousin, that I have in fact done
nothing so far to incur censure. A remarkable opera dress
is no more than that. A costume? Of lesser note. I will not
admit to being home to gentlemen, or otherwise, to whom
I have not been introduced."

Julien showed a rare frown. "Confound it! You are correct. Clever girl. Still, you may wish to be made known to
Mr. Somerset. He is Lord Bellaire's brother."

This remark caught Jemima by surprise that bordered on
panic. Could it be that Pru had contacted him and he had
come to ask about her? Oh Lord! What if he should know

the whole of the ruse she plotted against his brother? "W-why should he be here?"

"To admire Lady Hyacinth I should imagine."

Jemima turned to the window and looked out across the street to where a small group of gawkers waited on the square in a misty spring rain. "They are waiting to peck my carcass."

That thought brought her up sharply. All at once she knew she had to get out of the confines of the house or she would go mad.

She swung around. "Julien, send them away at once! Bar the door and let no one in!"

The wild fright in her gaze silenced Julien's sharp tongue. "It will be done, Puss." He left at once.

Jemima turned to her maid. "Bring my chip hat and umbrella. I am going out. But tell no one. Not even my cousin."

With surprising ease, she slipped out of the first floor via the servants' stairs and then out the back gate through the kitchen garden. With no clear direction in mind, she carefully picked her way down an alley that smelled vile enough to make her cover her nose until she came to the street on the next block. Here the streets were empty but for a single curricle drawn by a matching pair of grays. They rounded the block just as she, umbrella belled wide, stepped from the narrow alley into their path.

Startled by the sight of the large black "mushroom," the nimble pair stopped short and then lurched forward with a sudden nervousness that snapped the driver's head back painfully.

Jemima heard him swear as her wrestled to bring them under control. Then he swung his head toward her with a scowl. "What the devil—!"

Looking up, she saw that it was Lord Bellaire who drove

the gig. He seemed as startled as his pair had been by her appearance on the street.

"Lucifer's own luck," she murmured, and made to quickly cross the street. As she did so, a shout rose from the alley behind her. She turned and saw two young men running in her direction. There was nothing for it.

She turned back and looked up at the very angry owner of the gig and said, "Take me away from here, please!"

Chapter Fourteen

Beau's team was new to his high flyer, a pair of prime bits of blood with spirits to match their bloodline. He did not, as a rule, invite riders along until he was satisfied that a new team was broken in. In fact, prudent man that he was, he had not left to chance the possibility of an accident that might leave him stranded. As a precaution, a postilion on horseback accompanied him at a respectful distance.

The morning's gallop along Rotten Row had not worked through the emotional turmoil that had sent him pounding down the lane in the first place. Sarah was in high dudgeon over what she perceived to be his desertion for the pleasures of Vauxhall Gardens three nights before. She did not care for politics but like all women in his experience did enjoy gossip. The appellation *Lord B——B——* in the gazettes had caught her entire attention.

She had greeted him the next day by tossing the paper at his head and exclaiming, ''I see why I was abandoned last evening! All London knows! A Cyprian! In boy's clothing!

Do you take me for a fool? I shall not be able to show my face anywhere! Damn you!''

His civil reply that there were other lords with the initials *BB*—"Bill" Blackstone and "Bingo" Byng to name but two—met with stony silence. He further elucidated that none knew of their "unofficial" alliance and therefore, even if he were the designated Lord B——B—— in question, it should not signify with her.

This, he should have foreseen, resulted in a tantrum he could only sustain in silence.

As she wept and threw about a good number of figurines, which she had claimed on other occasions to love, he stood glowering and wondering if it were possible to dislike a woman more than he did the one standing before him.

If only she had, instead, thrown her arms about his neck and drawn him down into her bed and given relief to the very strong urges he had been wrestling with since an ill-considered waltz. She might be beside him now, basking in a public admission that they were officially an "item."

Instead he was proceeding at a sedate pace toward the residence of Miss Jemima MacKinnon where, for three days running, he had left his card and was refused entrance. He had only to think of her and his lips began to tingle with the remembered passion of her kiss. He was attracted to her and, despite everything she said, he knew she returned the interest. He couldn't blame her for being wary. The most jaded of women would be daunted by the fact that as near strangers they had jumped hurdles that the most accomplished of coquettes strung out for weeks with her suitor of the moment. A waltz and kisses, both exercises to warm the manhood of any red-blooded gentleman with little formality into the bargain—it just wasn't done. Unless . . . the female was a complete and indiscriminate wanton.

It was scant comfort to his pride that no one else of his acquaintance could lay claim to having seen her abroad since the masquerade. Not so much as a rout or a supper found either her or St. Ives in attendance. So then he would give her a week to abandon her ninnyish attitude or he would abandon all interest in the lady.

He was musing over this bit of logic within a block of Miss MacKinnon's when she suddenly appeared from a side street under the frame of an umbrella. The sight had startled both him and his new pair and nearly brought all to ruin. Once he regained command of his skittish team, he was ready to cut her up with vulgarity. But to his surprise, he saw that two gentlemen were pursuing her.

She hurried into the street toward him, eyes wide with alarm. "Take me away from here, please!" she cried.

On the spot, he abandoned his intention of returning his cattle to the stables. He sawed his pair to a halt and signaled his man forward. After his postilion handed Miss MacKinnon up to the seat beside him, Beau turned into a lane that very quickly led out of town toward the countryside. For reasons he did not give much consideration, he wanted to impress Miss MacKinnon with his equipage and ability as a Whip.

He was perfectly at ease—well, nearly so—in his mind that this desire had nothing to do with the fact that he had recognized the two gentlemen chasing Miss MacKinnon up the alley as his own brother and cousin.

The startled look on their faces as they stopped short at recognizing him was priceless, if irritating. How had Guy and Richard come to know Miss Jemima? And what in heaven's name were they doing playing Fox and Hounds with her in an alley?

He was so satisfied that the image of them stymied in their pursuit had had no effect on his actions that he refused to bring up the issue. They were passing rural hedgerows from the center of Mayfair before the urge to speak came to him. Even then he resisted. The lady beside him seemed in no frame of mind for conversation.

For her part, Jemima could not believe her luck. As if from a tale of knights of old, her savior had appeared at the moment when she was most in need. Not precisely on a charging steed but in a marine blue high flyer with red wheel rims and a bright yellow undercarriage and a pair of dappled grays. It was as stylish an equipage as ever she had seen.

Still, she was in no hurry to thank her rescuer for then she would be put to the need to explain her actions.

Instead she gave herself over to a perusal of the country-side coming into view. In the distance sun spilled between the departing rain clouds, highlighting a meadow there, a field here. Farther on lay a lazy river upon which bargemen worked with long poles in hand to cart their wares upriver.

Her umbrella long abandoned, Jemima turned her face for a moment to the sun so that its warmth rested like an old friend upon her cheek. "How I miss my home," she said mostly to herself.

"I had thought you would much prefer the town." Beau glanced down at her upturned back, startled to find it so near. "You are a creature of the salon, are you not?"

"Oh no. I am most often found among my roses this time of year. And then there are the bulbs to be divided and reset. In another fortnight, I should be smoking the apple blossoms in the hope they will set well enough to provide the whole village with enough fruit for autumn pies and applesauce."

"You see to the business of your orchard yourself?"

"Of course. There is very little in my home that is not under my full control. The management of a house is fully as important as that of an army or a government. For there to be peace and prosperity, all parts must run smoothly."

"Well put." But Beau was surprised to hear a wanton speak so warmly of hearthside affairs. "Do you have a particular destination in mind this afternoon?"

She glanced at him and saw that the wind whipped his silver hair into his eyes and a slight sheen of perspiration slicked his tanned cheeks. But it was not his handsome profile alone that made her stare a bit longer than was polite. It was the fact that for the first time since coming to London, he appeared at his ease. "I feel I am abusing your hospitality."

"I am glad to have been of service. If you were in need of fresh air, you had but to send round your maid with a note."

Jemima dipped her head with a smile. "I was not aware until the very moment I left my house of what I needed." She turned to him finally with a smile. "What a saving grace that you should appear so opportunely."

"Was it opportune?" He glanced briefly at her for his cattle were requiring the greater part of his attention. "I gather you were being pursued by . . ."

He saw her pinken charmingly before turning away. "I do not know who they were. This has been an excessively distressful week."

He nodded in sympathy. "You once expressed your belief that your reputation was such that you should never attract a glance. Today would-be suitors pursue you. Does that not ease your fears?"

"Hardly. It is a falsity universally accepted that a single lady attached to a generous dowry must be in want of a husband," Jemima said roundly. "One may as well say the sole desire of a hen is to be roasted upon the spit. Often as that fate may claim such birds, you made depend upon it that the idea never sits fondly in the heart of the dear doomed fowl. Marriage is for the unimaginative."

"Here! Here!" Beau chuckled appreciatively. He was never bored in her company, and that was saying a lot. Unlike Sarah, Miss Jemima never expressed the commonplace or

merely polite. It gave him permission to be as frank. "Forgive my impertinence, but what of the want of children?"

"I should love to have a child." A frown drew Jemima's
perfectly arched black brows together, but only for an instant.
"Yet to soothe the maternal instinct, one need only look to
the streets of London where orphans are as plentiful as
leaves. True charity of the heart should compel one to choose
from among them."

"Surely you would not take in a street urchin to raise as
your own?" Beau ventured after a short pause to maneuver
his carriage around a slower dray in the road.

Jemima gave the possibility as little consideration as one
would a daydream never to be acted upon. "I believe I
would."

"Would you not fear to be murdered in your bed by the
rapscallion?"

"As a matter of fact, I only recently took a young woman
under my roof. She was homeless and soon to give birth."

He reared back to glance at her past the wall of his shoulder. "You've taken in a stranger with child?" He made
no effort to hide his censorious tone. "You are too easily
persuaded. Of course, there is no sire."

"Absurdity! Of course, there is a sire." The moment she
said it, recall made her furious. *He* was the vile seducer.
"He is no husband to her, if you must have it. He is a
seducer of the vilest sort."

"And still you give this woman shelter? Extraordinary!"

Jemima rode a moment in silence, alarmed by the ease
with which she could forget that the man beside her was
her sworn enemy. He had only to smile and say something
gallant and she was half beguiled into her former belief in
him as a gentleman without equal. How could he be made
of two so completely opposite parts? The composition should
not hold.

"I had forgotten until today what a pleasure it is to ride

for miles with only the wind and sun for company." He glanced at her with a complaisant expression. "It would only be surpassed by present company of the most pleasant kind."

He's flirting, she thought in faint alarm. Then she realized that he must be thinking as she was of their last encounter. It ended only after she had been folded in his very heated embrace hazarding kisses as freely as if they were chips in a card game.

Beau watched the play of emotions give vivid animation to her expression and found himself thinking that she was more fascinating than even the countryside. *Refreshing,* that was the word that came to mind as he gazed at her.

He had considered her from the first glance across the opera house to be a practiced seductress or a hardened schemer. Yet her look in this moment was that of an innocent he could not say he truly remembered meeting nine years before. Her cheeks were pink from the wind and beneath her bonnet her black hair had come undone and streamed in long silky pennants behind her.

Once again he was acutely aware of the emotional turmoil inside him. This time it had nothing to do with Sarah or Lord B——B—— or even his lustful leanings toward her. It came to him that St. Ives must be behind the wilder aspects of her character. He had admitted as much that it was his aim to turn his cousin into a unredeemable wanton. Beau smirked. He had not yet succeeded.

So then the burden of this young woman's character, unwanted or looked for, had fallen to him. The prospect was not wholly unwelcome. With Guy running amok and his own sense of world order in shambles, here was something direct and helpful he could do: save a young woman from the fall. The knowledge of a new purpose swept him with a sense of self-congratulation and a certain amount of pride in his accustomed role of protector of innocence, even if it was from his own feelings.

"You will do well not to return to Town for a time. You cannot know what London can do to the tranquility of the inexperienced. For instance, you should have made known at once that you would not countenance the circus atmosphere that now daily surrounds you."

Resentment pricked her. "I assure you, it is none of my doing."

"Ah, but that is precisely the point. A more skillful lady should have known how to avoid it." He sent her a very warm smile that lit up his dark eyes. "If you will allow, I shall take the matter in hand for you. It should not require more than a few days. In the meantime, I should be happy to see you to the seclusion of a country inn of your choosing."

She started. "You are offering me carte blanche, Lord Bellaire?"

The question cut so close to thoughts he was not allowing himself to entertain that he spoke from chagrin. "Don't be a fool!"

A blush hot as fire swept her as she turned to him. "I find that is what gentlemen usually say when a lady is making sense."

Beau glared at her in consternation. "Then you have not known enough true gentlemen."

"Another slur!"

"Curiouser and curiouser you become," he said between his teeth. "I have never known a lady to be offended by a gentleman who called her sheltered."

"You called me ignorant. There is a difference."

"Not enough to make a pie with," he answered in some heat.

Beau whipped his carriage around a curve and into a broadening lane that signaled the entrance into a village. Though it was midweek, and the middle of the planting season to boot, the village was far from empty. On the square a crowd had gathered, shouting and shoving and laughing.

"What is going on?" Jemima demanded.

"Nothing to disturb our day," Beau answered calmly. "We'll ride on."

"Oh, but it must be a fair day. I should love to see a pantomime show. May we stop? Please?"

Beau sent her a glance and found himself staring into her look of delight over the prospect of the simple pleasure of a traveling show.

"Very well." He reined in his team.

The sight of a high flyer with crimson wheels and yellow undercarriage momentarily drew the attention of several of the villagers at the back of the crowd. As they turned and moved back, Beau caught a glimpse of the center of their amusement. His face went blank as he reached for the whip and gave it a sharp crack over the heads of his team.

"What's wrong?" Jemima demanded in vexation.

"We will drive on," is all he said.

"No!" Jemima had seen a slight narrowing of his gaze as he viewed the spectacle she could not see. She stood up even as the carriage began to move forward. "I want to know what is going on."

Beau quickly mastered the horses that balked at his command to halt yet again then turned a stony glance on her. "If you must know, it is a bear-baiting."

"What?" Appalled, Jemima pulled her spectacles from her pocket and put them on, then strained up on tiptoe to try to get a glimpse. She had never seen the violent crowd-pleasing sport but had heard of it spoken up in the most shocked and disapproving tones by Henrietta's father. "But that is awful. They must be stopped."

Beau had not prepared for her next action. In fact, she had stepped down onto the lane before he could bark out, "What are you doing?"

Jemima looked back up at him, a determined expression on her face. "Can you not see? They mean to put that poor animal in some sort of torture."

"Perhaps." He knew it was useless to deny it. Bear- and bull-baiting were sports from the Middle Ages that were dying out only in recent years. "I don't see what that has to do with us."

She scowled up at him, every line in her pretty face behind those odious lenses arranged in schoolmistress disapproval. "I must stop it. They will kill the poor thing."

Beau smiled indulgently. "You cannot be serious. You—Miss MacKinnon!"

Jemima turned and hurried toward the crowd, brandishing her parasol and crying, "Hold! You there! Hold, I say!"

"Of all the devilment!"

Chapter Fifteen

Consternation was a polite word to apply to his feelings as Beau climbed down from his carriage. He tossed the reins to his footman. "See to it they don't overset the rig," he instructed as he started after Jemima.

The grim expression on his face was not for her alone. Crowds were as unpredictable as wildfire. There'd been an occasion recently when the newly named Regent himself had been afraid to venture forth through a hostile gathering. No lady in his experience would ever think to wade into one, certainly not one made up of ruffians who were not likely, in their excitement at the prospect of watching a violent end to a beast, to treat her as courteously as she might expect.

Jemima did not share Lord Bellaire's concern. Her sole sympathy was for the cornered frightened creature she had glimpsed from her perch in the carriage. By a series of "See here," and "Mind the way," she forced a path into the crowd and out through the other side. The sight that greeted her when she had done so at last gave her pause.

In the center of the square, chained to a tree, was a large black bear. Around him, a dozen hounds barked and snapped. Terrified by the multiple threats, the bear stood on its hind legs, paws raised in challenge, roaring warnings to those surrounding it.

In the center of the throng was a man in open shirt and leather vest. The sleeves of his shirt were rolled up to reveal biceps the size of smokehouse hams. Those arms marked him a blacksmith. He was cracking a whip over the head of the poor animal who cringed and shook his head each time as though he were being stung by a wasp.

Jemima looked about her at the ring of jeering, taunting faces and understood there would be no use in appealing to them for help. At that moment she heard the bear roar with pain as the whip this time snaked about his head.

Angrier than she could contain, Jemima rushed forward and struck the arm of the man holding the whip with her furled umbrella. "You will desist at once. That is evil and cruel!"

The brawny fellow swung around. "Here—bitch!" Then his eyes widened as he took in Jemima's fine clothing and her equally fine face, at the moment flushed by anger and her exertions. His glower became a wide-open smile. "Here now, ain't ye pretty as paint?"

Jemima lifted her chin in protest of his too-forward speech to point at the bear with her umbrella. "You must release that animal at once!" The look of complete surprise on his face made her reconsider. "At least you must stop tormenting it."

" 'Tis no business of yers. Off wid ye!" one of the women in the crowd cried.

"Off wid ye!" The crowd instantly took up the chant, but as the blacksmith lifted his arm again Jemima struck him on the head and this time heard the distinct snap of her weapon.

He moved quickly for a big man, grabbing her up by her dress front and hauling her in close to him. The yank dislodged her spectacles from her nose and they dropped away. "Ye want to play, ye'll have to wait. I ain't never turned down a slap and a tickle, but I'm busy here just now."

As the crows hooted and cheered Jemima struggled uselessly to free herself from his grasp.

Finally a calm but thoroughly masculine voice cut through the chatter. "Let go of the lady."

The blacksmith turned toward that voice and looked Beau up and down, judging rightly from his top hat to mirror-bright boots that he was a town toff. His sneer expressed his opinion of that sort. "This be none of yer business, guv'nor. Shove off."

"Gladly, when you've released my companion."

The blacksmith squinted at Beau a second time and then turned his leer on Jemima, whom he still held in his grip. "You his fancy piece?"

"I certainly am not!" Jemima answered with as much dignity as her situation would allow. He had her up on tiptoe and though both her hands were wrapped around the fist holding her clothing, she could not budge it a single finger.

"Then tell the gent yer wid me now, lovely. There's a girl," the blacksmith added as he shook her like a recalcitrant child. "I ain't got the fine gent's copper in me pockets. But I've else in me breeches to keep ye happy."

The shaking was too much for Jemima to bear with dignity. She released his fist, and making a pair of her own swung them with all her might to strike both his ears at the same time.

He yelped in pain and released her so quickly Jemima fell back on her heels and then tumbled backward onto the grass on her backside. As she did so she heard a decided crunch in her nether region. "My spectacles!" she cried in desolation.

Each act further delighted the crowd until they were crowing with laughter by the time he reached for her a second time and she scuttled backward desperately to evade his grasp.

Meanwhile Beau was doing a bit of sizing up of his own. He was not near the bull-necked laborer's size and weight, but he had been extremely handy with his fists since his public school days. Anticipation of *hors de combat* did not frighten him. Dealing with the unfair advantages possible in the crowd who might join in the mill did. He knew that he could have only one chance to drop the fellow. Freed of the brute's grip, Jemima, at least, could flee.

"You there!"

Beau squared off in a defiant stance and sloughed off his riding coat.

"A mill!" someone in the mill cried and again others instantly took it up. "A mill! A mill!"

Jemima scrambled to her feet. "No, no! Lord Bellaire, you mustn't—"

Beau did not even spare her a glance. His full attention was upon the iron-muscled behemoth before him who, understanding what the crowd now expected by way of entertainment, turned on him grinning as if he held the key to hell.

It happened so quickly that when she told the story later, Jemima could never be certain she had witnessed all of it. Almost before she could comprehend that a bout of fisticuffs was about to take place before her, the fellow lunged at Lord Bellaire. He charged head down like a bull. It seemed that he hoped to knock Beau from his feet with the sheer force of his weight.

Beau moved more quickly, sidestepping the intended tackle, and yet landed a blow deep into the soft middle of the blacksmith's belly. The man expelled a great bellows breath, staggered, and then fell like a slab of stone face-first onto the grass. After a moment of silent shock, it was clear to all that he would not rise anytime soon.

As the villagers crowded around, some shouting to one another that the inert blacksmith must be dead, Beau grabbed Jemima's wrist and then ran for his life, dragging her behind him.

He did not pause until they had reached his gig and then he grabbed her by the waist and hoisted here up onto the perch without pause.

"What about the bear?" she asked as he climbed up beside her.

Beau sucked in a quick breath and reached for the reins. "He is from a sideshow. No doubt he has been taught fisticuffs for a mummery. He will needs fight his own battle."

"You mean to leave him behind?" The indignation on her face was a clue as to what she meant to do. Still Beau experienced the shock of unreality as she reached for the carriage brake to steady herself as she started to climb down.

The moment she put a foot on the first spoke, he grabbed her from behind. "You little fool!"

He swung her about in his arms, too angry to say more, and dragged her in against him. The kiss was full of fury and disgust and consternation. But all of that quickly evaporated in the experience of the touch of her lips. He had expected her to fight him, but she did not. The kiss seemed to drive every other impulse from her mind as she quite unexpectedly collapsed into him, offering her mouth freely for his exploration.

Jemima heard him chuckle and wondered how he could find amusement where she found only shock and unnerving pleasure. At his touch something had come roaring to life within her; something she had never expected. Before she could martial another thought, he lifted his mouth from hers.

For a moment he gazed down at her bemused expression

with an equal amount of astonishment on his own side. "What am I to do about you, Jemima?"

"I don't know," she answered in complete honesty. Then she blinked. "My bear!"

"God give me patience!" He shoved her back unceremoniously onto her side of the carriage seat, then stood up and reached for the horsewhip.

Jemima shrank back in alarm. "You wouldn't dare!"

Beau looked at her with a scowl. "Don't tempt me." But his scowl wouldn't hold. He smiled. "Stay here. For the love of Zeus! Stay here!"

Chapter Sixteen

Jemima arrived at Julien's Mayfair residence with a passel of children running alongside Lord Bellaire's carriage. Though uncommon sites were common enough in this great city, the vision of a great black Russian bear riding footman at the back of a gentleman's high flyer was singular!

With the footman's help, the rescued bear had been tied to the carriage's back step for there was no other place for him. If the bear occasionally roared his disapproval of the arrangement, it did not signify. The delight on Lady Jemima's face each time she caught Beau's eye for the moment made up for the suspicion that he had been made a fool of, and then been asked to pay the price of admission to his own farce.

It had not been easy to persuade the bear's owner, a butcher who said he had taken the creature as payment from a Gypsy boy, to part with the animal. In the end, Beau parted with ten pounds sterling for the beast.

Then there was the matter of freeing the bear from the

tree without being mauled to death for his trouble. First, he
had to get rid of the hounds. To do so, he had paid for and
then upended a meat pie cart. The spilled fare diverted the
attention of the dogs to the feast now spread on the grass.
With a few pieces reserved for the bear, Beau had gingerly
unbound the animal and then fed him pieces to get him to
come along toward the carriage without further trouble. The
bear, it seemed, preferred mincemeat to kidney pie.

But now, riding through Mayfair with all the pomp and
circumstance of a parade, Beau could not but wonder at his
audacity and the resulting preposterousness of his position!
The gazettes would have a field day with it. His dignity
would take a thorough trouncing. At the moment, that did
not matter.

Beside him, gazing up at him from time to time with her
heart in her eyes, was the most contrary, inexplicable woman
he had ever met. Because of her he felt, despite it all, that
he had just had one of the best days of his life. Schoolboy
pranks had never been as much fun. And, at the end of it,
he had a tale to tell of a mill with a blacksmith whom he
had bested with one blow. So then, he did not doubt a
retelling of the day's folly would produce as much envy as
ridicule among his parliamentary associates.

He had also the last hour of basking in Jemima's approving
company to quiet his suspicions that he might be thought a
gull.

And so without a qualm he took her right to St. Ives's
door, as she had requested. They were in agreement that he
would see her again, this very evening. In the meanwhile,
he was more than willing to turn over the care and housing
of his extra passenger to the man he thought most deserved
the trouble.

After directing his footman to shackle the beast at the
hitching post before St. Ives's residence, he rode off with

a light heart and a tip of his hat to the lady left behind at his rival's door.

Jemima, too, was over the boughs with delight at the afternoon's events. Her vexation with London ways was forgotten. Her disillusion with Lord Bellaire was muted. Her anger with St. Ives was overlooked as she rushed into his home to inform him of her adventure.

News of her arrival prompted a quick response from her host, who had been occupying himself with a decanter of brandy in his room while he waited word of her.

St. Ives took the stairs two at a time, a look of black fury animating his daunting features as he descended to greet her. "Where the deuce have you been?"

"Julien, dear! I am so glad to find you home. I shouldn't have known what to do else. I've been for a ride in the country—"

"The devil you have!" Her marched right up her and took her by the arm. "With whom?"

Jemima pinkened. "Lord Bellaire. It was a chance thing, really—Julien, you are abusing my arm." When he released it, she began untying her bonnet to put her excess nerves to use.

"Bellaire."

Julien took her in a single scorching glance that noted every item from her cockeyed bonnet over loosened curls to the crushed condition of her traveling dress. There were thick splashes of mud on her hem and more encrusted her boots. Most damning of all, a wide swath of half-dried earth slicked the back of her from shoulder to hips. The reason was unequivocal. She had been on her back in the mud!

His gaze met hers with a disturbing force. "You've damaged your gown, Puss. Next time, ask your lordship to provide you with a pallet before he rides you."

Jemima blushed hotly, deeper than she might have if he

had been near the truth. "Don't be vulgar, Julien. It's been raining. I slipped in the mud when the smithy released me."

"Smithy." Julien's tone iced the word as his gaze moved back to the damning stain on her skirts. "You were tumbled by a smithy, as well?"

"I fell, Julien. Slipped in the mud. Lord, why do I bother to converse with you when you are in this mood?"

But he had rattled her and Jemima's hands shook as she stripped off her gloves and set them aside with her bonnet before hurrying into his salon to find a mirror. The sight of her reflection in the glass above the mantel was far from reassuring. Her eyes were wide, her cheeks deeply pink, dark hair tumbling into her eyes. She did look a wanton!

When she glanced back at Julien, she had the unnerving feeling that he was constructing in his mind a scene of such debauchery as she might never wish to imagine. She could not answer the look he gave her. It was too depraved.

She turned away and began reassembling her hair with quick fingers that reanchored the pins. "I shall explain all in due time. But first you must help me. You see, I have brought you a guest." She let that thought wash through her with calming effect. She did have an explanation to distract him, after all.

She turned to him with something resembling her usual smile. "You must find somewhere to put the poor dear until the proprietor of the Menagerie can be fetched. Though I suppose, in truth, he is my bear."

Julien stared at her as if *she* were a bear speaking to him. "Your *bear?*"

"Yes. A black Russian, we are supposing."

Determined that he should not backtrack into a conversation of Bellaire, she took his arm and steered him to the front window where he could look out on the street. "Look, just there."

What Julien saw was a large furry animal with a thick

leather collar about his neck scratching his back against a lamppost.

He reared back and stared at her. "Good lord! It *is* a bear."

Jemima nodded and smiled. "I know, it's all quite unbelievable. Lord Bellaire got him for me. Rather he rescued the poor unhappy creature from a most detestable exhibition. My apartments are too small for his needs. I should be very grateful if you will but allow me to leave him with you."

This time, for the first time, she saw she had truly astonished her worldly cousin.

Jemima looked away, amazed by how much it shocked her to have shocked him. "May we have tea? I am famished and as dry as stone."

"So you must see, something had to be done." Jemima paused in the middle of her explanation to sip her tea.

Julien had insisted that she trade her soiled gown for one of his Oriental smoking robes. Though it covered her as thoroughly as any gown she ever wore, she felt faintly decadent drinking tea in his boudoir.

Julien must have thought the same for he watched her through slitted eyes as he sat opposite her in a matching wing chair. "Go on," he said after a moment.

"Yes, let's see." She had omitted mention of her reasons for escaping from the house and how she had met Lord Bellaire. If Julien suspected it was an assignation, she would not counter the impression. He would, she knew, think more of her for slipping away for an indiscretion than an admission that she had run away. "Lord Bellaire was kind enough to fetch the bear from a crowd that would have killed it."

Julien's sour expression took a positively prussic acid turn. "Bellaire purchased the beast for you?"

"Oh no. He fought a smithy for him!"

Julien expelled a common Anglo-Saxon vulgarity.

Jemima didn't on this occasion think it wise to object. "It was really quite exciting, Julien. Perhaps I might have handled my side better, but I was determined to stop the creature's torture. The smithy would have none of it. He began to manhandle me in a most unfriendly manner. That is when Lord Bellaire came to my rescue. I had no idea a member of the House of Lords could be so handy with his fists."

"His fists?" This brought Julien upright. "Your gallant indulged in a pugilistic exhibition on a village green?"

Jemima nodded. "I was never so surprised. Landed the smithy 'one in the breadbasket,' I believe he later phrased it. The odious man dropped like a felled tree. It was thrilling for I was quite afraid Lord Bellaire would instead be pounded flat as a wheel rim."

Julien offered her a tolerant smile. "You frighten me, child."

The cries of the crowd on the street reminded Julien of his duty and he stood up and went to the window. "I suppose we should do something with your . . . new pet before the crowd gathering outside my windows begins a bear-baiting of its own. Is he partial to steak, do you suppose?"

"I should imagine so. He ate all the meat pies Lord Bellaire offered him." She went to stand beside her cousin and look out. "He does seem quite done in, poor thing. Water and meat should set him up. Where do you propose to place him?"

"In the back garden for the present." As Julien rang for a servant, he turned back to her. "May I inquire as to the present health of your two-legged companion?"

"Oh, he is fine. You should have seen him, Julien! He could go a few rounds in the ring, if gentlemen did such things."

"They often do, at Gentleman Jackson's. Perhaps I shall

take you there some day soon. It is quite a sight, gentlemen stripped to the waist trying to batter one another senseless. Bellaire might be persuaded to perform again for you.''

Jemima's mouth formed an *O* of surprise. ''I had no idea.''

''Why is Sir Galahad not with you? I should have thought he would take it upon himself to announce to me his heroic service to you.''

''I am certain Lord Bellaire need not flaunt his uses abroad,'' Jemima said carefully for she had not forgotten Julien's earlier innuendo that *she* was the reason for the contention between the two men. ''But I am not so much in his confidence that I could be in the way of knowing his thoughts precisely.''

Noting her reluctance to impart her feelings in the matter of Bellaire, he continued casually. ''This blood thirst is a new and unsuspected facet of your character. I should mark it down as a warning against my own health. Or is it only Bellaire you would have risk his life for your enjoyment?''

Jemima bristled. ''You know very well I did not enjoy a moment of the minutes I thought his life was in jeopardy.''

''Yet in the main, you had a pleasant sojourn,'' Julien said with some asperity.

''The best.''

''The best, she answers. You've devilish queer ideas of an afternoon's diversion, Puss. I begin to think you are quite lost to the reason that brought you to London.''

Jemima gave him an annoyed glance. It would be so much easier if Lord Bellaire would stop kissing her. It made her mind excessively muddled and then she could not quite remember why she disliked him so much.

As for her own feelings, she had not had time to sort them out but when she did, she was certain she would find that her interest in Lord Bellaire had more to do with romantic notions gleaned from novels than any personal attachment to the man himself.

Julien could read her like a well-thumbed book. Her eyes were melting with joy, her cheeks blooming like June roses and her hair enough of a mess for him to presume, had she been any other woman, that a tumble in the meadow had been part of her afternoon. Even so, he suspected Bellaire must be a better suitor than his high-handed priggish traditional exterior would seem to suggest. He could not, if pressed, answer in truth whether that pleased or angered him the more.

Jemima's voice interrupted his thoughts. "I have begun to wonder, Julien. Is it possible for a man to be all charm with one woman and all harm to another?"

"Without a doubt. You need but my example to prove it."

Jemima turned to face her cousin with a small smile. "I do not, you should know, believe all that you tell me of your wretched conduct."

Julien gave her a scorching glance. "I could so easily change your opinion." He indicated his bed, a huge canopied piece of furniture. "You would not like the lesson, but you would learn it well."

Jemima's smile faltered. "You are forever at the trouble to make me dislike you. I do not understand why."

This time he shrugged. "It amuses me."

"What if I should one day take you at your word and treat you accordingly?"

He smiled then. "Then I shall have to find other amusement, Puss." He reached for a packet on a nearby table. "Until then, we shall rub on as cousins do. A post has come for you. From the LADIES."

Chapter Seventeen

My dear Miss Jemima,

How we, our little group, miss you! Has it been only a Fortnight since you left our little circle? The LADIES certainly can think of no Entertainment to match your Superior Hosting. We are at a loss to know what to do with our Two Thursdays.

Yet, we have not been Idle. It has come to our Attention that Foolscap has continued even as you are away from us. To that Purpose I write to you today. We have newly discovered another example of the Mercenary Habits of Young Gentlemen. Amelia has had a most Unhappy Letter from a former charge at her First Posting as governess to an Irish Horse Breeder. It has been the Misfortune of her eldest sister to be Jilted!

A month ago a certain Gentleman from Hampshire

*who had a Weakness for Horseflesh came to her
father's horse farm in pursuit of a Prime Bit of Equine
Lineage for his Stables. When denied his choice, he
affianced himself to the daughter of the owner of a
Prize Sire he desired. A Deal was struck with the horse
proposed as part of the Marriage Dowry. The Horse
was to be brought to Haymarket to be Held until the
Marriage.*

*Alas, before the First Banns could be read, the prize
Horse was Stolen. At the news the Groom broke his
engagement, charging that the Father deliberately
spirited the Horse away to the Continent where it
brought a greater Price than in Britain. The Father
claims he was duped. The Gentleman is responsible
for the Theft so that he might Avoid the Wedding. The
Abandoned Bride, who knew Nothing of the Arrangement between the Men, is said to be Distraught.*

*'Tis our Consensus that Foolscap should Address
this Wrong.*

Henrietta Smythe

*P.S. Amelia says to Please Relate that her Charge Pru
has Settled in Nicely. Her Confinement Nears more
Rapidly than any of us could at First Suppose. This
has Curtailed her Walks into Town. A Blessing for
all.*

Jemima sat alone in her room a long time with the letter
Julien had given her, reading and rereading the lines until
she had conjured for herself the humiliation of the young
lady whose happiness had been bartered for horseflesh.

Very soon all her old feelings of shame and humiliation
bubbled up through the happiness of her day. The sick humiliations of seventeen were stronger than the joy of a twenty-
six-year-old's afternoon. Once more the helpless feeling of

having no ally in a world where friends were enemies and parental protection brought no relief from disbelief engulfed her.

Most often she threw off the inclination to relive her own humiliation. But today after a strangely perplexing yet excessively pleasant afternoon in Lord Bellaire's company—and in his arms—she knew it again had to be faced.

It wasn't horseflesh her suitor had been enamored of. It was her dowry of ten thousand pounds. It had been explained to her a dozen times the spring she turned seventeen and was to be presented at court. The difference between the mercenary and the prudent motive of a matrimonial proposal had to do with one's position in society. A younger son, in want of a dowry that would allow him to live in the manner that he had become accustomed before his majority, was to be her aim. A gentleman of high birth could think to raise a young lady's family connections through his kinship to an earl or duke. For such a fellow to condescend to wed, ten thousand would not be prudent or worthy. Twenty at least must be his goal.

On the other side, a younger son of a barony or knighthood would find himself thought mercenary, indeed, to seek to secure twenty thousand as dowry. It was sure to be an unsuitable match where he could never hope to keep his bride in the manner in which she had been reared. Ten thousand bought just so much, but no more.

Therefore, the younger son of a viscount was thought to be as good a catch as she could reasonably hope to aspire to. Even so, there would need to be the indulgence of affection on the gentleman's part. The son of a viscount might aspire to twice as much before the accusation of mercenary would cast a shade on his picture frame.

On her side, there need only be an inclination to suggest interest but no decided favor. Love was for poets and kings.

Perhaps if she had cared more about her family's future

connections or less about personal affinity she would have been more wary of Sir Jeremy Holton. That he paid his address to her so suddenly after Lord Bellaire's attentions at Almacks should have warned her.

"Indelicate," her mother later murmured of Sir Jeremy.

It had been excessively forward of the young gentleman to single her out exclusively after an earl paid address to a social wallflower. Particularly when only a few days before at a soiree, Holton had refused the opportunity to be made known to her. The high sticklers took notice. But there it dropped.

Jemima had been too enamoured of her first Season to heed the looks or the glances of the other mothers and their daughters. Perhaps if she had been in the know, she would have heard the murmurings as well.

A man in desperate circumstance, as she later learned Jeremy Holton to have been, had little time for niceties. The income promised by his grandfather had been revoked. The reason was never given yet the gossip of his disinheritance was not long in coming to her door. Her father merely smiled and said, "If we do not object, who should?"

Who, indeed? If one's own parents could not be counted upon? And so she had accepted Sir Jeremy's proposal because it was what her parents wanted and he was attentive and charming and if she suspected it was nothing more than the charm of an accomplished flirt it did not matter because he had asked for her hand. And she let him kiss her almost as often as he liked because it was thrilling and new and, once engaged, she was safe.

A high opinion of herself on the marriage market. That was only one of the crimes Sir Jeremy accused her of at the altar that was to have bound them in wedded bliss, but it stuck long after the shock of more inflammatory slurs wore off.

A certain uncertainty and curiosity were all that she could

name to account for her actions on the eve of her marriage. Sir William was Sir Jeremy's avowed best friend. They seldom appeared out of one another's company. Even while Jeremy courted her, William was seldom more than a room away. So then when she received a note through her maid from Jeremy, asking her to meet with Sir William in private that afternoon, she had slipped out of her home without hesitation.

Sir William was always droll company, with his perfectly placed curls rowed across his forehead and his penchant for every new bit of flippery. That day he smelled of lilac water and scented snuff. He had taken her up in his gig just beyond her garden gate, saying that he was taking her to meet Jeremy, and had then driven her out of London and into the country.

His conversation was always full of inconsequential news of the day and she'd smiled and laughed at his amusing patter until she realized she was far from home in an unfamiliar neighborhood.

Soon enough, he turned off the lane into a rutted path that led to a cottage standing at the back of small clearing. Tucked away behind hedgerows and brambles, it was completely hidden from view of the road. A trysting place!

"Jeremy set it up," he assured her as he handed her down. "This is your day, Miss Jemima."

Inside the cottage a fire was laid, along with a repast that was more than tea. She remembered thinking that Jeremy was fond of his food. Yet Sir Jeremy wasn't there. The explanation why was as swift as it was shocking.

Sir William took her bonnet and spencer before he sat her down and said in the most ordinary voice that he had been asked to bring her here to deflower her.

"Jeremy asked me to do the honors,' she remembered William saying as if he were speaking of escorting her into dinner or out on the floor for a first dance. "He detests virgins. Said the idea of one made him ill. Yet the marriage will not hold until the deed is completed. I offered to show you how it's done. Teach you the skills.''

"I don't believe you!" Shock held her rooted to her chair when every instinct urged her to flee.

"But certainly you must," he answered in a reasonable tone. "Jeremy asked in particular that I teach you the French art. He's very fond of it. But you do not even know what I mean, do you?' ''

Jemima only stared at him. She had understood nothing he had said and that lent the moment an air of unreality which kept her from running away in horror. This was Jeremy's friend, her friend. He could not mean what he said. That was not possible. Yet she did not doubt she was in danger. "I want to go back. Now."

"Not quite yet." He reached for the wine jug and began to pour. "Have some wine."

"I—I, no. I don't like wine."

"You will like this kind. It is made for afternoons like this." Something in his expression warned her that he was resolved in his mission. "Come, drink a little to steady your nerves. I will not harm you. We will sit and talk, drink some wine and then, if at the end of an hour, you still wish to go, I will take you."

She stood up, feeling the need for action that would not put her to shame. "I wish to go *now*."

He looked at her almost pityingly, as if he knew her rebellion would gain her nothing. "Half an hour?"

She had been brought up with manners so entrenched that she could not easily abandon them even under duress. No, because of it. Manners framed the world so that the unexpected could be managed. Manners would see her through this unexpected vexation with no harm done, as her mother often said of an unpleasant event.

"One small glass and then you will take me home at once?"

He simply nodded. That should have warned her.

Confused, hurt, unsure of herself or of Jeremy's wishes, she had sat down and accepted the glass. Deflower her? Why would Jeremy send his best friend on such an errand? She had never heard the like. But then she was a country girl, knew only country ways and even less of the ways of men and women. Perhaps in town among the *ton* things were handled differently. She could not now know. But her ignorance was not dissolved by his explanation. Native intelligence told her to refuse him, in every way.

But by then, she had sipped the wine and was lost.

The next day Sir William stood up in church to denounce her and her duplicity as reasons she and Jeremy should not be joined in holy matrimony. As proof, he described their embraces, their kisses and how she had been eager to any and all that he might ask of her.

Jemima could not remember. She could not credit as true a single moment of things Sir William recounted in detail to shame her so that the soles of her feet burned in her white satin bridal slippers. But she could not refute him. She could not remember anything beyond the wine and then hours later the scolding tone of her maid who found her sitting in her own garden under a tree. There were no words to use in her defense, only the burning assurance that if she were so ruined, she would know it.

Only much later did she remember that he did not look at her. Through the whole recitation Sir William never once glanced her way. Perhaps he could not do so and continue to lie. Perhaps more than repudiating her in a house of worship, he feared to meet her shattered expression.

But even in the moment she knew she could not hold forth his demeanor as proof of her innocence. Too much had been said. Too many details to fuel scandal and rumormongering and dissection of character had been set forth to hold her against slander. One might not believe it all true. But not believe any part of it true? One might as well argue the moon was made of cheddar instead of Stilton. When all was said and done, it was still made of cheese.

Of course, she would be infatuated with his handsome friend. Sir William was a better prospect, less in need of the ready. Of course, she might be foolish enough to accept an invitation to a tryst. Of course, she might have been tempted. And if so, was the groom not within his right to feel the offense most profoundly on this day of all days? Wicked, foolish, silly chit! To be so lost to decorum, dignity, and self-possession. It were better he learned of her weakness for perfidy now, before he made the error of a lifetime.

She stood through the litany of infamy like a stone until she noticed Jeremy's expression, the faint lift of his features. Too much to call it a smile. Too blunt to call it a smirk or sneer or simper. It was only really in his eyes that she read the truth. He knew what had occurred and he was glad!

She knew then, she had been had a gull, a pigeon, a flat to their sharpster tactics. But she did not know why.

She had expected he would challenge his friend for his calumny, fly at him like a man taken leave of his senses, plummet him with fists and boot tips, assault him in reality for the emotional battering of his bride in words of stinging condemnation. Why would he stand still for the humiliation they must now both share?

But Sir Jeremy did none of that. He simple turned to her and said, "Did you accompany Sir William Ainsley to his hunting lodge yesterday?"

She didn't think a lie would help. "Yes, but—"

"Enough!" He turned to the minister and said, "I repudiate this woman. I will not have her as a wife." Then he turned and walked away from the altar.

Jemima closed her eyes and let out a shaky breath. She

still felt weak and a little sick to her stomach whenever she remembered the days that immediately followed.

It was a week before she learned her father had lost everything, or nearly so, in a South Sea Speculation. Less numerous than the South Sea Bubbles of the previous century, there were still a remarkable number of ways that such ventures could end badly, wiping out fortunes in a single swath. Jeremy Holton had gotten wind of her father's ruin and cut his own losses. Ten thousand a year was the least he was ready to settle for. There would be other dowries with more certain futures. And so he and his best friend cooked up the scheme to dishonor her and thereby free him.

The collapse of his capital and her marriage put her father in the ground, or so her mother lamented day after day for the last six months left of her own life. And then there was news. The ruin was not complete. The ship, badly damaged in a typhoon, had survived and put into shore at a desolate location for months while it was rebuilt to survive the journey home to England.

But by then, the MacKinnons had no joy left for the riches long delayed. Both parents were dead and Sir Jeremy had eloped to the continent with a wool merchant's daughter.

Jemima wiped at the tears she had not given permission to fall. She was long past feeling sorry for herself. She was long past regret and anger and a helpless rage against lies she could not shrivel with truth. But that did not mean she could not use those feelings as fuel for her LADIES crusade.

When she had brought under control every moment of her own doubt and fear and shock and wretched disbelief and fury and despair, she picked up her quill and began to draw.

Surprisingly, her hand was sure and steady. She worked quickly, sketching the thoughts that came to her. Here in this moment, with pen in hand, she felt in control, powerful, aware of a secret strength she had not known before today, the power of a pretty woman's attraction. Oh, she was scath-ing! Seething with righteous anger for the supposed plain girl who had been barter to her father's lust for a coronet and her fiancée's lust for horseflesh. She soon had the caption. "Un-Bridaled."

The pun and wit that followed flowed from her fingertips. The ability to form opinions through design served her as never before. She would unmask the chicanery of the father and the would-be groom. Hold them accountable to the ridicule and condemnation they deserved. No method of deceit was beneath them. Therefore she would spare them nothing!

There was purpose in rage. It clarified the mind. Edified reckless fury with a method for revenge. Crystallized the design. Vanquished doubt, prevarication and timidity. Vengeance demanded one's all, undistilled by ordinary concerns.

The candle had gutted in its holder, her tea had grown cold and stale, and still she drew far into the evening. Perfecting her masterpiece. It would exceed all others, bring Foolscap general acclaim for the preserver of womanhood he was created to be.

By the time she had put the finishing touches on her work, she was too exhausted to dress for the rout she had promised to attend with Julien. To both her cousin and Lord Bellaire she sent round her regrets with very little real regret attached. She needed to think about what she had come to London to do, and what she should now do.

The afternoon's fury had exhausted her desire for revenge. Her grudge against Lord Bellaire had been blunted. She did not now know if she should trust it.

Much as she had believed herself to be in the right, she was now having second thoughts. They had nothing to do with Lord Bellaire's kiss or his gallantries. It had to do with fairness and the seeming character of a man incapable of the kind of duplicity of which he was accused. She and the

LADIES were the avengers of lost innocence, but she was not lost to the capacity for temperance.

Perhaps there were extenuating circumstances that, if they would not precisely exonerate him, would allow her to view the matter in a less objectionable manner. The man she had come to know in a few short days seemed incapable of the kind of cruelty to both a brother and a woman his brother loved. Yet how to learn the exact circumstance without prying directly into his lordship's affairs?

"There is the brother himself," Jemima murmured to herself, remembering that Julien had recognized him in the street before her house just before she bolted. Perhaps an opportunity would again arise for her to meet the young man. This time she would not hesitate. She did not expect he would speak to her of old loves, but she thought herself a good judge of character and might extract, from his feelings toward this brother, if any serious injury had been done.

She would not allow herself to think that a kiss and a scuffle in the mud were all it took to win her fickle heart to a handsome man. Yet she had to be certain that the latent remnants of leftover romantic dreams were not at the bottom of her propensity to think the worst of a man she once more admired. "And yet I do."

In one thing only this day, she felt complete assuredness. She smiled as she looked over the Foolscap rendering. It was a two-panel strip. The first showed a gentleman in racing stripe with an illegal rabbit net, lying in wait. In the lane a young lady in maidenly white led by a harness a unicorn with an Irish harp strapped to his back. The second panel showed the lady in the trap, the unicorn fleeing, and the gentleman left holding the empty harness. The caption read "Un-Bridaled!"

Chapter Eighteen

After Beau left Jemima at her cousin's, he saw his new carriage and pair into the good keeping of his groomsmen and then went round to his club. There he drank two bottles of claret and repined upon the vagary of mind that had allowed him, a usually rational man, to challenge a smithy to a pugilistic exhibition and then wrestle a bear of twice his weight into his brand-spanking-new curricle. All this to answer the appealing glance of a pretty woman.

Beau smiled to himself as he rode toward his home. As a rule, he did not like pretty women. They were too full of themselves and their consequence. One splash of mud from a passing phaeton and Fiona would have been in vapors, her day spoiled beyond recovery. She'd have taken to her bed and . . .

Beau shook his head, feeling as he often did when remembering his poor dead wife, that he had slipped free of an onerous bond for all he did not deserve it. Now for the first time in many years the possibility of something he had long ago turned out from his life was back. Joy, in the shape of Miss Jemima MacKinnon.

He knew her reputation. He was beginning to know her character. While the two did not make easy bedfellows, the paradox did provide clues to her unorthodox views. She possessed a kind of heedless compassion more usually found in the young and innocent, and the wrongly maligned. That, coupled with an overdeveloped sense of right, had shaped the day's outing.

From the moment she appeared out of the alley to the moment he dropped her off at St. Ives's, she had behaved without consideration for her consequence or the impression her actions might leave with others. That was remarkable, and quite refreshing.

Perhaps she was as he had once been, impassioned by life. And, in running headlong to meet it, had met with disaster. But society was not so forgiving of hoydens, as it was wastrels. She had paid a price far higher than any he had known.

Even now she trod in waters thick with danger. St. Ives's boast that he had not yet despoiled her held in it the direct threat that he meant to do so. Even if she were no innocent, there was still the air of innocence about her. Knowing her better now, with her fierce loyalties and strong protective instinct, he suspected that another betrayal by one she clearly trusted would hurt her more than any seduction and abandonment.

Beau shook his head. Of course, it was none of his business . . . unless he determined—again—to make it so. Did he still believe in romance?

It occurred to him that not once during his sojourn at the club had he thought of the kiss he had forced on her or her surprising response. It was not as if the touch and taste of her soft mouth had not surpassed his expectations and pleased him. To the contrary. But such things seemed almost inconsequential in light of . . .

As he turned the corner he saw that the front windows of Cochraine House were ablaze as if for a party. And drawn up before it was a traveling coach from which a trunk was being handed down. "What the devil?" he muttered.

"Thank goodness you're home, milord." Beau's butler seldom ever looked the least distressed. At the moment he appeared positively anxious.

"What's wrong?" Beau demanded but an alarming ruckus coming for the main salon, followed by a crash, cut him off. Black brows lowering in temper, he strode past his retainer toward the room. "Never mind!"

The scene that greeted his eyes as he pushed into the room brought him up short. The remains of a late tea were spread upon his best Aubusson rug. From an upended silver pot, a brown trickle of tea came running toward him. In the midst of this two large Irish setters stood lapping up sugar and cream and the last of the biscuits.

"What the deuce is this!" Beau's famous oratory voice acted like the blast of a trumpet. The dogs shied, turned tail and hurried over to the far end of the room where they leaped up and made themselves at home on his two best Queen Anne chairs.

"I'm sorry, Father."

Beau swung round to find his daughter, Emma, a short distance away, looking small and pale and resolute, hands clasped before her like a supplicant in a convent.

"Emma? What are you doing here?"

"She's here because I brought her." Susanna York, his sister-in-law, came sailing into the room from another entrance. "Thank God you're back, Bellaire. I've been away long enough already. But I needed to bring Emma to safety."

"Safety? What is wrong?"

"There's illness in the house, scarlet fever. Beth and Winthrop have come down with it. I expect others will, as well. Dr. Shelton ordered a quarantine."

"Then what the blazes are you doing here?"

Susanna bristled up, her face flushing with strong emotion. "He ordered it as I left. Emma has been in the country with my cousin Miriam this last fortnight. She certainly cannot return to our home at present."

"So then, why not send her back to Cousin Miriam?" Beau was aware of his ungracious tone and his daughter's rapid blinking, a sure sign of nerves, but he had had a hard day, too. "What I mean is, I'm not ready to take on the duties of a child at present."

"That's all very well for you to say but it cannot signify. Miriam cannot keep her any longer and I have had sickness beneath my roof. You will have to rub on somehow." Susanna's strong chin began to tremble. "I cannot afford to be away. Even now, one of the children could be succumbing to noxious fever and I am not there to—to—"

She burst into tears without ceremony, bathing Beau in shame at his ingratitude.

He went over to her and put an arm about her. "Damn me for a rotten temper, Susanna . I am sorry. Truly. You have done what you must. Come, sit down and calm yourself. I will get you tea—more tea." He glanced at the mess on his favorite rug and then lifted a pointed brow in the direction of his butler, who nodded once then hurried off.

But his sister-in-law, usually a pillar of strength, had succumbed to a fit of weeping that would not quickly be stemmed.

Wishing his ill luck at the devil and himself anywhere but here, Beau continued to talk in order to keep alive the sense that he was in control. "Dear Susanna, do calm yourself. Of course, Emma is welcome at any time for any reason. This is, after all, her home."

He was babbling, talking almost as much as when he was

a boy in trouble. He glanced uneasily at his daughter. "You have grown," he said more heartily than required. "Come, let me look at you."

She came forward reluctantly, head bent at an angle that betrayed weariness and anxiety. When had his child become so shy? Or was she ailing?

He put a hand to her brow when she was close enough. It was chill and damp. No fever. "Where is your nanny?"

For the first time she smiled. "I don't require a nanny, Father. I have a maid."

"A maid." The very idea shocked him. When had she grown old enough for a maid? "Very well, tell her to undress you and put you to bed. No, you will be in need of supper. And then bed." He frowned. "That is what you require, isn't it?"

She nodded. "Yes, Father. Thank you, Father."

There was something august in that word *father,* as if she were addressing the Lord Magistrate and not her own flesh and bone kin. Always before she called him papa. He didn't like the change, but he couldn't say why.

"So then, what do you prefer? Dinner with me or a tray in your room?"

True, he had emphasized "in your room," but he was still relieved when she said softly, "A tray, please."

"Thank you, Bellaire." Susanna gave a great heaving sniffle and then blew her nose into her handkerchief with more vigor than seemed required. But he supposed she had been greatly overset by the sickness descending upon her house.

"You will of course spend the night, Susanna. You may make a fresh start in morning."

She popped to her feet. "Oh no! I've been gone too long already. I waited only for your return. I must leave at once."

She glanced at the girl. "Mind all that I've told you. Your father is a very important and busy gentleman. He shan't have time for games such as Making Cheeses and Go Fish. You must look to yourself for amusement and be very brave. I will send for you as soon as I can.''

The child nodded solemnly. ''Yes, Aunt Susanna.''

But then as Susanna turned way, Emma suddenly rushed up to her and flung her arms about the woman's waist and began to cry. ''I know, dear. I know. But you shall find lots of things in London to your liking.'' She glanced across the top of the girl's head to her father. ''I'm sure of it.''

''Of course.'' Beau said it automatically because it was expected. ''We shall rub on famously. You shall be proud.''

But when Susanna had disentangled herself from Emma, the girl looked even paler and smaller than before. Her red-rimmed eyes seemed too big for her delicate face.

Yet she did not cry again or even beg to be taken back. She squared her shoulders and said quietly, ''Good-bye, Aunt Susanna.''

''Good-bye, child.'' To Beau, Susanna offered her cheek. ''She is a dear, Bellaire. It's time you two got to know each other.''

''Of course.'' Beau escorted his sister-in-law to the door, feeling as if his world had been knocked at sixes and sevens. A child beneath his roof when he had not hired the requisite tutors and music teachers? And he had a previous engagement tonight.

''Good lord!'' He would have to send round his regrets to Lady Jemima with a promise of an explanation on the morrow.

When Susanna was handed back into her coach and it had set off, Beau wandered back into his salon, his chin sunk in his collar as he mused on the feeling of thwarted hopes plaguing him. He had hoped to share a private supper with Lady Jemima after the rout. Somewhere secluded, replete with the requisite atmosphere for a tryst. He had not planned to offer her a slip on the shoulder but—

The pair of beasts that had slipped his mind suddenly appeared before him, yelping and leaping upon him as if he was their long-absent owner.

"Down!" Beau cried with a force that trembled china teacups on the carpet. Then looking like thunder, he ordered the butler, "Take these beasts to the cellar."

No!" The cry of distress sent a chill through Beau.

Emma came running up to him. "Oh Father, please, they always stay with me. To keep me safe."

"Safe from what?"

Instead of answering, she hung her head. The abject posture did not improve his mood. His daughter behaved as if she had been browbeat daily. He nearly insisted she understand that she had no need of protection while under his roof but relented when one of the dogs came up to her and thrust his big shaggy red head under her arm, seeking the comfort he sought to give.

"Very well, Emma. You may take them to your room. But keep your door closed. I do not want them roaming the halls at night."

She looked up with a tentative smile. "Thank you, Father."

"Just so," he answered, but he was not at all happy with the sudden turn his life had taken. In the morning he would set about to turn the momentary stone in his road back into a smooth stretch of macadam.

"I say, that was damn agreeable of St. Ives," Guy said when their host had departed. "Come round to offer us dinner and extend his cousin's apologies when we ain't even been properly introduced yet."

"Yes," Richard replied with a significant reduction of his cousin's enthusiasm. "One wonders at the reason for it."

"You heard it." Self-satisfaction gilded Guy's expression. "She is most particularly interested in the association."

"She is a bit old," Richard ventured with a glance at his charge, for now that he understood exactly who the lady was, he wanted nothing to do with her or her cousin.

Guy smiled complacently. "She should be far more, well, practiced in the amatory arts. Wasn't that your advice to me? Find a woman able to set a man's appetites up better than a chaste young girl." The final thought, unexpectedly, made him frown.

Richard knew exactly the direction his cousin's thoughts had taken, though he would wager "innocence" was his former love's stock-in-trade. So far that was only a theory. Guy had yet to bed anyone, even a whore. Thus the "learned" mouthings of the uninitiated did not impress him.

"I'd not look there for much attention. St. Ives keeps a tight leash on his protégées. For all you know she is a whore in training."

"That cannot be. Beau would have nothing to do with her."

"The folly of youth!" Richard leaned forward. "I do not share your belief that your brother is but a shade from the parson's life in his disinterest in the fair sex. He is flesh and blood, and both rise at the sight of a pretty woman. Yet else do you suppose he took her up in his carriage?"

Being reminded of the sight of Miss Jemima climbing up into his brother's new carriage did not soothe Guy's temper. "You are saying I have lost her to Beau already? How is it possible that he has a oar in every pond?"

Richard leaned back. "I do not have your brother's confidence anymore than you. Perhaps it is only a passing interest." Beau was not his concern. St. Ives's motives worried him.

"As for St. Ives, I should not be surprised to learn he dangles the possibility of the lady before your eyes because he believes you are too young to do more than drool on her. Perhaps he thinks she needs a lap dog as contrast for his own more refined tastes.''

With a roar of resentment, Guy upended a silver platter of cracked oysters over ice on the table between then. ''Must you ever be at me, pointing out my deficiencies? I have a brother for that!''

''And that is why you prefer my company,'' Richard said calmly, righting the plate of oysters and scooping up one pearly gray creature for his consumption. ''Be wary of St. Ives, that's all I'm saying. The lady is his cousin. I should have remembered her sooner, but I was scarcely out of swaddling myself when she came a cropper her first Season.''

''Whatever are your prattling about?'' Guy asked in boredom.

''Miss MacKinnon.'' Richard hesitated only a moment before he gave up trying to be subtle. Heads like Guy's required a sledgehammer's crack if a thought was to be placed inside. ''She is notorious!''

Quickly he related details of the aborted wedding similar to those Beau had discovered at his club earlier in the day.

''By Jove! To swive a man's best friend on the eve of his wedding! She must be a real wanton!'' Guy's long-lashed gaze had kindled with interest. ''You think she's sleeping in St. Ives's bed?''

''For the love of Zeus! Do not put it about that he has despoiled her.'' Richard now wondered how he had thought his story would dampen the interest he had inadvertently fired. ''Else one or both of us may soon be meeting St. Ives over the business ends of rapiers.''

''But she comes with rumor of infidelity attached.''

''And you may be certain St. Ives does nothing that is not worked out to his advantage,'' Richard answered. ''Not even take a piss.''

Guy frowned in confusion. He did recall St. Ives relieving himself in the chamber pot in the corner of the room as he gave a quite depraved description of a ménage à trois he claimed to have witnessed the month before at the country house of mutual acquaintances. The size of his member could not have gone unnoticed even if he didn't continue to talk in terms that kept his audience's attention raptly upon him as he did his necessary. It was an impressive demonstration that Guy doubted any in his acquaintance could match, even if gentlemen made no such comparisons beyond public school days.

How surprised St. Ives seemed to be when he learned that, contrary to the direction he had been given to understand, Guy did not keep rooms in the club they were frequenting.

St. Ives had been most helpful in pointing out that a man about town should have his own quarters for, well, because of the ease of coming and going without question or consideration of others.

Guy smiled, thinking of the idea with renewed determination. "I'm thinking of taking rooms at my club." He liked the sound of that. "Every gentleman of consequence has his own private place away from the care and tribulations of home life."

"I agree," Richard concurred. " 'Tis the only life for a gentleman. But it is an expensive venture."

Guy flushed with anger. "Sequestered behind Beau's roof these last weeks, I've felt like a boy in short pants. Gad! Beau had dared mention talk of a tutor to keep me abreast of the classes I'm missing. As if I need schoolroom lessons! I'm nearly twenty. Time enough to strike out on my own!"

"You cannot strike out without the ready. It just so happens, Cousin, that I may know how to help you there."

Guy sat forward. "How do you propose to do that?"

Richard laid a forefinger beside his nose. "The Derby is coming up, don't you know? The field is wide and varied. A prudent man would take care to cover the field with a few well placed wagers. And I know where they may be put.''

Ever ready for a wager that had in it the hopes of high reward, Guy licked his lips. ''What have you heard?''

''Enough to convince me that a tidy sum is to be made for a price.''

''A percentage? From whom?'' Guy drew back. ''Not a cents-per-center?''

Richard *shushed* him. ''Will you moderate your tone? I speak of professional ring men,'' he continued when Guy had leaned in close. ''Former jockeys know more about a filly's chances than any number of breeders. We pay a leg man for his best tip and then share in the winnings.''

''I dunno. Beau warned me against gambling above all.''

''That is because he's not good at it.''

''Really?'' This tidbit of information seemed to set Guy up. ''Beau's not good at something?''

''I'm not saying he can't play the hand he's dealt. But he doesn't share the enjoyment of the sport of the wager that some gentlemen do.''

''Gentleman such as we!''

Richard smiled. ''Precisely.''

''Then count me in.''

''Happy to, Cousin. But with what ready?''

Guy screwed up his face trying to think of a place where he might come into a bit of cash. ''I am to come into a small sum upon my twentieth birthday. My mother's personal funds were left to me. Would a loan against future income do?''

''Perhaps.'' Richard rapidly calculated his chances of pulling the venture off without Cousin Beau detecting the tremor of its passage. ''It might work. You are certain of the sum?''

''Five thousand.''

''Five—'' Richard grinned. ''Done!''

Chapter Nineteen

The Derby marked the highlight of the racing season for Londoners. Of course, in a few weeks there would be the Ascot, at Queen's Anne's course near Windsor Castle. A much more exclusive race, it was open only to aristocrats and a few chosen others. But "The Darby," open to the public, was overwhelmingly the more popular. Even Parliament adjourned for it. Not surprisingly, though few members of that august body bred animals for racing, nearly every lord and commoner wagered on the outcome.

The one-mile-and-four-furlongs course open to both three-year-old colts and fillies became established in 1779 at the behest of Edward Stanley, twelfth earl of Derby. All very fascinating stuff, to historians and members of the Jockey Club. But any man Jack on the street could give the real reason for its success. And that was wagering!

From its very ancient beginnings in the Far East, gambling pumped the heart's blood of horse racing. The avid hope that Lady Luck would ride sidesaddle with a man's wager filled the countryside of Surrey on this bright June morning with a throng of hundreds.

Horseflesh, while of primary interest, was not the only thing on display this day. As on any occasion when the commoner and the aristocrat came into contact, the Derby set the stage for wives and mistresses to observe, and among themselves, discredit one another.

Beautiful women in elegant carriages with the tops down rolled through the meadows, smiling serenely and flashing coquettish smiles at the Corinthians on horseback. Their umbrellas, like their gowns, were ornately embellished to draw the eye. Once drawn there were other delights to notice, like gowns cut so low they revealed bare shoulders and expensive jewelry clasped about swanlike necks. This display was both invitation and advertisement of availability but at a cost only the most well-to-do might hope to support.

If a lady occasionally recognized among the pretty faces one who had previously been pointed out to her at the opera or the theater as a notorious courtesan, she pretended not to notice. But she did keep an eye on her husband, curious to know if he were as well acquainted with the woman's reputation as she was.

For their part, the mistresses came this day as close as they ever would to legitimate acknowledgment. While they could not proclaim the crests and colors of their protectors, they consoled themselves with flaunting the gowns and jewels and carriages those gentlemen provided. The jealousy that moved on silent darting glances between the women in the lives of these men provided a frisson of vitality to the very air. Occasionally it erupted into something more tangible.

On this particular day one enterprising *chere amie* chose to wear a gown in the wine and biscuit "silks" of the horse her protector had entered in the race. Once she was spotted, a voluble discussion had broken out in the carriage of the wife, whereby she promptly screamed and fainted. Moments later the much put-upon husband marched over to the vehicle of the offending demimondaine. After delivering her a slap that drew the attention of half the crowd, he sent her packing back to London. Instead of being snubbed, the gentleman was applauded by his peers. It was all very droll and very entertaining!

There were others, however, who did not need to look beyond the confines of their own vehicles for dramatic sport. Just such a one was the elegant barouche bearing the crest of the earl of Cochraine.

As his carriage rolled into Epsom Downs, Beau looked as ill at ease as a man with his foot caught in a poacher's trap. Since the outing began, he had twice abused the ears of his coachman and footman for minor errors. He had tossed his lunch in a passing stream and been sore put not to drink more than was his limit on such occasions. For once his admirable aplomb was undone, thanks to the actions of an eight-year-old.

Stiff and withdrawn, Lady Sarah occupied the seat across from him. Beside her sat his daughter Emma, as quiet and pale as death. An outing was just what Emma needed, Beau had thought only the day before. Now he wished he had stuffed the pair of them in a pickling barrel and come to the race on his own.

During the past week he had learned some disconcerting things about his daughter. She did not, as he supposed, know what he did with his days. She cried when he left and again when he arrived home to dress to leave again. It was an unnerving experience to discover that he had as little under-standing of her as she of him. They were daughter and father, but in every other way they were strangers completely.

Always before, he had planned for her visits by hiring a staff to look to her every need. She was then presented to him at breakfast, if he had the leisure to dine in, and after dinner, at the requisite hour when children were seen but not heard. But the Season was in full flow and every tutor, dancing master, and governess worthy of the title was "otherwise engaged." So he was left to deal with Emma and her abigail, as shy a creature as Nature ever formed. Abandoned by fate to their own devices, there was a great deal of silence and sighing and general discomfort.

Nor did he share the ubiquitous Englishman's fondness for dogs. Never before had he been host to the pair of hellhounds Emma called pets. Susanna had always been so obliging as to keep them in the country. He realized at once he must have done something to upset Susanna, though he could not think what, for her to sic them on him on this occasion. The dogs had a fondness for all things leather and feather. Between them they had chewed up his favorite Wellingtons, consumed the better part of a leather scabbard given to a great-uncle for service to His Majesty Charles II, and pulled the goose-down stuffing from a pair of mounted pheasants. After they gnawed through the legs of a Queen Anne settee belonging to some great-grand-aunt or another, despite Emma's teary pleadings, he permanently banished them to the basement and back garden.

Nor was he any good at child's play. Chess was not, he had discovered after an aborted effort at the board, a lighthearted game for father and daughter to smile over. Particularly when he kept seeing her king as the Regent, who had betrayed his former Whig friends when he assumed the post. The Tories still ran the government and his all-out assault against a novice player had ended predictably, if so noted only after the fact. Emma cried after the trouncing and ran away while he sat and stewed over her poor sportsmanship and the doubtful duties of fatherhood.

Abandoning the idea of fatherhood to his musty closet of dubious enterprises, he had determined to move to his club for the duration of her stay. But Guy usurped that option by announcing that he was moving into a club.

"Away from the nursery clatter of children and animals," he'd said with bags packed. "A man must have his peace, you know."

Beau still wondered how his brother had managed to engage rooms with little income to speak of. His majority was yet two years away. But he did not scotch the idea. As little as he liked having his home invaded, he could not in good conscience chide Guy for taking the escape he sought. Instead he gave Guy a line of credit for "necessities only." Then he set Richard more particularly than ever to be his brother's confidant and companion. Guy on his own in London sounded like misfortune waiting for chance.

He did not abandon Emma. He simply gave up trying to have conversations with her. So then it was by chance that he encountered her one afternoon in the park on the square with her maid playing with her dogs. On that occasion he discovered that her French was tolerably good. The dogs, it seems, understood only French and were much better behaved when shouted at in the Gallic tongue.

"Merde! Les gros chiens!" quickly became a popular epithet from him.

That day, too, he learned of her interest in horses. He had just returned from riding in Rotten Row with his team and gig. She was a wonder with his new pair. They allowed her to rub their noses and ate from her hand. It was then that he conceived the idea of what had seemed a wonderful outing for her, a trip to the running of the Darby.

But he knew through a week's harsh experience that he would need an ally: someone usefully female.

For one wild distracted minute, he considered inviting Lady Jemima along. But the social implications of that would be so numerous and onerous to his reputation that he could not support it beyond the thought. No, he needed respectable unremarkable companionship for his young daughter. He could conceive of no other than Lady Sarah.

Delighted to be included in the day "en famille," Lady Sarah had promised to treat his daughter to "a delightful day complete with an alfresco meal on the way."

Despite her assurance that she understood and was equal to the "wayward nature of small children," Sarah quickly retreated from her friendly overtures as the trip progressed. Emma found nothing in the picnic fare to her liking. She complained that strawberries gave her spots, that the ham was too salty, and that the pickled eggs were bitter. The greatest transgression was her opinion that Lady Sarah's prized French chef's liver paté tasted like pig dung.

Judging the child's attitude to be criticism of her, which in her opinion Beau did nothing to assuage, Sarah went from mild shock to indignation to haut frigidity in the space of an hour. By the time the racecourse of Derby was in view, the three occupants of the Cochraine carriage had formed a threesome of Dislike, Distrust, and Disdain.

"Ah, we are in time to view the horses," Beau said more heartily than he felt as they rolled onto the grounds.

They smiled and nodded at several friends and a few more acquaintances. He noted the lingering looks and wondered what his desperation would cost him. As a rule he was very discrete where women were concerned. There was talk, of course, of his affairs, but to his credit no names of ladies of rank had ever been linked to his by word or look or breath of scandal. Until now. Lady Sarah was all but preening as she took note of the second glances of the *ton*. The news would be back in London before they were. Lord Bellaire was squiring Lady Sarah about with his daughter. Speculations on the day of the First Banns would be laid at White's by morning.

Beau sighed inwardly. He should have thought of how he might spare Sarah the inevitable fight and humiliation of his abandonment after this enterprise. If only she and Emma had gotten on better, he might have reconsidered a future with Sarah. After all, a girl needed a mother. But after a few hours in their company, he had lost all illusion of the possibility of a match. Sarah and Emma did not suit!

He was casting about in the sea of faces for a masculine acquaintance that he might beg leave to speak to when his gaze was arrested by the opposite. There, several vehicles apart from his, sat Lady Jemima MacKinnon.

He had not seen Jemima since the afternoon of the outing that had produced fisticuffs and a bear as prize. She looked—quite wonderful. Dressed in soft pink shades that made her cheeks bloom, she wore a lemon-colored straw hat with a wide brim and curly ostrich feathers that drew the eye to her pretty face.

A sudden resentment took hold of him as she looked right past him until he remembered the incident with her spectacles. Of course, she could not at this distance recognize him! It was all he could do to stop himself from waving to gain her attention. The thought did not improve his mood and he guiltily turned his gaze away from a pleasure he could not today indulge.

If she wished to see him, she might have done so before now. In fact, he could think of no good reason she should not have sent round a note telling him she would be here. After all, they had agreed to meet the night Emma arrived unexpectedly. As a matter of fact, as he now recalled it, she had begged off as well. That thought gave him pause. Why? Emma was the reason he had sent his regrets. He did not know hers.

Chagrin crept over him as his pride made a tardy appearance. Why on earth was he fastening his desire on a woman who clearly did not hold a very high opinion of his regard? He hadn't even liked her when they met, had found her rude, disobliging, even vindictive. She had upbraided him for his refusal to intervene in that madness of the bear. Later, when she had been a victim of her mistake, she'd been abashed. But that didn't excuse her conduct or make her any less to blame for it. They both might have been murdered.

Chagrin and resentment made a dangerous cocktail for his already abused ego. The devil of it was, he couldn't erase the vision of her glorious gaze as she looked up at him, temper flaring. And then the way she had simply melted against him when he kissed her.

The memory of that kiss, the willing offer of her mouth to him, rose inevitably to mind. Beau sucked in a breath. Why then had she not contacted him since? Then it might have been her, not Sarah, who occupied his carriage.

"Look!" cried Emma as she sat up in interest. "That lady has a bear for a companion!"

"Whatever do you—oh my!" Lady Sarah, too, had taken notice. "Bellaire, look there! That woman has taken up a bear in her carriage."

"By Jove!" Beau could not quite believe it. He had been so intent upon Jemima that he never thought to question that her companion was not St. Ives in a disconcertingly warm fur coat but—surprise of surprises—the beast he had rescued a week ago!

"Well, I never!" Sarah turned a shocked face to Beau. " 'Tis positively outré. Do you suppose she is an actress?"

"Hardly." Beau composed a bored face to match the tone of a man with no connection to the lady in question. "That is Miss Jemima MacKinnon."

"Really?" The altered expression on Sarah's face bode him no good. "You know her by sight? Then you are acquainted?"

"Only indirectly and of long-standing." Beau refused to adjust his neckcloth though it seemed more uncomfortable than a minute before. He nodded at Jemima, for he could hardly do else as her carriage was now coming their way. "I had the honor at Almacks some nine or ten years before."

"And you remember her even so?" The comment had

the sting of annoyance that only a jealous woman could give it. "How admirable of you to remember a green creature of so long ago."

"Might have met her since," Beau hedged, wondering how to cut his losses as St. Ives's carriage rolled past them toward the paddock.

Jemima inclined her head slightly in greeting as she noticed him. In response he could not stop a silly smile from sliding across his face. Her broad-brimmed hat, he noted with masculine appreciation, offered a flirtatious angle for every movement of her head. That was all it took for his opinion to take a stance opposite of that from moments before.

The night of the opera he had thought her crass and obvious. Today he believed he had never been more wrong. She was as subtle and sure of herself as Solomon, and as artlessly seductive as Salome.

"She seems to know *you*." The point Sarah put on the word could have been used to stab Caesar. "Who are her people?"

"She is a relation of St. Ives," Beau heard himself say before he considered the implication.

"St. Ives—?" Sarah began on a note of disapproval and curiosity. "The Black Sheep—"

"Just so," Beau cut in sharply with a warning glance at her.

"Oh yes, the child. Of course." But the look Sarah gave him told him this was not the end of the discussion. *"Quelle outré."*

Beau set his jaw. When agitated, Lady Sarah invariably turned to French phrasing. The affectation annoyed him at the best of times. Today it grated.

As they were finally ready to alight from his carriage, Beau turned to Emma. "What should you like to do first? See the horses or have an orange?"

"I want to go and see the bear. Please, may I, Father?"

"Yes, Bellaire." Sarah instantly took up Emma's chorus. "Do ask your friend if Emma may view her bear."

"I don't think it would be a good idea," Beau answered in a neutral tone.

"But, Father, you said I would have fun at the races. I want to see the bear."

Beau swung his gaze toward his daughter, intending to answer her mischief-making with a scathing reply. But what he saw stopped him. All morning long the girl had looked miserable. Despite her quite lovely walking gown with pink sash and grass green ribbons in her bonnet, she had looked all but ill. Now her face was shining with expectation and delight. He could not deny her.

"Very well. I shall go and inquire while Lady Sarah takes you to buy an orange. But do not be disappointed if the answer is no. Bears are dangerous creatures."

"As can be their mistresses," Sarah answered with a challenging look at him.

Dreading nothing so much as the rest of the day, Beau climbed out of his barouche and directed his coachman toward the paddock where a few of the competitors for the day's racing were warming up.

Beau was only mildly surprised to find himself smiling as he moved away from his companions. He had not allowed himself to think there would be an excuse to speak to Jemima today. But here it was, and none of his making. The day was looking up!

Chapter Twenty

Jemima spied Lord Bellaire at the same moment he noticed her. Unlike him, she had no trouble recalling the details of last time they met and how it had been left between them: mutual begging off of an assignation and then a week of silence. The difference was, she had had little else to think about while it appeared quite evident from his startled glance that he had been thinking of anything and everyone *but* her. If she needed further proof, it was there in his carriage. He had a lady with him. And a child.

He's with his mistress and bastard! The thought stuck her between the eyes with all the force of a mule kick.

Staring at them far longer than was necessary, even without the aid of her spectacles, she forced herself to see reality. The supposed new rapport between them had been nothing but a sham. One afternoon in the country and a stolen kiss did not a romance make.

Her heart began to beat in slow heavy strokes that seemed to shake her body. She knew the ways of gentlemen! Had a treatise tucked away in her desk on the duplicities of rogues and roués and seducers. Still, she had allowed herself to be taken in. For what? The want of an ideal she now suspected no man capable of.

So then this was the true Lord Bellaire, the libertine who dared flaunt his lifestyle before the *haute ton.*

Jemima bit her lips to stop the foolish, unwanted sting of tears. She would not give him the satisfaction of her pain. No indeed, she would look upon the sight of him until it no longer affected her. In fact, she must give Lord Bellaire his due. He had not lied to her. Perhaps he had not been given the chance, but one could not convict on conjecture. What he was doing today was nothing less than honest.

"Odious man," she'd whispered to herself as their carriages brought them past each other. She had not come here expecting to meet him, but she had not been unaware that she might.

Here he was, in the open among the *ton* with his little family, smiling at her as if she were the cash prize in the day's race. If he expected any reaction from her, he was soon to be disappointed. He had not the least idea of who she really was and what she thought of such conduct. Still, she supposed she must give the devil his due.

She smiled and nodded just enough to make known to him her observance of him as their carriage passed but then she looked away. Before she did so, she raked a quick gaze of the woman with him, who looked as though she had tasted spoiled milk

Jemima felt her heart ease its drumbeat.

Lord Bellaire had smiled at her. It was as untroubled as any he'd ever given her. As if he were perfectly at ease.

His *savoir-vivre* could not but be admired. Rare was the gentleman who could acknowledge both mistress and bastard in a single afternoon without turning a hair.

The thought of his refreshing honesty brought her a doubt-

ful kind of satisfaction. Her views were radical enough to
applaud such a departure from the duplicitous furtive actions
of most gentlemen. Yet she felt a bit sick and, to be ruthlessly
honest with herself, a shade jealous.

Lord Bellaire could mean nothing to her.

She had had a long miserable week to repeat the litany
to herself and believe it. And if she was no longer prepared
to bring him down with public scandal, she had best go
home. Yet she remained in town while St. Ives wheedled
and teased and made sport of her indecision. If only St. Ives
had not begged off from the Derby at the last moment,
she would have had an ally to protect her from Bellaire's
attention. No, it was just as well that her cousin was not
here to read in her expression how very unhappy she was
at this moment.

Lord Bellaire's nature was such that he might be father
to half a dozen by-blows and none to question it. Perhaps
he would not be offended by the public declaration of
another, the one whose mother still lived beneath her roof.
So then she'd come on a fool's errand, after all. No need
to chastise the openly immoral. She had other fish to fry,
in the form of an Irish horse breeder.

Yet as the Cochraine carriage had rolled past, Jemima
could not but notice that the young girl looked as excessively
unhappy as the lady had looked so very cross. Something
here was amiss!

Jemima leaned forward and poured a handful of dried
currents into the paw of her companion. The bear quickly
stuffed them between the spokes in his muzzle and into his
maw, then stretched in his seat as though preening.

The menagerie was full up with bears for the present,
she'd been informed. St. Ives suggested she sell him to a
circus or street performer, but the sight of the village bear-
baiting was too fresh in her mind for her to abandon him
to the possibility of that sort of tortured death. And so she

had kept him. It was nothing short of a shock to learn that he was quite tame, as long as his belly was full and he was kept away from dogs.

She had named him Monsieur Bête Noir, the Beast. He was unpredictable but had reserves of intelligence and a wily understanding that she was likely the best mistress he would ever encounter. So he took up residence in St. Ives's garden, for her rooms were temporary. Only once had they risked losing him. He had gotten free of his chain and climbed a tree in search of a beehive. He had only been persuaded to come down by the sound of a marching band passing nearby. As the sound of trumpet and drumbeat neared, he had scurried down the trunk and proceeded on the tile walk of the garden to dance a jig, or very like it!

It was not her idea to bring the bear with her. But St. Ives assured her that without his presence to ease her way, the best way to make certain she attracted the attention of the person she sought was to attract all attention at once. The bear would bring many to speak to her and she could ask them about the man she sought.

There were times, like today, when she suspected her cousin of manipulating her, much like a puppet master who operated her strings with ruthless efficiency. She could not be certain it was true but certainly he seemed to know the very thing that would fix her mind upon a course. Like the jilted Irish bride.

She had come here today to learn the fate of the daughter of the Irish horse breeder Foolscap had written about eight days ago.

Not even through St. Ives's connections could they discover if the young woman in Ireland had learned of Foolscap's defense of her. Unlike all the times before, rumor about the bartered bride had been a three-day wonder.

"It's the Irish association," St. Ives had informed her. "Everyone knows the Irish are mad. What else can one

expect from lunatics other than farce and bathos? It does
not serve to ridicule the ridiculous.''

And so it had been left for her to await word from Chapel
Hill through Amelia's former charge. Yet, so far, no word
had been forthcoming. The Derby gave her the only chance
to learn more.

When her carriage had parked some distance from the
rest of the crowd, two of St. Ives's stout footmen helped
her and then the bear alight from the carriage.

Today, Monsieur was firmly chained by a thick leather
collar and dressed in a vest and flat oriental-style hat with
a tassel, a flourish Julian insisted he wear. The bear had not
seemed to mind the journey as long as she provided him
with a succession of sweet meats and nuts. Her skirts, when
stood up, shed a dozen bits of dried fruit and shells.

She was watching him being chained to a tree in the shade
when she heard someone being hailed. She turned to find
Lord Bellaire striding toward her with hand raised in greeting. That he had come in search of her was an unexpected
miscalculation she was not entirely certain she welcomed.

"Good day, Miss MacKinnon," Beau greeted more
jovially than he felt for he was reluctant to seem eager. Then
just to adjust that perception, he frowned and said, "I did
not expect to see you here."

"So I see." She glanced deliberately over his shoulder
and into the distance where Sarah and Emma stood watching.

Begrudgingly Beau noted her gaze. "That—they are not
the reasons."

"I should expect not." She folded her hands and said
primly, "Though I suppose you may bring your mistress
and her child out on any occasion you deem appropriate."

"That is not *her* child," Beau said roughly. "Emma is
mine."

Jemima sucked in a quick breath but quickly regained her

poise. "How refreshing to hear a gentleman freely admit his indiscretions."

Goaded beyond his good intentions, he answered crossly, "Emma was not an indiscretion."

"So then, you mean to marry the lady?"

"Of course not! No—you misunderstand. Emma is my child by my late wife."

Jemima digested this without daring to glance again at the child. "And the lady? Not your mistress?"

This time Beau refused to answer for no good could come from any sort of reply he could think of.

"Just so." Jemima smiled but it did not meet her eyes. "I wish you good sport of the day, Lord Bellaire. Goodbye." She turned and started away.

"See here." He took a step after her though he was aware of how it might look to those observing them. She angry. He pleading. All the elements of a lovers' quarrel.

Thankfully, she turned back with a mild expression that none but he would judge as pique. "My daughter, Emma, would like to observe your bear."

Jemima looked past him as if the sight of his face disturbed her. "I do not recommend it. He is a tiresome creature, prone to odd starts and fits. He has ridden a good distance today. Perhaps another time." She gave the go-ahead signal to the footman who was about to unmuzzle the bear. "He is about to be fed."

"I seem to recall he is fond of meat pies."

Despite her better judgement Jemima allowed herself a glance at him. "He is equally fond of apples, mincemeat, and jam pots. He cracks them open as if they were eggs and eats the contents."

Beau smiled and then she smiled, and he remembered why he liked her so much and why that liking made him uneasy. "So then, a moment with Emma, if she brings him a pie?"

"If you will be her guard. I seem to remember that when pressed into service you portray the protector rather well."

Beau turned away before she could see the grin of self-satisfaction blooming on his face. He felt forgiven for his abrupt and prolonged departure from her life. For reasons he did not want to question, he was relieved.

A few moments later the sight of Lady Sarah wilted his grin, for her presence reminded him how little that forgiveness could mean to him this day.

When Emma got the news that her wish would be granted, she was beside herself with joy. Wearing a smile so big it threatened to split her thin face, she watched impatiently as her father purchased three meat pasties from a vendor and then followed him across the lawn to the shady glade where the animal was being kept.

When Jemima saw the happiness that lit up the girl's eyes until they seemed to shine from within, she was glad she had relented. Whatever her thoughts of her father's choice of companions, the girl should not be punished for it.

Very quickly it was all arranged, even the introductions between Lady Sarah and Jemima accomplished.

"*Miss* MacKinnon." Sarah's tone said all. "That name is known to me but slightly. Have we met before?"

"I doubt that. I have not been in London in nearly a decade."

"A decade? Truly? I can never long be away from Town." Sarah turned a fond glance on Beau. "There are so very many lovely things to do here. Whereas the country is, well, so rustic."

"How aptly put," Beau cut in quickly. "So then, we are assembled to introduce Emma to Miss MacKinnon's bear."

At that moment Lord Bellaire's footman came running up. "The race will begin in a quarter of an hour, milord."

"And I have not made my wager," Lady Sarah said testily. "Have you set yours, Bellaire?"

"Back in London." But Sarah's forlorn expression told

Beau that his answer would not suffice. There was no help for it. He needed to accompany her back to the track to place her bet before the race began.

He looked at Jemima. "If you will be so good as to see to Emma?"

"Of course. We shall be right behind you," Jemima assured him.

He watched several moments longer as Jemima encouraged his daughter to approach the bear. Her soft pink skirts belled in the breeze then molded to her legs as she directed the girl forward, revealing the tantalizing shape of limbs, softly molded thighs, and rounded hips. And still he left them and that sight for a race that had suddenly lost interest for him.

"Oh, but Monsieur Bête Noir is soft," Emma declared when she had fed the bear a pie and was allowed to stroke him.

"Yes, but Monsieur is not a toy," Jemima reminded the girl. "You must never be at ease around him. He is very strong and might cause you harm though he would not mean to."

Emma cast a doubtful glance at her. "You allow him to ride with you in your carriage."

"Yes, but then he was muzzled. As to that, I should think many would yet believe I do not have so sound a head. Your father is among them."

At the mention of his name, Emma's happiness dimmed a little. Her expressive eyes seemed too big for her face and her sallow complexion spoke of a kind of permanent unhappiness. Jemima scotched the impulse to inquire into the matter of that same unhappiness she had earlier spied on the girl's face. Lord Bellaire would not thank her for meddling in his life, and truly, it was no business of hers.

Before she could find another more suitable topic, the

blare of horns sounded the beginning of the race. "Come, then, they are calling for us."

Emma quickly held out to the bear a second pie, dancing back in alarm when he grabbed it more quickly than she expected.

"He seems an indolent rascal, but he can move quickly when provoked," Jemima reminded her charge. "Come on. Oh dear! However will we find your father in this crowd?"

Jemima and Emma did find Lord Bellaire a few minutes later. His silvered head was impossible to miss under the June sun. A place near the starting gate had been reserved for him. Lady Sarah, surrounded now by friends, affected not to see Jemima and Emma's approach.

Despite Emma's grumbling that she did not have time to feed all her pies to the bear and that she was hungry into the bargain, Beau could tell that she was happier than before. So he treated her to two more pies.

While Emma ate and jabbered on about the bear and his antics, Jemima moved a little away so that she could have a better look at the famed race course.

"Oh, but they are beautiful animals," she murmured to herself as the thoroughbreds came prancing to the line.

"You know horseflesh, Miss Jemima?" Sarah inquired stiffly, for she could not long ignore the woman Beau had invited up beside him in the stands.

"No. But I can appreciate a beautiful animal when I see one," Jemima answered as she watched Beau hoist Emma up on his shoulders for a better perch from which to view the race.

"Then you should know that the even most beautiful animal can hide faulty bloodlines. You would do better to know the pedigree of each."

Jemima nodded. "Perhaps that is London's way. But that would take away the romance of the eye."

Sarah gave her a strange look. "What exactly do you mean?"

Jemima glanced at the lady whom she had at first thought lovely. The lines of anger about her eyes and mouth now spoiled that impression. "Do you read Foolscap, Lady Sarah?"

"I do, indeed. Such a scamp! I particularly delighted in the most recent one about the Irish horse breeder's daughter."

"Why particularly?"

"It was most famously done. Though I must own I heard an ever so clever on-dit to counter it. Some Wag has put it about that it was the daughter who was the Dowry for the horse."

"A judgment you share?"

"Who can know?" she answered archly. "The Irish are no better than they ought to be. Very little morals when it comes to trading. I don't doubt they'd barter a daughter for horseflesh. Why it's said they prefer to bed down in the stables rather than under a decent roof."

"Yes, the lowborn Irish. Nothing is beneath them. Of course, the fact that an English aristocrat stooped there to gain a Thoroughbred horse is of a different shade." Jemima tried to keep her tone light but the righteous indignation that was ever at the back of her thoughts broke through. "One understands how very difficult it is to obtain a really fine thoroughgoing racehorse. If one must promise to wed to be delivered of one in dowry, who can blame him?"

"Yes, well, I do see your point . . ."

"Do you? A pity I do not share yours."

Jemima looked away before her anger lost complete control of her civility. She did not glance again at Bellaire for fear his expression might goad her into saying more. But she had the distinct impression that he was shaking very slightly with mirth.

She told herself there was no point to dueling at daggers' points with his companion. She did not care that the lady was Lord Bellaire's mistress or wife-in-waiting, or whatever the devil she was. If thoughtlessness, superciliousness, and a touch of stupidity were all that London gentlemen required in their ladies, it was no business of hers.

The crack of the pistol and the race was underway.

The crowd cheered and cried encouragement to the various colts and fillies they had backed. Some even ran alongside the railing to better keep an eye on their favorites. It was all quite invigorating. Despite her lack of interest in a particular winner, Jemima could feel her heart begin to race in time with the galloping animals on the oval track. One simply could not watch with indifference the bunch and ripple of muscles under satin horseflesh. Very soon she felt one with the jockeys wearing the bright silks of the various owners as they rode in a crouch, brandishing whips and words of encouragement to their mounts. Only one could win, but the anticipation of it being one's wagered favorite drove the crowd to frenzy.

Though she had not wagered a single farthing on the outcome, Jemima was delighted to see her last-minute choice, the duke of Grafton's horse Whalebone, cross the finish line first.

The lift given her spirits by the roar that went up from the crowd was quite enough to equal any small amount she might have won. Or so she thought until Lady Sarah and her friends flew into raptures when it was learned one of them had won a hefty sum. They were quite over the boughs about it. Fourteen thousand pounds was the sum won on a seven-to-one wager!

Jemima felt suddenly ill. Such an amount would keep the village of Chapel Hill in bread and cloth for years. And to think it might have been lost!

The spectators went in several directions. Some to congratulate the winners; others to collect their winnings from professional leg men and other more friendly wagers between gentlemen acquaintances.

"There go the less punctilious losers," Beau observed to her with a nod in the direction of the meadow behind them.

Jemima turned to see a few gentlemen scurrying toward their hacks and horses.

"They've the need to outdistance their creditors until a more favorable outcome from some other wager will once more plumb their pockets."

Jemima had heard of such things, but never before had she actually seen someone with the gall to publicly decamp before settling a debt of honor.

"This calls for champagne," Beau said to her, but it was Lady Sarah who answered.

"Lud! Yes. Do bring enough for the party. I am parched beyond endurance."

Jemima saw Lord Bellaire's expression stiffen, but he merely said, "At your service," and moved away to do his lady's bidding.

Feeling that champagne would be no match for the natural exhilaration of the day, Jemima turned instead to look for Emma, whom she had lost sight of at the end of the race, in order to say good-bye.

It was only after she had searched fruitlessly among the milling crowd that she realized she could not see the girl anywhere.

"Where is Emma?" Jemima finally inquired of Lord Bellaire's party.

Sarah looked down at Jemima with a hint of temper in her tone. "She was right here but a moment ago. Has the disobliging child wandered off?"

As the woman spoke Jemima's gaze had gone naturally to the source of her worst fear and saw it was a reality. Emma had crossed the field and was approaching the Monsieur.

"Dear lord!" She set off at a run, grabbing up her skirts that she might cover the distance quickly. "Emma! Get away from there! Emma!"

Chapter Twenty-One

Perhaps it was the sound of his daughter's name, but Jemima's voice penetrated the din of Derby revelers to reach Beau. He turned and saw at once what had caused her cry.

Emma was approaching the bear, which was dozing unattended at the base of the tree.

"The devil!" he bit out and hurried across the lawn in Jemima's wake.

The hue and cry of alarm was enough to cut through the revelry of many of the sporting set and they, too, turned their attention in the direction of the alarm.

"Oh dear lord! He's going to kill her!" Lady Sarah cried in a clear carrying voice.

"Get a musket!" someone else cried, as the crowd split between those in fear of their lives and the avidly curious who wished to view firsthand whatever terrible event there might be about to unfold.

Jemima was far enough ahead of all of them to know exactly how dangerous the situation had become. She saw

Emma walk right up to the Monsieur and bend to poke him with a stick.

"No, don't!" But her warning came too late. Monsieur sat up.

Surprised by his quick movement, Emma dropped her stick.

"Emma, don't move," Jemima cried out, slowing to a trot as she neared the pair. "Don't move."

Emma looked up in blank surprise. "Miss Jemima. I—"

The bear suddenly lunged, snatching from Emma's hand the last of the orange she had been eating.

Emma, who now realizing her danger, cried out in fright, "Papa!"

Her cry startled the animal and it suddenly reared up. Instead of moving out of its reach, Emma screamed and shrank back toward the tree trunk, to which the bear was tethered, effectively blocking herself from easy reach.

Swallowing her own fear, Jemima slowly moved closer. "Monsieur Bête Noir, you are being a very inhospitable host," she said in French. "You are frightening your guest."

The bear lowered himself to the ground then lumbered slowly toward Emma. When he was close enough he made a swipe at her middle with his paw.

"I've got a pistol!"

Jemima looked up into the horrified expression of Lord Bellaire. He was holding a dueling pistol in his right hand, his arm outstretched as he pointed it in the animal's direction.

"No! You might miss and there's Emma." Jemima pushed him back with a firm shove and then stepped forward to spoil his shot.

Hoping her voice carried the conviction of her thoughts, she said in a loud but level voice, "Emma. Monsieur is frightened. That is all. We must make him feel safe. Do you hear me, Emma?"

The child nodded, but she had gone gray as smoke.

"Very well. I need you to do something very simple for me. I want you to sing, Emma."

"Wh-wh-what?"

"Sing for Monsieur Bête Noir. He loves music. Do you know, 'Hot Cross Buns'? Of course, you do. Let's sing it together. 'Hot cross buns! Hot cross buns! One a penny, two a penny! Hot cross buns!' " Jemima clapped her hands in time to her own wavering voice to mark the beat. "Come, sing, Emma. Please."

After a moment, Emma began to sing in a reedy soprano that gained a bit of volume after the first notes escaped her.

Singing as loudly as if her very life depended on it, Jemima turned to the onlookers and gave them the signal to join in. She did not dare glance at Lord Bellaire for she knew he thought her a madwoman and a fool. But she had to do what she knew how.

"Please sing," she begged the crowd. After a few seconds two gentlemen took up the tune. And then a leg man pulled a penny whistle from his pocket and began to pipe the tune in a dancing measure. Very quickly others joined in to make a rousing chorus.

When the music turned full-throated, Monsieur eased around in surprise. Then very slowly, as if he had the gout, he raised up on his haunches and lifted his paws in the air and began a ponderous bouncing from hind leg to hind leg as his head rocked from side to side. He looked like a drunken sailor in a rough sea, but he was clearly dancing.

"Doe anyone have a morsel of food?" Jemima asked of her choir. Immediately several pieces of foodstuff were pushed forward into her hands and she made a semicircle with them before her Monsieur.

The bear bent and picked up the first piece then continued to dance.

When she judged it safe to do so, Jemima darted in and scooped Emma up from where she had collapsed onto the tree roots. Crushing her tightly to herself, she hurried away out of the reach of the bear's chain.

Immediately a shower of stones was thrown in the bear's direction, and the animal roared in pain as several found their mark.

Jemima shoved Emma into Beau's outstretched arms and cried, "Stop them! Please! They will kill him."

Beau gave her a grim look but lifted his pistol and discharged it into the air.

The stoning stopped in the general confusion to understand why the shot had been fired. "Leave the beast be!" he shouted. "My daughter is safe."

The general grumbling followed this call to reason but as none could think of another excuse to continue, they put heads together to compare opinions or scattered to return to their previous interests. As they departed, the St. Ives's footmen hurried toward the bear with muzzle and cudgel in hand.

Feeling very ashamed and guilty for having not seen to the animal's muzzling sooner, Jemima sent Beau a regretful glance, which he ignored. Then suddenly his face changed.

"You are bleeding?" he said in alarm.

Jemima looked down at her gown that was smeared red. But she knew at once that it was not blood. She touched the spot. " 'Tis jam." She looked up and saw a similar stain oozing from beneath Emma's pink sash.

Emma turned a deep rose shade as she reached into her sash and pulled out the remains of a crushed pastry. "It's a raspberry pasty. I was saving it for later."

Jemima laughed in relief. "That explains why Monsieur was so interested in your middle. He could smell the pie in your sash and wished to help himself."

Emma thought about it for a moment and then nodded. "I wanted to save a part for myself. I am sorry."

"Oh, darling, don't be." Jemima took the girl's face in

her hands. "But you must never bring food within sight or smell of an animal if you do not intend to give it away. It is a tease, you see. They cannot understand explanations that the food is not for them."

"I understand. I am sorry your bear was hurt."

Jemima glanced at Monsieur, who had been muzzled by her footmen and was trying unsuccessfully to lick his side. "He was not so very badly hurt, I think. But I was very careless in bringing him here."

She cast another doubtful glance at Lord Bellaire, who only regarded her with a cool tolerance he might have shown any miscreant found guilty of a crime.

"I can't imagine why such a person was allowed to bring that wild beast into civilized company. *Mal à propos!*"

That ringing feminine voice needed no introduction. Standing a little distance away among her friends, Lady Sarah looked as furious as she sounded. Her color was mottled by hectic feelings. "That woman should be sent away at once. *Mauvais ton!*"

"I think you are making a great deal of very little," Beau answered evenly as he approached Sarah.

She blinked, looking a little unsure of herself for the first time. "I am only thinking of your poor Emma. Just think what that great beast might have done!"

"It is over." Beau's tone brooked no argument. "Emma is tired and needs to be taken home."

But his own heart was still beating very fast as Beau carried Emma back toward his carriage. Much as Sarah's remarks annoyed him, she was not entirely wrong. Jemima had been reckless in bringing the animal to a place where the crowd might frighten and distract it. Yet somehow the way she had responded to the emergency made him feel that she was within her rights to do so.

Jemima followed a little behind father and daughter, ignoring the black looks Lady Sarah gave her as they crossed back to their parked carriages. Nothing could punish her as much as her own regrets over the incident. That it had turned out well was a miracle. London was no place for a person like herself. Bears on chains! It was an affectation more worthy of Cousin Julien. Really, he was turning her into a creature she did not recognize at all. Notorious women must be made of sterner stuff than she.

When Emma and then Lady Sarah had been handed up into their carriage, Jemima stepped up to speak to Emma. "Miss Emma, 'twas a pleasure to meet you."

Emma smiled readily. "Will we see each other again in London?"

Jemima smiled a shade more reservedly, not wanting her father to think she was pushing the acquaintance for his association. "Oh, I don't know. London is a very great city."

Emma looked at her father as he climbed aboard. "But I should like it above all else."

"It is not polite to force your association on Lady Jemima," Beau said sternly and sat down without a glance at Jemima.

Jemima turned to him. " 'Tis no hardship to be in your daughter's company, I assure you." Only then did she notice the tight look on Lady Sarah's face and surmised the lady could not say the same. Poor child, the day must have been an ordeal from the outset.

Jemima smiled again at Emma. "You are welcome at my home at any time. Lady Sarah. Lord Bellaire." After offering each a slight nod, she turned away.

"Now look what you've done!" Lady Sarah said as Emma tried to rearrange her soiled skirts. "Thoughtless child! Now I am smeared with jam."

Beau glared at her. "Have your modiste run up another frock and send the bill to me." The look he turned on his daughter thawed instantly. "Come sit by me, Emma. I'm not afraid of the jam pot."

When she had done so, Emma smiled tentatively at her father. "Do you suppose we shall see Miss Jemima in London?"

Aware of Sarah's narrowed gaze Beau merely said, "I should not be entirely surprised."

After a moment's silence Emma leaned against her father's arm. "She's a wonder."

"Yes," Beau said absently. "She is."

"Well, really! You are a pair," Lady Sarah observed with asperity. "To be over the boughs about a woman with a wild beast who might well have eviscerated the one and deprived the other of an heir."

For the first time since they set out, Beau smiled easily at Lady Sarah. "You are correct. We are a pair." He patted his daughter's shoulder, feeling for the first time as though they had formed a bond, if only out of mutual regard for another.

"Done up? How can that be?" Guy stared uncomprehendingly at the bits of paper on which Richard had been busily figuring in the private parlor some minutes from Derby. "You said we won."

"We won some bets," Richard said between his teeth. "We did not win all or even the greater part." He raked a shaky hand through his red curls. "Not nearly enough."

Though it was not commonly known, the better part of Richard's income derived from gambling. Therefore he could not afford to neglect any possible source of cash. He had thought to lay a spread with Guy's inheritance and thereby increase the odds of the possibility of their winnings across the field. The play should have gained them several times over what a single bet could gain. To that end, they had taken rooms nearby the race grounds the day before so that they might meet with ring men as well as other like-minded gentlemen for wagering. They had bet not only against the Derby winner but also one animal against another within the race, and also various combinations of win, place, and show. In all they had made twenty-five separate wagers on the same race, laying as well as taking odds.

In the distance they could hear the celebrating of those gentlemen who had been most fortunate on the track this day. Unfortunately, they were not inclined to join them.

"It was supposed to be foolproof!" Richard murmured as the damning numbers swam before his disbelieving eyes.

On paper it had all looked well enough. But before him now were the financial implications of each of the given results. The worst disaster could result from a win by the favorite, Whalebone. Yet, at the last minute they had rashly laid odds of five to one against him.

Now, the implications were fact. Whalebone's win had cost them not only the five thousand they had laid out, but put them under the hatches for ten thousand more.

Guy wiped his mouth with the back of his sleeve, sweating as if he had run the race himself. "What shall we do now?"

"Do?" Richard looked up, his eyes a little wild. "Why we run like hell, Cousin. We must flee to the hinterlands. We must decamp, abscond, take French leave. In other words, old fellow, we must be gone before we are run to ground by those hellhounds, the creditors."

"But you promised!" Guy groused like a boy whose promise of an outing had been spoiled.

"I promised a fair chance." Richard gazed down at the papers again. "If only the Dandy had come in first. Or fourth. But second? Don't you see? It changes all. Blows every advantage of our scheme."

"I do not see it," Guy proclaimed. "But that you have

beggared me, that I see plainly. I shall tell Beau what you've done.''

Richard rose slowly, his wild gaze on target at last. ''I would not advise that. In fact, I would counsel the opposite. Who do you think the creditors will come for first? 'Tis your name writ on the chits.''

''But you laid the bets.''

''With your blunt.''

''You cheated me!''

''I wagered to free you from your brother's domination.''

''But now I am worse off than before.''

Richard shook his head. ''You are a right whiner. No wonder Beau asked me—'' Too late he heard him disclosing a bargain he had promised to keep. That truth registered as an arrested expression on Guy's face.

''Beau what? Sent you like a sheepdog to herd me?'' A terrible look came over Guy's face. ''Was this all an elaborate plot to cheat me of my money and freedom and tie me even more closely to him?''

''Don't be daft!''

''Daft, am I? A fool! A buffoon! A source of amusement for you and my brother? Damn you both!''

Richard stood up as Guy sent yet another piece of furniture, the desk this time, tumbling over. It was getting so the cost of furniture repair amounted to a significant portion of their visits to public establishments. But this time, Richard was too overset by the day's circumstances to reel in his temper.

''You're foxed!'' he declared in disgust with himself and his companion. ''And a spoiled puffed-up cockscomb! A gentleman takes his shot and bleeds in silence.''

For a moment Guy swayed unsteadily before him with cravat askew, his gaze unusually bright and his finely chiseled mouth blurred by slack muscles. ''You lost it all,'' he said thickly. "All! I'd not have thought even you were that stupid!"

Richard bent to gather up his walking stick and hat.

Guy took a staggering step toward him. "Where do you think you are going?"

"To perdition, most probably." Richard set his hat on his head. "But as of today I shall get there on my own."

Guy's lower lip began to tremble. "What then am I to do?"

"Appeal to your brother for relief, I should imagine."

"My dear brother! My supposed benefactor! He won't help me."

"Most probably not." Richard paused at the door. "So then you must grow up, Guy. 'Tis about time you did."

When Richard was gone, Guy went over to the sideboard and poured himself a very large brandy, which he drank without tasting. Richard was right. He must pull himself together. Only, he didn't know how. He must also leave the premises before the first of their creditors thought to look for him.

"I will go back to London." The sound of it stiffened his spirits. Until another voice intruded.

It was Beau's voice, raised in anger only a week ago after a discussion of his allowance. "If I learn that you have been obliging a moneylender in order to maintain yourself, I'll take a whip to you."

The remembrance caused nervous laughter to escape Guy's lips. Beau must not find out about the hash that he and Richard had made of things. If Beau ever found out—

"He won't!" Guy muttered. Not until he had found a way to bring his high-and-mighty brother down to his own humbled level.

Chapter Twenty-Two

Wishing to leave the Derby grounds and accomplishing it quickly were very different matters, as both Lord Bellaire's and St. Ives's coachmen discovered. The lane that led to the highway back to town was jammed with horses and carriages of every description. For the next hour the procession moved at no more than a snail's pace.

To protect her pet from the annoyance of too many animals in close proximity and to avoid the noise and odors attendant upon bringing up the rear in such a convoy, Jemima had her coachman take a circuitous route through other hamlets.

While traffic moved more freely on the less travelled lanes, the added distance required to escape the main traffic added hours to the trip. All in all, the day had been a near disaster.

Through it all Jemima sat in distracted bewilderment. But for meeting Lord Bellaire's child, and the race itself, she could not say she had enjoyed a single moment of it. Worse yet, she had not learned a thing about the fate of the young

Irishwoman, a subject that had gone clean out of her mind in the midst of the excitement of the race and then the accident with Monsieur.

Monsieur had long since fallen into a deep slumber that seemed more like winter hibernation. Looking at him now Jemima marveled at her own capacity for folly. Never again would Julien pull her strings.

Finally, an hour before sunset, Jemima called to the coachman to put up at an inn coming into view.

"London be only another hour," the coachman called back in encouragement.

"I do not care if it's ten minutes, I must have a stop."

The red-brick Georgian inn was large and well maintained. Candles flickered through every open window, a sure sign of prosperity. The reason for such abundance was easy to understand. The coaching yard was full up with barouches and carriages and saddled mounts. No doubt, like she, other revelers returning from Derby sought a repast and a pint to stave off the hunger and thirst of travel.

A blast from the mail coach's tin horn signaled that the vehicle was ready to depart, relieving the yard of some of its clutter as the heavy team pulled its coachload of passengers and mail back onto the road. She did not envy them. Night travel, called Black Work by the coachmen, was the worst sort of inconvenience and the most dangerous.

To preserve her pet's restful state, she had her driver pull off the highway opposite the inn and she crossed the road alone while he and the footmen were left to look after Monsieur and water the horses.

As she had surmised, the tavern was busy. There seemed not an establishment along the highway that had not benefited in some way from the Derby. After a visit to a water closet, Jemima found herself gazing wistfully over the crowded tables full of jovial diners. The smell of roasted lamb and broiled sausages reminded her that she had not had a meal since the pocket lunch she had brought on the trip. She could wait until she reached London, but she did so wish for a meal.

When she inquired about the possibility of quick service, she got a speculative look from the innkeeper that was a reminder to her of the jam stain on her gown and the fact that no gentleman accompanied her. Ladies did not travel without a maid.

"There may be a private table in the rear," the innkeeper suggested with palm outstretched. "But there's be no bed here for ye."

"I shouldn't think of it!" Jemima dropped a few coins into his hand without touching him and then followed him through the throng toward the rear of the room.

In afterthought she said, "Send a meal across the way to the carriage bearing the crest of St. Ives. I've three servants waiting."

As she passed out of the main room into a hallway, she wondered if perhaps she was making a mistake. Stories circulated of unaccompanied women being cracked over the head to disappear and never be seen again. And then she heard voices coming from what must be private rooms curtained off along the hall. She was far from alone.

At the far end of the passageway, the innkeeper drew back one of those curtains. As she passed inside, she spied a familiar face seated alone at a table.

"Lord Bellaire? Whatever are you doing here?"

The innkeeper smiled and winked at the occupant. "Though ye might be in need of a bit of company, gov'nor."

Beau looked up from his wine to find himself staring into the face of the woman he had been musing over. "Miss MacKinnon?"

Jemima turned back abruptly, almost bumping into the innkeeper. "This will not do."

"No, stay, please." Beau quickly came to his feet.

Jemima gave him a very reserved glance. "I assure you, I did not follow you, Lord Bellaire."

His surprise mellowed into something more reasonably called bemusement. "I did not think you did."

"Then ye be knowin' one the other?" inquired the innkeeper with a widening grin.

"Do not think to play matchmaker for me." Jemima gave their host a look of such disdain that his smile wilted.

She turned the same withering gaze on Beau. "I stopped only for a meal."

He saw that uncertainty banked her expression and the last of his own confusion departed. "I am here because Emma became sick."

"Oh?" Jemima's frostiness evaporated. "Is she very ill?"

"Nothing serious. She ate too many raspberry pasties. The carriage ride overset her stomach and, well, here we are." He made a helpless gesture with his hands.

"I see." Jemima noted that neither lady of his party shared his table. "Lady Sarah is looking after Emma?"

"No." Beau's lips thinned. "She saw no reason to delay at the inn when she was offered to be taken up by friends. I agreed that she should go on to town."

"Who is looking after Emma?"

"I sent for her abigail. She is abovestairs with Emma now."

Jemima permitted herself a small smile. "Then you are mercifully free to dine in the silence of your own making."

He smiled back. "Precisely."

"I shall not alter your design."

"No, that is—"

Jemima held up her hand. "I must insist. You have earned the companionship of dining with your own thoughts."

"Very well. Adieu, Miss MacKinnon."

Beau slid back into his chair, pleased that she understood so precisely his feeling in the matter. He did wish to dine with her, but not after the day he had just had. His emotions were worn through by caring for a pair of remarkably disobliging females. And if the temptation to add the company of yet another lady to his evening prodded him, he was wise enough to leave the provocation alone. A coaching inn was no place for the assignation he had in mind.

The innkeeper soon had her settled at a small table back in the main room, so small in fact that plate and wine goblet could scarcely keep company on its surface. Yet she was too hungry and thirsty to complain. Despite the halo of tobacco smoke ringing the rafters, she ate her supper of roast lamb and potatoes with a healthy appetite. If she occasionally felt the eyes of the company upon her, she pretended not to notice.

What she could not close out completely were the many voices speaking all at once on topics ranging from the day's racing to the rising price of Madeira due to the continuing continental blockade. Most of the time, they blended together in a hum punctuated by sporadic laughter. Occasionally the din dropped and a single voice could be heard distinctly above the others. As she wiped her mouth on her napkin in preparation to leave, one such gap in conversation appeared.

" 'Tis true! I heard it only today from my groom. The girl who was dowry to a horse drowned herself!"

Jemima shot to her feet, feeling as if the room had been given a vigorous shake by a giant hand, and turned toward the voice. At a nearby table sat four town toffs and a pair of women dressed in the obvious finery of the demimonde.

Unaware of her sudden interest in their conversation, they continued to talk freely.

"The father blames himself."

"I shouldn't wonder!"

"Could not be buried in consecrated ground."

Unable to bear the suspense any longer, Jemima stepped

up to one of the ladies. "Forgive my intrusion but I could not help overhearing. To whom do you refer?"

The older of the gentlemen glanced up in displeasure at being interrupted. "Do I know you?"

Jemima curtsied. "No, of course not. But you were saying, about the dr-drowned girl?"

"We were speaking only of a foolish Irish gel," the eldest of the women replied in cold tones. "If it's any business of yours."

"Say!" The heavyset gentleman reared back in his chair and squinted. "You're the gel at the races with the dancing bear, ain't you?"

"Yes," Jemima answered shortly. "You were speaking of an Irish girl?"

"Quite." The fellow frowned as if gathering his thoughts took effort. "Bad business, that. Drowning herself! As if that would do her reputation any good."

"Put a cap on it, rather," said another with a sage nod.

"You are not speaking of the Irish horse breeder's daughter, surely?" Jemima pressed.

"The very one." By his accent, the fourth male member of the party was clearly not a gentleman, but he was the most eager to converse with her. "They say she done it on account of a cartoon that appeared a fortnight ago. Who's the fellow what done it?"

"Foolscap!" answered another of the party.

"That's the one! Served the lady a bad turn on that one."

"In what way?" Jemima demanded.

The older gentleman cocked a jaundiced eye her way. "Way I heard it, the bride knew nothing of the marriage arrangement made by her father."

"Fancied herself in love with a stable hand," volunteered a man from another table.

"I heard the very same only today," said the woman Jemima first addressed.

"Are you cert—?" Jemima began, but her voice was much too faint to overcome the excited voices as more of the tavern's patrons joined in to show they too were up on the latest on-dit.

"The lad first learned his ladylove had been affianced away when Foolscap's cartoon showed up?"

"Poor blighter—!"

"Say he felt betrayed—"

"Up and deserted her."

"So she goes and casts herself into the river!"

"Damn waste, says I!"

"Irish gentry have no breeding."

"You'll not find an English lady to drown herself for love of a gentleman. It's just not done."

"Here's a riddle. How do we rid ourselves of the Irish problem?" The speaker waited a heartbeat. "Let Foolscap draw them a cartoon!"

Amid the general laughter, Jemima felt the room take another sickening lurch. All the warmth and sunshine seemed to vanish behind a gathering darkness that gripped her in icy claws. She felt her knees unlock.

Then, amazingly, Lord Bellaire was there beside her, his hand taking a firm grip on her elbow. "Oh, there you are, Miss MacKinnon."

Beau had been passing through the room on his way upstairs when he saw her sway. He knew he risked drawing unwanted attention to his acquaintance with her by moving to her side. Yet he suspected that if she fainted it would attract even more if he were forced to lift her from the floor.

"You have had a trying day," he admonished in a voice that carried plainly to all who wished to hear it. "In saving my daughter's life, you have plainly overset your nerves. Allow me to escort you to Emma's room that you may see for yourself that she is well enough."

Jemima blinked as she looked up at him. Her complexion

was dull as ash, but when she spoke her voice was stronger than he expected. "Yes, of course."

By exerting pressure on her arm, he steered her past the others and out the main entrance of the inn. When she would have turned from him and gone out the door, he pulled her along toward the stairs.

Leaning in close, he said in a request that brooked no argument, "Climb."

Hardly knowing where she was or where she was going or why, Jemima followed his command. But her thoughts were far from quiet. They screamed at her!

Dead? By Foolscap's hand? Was it possible that she was to blame for the drowning?

That thought made her stumble on the stairs.

"The devil! You will not cause another scene this day!" The grip on her arm tightened painfully.

Tears blinded her, but Jemima did not stop climbing until she reached the top. Then quite suddenly she was thrust through the door of a room and then heard it close behind her.

She whirled around, astonished by Lord Bellaire's actions only to have him say in great distaste, "What the devil are you about now?"

That was all it took. Suddenly a great heaving sigh escaped her and she burst into tears.

Beau could not have been more shocked if she'd slapped him. He stood still for a few moments while she sobbed, hoping the emotional torrent would end as quickly as it had begun. When it did not, he took a step toward her.

"I do not understand you," he muttered in an anger he could not name. "You have faced down a bear and accosted a smithy, and both times kept your head. Yet the news of a poor misguided girl's drowning in another country causes you to swoon like a missish school girl."

"You do not understand—!" Jemima began only to abruptly break off and turn away.

"Oh no. You will not turn Wet Goose on me again." He grabbed her by the shoulder and swung her about to face him. But she jerked away so hard that he had to grip her by both upper shoulders to hold her before him.

"That is better," he said when she finally stopped struggling and merely glared up at him. "Now, I will have it. What is this mystery? Explain it to me."

He saw her lips quiver and had the sudden watery gut feeling that she was about to burst yet again into tears.

But she sucked in a steadying breath and said in a voice devoid of all emotion. "I am responsible for her death."

"Don't be absurd!" He shook her a little to dislodge the foolish notion. "You are no more responsible than I or your Monsieur Bête Noir."

"But I am!" Jemima answered a little desperately. "You do not know. You cannot know—!"

"Then tell me, Jemima. Tell me."

She looked up at him, her gaze steady on his at last. "I am responsible for her death because I am Foolscap."

Chapter Twenty-Three

"You are Foolscap."

It was not a question, but Jemima felt compelled to answer. "Yes."

Quite certain that one of them had suddenly gone mad and because Beau was fairly certain he was still in full possession of his faculties, he released her and pulled out the single chair that stood by the table in the room he had rented for the night. "Sit down."

Jemima shook her head.

"Sit down before I tie you to it!" He regretted that the command might easily be heard below, yet there was no help for it. This woman was driving him beyond all endurance.

His voice rang like a clap of thunder in her thoughts, but Jemima was not so lost to herself that she could endure being ordered about without protest. "Very well, I will sit for a moment. But I must presently see to my bear."

"Bedlamite," Beau murmured under his breath and he searched in the darkness for flint and timber with which to light a candle.

When he had done so, he took a turn about the room. Small as it was, that required only a few steps away and back to bring him once more before her.

She was perched uneasily on the edge of the chair, her features mostly hidden in the deep shadow cast by her bonnet. He could not judge her expression, and he had no intention of provoking another outburst. "I will not ask you to refine just now upon your recent babbling. You are in no fit state for reasonable discourse."

"So say you," she answered coolly, but he saw that she had begun picking at the dried jam on her skirt and suspected that she was very close to another outburst.

Feeling justified in his assumption that she would respond best to firm authority, he said, "I have taken this room for the night. You may have it. I will make do in the common room."

"Thank you. No."

She started to rise but he moved more quickly, pressing a hand on the top of one shoulder. "I beg you, do not try my temper again this day."

Had the room below them become quiet or was he simply feeling exposed? He was a Member of Parliament, after all. A certain amount of decorum was required of its members no matter how messy their private lives might be. There were those who would delight in finding him embroiled in a compromising circumstance.

Feeling a sudden revulsion for spies and snoops of every kind, he said, "Nasty business, scandal. I thought you shared my abhorrence of it."

A sudden stricken look came into her face as she tilted it up to his. "You do not know what I have done! I must return to London. There are people I must inform."

"What people?" He came suddenly alert. "St. Ives?"

"No. Yes." She looked away. "It can be of no moment to you."

"Can't it just?"

This time when he reached for her, it was to drag her from her chair and up against him. "Against my will and inclination, I have been drawn into the middle of your every caprice this past fortnight. Since I cannot be rid of you, I will at least have the satisfaction of knowing why. What the devil has that man gotten you up to?"

She saw his eyes darken, but the warning of his rising anger only fueled hers. "My relationship with St. Ives is no business of yours, whatever it may be. Now let go of me!" Jemima whispered furiously.

But Beau wasn't nearly ready to let her go. He could feel her shiver under his hands. Her angry breath caressed his cheek. The soft contours of her breasts rubbed against his coat front. All at once what he wanted and what he had thought he wanted were not the same.

He was a man long accustomed to resisting temptation. He was a man who prided himself on honor, decency, and fair play. He did not take advantage of hysterical females who, however misguided, closeted themselves in a room with him. He was . . . lost.

He wanted her. Wanted to kiss her mouth and her eyes and then her breasts. He wanted to lose himself in her sweet body, indulge and then obliterate the agonizing longing that had plagued him from the moment he glanced across the opera house and saw her. To hell with his honor, decency, and sense of fair play!

Jemima saw his intention reflected in his eyes a scant instant before he lowered his head and so dodged his kiss by turning her head aside. "I do not want you to kiss me."

"Liar." His hand moved to her chin, drawing her face back to his. When she could no longer deny the sight of him, he smiled sweetly. "You will die if I do not kiss you." And just to prove his point he bent to her and did that very thing.

It was a hard kiss, an angry kiss, but in it Jemima felt a desperation to match her own. For a moment that struggle between them blotted out the horrid news she had just received below. For that reason, she did not resist the temptation to once again taste the passion between them even when she knew she should.

She might be very much afraid of betraying her feelings for him, and Beau was equally afraid of betraying himself. This battle of wills could have no good end; yet he did not know which he thought should prevail. He only knew he did not want to lose.

Heaven help them both, he decided as he buried his mouth in hers.

As her soft mouth trembled under his, he quickly decided it no longer mattered who fought what, only that neither of them lose this moment.

She was warm beneath her gown and he could feel an urgent tension in her ripe body as his hands slid down her back and over her hips to cup her buttocks. She did not smell of the heavy perfumes Sarah preferred or the stringent soap of his former wife. Jemima smelled of something altogether different, a womanly scent of lavender, perhaps, and powder. But it was bound by another fragrance that was both sweet and musky, and undeniably feminine.

As his mouth opened on hers in hungry urgency, Jemima could not catch her breath and after a few seconds she gave up. Pleasurable sensations alien to any in her experience became so strong that she didn't fight the urges suddenly rising up in her. Fear, anger, and despair melted away, leaving in their wake the white-hot persuasion of his kiss. In a moment fraught with shame and uncertainty came a desire so powerful she did not want it to be snatched away. With a pleading murmur, she raised her arms to encircle his neck to hold on to the only good thing in a suddenly bleak world.

At her touch, Beau felt the last of his restraint vanish. She wanted him! And that was enough.

He reached up to jerk loose the ribbons of her bonnet and cast the garment aside. Then his fingers were tangling in her hair, sweeping the confining pins before them as they plowed through to cup her head and hold her mouth to his. He thrust his tongue between her lips and, glory of glories, she opened willingly to his invasion. His groan of satisfaction drowned out her sigh of surrender as he plunged his tongue repeatedly into her mouth, in a primitive rhythm that her body if not her mind understood all too well.

When he finally paused for breath, he wondered if he had been too rough, his demand too fervent for a tender soul such as she. Then he felt the surprise of her tongue press forth against his mouth. In relief, he opened at once to her entreaty. She was not so skilled as he, yet he delighted in her effort. When she grew tired, he drew her tongue back into his mouth and sucked greedily at the tip until she was gasping and sighing as only a woman in full passion does.

After a moment she felt him shift her body and then lift her. She had never thought much about his superior size, but now, as she was swept so effortlessly from the floor, she was reminded of the mill with the smithy and marveled that she had ever doubted his strength and power. And then he was laying her on her back on the bed she had not even noticed in the room. Before she could more than think the thought, he was following her down onto the coverlet until his body half covered hers.

She stiffened at this, but his hands came up to frame her face in a gentle embrace.

"Please" he said. "Please don't deny me. Us."

Staring into his passion-darkened face, Jemima followed the sinking shaking sensation tumbling through her body to its core. What matter that this man was once to have been

her enemy and she his Nemesis? The tables were overturned
utterly.

Even as the last of her intellectual powers drained away
under the pressure of sensual sensation, she retained a final
fleeting thought. The word *Nemesis* had many meanings.
In this moment, wrapped in this man's arms, any and all
definitions seemed equally possible. He might be her fate,
her destiny, her kismet, or her doom.

She felt his arms go around her, searching for the buttons
and laces that would free her from her gown. The shock of
his act sent warning bells jangling along her nerves. What
madness was this she encouraged? To be taken like this, in
an hour when she had never felt less worthy of . . . love.

"No." She put her hands up against his chest and felt
his fingers still on her back.

With great effort, Beau dragged himself back from the
abyss of desire to the edge of reason and opened his eyes.

If she had seemed shocked and vulnerable before, it was
nothing compared to the look on her face now. Desire and
a longing to match his heated her gaze, but deeper still was
great surprise and fear. Of him? Or of the unknown?

"Don't fear me. I will not hurt you." He smiled at her
uncertainty. "Here, you may take the lead if you like." He
reached for her hand and placed it against his shirtfront.
"You may undress me first."

"No!" She pulled her hand away, but she did not push
at him again.

"Then allow me to help you."

The buttons of her gown came free quickly beneath his
fingers. She knew she should protest, but he pressed lingering
kisses upon her as he acted to undress her, so potent she
could think of nothing else. Then his hands came back to
lower her bodice and he bent his head and kissed each
welling mound above her chemise.

Raw lust streaked through Beau as he heard her artless

gasp of pleasure and felt her arch up under him. He pulled her chemise down and lowered his head to nuzzle one of the rosy peaks he had revealed.

He heard her gasp again, a ragged sound that mixed astonishment bordered by fear. "Please," she whispered and grabbed handfuls of his hair to halt the tender assault of his mouth on her breast. "Please! Oh, what are you doing to me?"

Her nearly inarticulate cry by his ear penetrated slowly the red curtain of desire that cloaked his senses.

And then it hit him, like a stone, where he was and what he was doing and with a gathering as witnesses. His daughter lay ailing the next room. Gentlemen he accounted acquaintances sat below, no doubt with an ear cocked to the doings abovestairs.

Beau lifted his mouth from her breast, breathing hard as he fought for control of his raging passion. He had not meant to go so far. This was scarcely the time or the place for passion of any kind.

"We must stop!" He said it forcefully, almost angrily, as though it was for his benefit alone. He saw her turn her head away and then a tear escape from beneath the shelter of her lashes and slide into the hair at her temple.

He reached for her hand and pressed it to his check. "We must stop," he said more slowly this time, with a resignation his body had yet to submit to as defeat.

He rose up off her so quickly Jemima shivered as the cool touch of the night air met her bare skin.

He turned toward the window as she sat up, knowing that if he did not deny himself the sight of her open bodice, he might not even now let her escape. He went to the window and looked out on the moonlit night.

"I know you have no reason to believe me when I say I would be your friend." He glanced back after a moment to find to his relief that she had struggled back into her gown.

"And not for what has just passed between us. You may be certain none shall ever hear of it."

"Because you are a gentleman and gentleman can always be counted on to protect a lady's honor?" Her voice was flat and unemotional, whereas his had been strained by barely governed desire.

"No, Jemima, because you deserve it."

She did not look at him. Her hands shook as she reordered her clothes and then began collecting the hairpins that lay scattered on the bed about her. She looked then so young and so innocent and so frightened. But when she spoke, her voice was distant and hard as ice. "I wish you would not be kind to me. You may live to regret it."

Surprise shot through Beau. But even as he moved toward her to ask what she meant, he heard voices in the hall. More urgent than his curiosity was the fact that they not be found together.

He quickly pulled his clothes straight, after a fashion, and ran his hands through his hair. "I will go below. You may take the backstairs after five minutes. My footman will be waiting there to escort you to your carriage."

She only nodded.

He moved quickly to the bed but as he reached for her she drew back.

He smiled. "Would you play the coward now?"

It was the provocation she needed. She lifted her head, her gaze suddenly bright with indignation.

He smiled at her. "That is my Miss Jemima. Keep your head a little longer and we will see this through."

He did not dare remain a moment longer near her and so went to the door and opened it. Though the hallway was poorly lit, he recognized the man in the hall.

"Giles!" he greeted with false cheer. "I heard you wagered well today. Buy me a flagon of ale and I shall believe it."

* * *

Jemima sat on the edge the bed and wished herself at the devil.

Of all the things that might have occurred this day, there was one calculation she could never have made. She had left Lord Bellaire's embrace with the knowledge that her feelings were appallingly apparent. Those feelings were exactly the reason she must never again allow him to touch her. She was in love!

Despite his appalling exhibition of the day, parading his mistress at the Derby for the world to see, despite every scrap of reason and good sense she had supposed she owned, she had gone willingly to bed with a man she scarcely knew and did not understand at all. All for the sake of his kiss and his caress.

Thoughts of the poor drowned girl came back, breaking the last of the spell in which his lovemaking had held her. Was this what the girl feared losing in the desertion by her stable boy? Had she known such passion and been driven to a mad desperate act as the only resolution to a life without it? Still shaking with the eddies of departing desire, she could begin to understand the magnitude of the loss, but not the despair. Even now with the specter of another jilted woman's ghost as company, she could not wish for more!

Shame stung her cheeks and burned her eyes. She, a wanton? She would never have believed it. But it must be true. Yet else would Lord Bellaire have risked so much to bed her: his daughter's knowledge, Lady Sarah's public humiliation if she should learn of it. His own reputation for taking a woman in an upstairs room of a coaching inn as if she were a common whore.

And she had let him!

Jemima groaned aloud and then buried her face in her hands.

"No, it is myself I do not understand," she whispered furiously between her fingers. She was out of her depth, over her head, treading in swift currents of unfamiliar waters. If she did not extricate herself immediately, she would be swept out to sea and lost forever.

She was on her feet and into the hall without thinking. Luckily there was no one there. She fled to the back of the hall and found the servants' stairwell and plunged into its steep narrow darkness. But even its enveloping umber was not enough to stop her blushes.

Was this the Jemima whom Julien saw and responded to when he looked deeply into her eyes with an expression he most often reserved for his favorite apricot tart?

Julien! She could not go back to London and face him. Not after this, not when he would see with an accuracy that frightened her every detail of the last hour written in her eyes. He liked to outrage her with his lewd speculations, but always before she could refute them. Not after tonight, not after she had bared herself for a man's lips and fingers and writhed under him in the pleasure he gave her.

"Oh, I wish I were dead!"

Liar!

Jemima started in the darkness as if someone had actually spoken to her. But it was only her conscience and she knew it.

She did not, despite all or rather because of it, wish she were dead. She had never before felt so alive. The blood sang in her veins; her pulse beat a measure she could easily dance to. And her lips, still full with the pleasure of his, ached for more and more kisses. She was not a wounded spirit. She did not wish for death. She wished for life. A life with the very last man she could ever hope to share hers with.

She had no doubt when his senses cleared of the carnal craving that had ensnared them both that Lord Bellaire would come to see their transgression as her fault. She had led him on. She had not resisted. She had allowed every indiscretion and would have offered more had something—his conscience?—not stopped him. That was how men thought. She had repeated proof of it. They blamed the women in their lives for their troubles and problems. An easy woman was a delight until the sun crept over the windowsill. Then she became the bewitching creature who snared a helpless man in the trap of his own lust. And in order for him to think himself innocent, it must be she who paid a price for his lust.

"Lust!" Jemima repeated the word even as everything within her recoiled from that designation. It had not been lust alone that drove her. But she could find no other explanation for Lord Bellaire's actions.

So then, this was the lust that men boasted and despaired of. She did not blame them. If they were creatures enslaved to so powerful an emotion, she did not doubt they would more willingly repudiate the supposed author of their entrapment.

And yet, there was free will. Perhaps men should share equally the shame of the past hour. She knew she was not alone to blame. She had seen in his expression as he left her a flicker of relief, as if he had feared he could not leave her. And that he would not be able to keep away from her if he did not. He seemed poised for flight and then he was gone.

Of course that must only be fanciful thinking bred in the maelstrom of her overwrought emotions. Lord Bellaire did not seem the type to run from anything, or anyone.

She found the back door just as a young man in livery carrying a lit lantern was about to enter.

"Lord Bellaire's man," he said in a respectful tone. "To see Miss MacKinnon to her carriage."

"Yes, I am she," Jemima answered, and followed him out into the darkness.

There could be only one destination for her now and that was home, though it would be near morning when she reached Chapel Hill.

An hour later and a more-than-a-little-drunk Beau stumbled back to his room and closed the door on a ragged breath. He had not enjoyed an instant of his drinking with fellow patrons, but it had given him a chance to catch his breath and for a short while obliterate all thoughts of Jemima MacKinnon. The moment he stepped over the threshold, however, a dozen little things reminded him. She had left behind her bonnet and several hairpins, and her scent. It was a blow to his ego to find the experience so easily rejoined.

She had been all cool flame in his arms. No woman had ever been so responsive. He had thought himself if not a connoisseur, a thoroughly experienced lover. But Jemima had turned him once again into a randy schoolboy as nervous about his own abilities as he was eager to please.

Beau drew in another harsh breath. And please her he had! She had incandesced in his arms, her mouth as seductive a design as any in his experience. No, singular. No other woman—he could not even conjure a single instant of a past liaison that could equal a kiss from Jemima MacKinnon's mouth. Everything he thought he knew about carnal pleasure was new and inexperienced again.

His hand shook as he reached for the door latch. He had nearly had her in the rough circumstances of a traveler's bed when she deserved silky sheets and roses and champagne and . . . love.

The word stopped him midway across the threshold. That was the source of unfamiliar disquieting knowledge circling his brain. This wasn't mere lust scorching him from head to toe and every vital organ in between. This felt like that long denied emotion he had once called love.

He returned to the room and crossed to sit down heavily, as if this new knowledge of himself was too much to be borne upright.

Could he have fallen in love again? No, this was nothing like the honorable tender emotions Fiona had once inspired within his breast. She had seemed to him perfection, pure and inviolate.

Jemima was strong and proud. She could hold her own in doubtful odds. Yet she beckoned his touch, no, melted at his touch. That was the response of a wanton, surely.

And yet, he could not forget the wondrous look in her gaze when she looked up at him from the bed as she asked what was happening to her. She had left to him her fate. And he had answered it with the instinct to protect.

One matter was perfectly clear. He had to get her away from St. Ives's influence. He did not know the tie that kept her bound to the man, but he would find a way to break it. She must be saved from her own allure. And after that?

Tonight in this room, Jemima had reminded him of all that he had once dreamed of and lost. All that he had turned his back on long before Fiona left this world. And now he wanted it back. Every scrap of boyish daydreaming of a perfect love. And all Jemima had to do to make him realize that was to kiss him.

His laughter was self-indulgent. Miss MacKinnon prided herself on managing every contingency in her life, even the wild beasts that ventured into her range. Yet now she had wakened a beast she might not know how to deal with.

Chapter Twenty-Four

"I knew it would come to this! We must abandon our enterprise immediately." Amelia looked a little green despite a fortification of cake and ale.

"I do not agree"—Henrietta began only to be interrupted by, of all people, Ianthe.

"It was a mistake! A prideful mistake to presume that we should have the right to castigate another's character!" Ianthe spoke more passionately than she ever had any other utterance. "And now be found to be the cause of another's despair? The taking of a life!" She shuddered and looked away.

Henrietta turned to the lady seated beside her. "What say you, Miss Jemima? Is the good Foolscap has done now overweighed by the harm?"

"I do not know."

A forlorn feeling passed through Jemima. She had returned to Chapel Hill by hired coach in the wee hours of the morning while the St. Ives's vehicle had been sent on

to London with Monsieur. The dreadful news she bore could
not wait upon a night's rest. She had called an emergency
meeting of the LADIES for tea and waited only until they
were served and refreshed to impart it.

"I acted on the information Henrietta sent. It did occur
to me that I should apply to you all for approval. Perhaps
I should have done so. I thought only of the good we would
do by Foolscap's portrayal of the villainy done the girl. But
now that we have such terrible news ... I can only regret
most terribly that I had any part in it."

The four members of the party lapsed into silence. The
remains of cakes and ale that had made up their tea now
lay neglected as each sank into reflection upon the adage
that the road to hell was paved with bricks of good intentions.

"I agree it was most ill-done," Henrietta ventured after
the silence would seem to hold sway. "But if there is fault,
we must share in it equally. Foolscap did no more or less
than we previously consented to."

"Perhaps we must reconsider our purpose." Ianthe looked
to the others for consent.

"We are not responsible for the consequences of the
truth," Henrietta replied firmly. "How long do you suppose
it should have been before the girl learned all through another
source?"

"How ever you divide it, it does not excuse our part,"
Amelia maintained in a embittered tone. "We should never
have been embroiled in affairs beyond our ken." She cast
a meaningful glance in her hostess's direction. "We should
all have been informed of Foolscap's latest effort before-
hand, as always before."

"The trouble was, we were not in possession of the full
facts," Henrietta said.

"But that is the very thing we strove to remedy," Amelia
answered, sounding more resentful than ever. "Miss Jemima

herself said that gossip runs on speculation and half-truth. The LADIES were formed to admonish rumor with fact.''

"I accept all the blame," Jemima said at last. "Whatever good or ill, it is all my doing. And I should make amends, if only I knew how."

"I will not take part in another LADIES meeting," Amelia said primly. "We should disband."

"Or go back to knitting mufflers for soldiers," Ianthe suggested. "Mother said that winter will be here before we know it and the army will be in sore need of socks and scarves for the Peninsular."

"Mufflers and socks!" Henrietta murmured. "I suppose we should. Though I did so enjoy pricking a few bubbles."

The four women eyed one another guiltily, though only Amelia's expression lacked the wistful glance of what-might-have-been.

When they were disbanded for the day, with no determined meeting time set in the future, Jemima saw Ianthe and Henrietta to the door. When she turned back from it, Amelia was waiting in the hallway for her. "Yes, what is it, Amelia?"

"There is a certain person asking for you."

"Pru." Jemima had been too tired and preoccupied to do more than check briefly on her houseguest, only to find her still abed at noon.

"She's complaining she has nothing to wear. And after all those pretty things you gave her."

"What pretty things?"

Amelia's brow lifted in question. "I did wonder . . . But she said you had given her permission."

An unpleasant thought came to mind. "You suspect she has been stealing my clothing?"

Amelia shrugged. "They're still here, in a manner of speaking. They needed to be altered to fit. She's been asking after you every day. She should be up and about now. She rarely lifts her head from the pillow before four of the clock.

I shouldn't be surprised if she can no longer walk. She eats from the moment she wakes until she falls asleep again. And she drinks wine. I've kept her out of the cellar but only just. Cook threatened to write you in the matter. She's ask to see you to discuss it.''

"I see." Jemima shook her head. "I am not up to domestic concerns today. Yet I suppose someone must see to her needs. Amelia, would you be so kind?''

"No, I will not.'' Amelia's usually sallow complexion flushed as she crossed her arms before her chest. "She is a lazy, disobliging, and very vulgar baggage, and I want no more to do with her.''

Her cousin's whining complaint was the very last thing she wanted at this moment. Tired and achy from her long journey, she longed for her bed and a good night's sleep. "I had no idea you felt so. Why did you not say something before?''

"I could not, could I? Not without jeopardizing the position to which you obliged me by the loan of a cottage.''

Scalded by her cousin's anger, Jemima answered shortly, "I never asked a thing in return for that but its upkeep.''

"Did you not? While you gad about London, I am left to deal with the disagreeable impression you created among the villagers by bringing that female under your roof. Yet there was no other way I could repay you than to discharge the duties set me, however distasteful. No, I must chew my crust and be grateful for it.''

"Amelia!'' If a mouse had run from its hole and stood on its hind legs and spoken to her, Jemima could not have been more shocked.

But the mouse had only begun to roar. Amelia took a step toward Jemima, her face distorted by an anger held too long at bay. "Do not attempt to thwart me. I must this once speak my mind as I should have done beforetimes. You think yourself a great and blameless lady because you need not stoop to the toadying of others. You ply us with cake and fine wine and bask in our pleasure.''

She thrust up her chin, jerking her mob cap askew. ''Few of us would be the meek lowly creatures we are, given your wealth, beauty, and ease of life. But then you would not know anything of hardship and suffering.''

''How dare—''

Amelia took another step toward the startled Jemima and wagged her finger at her cousin. ''You claim to be one of us, a poor mistreated spinster with no hope of joy and no escape from loneliness. Yet all Miss Ianthe, Miss Henrietta, and I have had these last weeks are your endless postings from Town filled with descriptions of fine gowns and of the places you have been. The opera and Vauxhall Gardens! If you suffer as I do, I cannot think why unless it is that you are too ungrateful to appreciate what has been given you in life!''

Jemima could not quite believe her ears. To be so scolded by a relation she had striven to help! Perplexed and vexed beyond all reason, she responded with what she felt was equal frankness.

''I—I am sorry that you feel this way, Amelia. Had I known you were resentful of my efforts on your behalf, you may be certain I should not have pushed my attentions upon you. I should have allowed you to live as you preferred though I doubt it would be as comfortably as the cottage you inhabit. And most certainly, I should not have looked to you, a relation, for help with Pru. To be bound to so onerous a duty through kinship must have been a hardship, indeed.'' She saw that her words struck chinks in Amelia's emotional armor and continued. ''You may be certain I shall not further impose upon you now or in future. I think we have said all that needs be said on the subject.'' She inhaled a stiffening breath of righteousness. ''Now if you will excuse me, I must take a draught for my aching head.''

Holding her head as high as she could, Jemima passed her browbeaten cousin and took the main stairs up to her room.

As she climbed she exclaimed incredulously, "Of all of the ungenerous— Unnatural— Unexpected—"

She passed into her room on a storm of fury, nearly knocking over a small table in her path. After all she had done, all she had risked, all she had endured to help the LADIES achieve their goals! Had she not taken it upon herself to . . .

Jemima paused in the middle of her room, arrested by sudden new knowledge.

The image of herself as injured party would not long hold. There was enough truth in what Amelia claimed to instantly crack her injured affront and expose for her examination an unsuspected flaw in her nature.

Was she too sure of herself and her place in the world? Had she wrapped herself in a mantle she did not deserve? Surely, she had been disappointed in love in a manner that was equal to their stories of love lost—stories known but for Amelia's. Certainly, she was wealthier than her three friends combined, but that was none of her own doing. And if she used her superior social position to influence them, that was to be expected. After all she knew more, understood the world better, had more experience . . .

And that was why she thought she, better than anyone, knew how the world should work. The only word to apply to such an assumption was arrogance!

Jemima subsided into the nearest chair with the sudden sensation of having made yet another error in judgment. This one without any temporizing circumstances.

She had thought because she did not complain that Amelia would enjoy playing lady of the manor in her absence. She had not seen herself going off to London to be the better part. And the gowns, they were Julien's idea, as were the opera and Vauxhall Gardens. She had suggested none of it, had not wanted to go. Yet seen through the lens of Amelia's point of view, she could not now doubt that she had reserved for herself the better part.

She *had* been highhanded in her manner toward her friends. Perhaps even smug, though she did not consciously think of it that way. She was Lady Bountiful in the guise of Foolscap, going about pointing out the flaws in the lives of others too foolish or stupid or unlucky to notice them for themselves. High-minded though the tactics might at first have seemed, Foolscap was a cloak for her own egotistical strivings. She had only to reflect upon the joy she experienced as she conceived her little drawings, how much pleasure they gave her, how witty she thought herself. And how safe from the very censure she sought to impose on others. She had hoped to teach society a lesson. At the moment her stung cheeks and deep mortification were lesson enough for herself. She had become the very thing she detested most, a meddling, interfering gossip!

However unwelcome this illumination of her character, Jemima could not but judge herself in the light of Amelia's candle. She had been selfish and thoughtless and self-congratulatory in her pride that she knew better than others what was good for them. She had once thought she would have welcomed the intervention of a well-meaning person when she was castigated falsely. But looking at it now, she would no doubt have resented the interference, objected to the presumption of another to know what she needed, and rejected any offer of aid.

It was a lowering admittance. The more she sank into reflection of it, the worse she felt. By suppertime she was fretted by so vicious a headache that she took to bed without supper the shameful realization that she was to blame for more misery than she had heretofore suspected.

* * *

After a late breakfast and two cups of cocoa, Jemima felt more the thing the next morning. It was time to visit her houseguest and learn what Amelia, who had decamped for her cottage before supper the evening before, had found so disagreeable about Pru.

She was sitting up in bed wearing what had once been Jemima's favorite wrapper, green silk embroidered with gold thread pagodas. Her yellow hair was twisted with papers and bound up in a scarf Julien had once given Jemima as a birthday present. The room smelled of too much perfume. But Pru herself was the greater surprise. A great transformation had taken place. Her once childishly pretty features were swelled and puffed out of proportion. Her pouty mouth was squeezed between her moon cheeks like the opening of a bladder and her eyes were no longer bright and clear. They were red-rimmed as if she had been crying or drinking too much.

"Oh there ye be, my lady," Pru greeted her as casually as if she were the lady of the house. "Have a cup o' tea with me?"

"No, thank you." Jemima looked about for a place to sit but there was not a piece of furniture in the room that was not draped with what appeared to be very nearly the entire contents of her wardrobe.

Noticing Jemima's perusal, Pru attempted to give a reason for the disarray. "Oh now, my lady, I can explain. I was just trying a few things on, in case ye'd not be wantin' them all. I had only the clothes on my back, and as they was all hanging there unused . . ."

"Yes, they were once hanging." Jemima looked back at her guest. "They are my winter things; that is why they were put away in this room."

Far from being abashed, Pru dimpled up in a smile. "I

did wonder, what with all them heavy silks and velvets. What's a girl to do for summer? thought I. But then I could not wear them anyway. And I did so want to be pretty for your return, so you'd be proud of me.''

"If you needed clothing, you might have inquired. Miss Amelia would have had a maid make something simple for you.''

"That's me, a girl of simple means.'' Pru's expression altered as swiftly as shifting sand to a pout. "I just miss pretty things. I was to have lots. But now I'd swung like a sow, I cannot think I'm pretty any longer. I can't wait to be shod of it.'' She paused to pat her belly, drawing Jemima's attention to the amazing increase in her girth. Had it been only four weeks? "My little stranger what's coming.''

"You have grown.'' Jemima frowned as she spoke. "By what date do you expect the child?''

"September,'' Pru said promptly.

"As soon as that?''

Hearing surprise in Jemima's tone, Pru frowned suddenly. "Well, I can't say for certain. I was never good with figurin'. What would be a good number of months?''

"Why don't you tell me when you think you were got with child and we will measure from that.''

Pru tucked her chin to her chest. "I would say it was about March. The week before Easter or a bit, most like.''

The thunderclap of realization inside Jemima's head momentarily stunned her. "Then your child could not possibility be Lord Bellaire's.''

Pru's head jerked up. "What do ye mean?''

"You could not possibly be so far gone if you conceived only three or four months ago. Your child would not be due until . . . Christmas.''

Pru smirked. "Mayhap he'll come a great bruiser, like his father.''

"That's as may be, but the father will not be Lord Bellaire."

Pru screwed up her face and crossed her arms before her now too-ample bosom. "So what if he ain't? That don't clear him of what he done to me, and me own dear boy. Forcing me into his bed so we could be found out in a com-compre—"

"Compromising position," Jemima offered, and could have kicked herself for her willful blindness of a month ago. Doctor Wesley had tried to warn her.

When the young woman swung her legs over the side, Jemima noticed in alarm that her feet were puffed like balloons and the veins were distended.

"Have you injured yourself or are you in pain?"

Pru huffed and puffed to heave herself to her feet. "No, but me back aches something fierce. And me feet!"

That was all that Jemima needed. She went and pulled the bell for the maid.

"What are you doing?" Pru asked as she tried to steady herself on her thick feet.

"I'm sending for the doctor."

"She has the swelling sickness. A kind of dropsy, if you will. There is no cure but the delivery of the child. I advise you to send to her an almshouse. They will know how to care for her until her confinement."

Jemima shook her head. "I cannot."

"Now, Miss Jemima—"

"I do not dispute your good advice on this occasion, Doctor. I should have heeded it when we first spoke about Pru. But now things are different. I have made her my responsibility, and I will not abandon her because difficulty has developed."

The doctor gave her a shrewd look. "I still do not approve, but I hope if I should ever stand in need that you are by."

Jemima smiled. "Tell me what must be done."

"You must order your cook to eliminate from the woman's diet every bit of salt and wine and cheese. No ham, no salted meats. No heavy puddings. It's custards and coddled eggs for her, dry toast and tea."

"She has developed a decided partiality for strawberries and cream."

"Strawberries but no cream. Nothing rich to encourage the swelling."

"What about the babe?"

The doctor wagged his head. "I cannot tell. Perhaps it will be delivered with no harm done. But we should prepare her for a stillbirth."

"Oh no!"

"It is not her doing, for all she has tried to drink herself into stupefaction. It is this noxious ailment. We could bleed her, but she won't hear of it and I am loath to press the matter in her condition."

"How long before she delivers?"

He shrugged. "It could be a month or a week. Sometimes the babe comes earlier and cannot thrive, but the mother is saved. We can only leave it to Nature to decide."

She followed the doctor back into the room and stood by as he explained to Pru her illness. Badly frightened, the girl had wanted him to take the baby at once and save her life. She seemed strangely distraught to be told she must wait upon Nature. She began to cry and scream and make herself hysterical until Jemima began to worry about the fate of the child within. Only a laudanum dose calmed her enough for them to leave her in the care of a maid.

She dressed for comfort and went out. She needed to be out of doors in the fresh air that it might cleanse the cobwebs from her mind.

As she walked, she mused on the ways that her life had turned upon an instant into something quite different from what it had seemed before. Amelia resented her. Henrietta and Ianthe felt betrayed by her. Pru had lied to her. And Lord Bellaire, well, she could not think about him at the moment without the threat of tears.

So she walked a little faster and a little more purposefully. She no longer believed Pru's tale of ruthless seduction at Lord Bellaire's hands. It was not only that she felt she knew him too well to believe him capable of the act. But that did not mean he had not shared her bed. Yet, none of it mattered. She was bound by a rash action to see the business of Pru through until she could be delivered.

On the edge of the village, she spied the vicar's cottage and immediately turned down the lane toward it. She needed to confide in someone and Henrietta was the most sensible woman of her acquaintance.

"What is wrong?" The look on Henrietta's face when she recognized her visitor sent Jemima's heart plummeting into her slippers. "Is there more bad news?"

"You've been gazetted," Henrietta stately flatly.

"Whatever do you mean?"

Henrietta hesitated only a moment before she opened her door and directed Jemima inside. After a quick glance up her lane, she closed the door.

"Who is it?" both women heard the vicar call from another room.

" 'Tis no one of importance," Henrietta answered and glanced upward as if asking for forgiveness. Then she put a finger to her lips as she directed Jemima to the opposite end of the small parlor.

Finally Henrietta said in a very low voice, "You should not be abroad today, Miss MacKinnon."

"Miss Henrietta, you are alarming me. What has happened?"

She did not offer Jemima a seat but went directly to her knitting box and pulled out several folded papers and brought them back to hand to Jemima.

"These came in the morning post. I have kept them from Father, but you may be certain he will soon hear of it. The postman said they were franked to every household in the village."

"To everyone? Why ever should anyone do that?"

Henrietta blinked nervously, but her expression remained quite blank. "When you've seen them you may tell me."

Jemima looked down at the newspaper she held. It was not one of the prestigious gazettes but one of the more execrable sort. "High Jinks on Derby Day" the headline read.

"The inside," Henrietta prompted after a moment.

Jemima opened the broadsheet to the cartoon that took up half an inside page. It was a wretched piece of buffoonery. The merest scrap of skill had gone into its creation. Yet it was devastatingly effective. The panel showed a young woman, presumably herself, leading a capering bear about on ribbons. Behind the bear trotted a silver-haired gentleman, also on leading strings, with a broad foolish smile on his face. Beside him a young girl was tethered to the gentleman. She, too, was dancing. A little distance away, in a carriage marked with a crest stood a lady with her arms folded, looking quite vexed by the procession. Underneath the cartoon were the words: "Cross as a bear?"

It was an unfaltering portrait of all of them, particularly Lady Sarah. Jemima peered at length before murmuring, "I did not remember her nose as quite so long nor her chin so prominent. This was done for spite."

Yet she could not comprehend a good reason for it. The only person she suspected of wanting to show her up in a poor light was Lady Sarah, yet she could not conceive of Lady Sarah allowing herself to be portrayed so unflatteringly for the discomfort of another. So then, someone else was responsible. But who, and why?

She studied again the foolish expression on Lord Bellaire's face. He seemed to be in the throes of a kind of ecstasy. Was he supposedly besotted by her? And she leading him on a merry chase?

"There is worse."

When Jemima looked up Henrietta handed her a second paper.

This time there was no mistaking the malicious intent of the illustrator. The cartoon depicted a large coaching inn. From its open doorway spilled drunken revelers, their pockets overflowing with pound notes. This scene was nothing compared to the portraits in the open upstairs windows. Through one window a gentleman could be seen being robbed at pistol-point by a cents-per-cent. Another showed a young girl in a nightcap retching into a basin held by a servant. The most prominent panel showed a fashionably dressed gentleman and lady tumbling into a bed, her skirts tossed over her head and his pantaloons loose about his hips. If that were not damning enough, outside and below the window a bear in hat and vest danced a jig to the accompaniment of a brass band. The caption read: "The Wild Ride on Derby Day."

"Oh! Oh! Oh!"

Chapter Twenty-Five

The villagers of Chapel Hill were in turmoil. The tale of the wayward Miss MacKinnon took the whole of the week's news. By the end of the first day, every one of the adult inhabitants had seen the gazettes. Yet there seemed not a soul in the entire village who did not have a claim to other knowledge about the matter. And the first stirrings were of outrage for a scandal that could not possibly be true.

"What a clanker!" replied the MacKinnon cook to the question put forth, however tentatively, by the butcher. "My mistress would no more be found in a coaching inn with a gentleman than she would riding a broomstick!"

"Our Miss MacKinnon? Squiring about a black bear?" suggested the grocer. "She don't even keep dogs."

But gradually the denials were undercut by a letter from a cousin here, a family friend there. Miss MacKinnon had, indeed, been at the Derby with a dancing bear. There were others to tell that she had kept company with Lord Bellaire and his daughter. And while the gentleman was imminently respectable, the women of the village sucked in their cheeks and exchanged glances that said none of them had ever met a man what was better than he should be when he was with a woman. And a man was a man, after all.

Within a day or two, the mood changed. Discontentment reared its head. There were two fights at the market over the quality of the new shipment of beef. And at the tailor's, a bill left unpaid these five months caused an altercation that was to be turned over to the magistrate. While the more reasonable citizens debated the causes of this sudden dissension in their midst, the chuckleheaded and the addlepated came to agreement on the point. The growing general discord could be laid at the door of their once august citizen. Scandal was infecting the whole community. And the feeling that something should be done about it took instant root.

The vicar was beset by requests that he immediately go forth and commiserate with Miss MacKinnon over her fall from grace. A public display of remorse was demanded by the more extreme. It was one thing to hold unorthodox views. Another to rub the faces of the entire town in her lascivious ways. After all, who was she? An unmarriageable spinster with a history of scandal that kept her from polished society of her own kind. There was only so much poor, honest, God-fearing when-it-pleased-them people could allow and look one another in the face!

Everyone knew that contemptible deeds must be done in the dark, hidden from view, paved over with the appearance of right-thinking and right doing. True, Mrs. Bacon had slipped up and borne Mr. Hopskin a son with Mr. Bacon none the wiser. True, too, that Miss Phillips enjoyed rather more than a temperate amount of Blue Ruin when she had locked her door for the night. And if Mr. Budgie now and again dipped a sticky finger into the collection plate, as long as there were no witnesses, the deeds were as good as not done.

But Miss MacKinnon had done the one thing which no other guilty party could forgive. She had flaunted her throwing over of convention and seemed quite happy with the results.

And so a few days after the gazettes had been distributed, the men of Chapel Hill gathered as usual round their ale pots and grog jars one evening and shared the village news. At first they seemed embarrassed. They shook their heads and murmured about the Miss MacKinnon they thought they had known all her life. As the liquor went down ever more smoothly they began to speculate, with the aid of the cartoons tacked up behind the bar to spur them, on the type of woman she must actually be. A few whispers drew the first titters. Soon the more cocksure expanded into ribald theories that resulted in great guffaws of rough laughter. Their language turned ever more crude and lewd until even they did not know where truth ended and speculation, ever alive in the minds of men with a bit of spit still in them, began.

It was only after they parted company and turned their reddened countenances toward home that their consciences pricked them and they grew quiet and morose and sullen. By the time they stumbled over their thresholds, all the grievances of their humble existence had begun to gnaw at them. They had no pretty Miss MacKinnon to tumble them into bed and tickle their fancies. Instead angry termagants, smelling of smoke and sweat, met them at the door. Mrs. Hollingsworth demanded to know why Mr. Hollingsworth had been so long. Mrs. Dodge met Mr. Dodge with the news that dinner was cold and their youngest was sick. Both men mumbled under their breath and went to sit in silence before their hearths. Other, less indulgent men knocked a few heads together and backhanded their wives until their families quailed before them in wary silence.

The wives, for their part, felt no better served by the new knowledge of the lady in their midst. They had never known other than that life for a woman was hard and brutal and often futile. Men might gather in their taverns and drink away their sense of injury and injustice at their lot. Wives could only look to the fire and tend the children they bore too often until there were too many to do anything with but scold and box their ears and put to bed without supper when times were hardest. What they thought they shared with their beloved Miss MacKinnon, until the gazettes proved different, was a kindred misery that life treated even the best among them no better than the worse.

Now they knew different. Miss MacKinnon had proved herself to be above them. Unlike them, she had the means at her disposal to change her situation. She had ridden off to London and begun to enjoy life. And that had made her in their eyes a Traitor!

And not even her friends could forgive her for it.

Starting on the evening the gazettes arrived, Miss Henrietta would sit with her little lap desk and turn the key in the lock and then pull from a secret compartment an old yellowed letter postmarked from the once colony of Massachusetts. She would read again the scant lines from Her Tom that informed her that he was not coming home. He had married a colonial lass. They were expecting their first child. And when she had read it through three times, she tucked it away again and locked her box and went to bed to smother her tears in her pillow.

Down the road a different skit was underway. Since the news had been published abroad that Miss MacKinnon was nothing less than a loose woman, Widow Strickland had forbidden her daughter to ever again speak to the lady.

"To think that someone I account an acquaintance could be so lost to dignity, decorum and good character! Comporting herself like a common strumpet in public with an earl!

Her character has been dished up! She is ruined! I'm not one for gossip but one should always heed the whisperings. The truth was in the wind some nine years ago. Character will out! No good comes from idle hands. No wonder she took in that baseborn trull breeding a little Satan, I don't doubt! And that ladies' club of hers— Gracious, Ianthe! You might have become infected with her scandalous ways. No, I shall not hear another word on the subject. You are never again to go near the MacKinnon person! I shall never get over it! Never! Quickly bring my smelling salts, I feel the vapors overtaking me!''

Strangely enough, her mother's ranting had, this time, the opposite effect on Ianthe. Instead of trying to calm and soothe her every waking moment, Miss Ianthe began to listen a little less intently for her mother's voice to make known her demands. She began to neglect her duties and go and sit in the tiny space that served as a garden just outside the kitchen door. The first day she waited three whole minutes together before she stirred to do her mother's bidding. In a few days' more, she affected not to hear her mother at all for as much as half an hour at a time.

"Daydreaming!" her mother scoffed in suspicion that her daughter could find anything of more pressing urgency than her mother's health. "Woolgathering and star-gazing!"

It was not woolgathering that held Ianthe more and more in thrall to her own thoughts. It was the gathering suspicion that she had been a fool!

Quite some three years ago, the widow Strickland developed a heart condition that had doomed Ianthe's then engagement. After all a young man, even one as much in love as Captain John Morley of His Majesty's Navy, could only be expected to wait so long for his intended. Yet how could Ianthe abandon a mother with a formidable list of symptoms that were likely to assert themselves at any hour, but usually when Ianthe dared make plans of her own? Alas, the captain soon sailed away to other arms. Now Ianthe could but wonder how her life might be if she had sailed away with him. Her mother, helpless when her daughter did all, had lately been found belowstairs entertaining a few ladyfriends when Ianthe was out.

The infectious discontent reached even to the little cottage at the back of Jemima's small estate. Who could say where the discovery of infamy in their midst might lead next?

"Where, indeed?" Amelia wondered in anxiety.

Since just after Eastertide, she had been at the august task set her by Jemima to read at least one work of England's most famous Elizabethan playwright. *Hamlet, Prince of Denmark,* had been her choice when she learned that the hero was unmarried and a prince to boot.

Three months along and several scenes into the play, she had so far seen little that was heroic in the Danish scion. He seethed in endless despair over matters quite beyond her ability to grasp.

Then the day before Jemima's return from London, Amelia had opened a posting from her last position as governess. When she had read it, she understood all too well Hamlet's dilemma. The letter was the reason she was so out-of-reason cross with Jemima when she returned. Her continued agitation had little to nothing to do with the gazettes. It came from being forced to remember that, like Hamlet, her own inaction might have been the cause of a death.

The eldest daughter wasn't even her business. She'd been hired to stick a bit of learning into the younger sister's head. In a gentry family that boasted an eldest and youngest girl child with four robust boys in between, the governess had played only a minor role in her new family's life. The eldest, Jane, was pretty with wide blue eyes and soft brown curls and a manner that surely suited her for a better match than her village could offer. Mary, the youngest, was plain and quiet and quite clever.

Then one night last winter Amelia's charge Mary came to her, saying that Jane was feverish and ill, and was asking for her.

Jane lay in her bed shaking with fever and chills. It did not take long to get the truth out of her. She was bleeding. She had been to visit the Gypsies in the hills. And the soothsayer had given her something to prevent a child. Amelia must please do something to help her, but no one else must know.

Tell no one. It would disgrace her family. She would rather be dead than face them. But Amelia must do something. So she tore bedsheets into bandages and packed the girl as best she could, and waited.

The next morning it was put about that Jane had a noxious fever. It might be catching. Amelia offered to nurse her. She had seen it before. No need to send for a doctor. These things usually ran their course in a few days. The family readily agreed. Let the governess take care of it. She was inured to the dreaded diseases of childhood. Three long days went by while Jane rallied twice. But in the wee hours of the third morning, she simply heaved a great sigh and died.

That next Sunday, across the altar of the church, Amelia met the eye of the young vicar, who looked like a man condemned to the cross, and *knew* who was responsible. And still she sat and said nothing, for there was nothing to be done behind a wasted life. No good revenge for the dead.

But ghosts, as Hamlet learned, will not be still. And her part in the girl's death would not allow her peace. She began to shake for no reason, to forget where she was and even the next word she meant to speak. The family took it as evidence of the same ineptitude that had cost them their eldest daughter's life and quickly sent her packing, the lie they did not know they should guard sent to safety in Chapel Hill.

Amelia thought she had put it all behind her, until Jemima

took in Pru. The pregnant girl, who had no shame and no morals, would live while sweet gullible Jane lay moldering in a grave.

And then the post arrived, after all these months, containing a letter of recommendation for employment and, who would have guessed, one hundred pounds. They knew! Or guessed. Or had been told. And this was a bribe, hush money for the ghost who plagued her.

And so Amelia began again to read *Hamlet* by candlelight, accompanied by a bottle of brandy. The more she read, the more she drank until the complex guilt and misery of the Danish prince became her own.

Could she have saved the girl by proclaiming the truth that first night? Or was she honor-bound to the girl's dying wish? Was she a loyal friend or a gutless servant? The guilt and uncertainty bound her up in such resentment and jealousy that her cousin's foibles seemed of no great moment. Jemima had wealth and beauty and a good mind. She would survive. Amelia was very much afraid she would not.

And so it went throughout the village. Not a soul who had a secret to keep could refrain from thinking that it was somehow about to be exposed by the indiscretion of the lady among them. Once the revelations began, where would it all end?

When the gossip had been chewed dry, there was nothing left to do but join sides.

By the end of the week, the butcher became uncertain that he could fill Miss MacKinnon's weekly order. The apothecary could not find the ingredients needed to mix a purge for Miss MacKinnon's ailing houseguest. The reasoned opinion that the merchants should soon all starve without the patronage of Miss MacKinnon was tempered by the rage with which they were met beneath their roofs each night.

"A ten-day wonder," became the fervent if silent chant of every shopkeeper. And then life in Chapel Hill could return to normal.

The only man in town who seemed unburdened by the revelations of the last days was the smithy. One might even say he waxed philosophical about it all.

"The aristos will have their bit o' fun," he said to one and all, "or why else be them?"

The third morning of the day following the arrival of the gazettes, Jemima was awakened with the news that she had a gentleman guest from London waiting below.

Thinking it must be Julien, she went below without bothering to do more than put on her wrapper. For the past five days she had not been able to bring herself to venture past her own gate. Miserable and ashamed and unable to fathom out what to do about it, she was in need of advice and it was not the kind Henrietta could give her.

But, of course! She should have sent for Julien at once. Always before when she was most in despair it was he in whom she found comfort. She should have known he would not desert her.

She found herself smiling for the first time since Derby Day as she opened the doors to her parlor and hurried in.

"Oh—Lord Bellaire."

Chapter Twenty-Six

Beau rose from the settee, his top hat gripped tightly in one hand and a copy of the damning gazette clutched in the other. He had almost turned back twice while making the journey, uncertain why he had come here, after all, but unable to keep away. The last week in London had taught him that above all things, he was not a man who cracked under pressure.

Perhaps he would never face an enemy's musket ball or foil a French lancer's thrust. But he had without flinching withstood laughter, smirking faces, and dozens of sly comments made at the back of his passing. He had endured a lecture on a want of discretion by no less than a great-aunt and been made to smile at his own tomfoolery in the House of Lords. He had even faced up to the torrent of temper and tears that Lady Sarah rained on him. Shot and powder seemed nothing in comparison. Through it all, he thought only of Jemima and what she must be going through. It had taken every ounce of his will not to run to her side in defense.

No, he must stay in London and pretend that not a drop of truth could be found in any of the malicious accusations. Or worse, if there was a drop, he was not interested in where it fell. Cats did not long tease a dead rat.

And through it all he had grappled with a new knowledge of himself. He was in love with Jemima MacKinnon. It was that simple. That knowledge made him walk away from Lady Sarah, whom he didn't love though she was an eminently suitable lady to take as a bride. And here he was to claim—he did not yet know how—an infinitely unsuitable woman whom he ached to bed.

Which made Jemima's arrival into the room momentous. But not the pleasure he expected.

Her hair was drawn back in a tight, unflattering knob. The new spectacles perched on her nose seemed too heavy for her face. Her wrapper was unfashionably shabby, almost shapeless and of a dull-figured muslin. She looked outright dowdy and disgruntled. The image of Bluestocking offended him. It gave lie to the very things that had sent him hell for leather into the country without a thought for his dignity or his pride.

Because he confronted something less than his dreams proclaimed, he could think of no good way to begin what he had come to say, to demand. Instead, he felt betrayed by memory and his emotions. She was not the sort of vision a man risked everything for. In the end he could only muster a stiff unloverlike, "Good day, Miss MacKinnon."

To his astonish she did no more than glance in his direction before she said mildly, "So you've seen it."

Beau cast aside the gazette he held. "Then you've been informed as well."

"Yes." She pushed her spectacles back up to the bridge of her nose. "I should have lived quite happily without the news."

He had thought to find her distraught, or been prepared

to console her shock when she had seen the infamy printed about them. Yet she seemed nothing so much as unconcerned. After the week he had endured, it did not seem fair that she remained untouched.

"Is the matter of no moment with you? Are you undisturbed by this venomous assault on character that could be ruinous to us all?"

She fixed her gaze on the carpet two feet before his boot tips. "Aside from myself, I do not see that ruin can be the result for anyone else."

"Then you do not understand the damage ridicule can do." Annoyed that she would not allow him so much as a second glance, he went on the attack. "It has smeared many. Lady Sarah, not the least. She has been forced to leave town."

At last she looked up, but he could not tell through her confounded lenses what emotion her gaze held. "The humiliation of public mockery has completely wrecked her nerves. Her physician recommended a complete rest at her country estate for at least three months."

"Oh dear," she murmured. "Considering how little she likes the country, the cure would seem worse hardship than the ailment."

Another time he would have smiled at her wit. This time he felt she was in no position to criticize a lady they had both, in a manner of speaking, done ill. "I would have thought it beneath you to make fun of another."

"Yes, of course. You have never done so, I'm certain." With a distracted gesture, she pushed her spectacles up a second time, making him wish to snatch them from her.

He gave her a hard look instead. "Do you think *I* enjoy seeing myself being paraded about like a Jackanapes? However careless you may be with yours, I have a reputation to protect."

Jemima let the remark settle over her. She could not begin

to tell him how offended she was by his appearance without first informing her. And then for him to castigate her with his first words! As if she were a lost cause and only his future was jeopardized by the slander! It was unsupportable.

A white-hot heat that had nothing to do with the warmth of the day raced up her bosom and neck into her cheeks as she looked up at the handsome strong-willed man she loved but could not have. And that realization made her take up the only defense she had against him, her wit.

"Your reputation," she said slowly. "You might have thought of that before you forced me into that bedroom at the inn."

The reasonableness of her statement further infuriated Beau. How could she stand before him so calmly when last they met she had lain half-bare in his embrace?

"Am I alone to blame? Did you do nothing to encourage it? I do not seem to recall your protest in any action that took place abovestairs. In fact I seem to recall the exact opposite."

"Then your memory selects what bests suits your humor."

Goaded beyond his reserve, he reached out and caught her by the wrist. "Tell me I abused you, forced you against your will?"

His touch caught Jemima totally unprepared for the silly reckless pleasure that burst through her. Did he know that she could not remain polite and distant when he brushed his thumb along the tender inside of her wrist? Could he feel the place where her pulse beat much too strongly? It was as if her heart had not heard her vow never to see him again.

"Your familiarity grows tiresome, Lord Bellaire." She tried to free herself, but he clamped strong fingers about her and would not let go. She tried to turn away from him but his expression would not allow that either. He looked angry, of course, but a new expression overlay it. And that was hurt!

"To think that I am seen as a man too easily led about by a pretty face! I will not have it!"

Jemima saw at once that his anger, fiercely roused though it was, was no longer aimed at her. But of course, his precious reputation would have made his last days in Town difficult. "I think, my lord, you overstate the case. In certain quarters, your reputation may even be enhanced by the notoriety."

She was correct, as usual, but Beau was too offended by her indifference to admit it. He dropped her arm as though it, too, offended him. "You think my reputation alone is what I care for?"

Jemima stepped back and gave him a cool glance. From the moment she walked in the room all she had wanted to do was throw her arms about his neck and kiss him until neither of them cared what the world thought of them. Because she could not do that, she withdrew into the shelter of disdain.

"I do not know you well enough to judge properly, Lord Bellaire. But yes, if pressed, I suspect you are the veriliest prude. A pompous self-righteous prig who cares more for appearances than the truth!"

His face contorted in fury. "Damn you!" he roared, more angry than if she had accused him of being a seducer and roué.

He advanced on her slowly, his footsteps punctuating his words. "Prig, am I? Prude?" He let his gaze rake insolently over the low-cut neckline of her wrapper that spread open as she took equally deliberate steps back from him. Her bosom, which he had seen only in meager candlelight, caught his full attention. The luscious display made him even angrier as he searched for the words to hurt her.

"I am no bluenose. 'Tis only that I am more fastidious

in my choice of bed partners than your—ah, confidant St. Ives.''

In stunned affront Jemima realized he was indirectly accusing her of an improper relationship with Julien. She balled her hands into fists until her nails bit into her palms. Well, she would not give him the satisfaction of denying it.

''You should then be pleased to be rid of me. I have left London for good. You may be certain I have no claim on you, nor do I wish to make any.''

''So say you now.'' He smiled but it was not a nice smile. ''You were not so reluctant to make claim to me on Derby Day.''

Jemima felt her cheeks warm with the rise of her blood. Need he stand so near? But the settee pressed the back of her knees. There was nowhere else for her to go. Words were her only weapons. ''Since when do gentlemen mistake passion for possession?''

He leaned in toward her. '' 'Tis you women who most often use that weakness against us.''

''Weakness?'' That brought her back up though she had to lean away to keep from bumping her brow on his chin. ''Then by all means take your leave of me. Flee if you must. I should not, above all things, seek to be the cause of your unmanly conduct.''

''My unmanly—'' Beau tossed his hat away and took her by the waist. ''Do you not yet understand how very much your presence emboldens my manhood?''

The proof of his statement pressed against her was shocking.

Jemima lifted her chin though her legs felt unsteady. ''Insults! You yield to them on every occasion you are being bested.''

''Insult?'' Beau bit out a curse that ended with, ''God give me patience!''

''God grant you a more civil tone!'' she shot right back.

Half the time Beau did not know whether he wished to swat or swive her. At the moment both impulses rode him hard. She was made for love, he thought as lust hammered in his veins, and she must be his!

His mouth did not engulf hers as it had in the past kisses. His lips touched hers softly, lingered a moment, and lifted. It was only a tiny a spark of passion that leapt between them. But the spark set fire to her whole being. And like a flash fire, the resulting raging inferno threatened to burn down the last of her pride and self-confidence. He had found the method to best her. And he knew that, damn him! She saw it flare in his gaze.

"Let go of me!" she choked out at last.

Her expression became one of such intense dislike that Beau released her and took a step back.

"You may think every ill of me." She spoke with a breathless urgency, as if every word cost her a great deal of effort. "But I won't be fondled by you as if I were a strumpet."

Her words stung but Beau had felt her reaction and he wasn't about to admit he had acted wrongly. "What I am to think? One moment you kiss me with the practiced skill of a courtesan. The next you bristle up like a frightened virgin. What sort of woman are you?"

"An independent one." Giving up the fight to keep her spectacles perched on her nose, she snatched them from her face. "Get accustomed to us. We shall not forever be a rare breed."

"Then God help mankind!"

"Become more like womankind, I should hope."

She stared at him, angry and obstinate, but that was not all. Behind her defiance, he saw now a hint of trouble in her unfettered gaze. Like cloud shadows on a pond beneath a sunny sky, anxiety, wariness, and even fear sailed across her gaze.

Watching the subtle and bold expression of emotions on her face kept him from replying at once. She had insulted him with the brass confidence of a duchess. Yet now she was blushing like a debutante. He wondered fleetingly if he spent the rest of his life in her company if he would ever understand her, and doubted it.

Belatedly he remembered that she might have endured troubles of her own this past week. The ugly epithets that had spewed from Sarah's mouth when she brought him the damning gazettes quite appalled him. What had Jemima, a woman alone, endured? And what further trouble might he be stirring up for her by coming here today?

"Jemima, I—"

Jemima jerked back from his reaching hand as if it were a snake about to bite her. "I don't understand you. You don't even like me!"

She sounded as mystified as he felt. But he had more experience with the tangled skein of emotions she evoked in him. He had thought about it many times during the last week. "I don't know that liking has much to do with what is between us."

As he watched her move away from him, the natural instinct for self-protection told him to back away from her, as well, to leave her to her own devices. She had not asked anything of him. Did not ask anything now. She had been a stranger one short month ago. Surely in an equal amount of time he would forget her. In one thing she was correct. Without her in Town to keep the titillation fresh in mind, this scandal was already ebbing. Talk of the Regent's ball had again assumed prominence as it neared.

Then, too, he had problems closer to home that required his attention. Between them, Emma and Guy threatened to ruin what was left of his once-peaceful life. Yet he remained rooted to the spot, wanting nothing more than to snatch the pins from the knot that held her lovely hair prisoner and run his hands through it as he had only a week ago. That night she had been full of woe, but in her pain she had turned to him.

And that reminded him.

"You said some very perplexing things to me when last we were together. You were distraught over the news of the Irish lass who'd drowned herself. Will you tell me why?"

Jemima's gaze darted away. "No."

"Then explain why you claimed to be the author of Foolscap?"

Jemima shook her head. Mercy! Had she really confessed that to him? "No."

Beau let out a slow breath. Her tone was not civil but it was no longer gusted by anger. Taking that as a cue to remain, he moved over to her mantel and set his boot on the grill.

"I was of a mood to believe that you were more than agitated beyond reason at the time. But now I wonder. You must know something of the man."

He moved to scoop up the papers he had thrown aside and held them out to her. "Someone leaked this on-dit to the illustrator. I will have satisfaction for this slight. But before I can do that I must know who is responsible. Before I leave this house, you will tell me what you know. Or you may be certain I shall make inquiries until I have dug up the truth about Foolscap and published the full abroad."

That brought her gaze back to him. "You wouldn't?"

But she saw a determination to match her own in his gaze.

"Very well." She turned her back on him. "But the truth involves others who are completely innocent. I must have your word you will not speak of it again outside this room."

She glanced back over her shoulder when he made no ready reply. "I never meddle in the affairs of others," he answered. "But I reserve the right to have satisfaction for this slander from my accuser."

"Very well. Foolscap had no part in the cartoons you hold."

"How do you know this?"

Jemima turned to face him. "Because I am Foolscap."

Something in her expression kept him from laughing in her face.

"Tell me."

For the first time since he'd known her, she smiled and turned upon him an expression of artful coquetry. "You will think me a silly woman—" But then she stopped herself.

Perhaps it was his arrested expression or her girlish tone sounding falsely in her ears, but her smile vanished. She straightened to her full height and took a step toward him. "Have a seat, Lord Bellaire. It is a long tale."

As succinctly as she could, she laid out for him the origins of her group of female avengers and its purpose.

Though he peppered her recitation with the occasional "By Jove" and "Damme!" Beau thought it to his credit that he did not once interrupt her with derisive snorts or outright laughter. A group of spinsters, to take it upon themselves to scold the haut *ton* on manners. It was absurd, worthy of a Drury Lane farce. But he saw by her expressive telling that she was genuinely committed to the madness.

In one thing alone, he found a new respect for her. "You are the artist, Foolscap?"

Jemima nodded. "I have the best hand among us. I thought we should use essay but few will sit still for a lecture. Cartoons seemed better suited to our purpose."

"I see." But he did not, completely. "This has been a delightful joke played by your little party and a sop to assorted grievances. A diversion whose purpose was, as you so picturesquely put it, to ladle scandal sauce on the Gander who first served it to the Goose."

"Those words are not mine." Jemima had been careful

not to mention any other names. "But they speak to the purpose."

As she spoke, Beau had lapsed into something just short of a sprawl on her settee. He drummed his fingers lightly on the arm of the piece as he contemplated her revelations. "So then your blunderbuss tactics by Foolscap have nothing to do with this present matter."

"Certainly not." Jemima eyed him impassively. "Yet I must take exception to your phrasing. We have been quite organized in our methods. We even have a name."

Beau smiled indulgently. "Yes? What is the name of your society?"

"The LADIES. It stands for Ladies Against Deceivers Infesting Elegant Society."

His lips twitched. "Rather say Ladies Abandoning Dignified Instructive Ethics Society." He sat up, warming to the subject immediately. "Or perhaps a more apt title would be Ladies Annoying Daily Individuals Everywhere Society." All at once he laughed. "What about Ladies Against Delicious Intercourse Enjoyment Society?"

Jemima blushed scarlet. "Sir, you are too vulgar."

But Beau was enjoying himself too much to notice the warning glare in her gaze. "Very well. Ladies Avidly Detesting, Inveighing and Enkindling Envy Society."

"That has two *E*s."

"So it does. Ladies Abandoning Desirous but Inadequate Everyday Sense?"

"There is no *but*."

"Ah, I beg to differ. You butt in at every point."

"You have yet to make a point."

"So say you because you cannot refute it." He tapped a finger against his lips. "Ah yes, Ladies Abetting Delusional Insane Exaggerated Spite. And furthermore, Ladies Assuring Derision at Incalculable Expense to Selves!"

Mortified by his derision, Jemima retreated once more

into icy disdain. "One would think you had given this quite some thought."

"Madam, I have given it but a soupçon of my wit."

"That explains it." She turned on him a withering smile. "Little wit in, little wit out."

But Beau was much too relieved and enlivened by his humor to be angry. In fact, at the moment, he was diverted beyond all calculation. He stood, laughter making his eyes shine and his face more attractive than ever, and came over and took her by the hand to draw her to her feet. "Miss MacKinnon, there is only one way to rectify this matter. It speaks in answer to all necessity of your needs and mine. Marry me."

Jemima stared at him for so long that the sound of her hand cracking a slap across his face sounded a surprise a both their ears.

"How dare— Don't you— To so insult— I will not have it— I will not!" Jemima was moving backward and away from him as fast as her feet could carry her. "You have no right to so insult me!"

"Insult!" Beau's formidable temper had flared like the blood to his face, which outlined the shape of her hand along his jaw. "I insult you? You are a mad woman."

Yet he felt as appalled as she looked. He could not think why he had blurted those words. A proposal of marriage? Was it he who had run mad? He had a child to think of, and a political career. The kind of Bluestocking high jinks she had gotten up to could spell disaster to his future.

He pulled himself together with great effort, wrapped himself in the mantel of the injured party and spoke. "You must forgive me, Miss MacKinnon. I cannot think what madness of mind promptly my proposal when it was so obviously odious to you. I beg you ignore it. In fact, I had come to tell you that I can have nothing more to do with you. And only that."

Jemima watched him through eyes that burned with what she was certain were tears of righteous indignation. "I did not think you would offer me anything else. Your offer is withdrawn, which suits me perfectly. Now if you are done with your castigation of my character, I bid you adieu."

Beau could not decide which was worse—to have his proposal refused or to be given his walking papers by a chit who did not have the reason to know the honor he had done her by his proposal. Not that he wanted her to accept . . . but to reject it without consideration? That was lowering.

He picked up his hat and turned without leave for the door.

"Do allow me ask one question of you, Lord Bellaire."

Her tone bore him no good, but Beau was too much a gentleman to ignore a lady's pointed request. He turned back.

She smiled at him. "Do you know a simple country girl by the name of Pru?"

Jemima had expected the answer, yet she was still shocked to see him go pale but for the vivid mark of her handprint on his face.

"No, of course not" he managed after a moment.

"No, of course not," she echoed. "Good day, Lord Bellaire."

Chapter Twenty-Seven

The arrival of Lord Bellaire in Chapel Hill did not go unnoticed. It did take some time, however, before his name could be discovered. In fact, it was the back of him villagers turned out to view as he left Miss MacKinnon's gate on horseback and trotted off toward the Kings Highway.

So this was the silver-haired gentleman she had been discovered cavorting with! And here he came brazen as everything, in broad daylight, no doubt to carry on with more of the same. That he had remained beneath her roof for less than an hour did not stop tongues from wagging. Unfortunately, the head gardener had spied the lady taking leave of the nobleman at her front door, still dressed in her wrapper!

If Miss MacKinnon was not duly cowed by the outright snubs of her neighbors, then it was clear some "stronger demonstration" of their disapproval was in order!

The matter fomented until a second rider came down the same path less than two hours later and reined in at Miss

MacKinnon's door. Now this gentleman in his tricked-out finery was well known to all. This was Julien St. Ives, the scapegrace cousin to the lady. His familial attachment to her did not still the chatter that "another gent" had come calling on Miss MacKinnon. "What with the first scarce rid on his arse out of sight!"

Too many villagers were wed to their own cousins to halt new speculations that swelled the throats of those who gathered in the lane in twos and threes to discuss this newest turn of events. Two gentlemen in a single day! The lady had no shame! She flaunted her misbehavior and thereby invited every sort of indecent speculation and corresponding censure.

As the day wore on, the consensus that "something" must be done gathered substance and power like the storm clouds that had come to bank the southwestern sky. It waited only an excuse to be set free.

Unaware of the surge of vehemence outside her walls, Jemima accepted the arrival of her cousin with less than usual pleasure. For, after long delay, he had come to commiserate with her over her newfound notoriety.

"Well done, Puss. You have amazed even me." Julien's tone was all good humor. "I have swived hundreds and never once received so much as a mention on the back page of a pamphleteer's handout. Here you bed a single aristocrat and you are shown in flagrante delicto throughout the land. I am most jealous."

"Go away, Julien. I will not endure further insult this day, even from you."

He cocked a black raven's wing brow. "Do you deny it is true?"

"I deny nothing. There, you have what you came for. Now leave me."

Julien sat and cocked one leg over the chair arm, as if he had just been invited to stay for tea. "I don't suppose you are responsible for the cartoons? A pity. I never thought to self-advertise, but I see where a certain skill with a pen might do the trick.''

''Don't you have affaires of your own to organize?''

''My affaires are never organized. But it is yours I come to hear the details of. Tell me, what is the great Lord Bellaire like as a lover?''

For the first time in her life, Jemima loosed a vulgar epithet.

''Most unsatisfactory, was it?'' Julien gazed at her with mild interest. ''I'd rather hoped, for your sake, that he would be adequate to the task.''

When she began to move away, he rose with catlike speed to follow her. He beat her to the door and leaned a shoulder against it to hold it closed. ''Or is this pique of yours because he has thrown you over? 'Tis the scandal, isn't it? Has Bellaire been run off by a little heat from the flame of infamy? God's Body, I've been done to a turn by that fire a time or two. It is the mark of an unrepentant rake. Or is your lover so fragile a moth that he must care for singed wings?''

Jemima thought of a thousand answers she might make. In the end she chose the most goading truth. ''He believes you and I are lovers.''

''Does he now? How delish! Was he jealous? Did he ask you to describe in detail our antics? Or was it a demonstration he fancied?''

He saw that he had gone too far. The color drained from her face so quickly he thought she might faint.

He took her by the shoulders and squeezed slightly. ''I am sorry, Puss. Truly. Do you want me to call him out for the insult?''

Jemima shook her head.

''I would, you know. In a heartbeat. Do anything to

assuage your honor or please you. You have but to ask it of me."

She turned to look up at him and found his face only inches from hers. "Why, Julien?"

He saw the wariness in her gaze, felt her body stiffen in anticipation of his answer and knew at least that she was not indifferent to him.

"Because it amuses me." He saw the hope drain from her expression and wondered at his own cowardice. Here was the moment he had so carefully engineered. And he could not speak to it. Was he protecting her or himself? Both, his conscience whispered. Or at least he supposed it was so, for he was pretty damn certain he was born without such a device as plagued most other men's lives.

Jemima turned away and gathered herself together. "I have come to understand things I did not believe before. One cannot flaunt society's conventions without paying a price."

"Of course one can, if the price is of no moment. You and I, we are above the touch of the rabble."

She gave him a resentful glance. "The others have deserted me. The LADIES is no more."

He followed her back to the center of the room. "To be expected. You chose weaklings for your allies."

Jemima rounded on him. "They were good and faithful friends!"

Julien made a great show of looking first to his left and then to his right. "Then where are they, your good and faithful friends?"

Jemima did not answer.

"Be honest, Puss. You have but one friend. I am it."

Her gaze widened suspiciously, but she did not reply.

"In fact, I believe I am the best, most faithful friend you ever had." He smiled charmingly. "You deserve better, I don't doubt. But you are stuck with me."

"I am grateful, Julien, truly."

He shuddered. "That odious word again. *Grateful.* What is that to me? One shows gratitude to kings and confessors. I am neither as exalted as the one nor as inclined to mercy as the other."

Jemima thought she knew where the conversation was headed. "I cannot deal with any more of your vagaries of mind today, Cousin. I have had a difficult week."

"So have I." He seated himself on the settee this time. "More than you know."

She looked at him, her interest snared. "Why? What has happened to you?"

"I overplayed my hand last week," he said slowly. "And thought I had lost something very precious, something more than I could afford to lose."

Jemima crossed her arms. "You are in debt."

"I am in . . . love."

Jemima's expression lit up her face. "Oh, but that's wonderful, Julien! It is about time." She came forward and perched on the settee beside him. "Tell me all about her."

He smiled at her with more gentleness than she would have expected. "She is not at all my type. She is pretty but no Stunner. She is something of a Bluestocking, a bit of a prude but in her own way quite desirable. I am not worthy, but she doesn't see as many of my faults as others. If she knew all, she would take to her heels and I would be the last to blame her."

"So then you must seek to be worthy of her."

He reached for her hand and threaded his fingers through hers. "And how, pray tell, does a man of my much deserved reputation do that?"

"By good works," she answered promptly. "I believe you have a good heart, Julien. For all you mock me and try to make me dislike you, I see more of your goodness than you would like. And your weaknesses."

His fingers flexed over hers. "What, Puss, do you see?"

"A man afraid, who dares not give up his old life for fear a new one would not equal it. You fear disappointment and ennui. But if you choose the right lady, the two of you may make of your lives what you will."

"It would not be a cottage for two with rose trellises and ivy walls. It would be a wild mad dance, revelry of the senses in every sense until we are exhausted, spent of passion and ready for oblivion."

"How oddly you express it."

"Yes." His black eyes searched her face. "No easy life for my bride. Do you think a gently bred lady who dreams of love and family would not soon despair of me?"

"If she loved you—"

"Yes. If she loved . . . *me*."

He let his gaze stray downward to her bosom. The square neckline was filled by a filly bertha. "So prim in your ruffles. But what is the woman beneath like?" His hands found her waist and lifted her over onto his lap.

Startled, Jemima made a murmur of protest. Then she saw his expression. To her dismay, she recognized in it desire. Unlike with Beau, passion had no softening effect on Julien's harsh features. Instead, he seemed almost angry.

"You are thinking of him even now, are you not?"

Jemima could not think how to answer, for she had been comparing the two men.

"Damn me for a fool! I can't bear to see you suffer so." Julien leaned forward suddenly and kissed her. It was not a brief kiss. His mouth lingered.

Astonished, Jemima pushed him away. "Julien, no!"

Julien smiled at her as though he were seeing her in a whole new way. "Do you not yet know that you are as fine a creature as ever Nature fashioned for a man's delight? I have always known it. I will not allow the lesson to cost you everything. You pine for the loss of that wretched idiot, but I swear I can make you forget him. I love you, Jemima.''

''What?'' Jemima stared at her cousin, seeing in his avid an emotion she would have sworn only seconds ago was not possible.

''Marry me.'' He looked as stunned as she felt to hear the words spoken to her for the second time that day. But unlike Beau, a smile broke over his surprise as he repeated himself. ''Marry me, Jemima!''

She was too bewildered to answer but when he raised a hand to her cheek she flinched. ''No. I certainly will not. You have sworn never to marry and are a wretch to tease me.'' She said the words defiantly, afraid he might be as much in earnest as his expression.

''I think you should reconsider your position, Puss. Surely that paragon of a Whig who fancies himself as one day fit to be Prime Minister was man enough to show you the way of carnal matters.'' He cupped her breast before she could imagine his intent and said, ''What if you are already with child?''

''I am not with child!'' Outraged, she slapped away his hand. ''He did not touch me.''

It was not a complete lie, yet she blushed at the look that crossed Julien's saturnine features. Then he threw back his head and laughed. ''So then marry me, Jemima.''

''We are cousins,'' she maintained primly despite her compromised position on his lap.

He kissed her quickly before saying, ''Cousins wed everyday.''

''Not you and I. We are coconspirators. Nothing more.''

''Are you certain?''

He watched her with knowing eyes. ''You came to me to begin your game of revenge. That is because you recognize that we are of a kind. Did you not suspect that I would have an alternate design should things come amiss?''

He leaned close, his gaze lingering on the full curve of her lip. "You know I dare more than most. Did you not suspect that I might be the very sort of man who could allow you to be seduced by another, knowing that in your hour of need you would turn again to me? If Bellaire were not man enough to avail himself of the opportunity it is only my gain."

"But that is vile!" Her beleaguered senses erupted in outrage and she slapped him twice. once with each hand, before leaping from his lap.

He laughed and said again, "Marry me, Jemima."

"Never! Jemima moved a short distance away, wary now as she had never before been in his company.

Julien stared at her a long time, drinking in every detail of her expression. In it he saw anger and defiance and fear . . . but not passion. She loved Bellaire, damn him!

"The lady declines."

The derision in his tone contained the bitter reflection of lost opportunity. He had played his final card and lost all to an enemy he could not now in good conscience destroy without also risking destroying the good thing in his life, the only woman he'd ever loved.

He glared at her suddenly, wanting to hurt her, to force her back outside the dangerous emotional zone of his life that she had entered unwillingly. "So then, will you now lock yourself away again from life? Shall I send Monsieur to keep you company, the only male in your sad little nunnish life? At least you cannot use your supposed disappointment to lie to yourself with the old maid's sop that it was better to be untouched than ravished and left."

Jemima knotted her arms before her bosom. "That would make of me a poor dish, I suppose."

He rose to his feet, wishing her at the devil—himself. "What did you expect, Jemima? That Bellaire would love you for showing him his worst nature?"

Jemima closed her eyes to stop the fresh tears that would do no more good than the many others that had fallen this day. "He came here this morning." She could not mention Beau's proposal any more than she could let herself think about Julien's. "I asked him about Pru. I had to know the truth."

"Yes, you would." His tone matched hers, flat and final. "Will you be able to live with the results?"

Jemima turned away, her voice a husky whisper. "I don't know."

The answer hung in the air between them. So much regret in those words. She could not believe that love had found her at this advanced age. After nine years of isolation and solitude, to receive two proposals in a single day! Yet neither of them was presented in a manner she could accept.

She could not believe what Julien had attempted. No, she would not think about it! But her heart beat in a jagged rhythm that was fear.

"There is some compensation to be had." Julien had gone to the table and poured himself a whisky. He drank it in a gulp. "Only think what your Foolscap can make of the matter."

Jemima glared at her companion. "You would seem to find a great deal of pleasure in my lowest hour."

He tilted his head back so that in the gloom his dark eyes burned like banked coals. "I warned you at the beginning to abandon your scheme."

"Fustian! You said just enough to be certain I would pursue it."

"Hah! So now you will revert to womanly type. No doubt you will soon enact for me a scene from one of those abominable melodramas. 'Alas and alack, I am but a poor innocent maid led astray by a cad of a fellow!'" His mocking falsetto dropped back to its natural lower, more menacing, level. "You knew me to be no more than I am. Be brave, little Cousin. Admit you used me as much as you say I did you.''

Jemima opened her mouth to deny it but found she could not. Not when she had but to close her eyes to see again the look of stunned disbelief and then injury on Lord Bellaire's face when she told him she would not marry him. ''I will admit that women can be as devious and scheming as men. Yet there is a difference. We women are capable of bringing to disaster our own desire.''

Julien stared at his empty glass. ''A hard lesson, indeed. But if you believe 'tis the folly of women only, you are mistaken.''

For a moment their gazes met across the room and each recalled Julien's scandalous behavior of a few moments before.

Jemima looked away first, but she heard Julien expel a breath as if in relief. ''Do you not yet hope that the colossal ass you love can be persuaded to set aside his overly developed pride and accept his luck that you, silly creature that you are, find him worthy of your love?''

With no good answer for his question, Jemima lapsed into silence.

Julien moved toward the door. He did not need her agreement to know the answer. So then, if it were in his power, he would yet find a way to give Bellaire to her.

''You did not really mean it—about wishing to marry me?'' Her voice was small, as if she were not certain she should even ask the question.

Julien paused with his hand on the latch and smiled a wicked smile. ''It seems we shall never know.''

When he was gone, she stretched out on the settee and had a good long cry.

What was wrong with the people in her life? First Lord Bellaire and now her cousin, treating her as if she were some prize to snatch up. That Julien should think himself in love with her? It was absurd. Everyone knew her for what she was: a dowd, a scholar, not a fantasy for gentlemen's dreams.

Yet if any had borne witness to this day, they would have new spice to add to their scandal broth. Surely in all of London there could not be another who wore the label of "Thrice Jilt."

Chapter Twenty-Eight

"The weather's whipping up to be a right blow," Jemima's gardener said as they fought to stake the last of her roses.

It wasn't often a real storm brewed up over Chapel Hill, but the scudding drapery of rain clouds in the late afternoon sky promised a very unpleasant evening. Vivid flashes of lightning ran along the horizon, harkening the arrival of worse to come.

The first thick drops of rain pelted Jemima like small stones. One struck her painfully in the eye.

"Best make a run for it, my lady. I'll see to the last."

"No, leave them!" Jemima shouted, for a sudden gush of wind had come howling through the trees. "We've done all we can!" A second gust caught the brim of her bonnet and levered it back from her head. Another grabbed the edge of her garden smock and almost ripped it from her body.

Together they hurried toward shelter, she for the house and he for the gardener's cottage at the back of the formal gardens.

Trimmed bushes danced and bowed before the wind as Jemima hurried past. At the back of the house, primrose vines snaked out like live beings and wrapped themselves like whips about anything in their path. One caught Jemima by the ankle and she stumbled as tiny thorns cut through her stocking and grabbed hold of her skin. Dirt and grit from the road rose up in great gusts and pelted her face until it stung.

"It be like an Old Midsummer festival," said the maid who greeted her at the kitchen door with nervous laughter. "Cook says the sky is riddled with fire."

"Let us hope Nature does not see fit to include us in her revels," Jemima answered, and hurried inside to change her damp clothing.

The unnerving thought that this was no ordinary summer rain had crossed Jemima's mind, too. This was a Midsummer Brew that grumbled and belched and flickered like a prank set off by one of the Old Ones. Yet she knew better than to give voice to her flight of fancy. Pagan deities, indeed! It would only frighten the servants.

As she passed into the front hall, a vivid blue-white flash brightened the gloom of the house. For an instant, she held her breath. Then thunder slammed into the walls of her home, jarring every item and person within.

She heard a cry of fright from belowstairs, but it was instantly hushed by the raised voice of another.

"Unnatural," she murmured to herself, and turned back toward the kitchen to remind the cook to set aside several pails of water should they be needed to put out small fires.

When Jemima could once more head for her room and dry clothing, her maid met her at the top of the stairs. "Oh there you are, Miss MacKinnon. I've been looking for you. It's the girl Pru. She's taken bad with pains."

"Birthing pains, Mary?"

"She won't say. Only that she needs a doctor."

Jemima debated the wisdom of sending anyone out in the approaching storm, then realized that the weather was not likely to improve anytime soon. "Better go for Doctor Wesley. I will sit with Pru."

As a premature darkness set in over Chapel Hill, the villagers huddled in the gloom around their doused hearths. The poorest did not dare strike a spark for fears that a downdraft might send live cinders flying through the room and kindle a fire.

At first there was only a little splattering of rain and the occasional rumble of thunder in the distance. But the rain quickly gathered strength, sheeting down from the blackened sky like water through a broken dam.

Elder family members, who had noticed the date, murmured to themselves. This was July 5, Old Midsummer's Eve. Of ancient lineage, fire festivals were conducted on this date throughout England to strengthen the sun, drive out evil, and bring fertility and prosperity to the people and land. Torchlight processions, flaming tar-barrels, even wheels bound up in straw and tow were set aflame and sent rolling down steep hillsides until the night itself seemed to be afire. But on this eve, Nature came well fortified to produce her own ritual.

Those with more learning lit a single candle and read or smoked a pipe and waited. In Doctor Wesley's household, both had been done. He smoked and his wife read her Bible. When the knock came at his door, they could not at first be certain it was not the wind. When answered, the shape of Miss MacKinnon's rain-sodden maid loomed up out of the gloom. "Miss MacKinnon needs you to come at once. The girl Pru is having pains."

Mrs. Wesley harrumphed her opinion of that at his back.

The doctor frowned. "Tell your mistress I will come when I can."

When the door was shut again, Mrs. Wesley said, "Let Miss MacKinnon suffer the consequences for her sins, that's what I say. Why drag a good God-fearing man out into this evil night? As for that slut she cossets, if she didn't want the pain, she should have kept her legs together beforetimes."

"But Miss MacKinnon—"

"Must needs pay for her own folly. She should not have taken the creature in."

"Yes, my dear."

And because the doctor could think of no good reason why he should stir ill feelings beneath his warm dry roof to go out and become drenched on a thankless task, he sat back in his chair and picked up his pipe.

He did not share his wife's belief in a vengeful God whose wrath smote only the guilty. In his profession he saw too many innocents suffer to accept that it was the result of a so-called benevolent deity who meted out justice fairly. Rather he saw the world as full of acts of willful children who would not heed the good advice of their Father. And so he consoled himself with the knowledge that women had been birthing babies for far longer than man had taken science into the matter. Pru most likely would do no other than pay the price for her original sin.

Few heard the sounds of the gentleman on horseback who came riding in on the wind, as it were. None saw how his black cape flew out behind him like raven's wings until rider and mount appeared as one, a wraith on horseback pounding down the lane through town. Miss MacKinnon's drenched maid Mary saw the apparition rein in at last before Miss MacKinnon's gate and turn to canter up the drive.

The sound of the front bell echoed through the dark house. Jemima heard it in blank surprise. Who could it be? The doctor would have come back with Mary and entered through the servants' door to save time. The storm was nearing its height. Nothing less than mortal need would send any right-thinking person out in the blow.

"Amelia!" Jemima surged to her feet beside Pru's bed. Had Amelia's cottage perhaps lost its roof in the storm?

"Miss! Oh, Miss, it do hurt!" Pru's head stirred on the pillow. She had been dozing between pains. Labor had begun.

"I won't be long," Jemima assured her. "Perhaps I hear the doctor now."

"Bring him quick, Miss. I don't know as I can hold out."

"Of course," Jemima answered, thinking now of her estranged cousin with whom she had not traded a single word in a sennight. But blood was blood and if Amelia needed shelter she would surely find it here.

But when Jemima reached the top of the stairs she saw that Cook was trying to hold the door against a heavily cloaked man.

"You, sir. What do you want here?" Jemima called down in the sternest voice.

The man looked up. "I seek the lady of the house. It is imperative that I speak with her."

Jemima hesitated only a moment after hearing his culti-vated voice. Perhaps Lord Bellaire had sent the man. No, after a week of silence he would not suddenly be sending posies by messenger on a night like this. More likely it was a stranger passing through the village who found himself in need of shelter. "Let him in, Cook."

Jemima descended the stairs quickly, wondering what could be keeping the doctor. The sudden brilliance and heavy clap of thunder seemed to answer. She supposed he and Mary might be waylaid by the tempest.

When she reached the bottom of the stairway, she saw that a young man stood in her entry. Water sluiced from his hat brim, shoulders, cloak hem, and boots. A pond was gathering where he stood, but she supposed it could not be helped.

"Good evening, sir. Do you seek shelter from the storm?"

He stamped and shook himself like a dog before saying, "I seek more than that, if this is the house of Miss MacKinnon."

"It is."

He took off his hat and smiled. "I am here to see Miss Church."

"Who?" His was quite the most breathtakingly handsome face Jemima had ever seen. Though he was a stranger, there was yet something familiar in the shape of chin and brow.

He frowned suddenly and made an impatient gesture. "You need not dissemble. I know she's here. St. Ives told me I might find Pru with you."

"Julien?" What was the wretch up to now? No good, Jemima suspected, and instantly regretted her hospitality.

"Why should my cousin send a stranger to me?" She supposed she might take such a censorious tone with the young man who had forced his way into her home.

"I beg your pardon, ma'am." He snatched his sodden top hat from his head and offered a smile to melt sterner hearts than hers. "We have not been introduced, 'tis a fact. But I have a letter to do the do."

He reached under his greatcoat and pulled out a letter swollen with raindrops. He held it out apologetically. "I am sorry. 'Tis this dam—detestable weather." He glanced up in alarm as a crack of thunder shook the windows. "Does it often storm in Chapel Hill?"

"Never," Jemima answered and took the letter he proffered. "You may come in a dry out by the fire while I read your missive. But leave your wet things here in the hall." She glanced at the puddle starting to run back toward the door. "I will ring for tea."

Once shed of his cloak, he followed her into the salon. There was no fire lit for it was summer, but he went out of habit to stand by the mantel while he watched her sit and open the letter he'd brought.

Though rain had bled the address into unreadable streaks, the inside was relatively dry. Jemima recognized Julien's black scrawl immediately.

Dear Faithless Cousin,
   This is your Gelded Buck's Prodigal Brother. Make use of Him as you Will.

                                                            J

Beau's brother! Jemima refolded the letter slowly. What mischief had Julien thrown in her path on this night?

"You are Lord Bellaire's brother, sir?" There must be a considerable difference in their ages. He seemed young, no more than twenty-two.

"I have that dubious honor," the young man answered.

"Your name, sir. It is not writ here." Jemima knew she must sound a hundred years old to him but he deserved no graciousness for his conduct in her hallway.

"I am Guy Somerset, ma'am. I've come to see Miss MacKinnon."

"You have that distinction, Mr. Somerset."

The young man blinked and then smiled. "I meant Miss Jemima MacKinnon."

Jemima inclined her head. Only then did she realize that perhaps he had seen her in town in one of the glamorous gowns Julien had run up for her. Sitting here in her garden smock, mob cap and glasses, she must present an altogether different picture. The fact that it was writ so large on his face did not incline her feelings toward him. "You may close your mouth. We have no need of flytraps today."

He recovered himself quickly and came forward to make her a pretty bow. "I have clean forgot my manners. Most honored to meet you, ma'am."

Jemima nodded in answer. "You may be seated." She was pleased to see he chose to perch on a wooden bench by the hearth fender rather than a piece of upholstered furniture, for his beeches were soaked through. "Now, how may I help you?"

Guy flushed. He was not about the give her the true answer, that St. Ives, being a damn fine friend, had advanced him five hundred pounds so that he could take Pru away and marry her before Beau knew what was o'clock.

Luckily the tea arrived. While Miss MacKinnon served it, Guy sank into reverie while the strife of the storm outside punctuated his thoughts with light and noise.

He had been playing Toad in the Hole with creditors since Derby Day. If not for a fortuitous meeting in a gaming hell in the rookeries, he might not yet know Pru's whereabouts. But St. Ives took him up immediately, even gave him a room in his house. Cousin Richard was a fool. St. Ives had shown him nothing but a remarkable amount of attention without ulterior purpose. In fact, after a long night's drinking during which Guy confessed the whole of his love for Pru, St. Ives suggested that he should show his brother that he had a mind and will of his own, and how little he cared for Beau's opinion. In fact, St. Ives knew where his long-lost Pru was to be found. Now if that wasn't a jolly coincidence!

St. Ives had offered him "flight funds," as a boon from one gentleman to another. Once away, he and Pru could travel abroad, make their own way in the world. Precisely how, Guy had not worked out. But he was as certain of a bright future as he was of his love for Pru. The means would come to him. At least abroad there would be no creditors hounding him.

"So then, Mr. Somerset," Jemima began when tea was poured. "You may continue."

He nodded, locks of damp hair falling over his brow like some fairytale swain. "I don't know what Pru may have told you, Miss MacKinnon. But we were in love— No, are in love!"

"And Julien sought to aid in reuniting you?"

This is a trap, Jemima. One set for you. Julien had said those words to her when first she told him about Pru. The words came back to her now with new meaning. And she began to feel once more that he had been playing Cat's Paw with her for far longer than she knew.

"Forgive my presumptuousness, but why should my cousin seek to be involved at all?"

"Because he knows how brutally I've been treated by my own brother." Guy offered her an appealing glance. "You, too, must know a part of the story."

"I have heard some," Jemima said carefully, "Pru was reluctant to speak of her ordeal. Why don't you tell me what occurred?"

A gush of wind down the chimney sent soot rushing into the room.

Guy coughed behind his hand. "It's nothing for a gentleman to speak of before a lady." He added after a curious glance at her. "Still less to one who would be my brother's sympathizer."

Jemima ignored the lacework of ashes settling around them. "I pride myself on having opinions of my own making."

Guy sized up the lady before him, unable even by squinting to resolve the stiff-as-a-poker female before him as one and the same as the lascivious Cyprian dressed in breeches from Vauxhall Gardens. Amazing what paint and power could accomplish. Something to be remembered.

"So then, it's this way, Miss MacKinnon. I first met my dear Prudence at the beginning of Lenten term at Cambridge. Her father keeps a tavern nearby. But Pru was clean, a good girl. Never was a—" He suddenly blushed.

"A barmaid of the establishment?" Jemima offered helpfully.

Guy smiled. "Exactly so. Her father saw it to she was kept away from the rough and common. Wasn't allowed to serve the general customer. Only the gentlemen what paid for a private room."

"And that is how you met?"

Guy blushed again and Jemima suddenly understood why an older brother might have cause to worry about a younger son. His manner revised her opinion of his age downward. He could be no more than a very green eighteen. "I'd been drinking with friends one evening, got soused, drunk as a lord."

"Prat-faced, yes."

"I passed out under the table. Later the fellows said when they left, they clean forgot I'd been there. But that was the beauty of it, you see. When I came to, I was staring up into the prettiest face I'd ever seen. She'd found me and lifted my head into her lap. And there I lay, staring up into her glorious blue innocent eyes. After that I'd come round from time to time and she'd be sure to sneak away for a short time to see me. Her father was the mean sort. Threatened to take a strap to her so we had to be careful. Most times I took a room and then she'd come up the backstairs after her work was done. We talked and sometimes played chess."

Jemima regarded him with her head canted to one side, wondering if he really expected her to accept as truth the twaddle he was telling. "Do go on, sir."

"After a time it came plain, we suited."

"You believed yourself in love?"

Guy lifted his chin. "Certainly. But my brother, the great Lord Bellaire, would have none of it. Said it was calf love. As if keeping my grades up and not being sent down were to any purpose. A man may know his own mind in such matters!"

"I don't doubt." Jemima winced as lightning lit the interior with eerie white light. "But minds and hearts do change."

"Not mine. Not my—" Thunder rolled through the back of his words like a surge of storm-driven surf so that he had to pause and wait to repeat himself. "Not my love for Pru," he maintained stoutly.

"So then, what parted you?"

Guy tucked his head. "Beau would meddle. I can't think how it happened, unless Pru followed me to London. She was that much in love, you know."

"Just so." Jemima hoped she sounded more neutral than she felt. Hearing the tale a second time, from the suitor's point of view, did not improve it by any means. How could such fustian have taken her in? Had the name Bellaire not been attached, she doubted she would have allowed Pru to finish her lurid tale. It was the only reason she sat still for this retelling.

"So then?"

"I can't speak of it all. Not to a lady. But I was betrayed by a method most heinous. I will never forgive Beau for it. Never!"

Thunder at the back of his words seemed to underscore his theatrical avowal though Jemima did not think his feelings a sham. Yet from what little she'd seen of Lord Bellaire's relations, his brother's behavior seemed no more mature than his daughter's.

"Pru believes you abandoned her. She said you threw her over for an . . . indiscretion with your brother. Is this true?"

Guy surged to his feet. "You cannot comprehend the nature of the betrayal. If I could but speak to it— But, by my honor, I cannot." He glanced down at her. "Is she here? May I see her now?"

Jemima debated the wisdom of her answer. Young love, green or otherwise, could be put off by the merest trifle.

Pru's present condition amounted to much more than that. "I will ask her if she wishes to see you. How is that?"

His expression lit by another flash of lightning was triumphant. "She will see me," he said with the greatest confidence. "In fact, if she wishes, I will take her with me tonight. We are bound for Gretna Green." Only after he said it did Guy realize it might be a tactical error to tell his brother's latest cast-off mistress of his intentions.

"She may not yet be up to the trip," Jemima answered tactfully.

"Why? What is wrong? Is she ill?"

"Yes, in a way. Wait here, please. I will speak for you to her."

Jemima climbed the stairs and hurried down the back hall of the servants' wing led for the most part by flashes of lightning that made her candle unnecessary. The storm did not seem to be wearing itself out. But the wind had fallen into an low ominous mourning sound.

Pru's moans reached her before she opened the door. The poor girl was rocking from side to side with Mary trying to wipe her brow.

"Where is Dr. Wesley?"

Mary met Jemima's gaze across the room. The look said enough. "He will not come at all?"

"He says, miss, that he will be along when he can."

Jemima's lips thinned. She had lost all friendship in the village if Dr. Wesley could abandon her. "Very well." She moved toward the bed. "Pru, you have a visitor, a most surprising one. I have told him that you are not in the best health, that perhaps he should come back—"

"Pru! Pru, is that you?" Guy pushed through the door behind Jemima.

When she spied him, Pru tried to sit up. "Guy! Me own sweet boy!"

Guy came up short at the sight of the woman on the bed holding out her arms to him. "What the deuce!"

"Guy!" she cried, her mouth stretched wide in greeting. " 'Tis yer Pru."

Guy fell back a step. Nothing about this horridly bloated creature was familiar. His Pru had been a toothsome handful. This hag was grossly inflated, must be twice his weight. Her face was blotchy and swollen, as were her breasts beneath her gown. A bulging belly protruded where a neat waist should be. Only her hair was the right color, but it was bound up for the most part under a mob cap. The few yellow strands framing her face were dark with sweat. Gone were the soft mouth, melting blue eyes, and petal cheeks. This harridan with mouth agape in a pudding of a face seemed a nightmarish fiend. And then from that mouth came a cry to shrivel his heart.

"Arrrrgh! The pains, they're after murderin' me! Guy!"

"It is nearly her time," Jemima said softly, touching him lightly on the shoulder. "You will soon be a father."

"What?" Guy jerked away from her, looking dazed and disbelieving as he turned away from the stranger in the bed.

"She is with child," Jemima said more gently. "Are you not the father?"

"No!" His handsome young face was contorted in horror and revulsion. "This is none of my doing. 'Tis Beauregard's brat!" So saying, he turned and fled the room.

"Guy! Guy, sweet boy, don't leave me!"

Outraged by his reaction, Jemima went after him. "You, sir. Wait there! You cannot have come all this way to decamp at the first hurdle!" She would not allow it.

But he had longer legs and soon outpaced her. Still she followed, even when he sprinted down the stairs and flung open the front door. He did not even stop for his hat and cloak but ran out into the night.

Jemima debated the wisdom of following him, but she

was much too angry to simply allow him to flee. Gentlemen, in her experience, were never where they were needed. She did not doubt Julien would find this all a great joke but the young woman upstairs bore Guy's child—or Beau's?—and the brothers owed her something, if only recognition.

The sense of impending danger came in the space of silence as she ran out into a darkness more complete than normal night. The rain had ceased. Then she felt her skin tingle, as if the air had loosed dozens of ants to crawl hurriedly over her skin. The flash across the sky became so pure blue-white a light that at first she could not believe it.

She heard Guy's cry of alarm and then out of the darkness his body collided with hers and she was flung to the wet ground.

The crack of thunder came as a physical sensation, as if the night itself had been split by an ax, and then she heard a cracking of tree limbs and smelled the ether of the light that blinded her as it forked down in a dozen places around them.

"Stay down!" Guy cried roughly when she would have gotten to her feet. The thunder seemed to shake the ground behind them. Immediately upon its heels came a renewed deluge of rain, this time mixed with hard icy pellets.

Guy grabbed her then and dragged her to her feet. "Come quick! There's going to be worse."

Jemima held on to his arm, wondering what else could be worse. And then she saw at the back of her house near an eave a strange red-orange flickering light.

"The house is on fire!"

Chapter Twenty-Nine

The charred ruins of Haversham House smoldered in the morning mist.

Some said it should be so, a reminder to others of the wages of sin. But most saw it as a sign of their perfidy, so they kept closed their windows even in the heat of the day to block out the damning sight. The great cry that went up through the village the evening before had not brought out as many as quickly as it might, once the source of the blaze was located. But these were country folk with a thousand years of common ancestry in their veins. Fire was a common enemy no man fought alone.

And yet, last night, many of them had done nothing.

They murmured the next morning about how it was a devil's storm no rightminded man should have ventured out into. But they knew they lied. Had it been the stables or the parsonage or any other dwelling in Chapel Hill, they'd have turned out with rakes and shovels and precious buckets to form a brigade to fight the flames. And they might well have won.

The rain came down in torrents, dousing all the but most stubborn cinders without the help of those who did show up to fight the flames. All within were saved, owing to the rain. And the damage was minimal. Rebuilding would not be difficult.

But then, in the wee hours of the night, long after the gale had blown itself out and the night was quiet again, the blaze rekindled. This time the villagers turned over in their beds and pulled their covers over their heads and hoped that no one would come knocking.

Jemima sat on a stone bench in the back of her garden and stared at the remains of walls that had sheltered her from her very first breath. Within that house she had been a child and later she had learned to play the pianoforte and to dance. She thought of all the volumes now up in flames that composed the library of which she was most proud. There were her own writings. Her family's portraits. All gone. Even little things. A favorite bonnet, a porcelain figurine given her by her mother. A tin of biscuits by her bed. A volume of poetry. All gone. It would take days to pick through the debris and when that was done . . .

"What shall I do?"

Jemima leaned her chin into her hands. She had money enough to rebuild, if she did so slowly and modestly. But that was not the cause of the great emptiness inside her. She had lost far more last night than her home and her possessions. She had lost faith in those she had once accounted as friends. She no longer had a house. What was worse, she longer had a place to call home.

She could count on one hand those faces she recognized during the mad dash to save Pru and Mary and to wake the others in the household, if any had slept through the thunderous blast. And then began the arduous task of fighting the fire. The pond at the back of the garden was overflowing but without enough hands to form an adequate brigade, they had lost precious time hauling and slipping and spilling water to bring it up to the blaze.

She looked down at her hands, raw and bleeding from her efforts. She smelled of the smoke that streaked her clothes and still burned her throat and stung her eyes. Her hair was singed and her muscles ached from the futile efforts made mockery of when the fire rekindled.

Yet, in the midst of the travail, life had triumphed.

Pru had given birth to a baby girl.

They had moved her to the stable for safety when Amelia suddenly appeared. The girl needed a better place to have her child, she'd said without looking at Jemima. She must be brought to her cottage, at least until morning. Guy offered to carry Pru, but in reality it took the three of them to bear the laboring mother across the field.

She could not forget her last glimpse of Guy's face before he rode away. He looked like a man who had stared into the abyss of Hell and would ever after be haunted by it.

Poor gullible Guy, the look on his face when he saw what a tickle and slap under the covers could give rise to. Doubtless, he would never again be so cavalier in his avowals of love.

She felt sorry for him, deeply regrettably sorry. But in this instance, he had only himself was to blame for his loss of innocence. He had kept repeating throughout the night that he was not the father of Pru's child, would not even look upon the red wrinkled scrap of life that came roaring into being at five of the clock this morning. And if she had once believed his accusation and Pru's that Lord Bellaire was the begetter, she no longer did.

The mathematics of it was as old as time. Pru's daughter might be tiny, but she was fully formed. Nine full months had gone into her creating. That meant neither Guy nor Beau could be her sire. Long before Lenten quarter came to Cambridge, Pru had found the company of another man to her liking. Unlike Guy, he had no doubt left her without a backward glance.

And who was to say that Guy's love was not true, for all it was shallow? First love was often like a toe sunk into the river of life. Sometimes one caught a chill and withdrew. It took courage to dive in over one's head. Many people no more than waded along the shore their whole lives long.

She did not blame Pru for lying. She blamed her for being a fool. Men were caught by lies of this kind everyday. But they were seldom kept. Pru had done what she did out of necessity. That did not make her evil, but it did not serve her well. The future would not hold its hand out to her. For that alone, Jemima pitied her.

Against others, she did not feel so kind. The village had turned on her, deserted her, and left her with the charred remains of what had once been her citadel and her solace. All her life she had lived here amid general admiration and approval of her neighbors. Confident, safe, and content. But that was not enough. She had sought to educate them, edify them, raise them above their petty prejudices and jealousies and scotch the might of that social adder's tongue: gossip.

She thought she knew best. The LADIES would rid the world of deception and snobbery, of bounders and cads, seducers and debauchers. Foolscap had been a success. But it was not enough. Pride spurred her on to the one incalculable disaster.

Two short months ago she had gone to London to play a naughty game on a gentleman she thought deserved to be taught a lesson. Pride had first set her foot on this path to perdition. But it was prejudice that had set her against a man she could only now admit to herself that she had harbored a tendre for since the age of seventeen.

Now the skein of her motives was hopelessly tangled in her own cross-purpose of emotions. She was in love with the one man who would most despise her when his brother

got back to town with news of Pru, and her own duplicity
in the matter.

She had recklessly gone up against every social convention of her time, and lost. While she would like to pin her
fall on the complicity of Julien or even Lord Bellaire, she
knew she had only herself to blame. And now they all
despised her.

What folly her life had become! In this moment she felt
so solitary that she might as well be the only being in the
whole wide world.

And so she sat and stared at her loss and wondered what
would become of her.

"Father, may I have a bear?"

Beau did not look up from his book. "No, Emma."

"But Miss MacKinnon's bear has no one."

Beau did look up this time. Emma sat across from him
in her best dress feeding part of their breakfast to her china
doll. "I'm certain he is being well looked after."

"No, he isn't." Emma frowned. "I saw Monsieur in the
park this morning with Mr. St. Ives. He said Monsieur is
pining away for want of an owner."

"There is Miss MacKinnon."

"Oh no," Emma said very certain of herself. "She no
longer wants Monsieur."

"How do you know?"

"Miss MacKinnon told Mr. St. Ives. He said she said that
there is no place any longer for him in her life. That he must
see the Monsieur is found a good home."

"I see. Well, that is no cause for us to take up the burden.
No, Emma. That is an end to it."

She tucked in her chin, her face again solemn. "Yes,
Father."

Beau gazed at her a moment longer. He had found being

thwarted in love to be an edifying experience. The loss of
one pointed up sharply the many other deficiencies in one's
other relationships.

Like his relationship, or rather lack thereof, with his
daughter. He had been no father to his only child, only her
sire. It did not take much thought, when he finally came to
it, to understand the reasons. After Fiona's untimely death,
he had hoped to put all thought of her and their unfortunate
marriage behind him. He could admit it now. He had abandoned his child to another, a very caring other, but it was
abandonment all the same.

Oh, he could not have cared for a newborn or even a
toddler. But he might have sought in the intervening eight
years to provide her with a new mama to take care of her.
And if pride kept him from that, when she was older, he
might have had a succession of nannies, governesses, tutors
and dancing masters to help him cope with the responsibilities of having her live with him full-time. But he had been
first afraid and then indifferent, and too proud to admit either.
It took only an afternoon in Miss MacKinnon's company for
him to see how Emma blossomed when treated with kindness. Jemima and her silly bear, that is.

He glanced out at the spacious yard beyond the windows
of his drawing room. Emma deserved to be better served
than she had been by him. He would do better in future. He
had only yesterday written to Susanna to inform her that
Emma would be spending the rest of the summer with him.

"I am thinking of taking a month in the country. Would
you like to come along?"

Emma gave him a long considering glance. "Can we
invite Miss Jemima, too?"

"No." His expression grew serious. "She is a bit above
our touch these days."

"Oh." Emma turned back to her doll, but Beau felt her

withdrawal. No one approved of his handling of the situation with Miss MacKinnon. Not even, it seemed, his daughter.

She looked forlorn as she sat feeding her doll. Her hair had been brushed into a smooth dark band down her back. Her eyes were blue like his and her serious little face was almost an exact copy of his mother's. While he could not say she reminded him in any great part of Fiona, he supposed he should be grateful to Fiona for the child. Otherwise he might be utterly alone in the world.

Friends had withdrawn from him over the matter with Lady Sarah. She exerted more social pull than he would have imagined. Social invitations had almost dried up. But then he was in no mood for diversion at the moment. He knew it would only be a matter of time before the social ostracism lifted. He was a gentleman, after all, and a titled *unmarried* one. No social maven would want him long banned from her guest list.

Then there was the matter of his half-brother Guy. Another deficiency in his character laid bare by his dealings with Jemima. He had been no big brother to Guy. He had not led by example, carrying him about Town a bit in order to put a bit of Town polish on him, teaching him to spot cheats and sharpsters, and how to get on with the muslin set. No, he could only stand in judgment, issue orders, make demands and disdain every crackbrain idea youth was prone to. As if he had never made mistakes! Been gulled! Or rolled up. The poor fellow did need guidance. From now on, he would get it. As soon as he could locate his brother. Guy appeared to have disappeared. Richard could not or would not give him his own brother's direction. Debts, he was given to understand, were the reason.

When their tea was done, Beau set his book aside. "What do you suppose we might do with Monsieur?"

Emma's eyes lit up, but she quickly curbed her enthusiasm. "I don't know, Papa. What do you think we might do?"

Papa. She had called him Papa. A small thing to make his chest swell so broadly. "I suppose we might take him out into the country with us where he might have a large cage and plenty of fresh air."

"And plenty of raspberry tarts?"

"Yes." He smiled at his child. "Plenty of raspberry tarts."

He went to fetch his hat and cane. First he would get Emma her bear and then he would find his brother. Finally, he would seek to make amends to Miss Jemima. He did not know how he would do it or even if he could. But the possibility that it might be accomplished left a big fat smile on his usually stern face.

"I want to buy your bear."

Beau decided to tackle the most unpleasant business first, a trip to see St. Ives.

St. Ives had kept him waiting fifteen minutes. No other gentleman would have dared. Yet here he was, in shirtsleeves and stocking feet, a clear illusion to the fact that he had risen from bed. And not alone. The fragrance of roses that clung to him could not be mistaken for a gentleman's cologne.

St. Ives smiled at Bellaire but it did not reach his eyes. "Not for sale."

"But you told Emma—"

"That Monsieur pines for Miss MacKinnon." St. Ives smiled smugly. "Do not we all?"

"You should know that I intend she no longer be your business." Beau narrowed his gaze in challenge as he made his position plain. "I have asked her to marry me."

"Did you, damn you! So have I." St. Ives almost laughed

in Bellaire's face. How transparent the fellow was. Another man might not have noticed, but a rival could not afford to miss any sign of anxiety in his adversary.

Jealousy seared him, but Beau's voice was lower and softer than at any time during their previous conversations. "What did she answer?"

"The lady declined." St. Ives's smile could have cut glass. "I suspect you are the cause. Therefore, I must eliminate you." He whipped his hand across Beau's face, the slap no more than a formality. "You do duel?"

Tension drained from Beau's face, replaced by an unholy smile. "I do now."

"Dawn and seconds?"

"With pleasure. Might I beg leave of two days, to put things in order? I have a child."

St. Ives inclined his head. "But of course."

Beau reached the door before St. Ives said, "You will not find her in Chapel Hill."

Beau turned, his expression carefully neutral. "Where is she?"

"In a cottage nearby. Haversham House burned. To the ground."

"When?" The word sounded forced out of him.

"Two days ago. You are a neglectful lover, aren't you?"

Beau took a careful breath. "Was she injured?"

"Nothing serious. I believe you have your brother to thank for that."

"Guy?"

"You have more than one?" Hugely enjoying himself, Julien took his time extracting a cheroot from a humidor. "Your brother was with my cousin the night of the blaze. A storm blew him in, I'm told. If not for his quick thinking, she might have been struck by lightning and killed."

Beau felt his as he were tumbling backward down a well,

unable to see where he was going or calculate how deep his fall would be. "Why was Guy with Miss MacKinnon?"

"Why don't you ask him?" St. Ives produced a card as if by magic. "He has taken rooms under this name. The address is here."

"The devil he has!" Beau's mouth thinned in anger when he read the address.

"Yes, it is an unfortunate location. But when one wishes not to be found such places have their uses."

Beau studied his enemy with care for they had an engagement now that nothing could forestall. "You seem to have your fingers in a lot of pies."

Julien smiled. "And stirring, old boy. Stirring."

The suggestion that St. Ives had him in some coil confirmed Beau's half-formed opinion that the man should be shot. His choice? It must be pistols at dawn.

"You will excuse me," he said with all the stiff formality of parliamentary procedure.

"Certainly." Julien smiled. "You will not, however, neglect our social engagement?"

"My seconds will call on yours directly."

"Perfect."

"Damnation!"

Beau took in Guy's appearance at a glance. His eyes were red-rimmed and sunken. His hair stood in points on his head, and his finely chiseled mouth hung loose in surprise. The room beyond him appeared to have been tossed by a giant hand. The chamber pot, alas, had not been tossed often enough. To judge by the stench from those in the neighboring rooms, all were long overdue for an emptying.

Guy refused to be cowed by the stare bent on him. He had not intended to be found since returning from Chapel Hill. He had things to think about, lots of things, and his faculties worked better when liberally oiled by brandy. He had applied himself to this effort with a diligence to make most any other brother proud. But then he had had the misfortune to get Beau as a brother.

Standing in his doorway none too steadily, he matched his older sibling scowl for scowl. "If you've come to ring a peal over my head, consider it done."

"I should be glad to, if I thought you would heed my words."

Beau swung out an arm to stop Guy from closing the door in his face. "We must talk."

Guy swung away from the door and flung himself into a nearby chair. "'Od's body, Beau. A fellow may indulge his tastes in his own rooms if he's a care to."

"His rooms." The deceptively soft tone warned Guy of the blast to come. "You don't pay a farthing toward the upkeep of these rooms. 'Twould seem, according to the proprietor, the bill is weekly set against my account and so I will have the respect due me!"

Guy stopped just short of rolling his eyes. "Parsimonious prosing don't look good on you."

"Piety has nothing do with it. You may entertain the whole of Haymarket's whores here for all I care. As long as you do it with your own blunt."

Guy swung one leg over the other in an attempt at nonchalance. "Is that what's lit a fire under you? The bill? I am free to spend my allowance as I see fit. It has nothing to do with you."

"Your *debts* do. I don't know that you've spent tuppence of your own allowance this last month."

Guy smiled, reminded that he had come into a small inheritance on his birthday. The smile dissolved when he recalled how it had all flown away on the back of a knob-kneed horse on Derby Day. "I clean forgot."

Beau held back the blast of his temper. The fact that Guy

could barely speak went right to the heart of the matter. "You will behave as if you had not a care in the world. 'Tis time you grew up." He flung a packet into his younger brother's lap.

"What this?"

"Your colors. I bought them for you an hour past."

Guy sat up straight, his ennui departed in an instant. "You what? You could not—have not!"

"Could and have done. Perhaps a tour in the military will show you where your duty to yourself lies."

"Duty to myself? Are you certain it is not duty to you that is required?"

Guy flung the packet onto the floor. "You and your Whig friends are pressing for the war against Napoleon to continue. You would back Wellington on the Spanish Peninsula. Am I to be your battle flag? My life given in the glory of your political ambition?"

Beau grabbed his brother by the front of his coat and lifted him to his feet. "Listen to me, young whelp. I would pay twice that to preserve your hide from moneylenders and sharpsters—"

"I do not thank you for it!"

"I do not ask your thanks. Only that—damn you!—grow up!"

Guy jerked free of his brother's grasp. "I do not recall asking for your help in any matter."

"No." Beau swallowed his wrath. "But you should have and I should have been there for you to ask it."

Guy frowned, certain this sudden softening of his brother's tone must owe itself to the liquor that roared in his head. "What? Are you saying you will pay them?"

Beau smiled. "I will tell you all if you will tell me all."

Guy eyed him suspiciously as Beau stepped over items of clothing and bottles and settled himself carefully on the end of the unmade bed.

"Tell me why you went to see Miss MacKinnon."

Guy jerked. "What have you heard? Damn the bitch—"

A smile of pure satisfaction appeared on Beau's mouth as he clipped his brother neatly under the chin with his fist. He was prepared to be a wise adviser and good counsel, an older clearer head. But most of all, he needed to vent his jealousy that Guy had been to see Jemima. Guy had just given him the excuse.

He caught his brother before he collapsed into the rubbish on the floor. He pulled him close and patted his cheek before he laid the young man out on the bed as tenderly as any mother might her child. After all, this was his brother and Miss MacKinnon might just owe him her life. That made up for a lot.

So, when Guy came to and had recovered himself, they would sit together as brothers and talk and drink and learn a little of each other. Because it was time.

Chapter Thirty

"It is very kind of you to take us all in," Jemima said as she sat to supper with Amelia.

Amelia nodded once but did not look at her. "It is I who should be grateful that you have not put me out. It is your cottage, after all."

Jemima frowned to cover the quick stab of pain her cousin's answer gave her.

Amelia looked equally abashed but said nothing more, only applied herself to the scooping up of a potato from her soup.

The larder in the kitchen was mostly destroyed. What was left had been picked over by nimble hands during the night. Cook and Mary had come upon boys digging in the debris in the early morning after the first day and run them off. Since then Jemima had ordered her gardener to take a musket and his dog, and patrol the perimeter of the house each night until she could salvage what was left. In all else an otherworldly quiet had descended around her.

A cry from Pru's newborn was the only other sound in the house.

Amelia puckered her face in disapproval. "She will not even try to feed the babe properly. She lacks proper feeling. Wants nothing to do with it."

Jemima didn't answer. She, too, had noticed how seldom Pru looked at the babe and fed her only when others could not longer bear its crying.

"Perhaps she just needs time to adjust," Jemima said after a moment.

"She just wants a horse whipping," Amelia answered. "To have such a gift! And be ungrateful. After all you've done."

"And you are doing." Jemima added a smile to her words. "You are wonderful with the babe. You know just how to hold and swaddle her."

Amelia pinkened. "I've helped a nanny or two in my time. I once thought to have a child of my own."

Another plaintive wail wafted through the cottage, halting Amelia's spoon halfway to her mouth.

" 'Ere!" came an aggravated cry from the next room. "Give over yer squawlin'. Me tits is sore!"

Amelia set down her spoon with a force that splashed the contents of the bowl over the edge.

Jemima shared her feelings. "Do you think we should hire a wet nurse?"

Amelia looked up with a smile. "I'll see to it. We'll have to go beyond Chapel Hill."

Jemima nodded. Neither of them had spoken to the matter on both their minds. That was that their neighbors had allowed Jemima's house to burn to the ground.

But Miss Amelia stood up, as if her mission in life had just been handed back to her. "I'll walk over the hill. 'Tis midsummer. The sun will stay high for hours yet."

Jemima did not ask what her purpose was. They both cast guilty eyes at the bedroom where the new life among them wailed in discontent to find herself thrust so suddenly into this unfriendly world.

"How will we find room for a wet nurse and her child,

if she has one?'' Jemima cast a glance about the tiny parlor beyond the kitchen where they sat to table. It was tight quarters in the cottage with three women and a babe. Her servants had had to return to their homes. Only Cook came daily to make meals.

"I suppose we could contrive something in the stables until . . .'' She let the thought hang. Until what? She rebuilt Haversham House? Until she found another place? Where? Until she left Chapel Hill altogether? And went where?

The wounds were too fresh. She shook her head. She could not think of any of it yet.

"We could soak a clean rag in milk,'' Amelia said suddenly. "I remember seeing a doctor do that once, to get some fluid in a child who was too sick to drink. Mayhap the babe will suck a bit of nourishment that way.''

Jemima smiled at her. "Cook and I can see to that. You find us a wet nurse.''

It was still a shock. Though he was prepared for it, the site of the charred remains of a place he had visited only once shook him to his heels. To think that his lovely Jemima might have been burned up like it by the same heavenly blast that lit the inferno!

Beau shook a little more and dismounted.

He had instantly liked Haversham House very much. Like its owner it had been graceful and pretty without pretentiousness. Within its walls the rooms were friendly, worn with use and yet lovingly maintained. It boasted no gilt or elaborate finials or painted ceilings, but was lovely for all that. Not only a house but also a home. And now it was gone.

The roof and second story had caved in like the sunken mouth of a toothless old man. Thin fronds of smoke still uncurled from the rear, near the kitchen chimney, the only part left fully standing. As he carefully picked his way past the main entrance, Beau saw empty holes where lead glass

windows had hung only hours before. And his heart ached
for Jemima. Somehow he knew it was more than a monetary
loss for her. For nine years she had huddled away here,
nursing a pain none could adequately conceive of. He had
come here to change that.

If she would allow it.

He found her without looking. He knew that she would
not be far away. He thought to find her treading lightly
among the ashes, looking for salvageable items. He expected
to find her careworn and sad, tears standing in her eyes and
infinite grief in her expression. But the first hint he had of
her nearness was laughter.

She was on her knees in the grass, wiping a hand over a
framed portrait. She picked it up and he saw the painted
shape of a woman smeared by soot. As she approached,
Jemima handed it to a maid and said, "I found Mama.
Perhaps we shall find Papa's portrait, too."

As if he had called out to her, she suddenly turned and
looked directly at him. That is where the picture of a lighthearted lady ended.

She and her clothes were streaked with soot, making vivid
again how much she had been through. He hair was unbound
this once, falling down her back in a thick tangle. She looked
young and impossibly pretty. But for Guy, she might be dead.

The shiver that ran through him this time was not of fear
but from the power of the love he bore her. It had been nine
years since he had tried in earnest to make a woman know
how much she was loved by him. That time he had failed.
He must not fail again.

Jemima was not surprised to see Lord Bellaire, had only
wondered how long it would be, if he did decide to come.
He had come to see Pru, of course. Guy would have gone
to his brother with the news of the birth. While she now
knew it was not his, nor Guy's, she knew he would come
all the same, if only to gloat.

She moved toward him with a pleasant but wary expression. "I am sorry to meet you in my dirt, but there is no change to be had."

"No, of course not." He was amazed she had found even a portrait whole. "You must allow me to take you to an inn where you may wash and change. I am certain for a price the innkeeper can find clothes for you."

She smiled. "I am not made of so fine a stuff that I will crack or wilt with a dusting of dirt. I am fine. I have taken up residence with my cousin Amelia who lives in a cottage just there."

He swore under his breath as he noticed the broken blisters in the palm of the hand she pointed with, and reaching out, he took possession of her hand.

"They will heal," she assured him as he grasped her other hand to inspect it. It too was full of broken and bleeding sores.

Furious that she had been injured, Beau felt again the quaking inside him that he might now be mourning her bones instead of staring back into her lovely gaze. He lifted both her hands and kissed the back of each.

"Don't!" Alarmed by the simple touch, she tried to pull away but he would not release her.

He held her wrists carefully as he said, "Guy told me what occurred. And how the villagers did not turn out with aid."

She saw in his face a savagery more fierce than she would have expected; anger locked in an iron grip. She remembered how he had fought the smithy, swiftly, economically, and with deadly intent. She did not envy any man he would call enemy. But her cause was not his battle to fight.

She looked away. "A consequence of my fall from grace. I have been shunned by all these last weeks."

"They are ignorant, churlish, spiteful and full of malice. If there is any justice, it will come home to roost with them."

Jemima shook her head. "I am full-up with the matter of

vengeance and revenge. I have learned it is impossible to seek one without bringing the other upon one's head.''

He nodded in understanding. "So what will you do now?"

This time her smile would not hold. "I do not know. I do not think I can live here any longer. But I have nowhere else to go."

Beau almost mentioned St. Ives but thought better of it. There was yet a matter to be settled between them and he would not willingly throw her into his adversary's arms. "Emma would like to see you again. Why not take rooms again in London?"

Jemima frowned. "I do not think I should like being shunned by strangers any more than by my neighbors." She looked up at him, her natural reserve back in place. "But I suppose you think it no more than I deserve."

"Deserve?" Without any warning, he pulled her into his arms and kissed her quite soundly.

Jemima shoved him away when he gave her the chance. "If you think that one indiscreet moment with you means that I am never again to have say-so over the time and manner in which I might—"

He glowered down at her, his face all aggression and anger, the cause of which she could not fathom. But then his arms were sliding around her shoulders again to bring her tightly up against his chest.

"I am sorry, Jemima." One hand came up to smooth her cheek. "I am sometimes an impatient man. But what occurred here! It was cruel and unfair."

Jemima closed her eyes. His warm palm was like a fire on her chill cheek and she welcomed it. She had been wrong to send him away as she had. She had had two long miserable weeks in which to realize that her actions had been unjust to a man who had asked her to marry him. It was perfectly natural for him to want to hold her and console her. She wanted to be here, in his arms. But he must not know how frightened she was of the future. Knowing that her desires so exactly matched his own was far more dismaying than if she did not share his passion. For now there was no possibility of a future between them. When she had gotten over the shock of the past days, reason would reassert itself into both their minds. He could not wed her without the scandal of it ruining him. And she would not, though every fiber in her being denied that fact, become his mistress. And they would both face the impossibility of it all.

Beau's thoughts ran remarkably close to hers. Yet he remembered how he barged in on her two weeks before, indignant and wrathful, waving the gazettes that printed the damnable cartoons of them together and blaming her for problems there were in fact of his own making. He did not know how to apologize for that, or if any trace of his actions could be forgiven by her. He had thought his life in shambles. Looking at her just now, framed by the burned-out cinder that had been her home and refuge, he knew he had never at any time suffered as she did.

When he spoke, his voice was as deep and dark as the dusk gathering about them, and just as prosaic. "If you will not come back to London with me, allow me at least to buy you a good dinner."

Jemima looked back toward the cottage. "I cannot leave Pru alone." She turned back to him with a reserved glance. "Would you like to see the child?"

"It is not mine."

"*She,* you wretch. She is a girl."

"So Guy told me." He felt her shiver as his fingers trailed down the curve of her jaw, and he smiled. She was not indifferent to him. "For you to think that I could turn out a woman who bore my child!"

Jemima turned her face into his coat to hide her embarrassment. "I did not know you then."

"Yes, but now you do."

The question hung in the air between them for a few seconds. "No, I do not now think you capable of such enmity."

"That is something." Jemima felt tears gather as his hand slid, warm and comforting, to the back of her neck. "And for the other, that I willfully took her to my bed against her will?"

Jemima swallowed her emotion. "I do not doubt that it might not have been against her will."

"What about against mine?"

Jemima leaned back and looked up at him. His gaze was strangely lit by the evening sky.

"The jade had found a way into the house and helped herself to my bed. I found her there, naked, after I was undressed for the night. I suppose she decided after following Guy to London that gracing the bed of an elder brother would bring better rewards than that of the younger. It was the devil's own luck Guy barged in. When I saw his face and realized what he thought—" Beau shrugged. "It was unforgivable. But in that instant I knew he was cured of her. And that is what I wanted. She made no claim on Guy then. She must have discovered she was with child afterward. Guy has forgiven me. I hope you can."

And then his mouth was once more on Jemima's.

After a few moments, she turned away from his kiss. The tears came quickly, her sobs muffled by the fabric of his coat as he cradled her head.

Beau stroked her back and was silent.

When her sobs subsided, he lifted her face in his hands and kissed away the soot-streaked tears from her eyes and cheeks and then he took her trembling mouth in his.

She tasted of home. Not the kind made out of brick and mortar, but that place that every heart searches for until it is found, or the searcher is no more. Somehow he knew words were not adequate to the task of convincing her. But he had other persuasions at hand.

He picked her up in his arms and carried her to his horse.

"Where are we going?" she demanded as he placed her in the saddle.

He came up behind her and put his arms about her. "To show Chapel Hill how little a lady may be humbled by their spite."

And to her utter astonishment he did just that. Holding her up before him, he took the main road into town. He rode slowly, confidently, with his head high and his arms about her, steadying her against all the buffets of the world.

The children came running first, as if they sensed that this was no ordinary journey through town. As they reached the lane that led to the village green, a few adults hurrying home for supper stopped to stare. Not by glance or action did Beau acknowledge their presence. He rode slowly along, aware of shutters opening in houses on either side of the green, aware of murmurs as they passed, aware of the woman in his arms who shivered but did not cower.

Not a word was said on either side. But everyone knew why he did what he did. No one could look on the lady up before him in her soiled and tattered gown, smell the smoke still in her clothes and hair, see her sooty face and not know that, in part, it was their doing. And they were shamed by the knowledge.

When Beau at last turned his mount and headed back out of town, there was first silence. Then a hard word spoken between neighbors. More words followed and then accusations until guilt turned to anger and shame turned to resentment and doors slammed and suspicions flared, and the first of many uneasy days gripped Chapel Hill. They could not lie to themselves anymore. To protect their own secrets, they had turned against one of their own. Yet suspicion feeds on itself. They now knew they could no longer trust one another. Who would be next?

Chapter Thirty-One

"What is this place?"

They had been riding for almost an hour when Beau turned in his mount at a stile, and she saw in the distance a house with a candle in the window and smoke at the chimney.

"It is the country home of a gentleman friend. He's most often in Town. He lent its use to me for a few days."

"Were you that certain of me?" she asked in a small voice.

"I was that certain that you must have a proper place to rest," he lied. "You need a bath and food and a refreshing rest. That is what this place has to offer you. It is all prepared."

She moved restlessly against her shoulder. "What will you tell his servants?"

He had known the question would come. "That you are ill and that I brought you here to make passionate love to you while you are too weak to defend yourself."

She lifted her head from his shoulder in a quick motion,

and he laughed at the outraged expression she turned to him. "Would you rather I tell them that you are my new mistress and I've run off with you that we may tryst in peace?"

She started to laugh but it lodged in her throat and she could not match his bravado. "What will they think of me?" she asked when she had recovered.

He kissed her brow. "The world may mind its own damn business for a change!" Then more seriously he asked, "Do you really care?"

Jemima thought about it, remembering all the gossiping and sniping of the past weeks, and shook her head. "I don't think I can fall any lower."

He tightened his arms about her. "Do not say that. Nothing and no one will ever be allowed to hurt you again."

She leaned her head back against his shoulder, willing this once for him to take on the burden of her world. Time enough tomorrow to worry about the future.

She sat ramrod straight in her chair. It was one thing to be thought a mistress. Quite another to behave as one. Across from her Lord Bellaire was being served a pair of spit-roasted squabs. While he had waited below, she had very reluctantly allowed herself to be ushered upstairs by a very motherly maid who clucked over her soot and wounds and promised to have her "sorted out in a tick."

Amazingly, she had. There was a copper hip tub of hot water waiting for her. As she soaked there in half-asleep drowsiness, the maid washed the soot and cinders from her hair and then very carefully cleaned her hands and then bandaged them with linen strips. She was given a sherry for her health and then a cup of tea and biscuits. Then she was tucked into bed with sheets smelling of summer sunshine.

She slept only an hour, for she was much too nervous

about spending the night beneath the same roof as Beau to give exhaustion more than minimum due.

She awakened to find a clean chemise and stockings and gown waiting for her. Beau, it seemed, had thought of everything. He must have brought them from London when he heard of the fire. The gesture struck her as impossibly sweet. She had learned enough about suspicion and conjectures not to heed the tiny malicious voice that whispered, "Whose are they?" They were hers, because he brought them for her.

With her hands bound, she needed help getting dressed. As she stood and allowed the maid to dress her, she could not help but muse upon the advantages of becoming a rich man's mistress, if this were a foretaste.

He was waiting for her below, with a book in one hand and brandy in the other. He rose quickly at the sight of her, delighted, it seemed, with her appearance. But he only said, "You are awake. I rather thought you would spend the night abed."

Jemima could not meet his gaze as he said this, for they were not entirely alone with servants about. Something in the timbre of his tone told her he was teasing her in a suggestive manner.

"Are you hungry?"

"Famished," Jemima admitted.

He came forward and took her hands in his and examined the bandages. "Are you in very much pain?"

"Very little," she answered truthfully.

He said blandly, "I've always admired the Empire style, but I must confess that no other lady of my acquaintance reveals its full advantages in exactly the way you do." His gaze lowered to her bodice where the swell of her breasts rose high above the simple square-cut neckline of her gown. When his gaze met hers again, it was full of frank admiration.

"We must go to the opera sometimes. I seem to remember a gown I'm even more fond of."

Jemima ignored his compliment and moved past him into the room he had occupied. "It is a lovely place."

"Do you like it? Perhaps you would like to own it."

She held her breath. Was he offering her a slip on the shoulder so soon? "Is it for sale?" she asked faintly.

"It could be for the right price."

Nothing in his voice gave away his intention.

"Perhaps I shall inquire." There, let him make of that what he would.

And so here they sat, with the width of a beautifully polished table between then and enough food to feed her, Amelia, Pru, Cook, Mary, the undermaids and the gardener's family. But she could think of nothing but the handsome man across from her. He, too, had changed into an evening coat of deep blue and buff breeches. A simple set of folds formed his neckcloth. Informal country wear, but he gave it distinction. She did not know him in his world and suddenly she wanted very much to see him in it, at his side.

Under the guise of eating his meal, Beau admired her with a concentration he usually reserved for government business. Her cream silk gown suited her. He had chosen right. And he thought he would never prefer her hair other than it was tonight, brushed up and back to hang from a topknot in simple waves. Scattered tendrils had fallen about her brow and nape, softened the severe line. It made her appear younger even though she had reached no advanced age.

He thought again of how Guy had described her in mob cap and shapeless smock with those horrid spectacles perched on her nose and smiled. Old, he'd called her. A dowd! He could not imagine that women aged so swiftly or that beauty could transform to dowdiness practically overnight.

Beau chuckled to himself when he caught her eye. Young men had no imagination. They could not see beyond the obvious. It took a man of experience to see beneath the layers and discern the mysteries of the female form. For instance, at this moment, he was imagining in exact detail the shape of the breasts behind her bodice that he had only once held and tasted. The memory came so strongly he shifted in his seat.

"Tell me, Miss MacKinnon, what do you see as your future?" Beau asked at length when their meal was nearly finished.

"I had not in truth given it much thought." Jemima chose her words carefully. "I suppose I shall be first in need of a roof over my head."

"After that?"

"I am possessed of a goodly inheritance and so shall continue as an independent woman."

He noted her slight emphasis on the word. "You set a great store by your independence."

"Certainly. Gentlemen do so out of hand."

"Yes, but with our independence comes a great deal of responsibility."

"Do you mean labor? Or management? Ladies and certain women have great responsibilities in their lives. Men merely rule nations. Women rule the world."

"You, no doubt, seek an illustration to be made in that speech."

"Of course. Nations rise and fall; empires ebb and flow. But the life of a woman changes little, which means hers is the stronger, more important part."

He did understand her to a point, but because she was talking now more than she had since he arrived at Haversham House, he prodded her just to hear her speak. "I should think just the opposite supposition might be derived from your example. Women's work is so rudely simple that not even mighty events can topple it for it has no other foundation than bare existence.''

"It is so fundamental to life, I expect you mean," Jemima answer primly. "Without a means for food, clothing and shelter, there is no life.''

"Precisely. Men toil to build that roof, grow the grain, raise the wool.''

"And at the end of the season there is lumber, grain and wool. Women make of it a home, a meal and clothing. The rude elements are but an elaboration of what Nature herself provides. Women spin, weave, crush, mix, form and cook. They sew, tat, embroider, dye, foment and churn into being the things that make life little more than rude animal life.''

"And yet men are great creators. They build houses, roads, bridges, ships—''

"Munitions, war and ruin.''

"Governments, medicine—''

"First women's work. Call them witches, sorceresses, or seers, medicine was first women's work.''

"Philosophy, science, literature—''

"I should not wonder but that the first fabrication was told by Eve to Adam in connection with the apple. And that makes storytelling women's work first.''

"Touché, Miss MacKinnon.''

She smiled at him. The saucy exchange had put the color back into her cheeks. "You should not give in so easily, sir. You all but had me.''

"The night is young, Miss Jemima." Beau smiled a smile that made her blush. "But there you are correct. Men and women cannot do without each other for all they may rail at the necessity.''

He pushed back from the table. "Do you play cards, Miss MacKinnon?''

"Tolerably well." Jemima rose in answer to his lead.

"Shall we play for shillings?''

322   *Laura Parker*

"I have no shillings with me."

He smiled at her, admiring again how the sheer skirts of her gown skimmed her body with tantalizing effect. "Then we might play for other stakes."

Jemima took the arm, he offered her and they moved to where a smaller gaming table had been unfolded for their use.

She had not played V*ingte Et Un* in some time, though it was simple enough. Each player hopes to acquire cards that summed to no more than twenty-one but more than the sum of other player's hand. They had agreed to play for tuppence, the amounts to be kept on a pad for later tallying. Even so, she kept her gaze fastened on the table as though she played for her life.

Content for the time being to simply watch her, Beau lost several hands in a row to carelessness.

Finally she sat back in annoyance. "If you were not interested in the game, my lord, you might have said so at once."

Her consternation was so honestly bare that he could not keep from laughing. "Perhaps if the stakes were more to my liking, my interest might be more firmly fixed."

Greatly daring, Jemima met his mocking gaze across the width of the small table. "What do you suggest?"

The candlelight gleamed pure silver in his hair and threw in to sharper relief the heartily masculine angles and planes of his face. "I suggest a game where hearts are the wager. The winner takes all. The loser must submit all."

Jemima felt the push of nervous laughter at the back of her throat. "Are you propositioning me, Lord Bellaire?"

" 'Twould seem each would be equally at the mercy of the other. If you win, I am yours to command."

"And if you win?"

Beau almost felt sorry for her. Admitting to her own desire would be hard for her, perhaps the most difficult thing she had ever done. He knew her story, but he did not know her side. Knowing her but a little, he could not imagine her nine years younger having abandoned herself to a whimsy of passion with another on the day before she was to wed. If she had, and disaster overtook her, then coming to grips with desire in any form after all this time would be still more difficult for her. He wanted to make it easier, but he would make it possible.

He rose from his chair and came and stood before her. When he reached for her, she looked back over her shoulder toward the kitchen.

"They have been dismissed for the night."

The startled gaze she brought back to his made his voice even more tender. "This is no trap, no brutal seduction. I want to make love to you. And you, sweeting, proved on Derby Day that you want very badly to make love to me."

"I see you have reasoned it out thoroughly to your advantage," she said coolly.

"No, I have reasoned it out to our equal benefit. You will benefit, if you desire it."

Jemima at last refused to meet his eye. "And if I refuse?"

His hands found her shoulders and squeezed lightly. "I will not force you. I will not take selfishly what I hope you will want to offer. I'm considered an accomplished lover by those who've shared my bed."

"Letters of recommendation won't be required," she answered in a stifled voice.

He pulled her gently into his arms, smoothing a hand down her back so that she was forced to step in close to him. "I love you, Jemima." His arms tightened as she started to pull away. "You need not answer. I do not need assurances or lies. But I know you are not indifferent to me. Tell me what I must say and do to bring you across the line of your uncertainty."

"If you do not know, I cannot help you," she said under her breath.

He kissed her temple, which was by his lips. "Shall we sit again to table and play a few more hands of that damnable game? Or are you ready to move to the winner's circle and receive your prize?"

He caught her chin in his fingers so that she had to look at him. "What shall it be, Jemima?"

"Am I the winner?"

"By my reckoning. Or would you rather the option be taken out of your hands?"

"No." The novelty of the moment was not lost on her. "No, I believe I am up to the stakes." She lifted an eyebrow. "It is winner takes all?"

He smiled back. "And loser forfeits all."

"What sort of forfeit?"

"I am at your disposal."

Jemima thought about all the ways in which she might have come to this moment, as a bride in white nightdress, quailing on a bed, ready to submit to her new lord and master. The image had always left her feeling quite like a roast upon a platter. An unappetizing image when one was the supper.

But something in the way he phrased his challenge, this sense that she might be the diner as well as the dish, delighted a quite shocking aspect of her character that she had never before suspected to exist.

The wanton in her stirred.

"You are thinking rather long for a lady with a ready wit," he said after a lengthy pause.

She lifted her head. "What is good for the Goose is good for the Gander, you will agree?"

Beau felt the floor shifting under him, but something twinkling in the depth of her eyes made him suspect that the risk was going to be worth it. "I agree."

She lifted her arms up to loop them about his neck. "Then show me how to kiss you properly."

He grinned. The challenge was translated into action as he bent and placed his mouth over hers. He kissed her urgently.

Jemima shut her eyes, allowing herself to feel every nuance of his touch, to hold it, study it, try to understand why the simple touch of skin to skin could produce a sensation like spinning about with arms spread. Behind her eyes she felt the brush of his lips, warm and moist, first firm then seeking on hers. The wet length of his tongue moved strongly into her mouth and this time she did not retreat. She had asked for the lesson and as all good pupils do, she sought to respond in kind, to show that she was paying attention and could follow the leader.

"May I show you more?" he murmured against her lips.

"Yes . . . please."

Smiling his kiss, Beau pressed her more firmly to him, brought her legs against his and pressed the hard jut of his hip into the slim curve of her stomach. He wanted her to know all of him, learn all of him, just as he wanted to know her intimately and thoroughly.

Jemima felt his hand at her back, plucking the laces that held her gown together. Wherever they touched—her breasts, her stomach, her hips, her thighs—she felt a tightening of her body and a corresponding tautness in him. He was moving her backward in a kind of dance until she felt the game table press firmly against the back of her thighs. He moved his hands to her waist, spun her around, and then pulled her to him again, pressing his knee strongly between her legs, parting them. She caught her breath as the hard muscle of his trouser-covered thigh brushed the inside of hers and then his hip pressed close to the center of her desire.

"No . . . wait!"

Beneath her hands, the muscles of his neck and shoulders

became rigid with the effort to hold still. "What do you command, Jemima?" His voice sounded trapped deep in his chest.

"That you . . . I can't keep up."

His laughter communicated itself through his body though he made no sound. "Give me but a little time, sweeting, and you will surpass me."

His hands ran in a heavy caress down her back and over the flare of her hips where he began to gather the slim silhouette of her gown with his fingers. She felt the chill of the evening upon her calves, then the back of her thighs. This time when his knee parted hers, his long warm fingers were under her bare buttocks and he lifted her up astride his thigh. With his kiss to distract her, he held her there while she rode the long slow strokes of his leg that surged into her, teasing, demanding, begging a response. Then, in the secret darkness of her core, she felt the touch of his hand and yielded to the sweet waves of sensation flowing thick as honey through her body.

Aware of her every shuddering breath, Beau knew the instant she reached the invisible barrier between yearning and fulfillment. But he wasn't quite ready to take her there yet. She did not yet know what he was capable of, or what she was capable of.

He lifted his mouth from hers but held her high on his thigh so that her every shift, however small, eased and teased his arousal. "What now, Jemima?" His voice was a dark whisper against her ear.

Jemima gripped his shoulders, breathless, dizzy, and uncertain of what came next. She lifted her mouth to his, her tongue sweeping over his lips with deliberate slowness, her hands gliding slowly up and down his shoulders until the hypnotic rhythm smoothed the fraying edges of her courage. She did want him, wanted his kisses, wanted to know what it would be like to be loved by him. He had said he wanted to make love to her. It was what she wanted too.

"Show me how to love you," she said against his mouth.

"As you command," he answered.

He licked her earlobe and then plunged his tongue hot and moist into the orifice and as she shivered he said, "This pleasure is for you, my forfeit to your victory."

He pushed down the bodice of her gown and, before she could speak the instinctive protest he felt stiffen her body, he bent his head to catch a breast in his mouth.

In astonishment Jemima absorbed the moist heat of his tongue on her breast. And then he suckled her so strongly, it seemed he was drawing her up and out of her body into his. He had said he was the loser and so must forfeit his all to her. Yet everywhere he touched her, the reverse happened. With only a touch, he seemed to claim another part of her. She ached where he broke contact only to be consumed with desire in the next portion he then touched and kissed and licked and caressed until it seemed she was on fire from head to toe.

Finally he loosened his embrace, letting her slide ever so slowly down his muscular thigh until her toes touched the floor. "Much as I would like you spread upon the carpet at our feet, you deserve better. You must tell me if I may come up to your bed."

He knew he risked a great deal in handing the choice back to her. Her face was flushed with passion, but her eyes were wide with a knowledge of herself she had not possessed before.

Jemima looked up at him and spoke the truth. "I do not think I can wait that long."

She heard his chuckle and then he was cradling her head with both hands, first dragging his lips back and forth across hers and then licking at her, drawing shivery sighs from her with the velvet wale of his tongue.

As their mouths melted into another deep kiss, he caught her weight against him, murmuring incoherent promises as, by mutual desire, they slid to the floor.

The carpet was no sooner beneath her bare hips than he was pushing her onto her back. But she had work of her own to do. She reached for and found his cravat, tearing at the loops, and then she was pulling his shirt free from his trousers. It was a daunting experience to meet the heat and weight of his naked body emerging from the cloth. Yet he felt so good and strong and human that she could not resist touching him, rubbing her hands over his chest, smooth but for a few silky strands of hair and then his shoulders which seemed much broader when freed from his jacket. Heavy muscles strapped his back beneath his skin and then he was leaning over and on her and she stopped thinking and comparing. The Bluestocking deserted her for the shameless Sensualist.

She felt him reach under her gown, bunched at her waist, then his fingers were on her and inside her, moving with exquisite friction until she could no longer catch her breath but held it against the building pulsating tension she could not understand.

Then the first peak of pleasure burst over her and she felt the earth drop away.

Sensation rolled over sensation, each banking the other in a pleasure so strong and sweet she moaned in joy.

Beau moved quickly over her, prodding her legs a little more apart with his knee. He kissed her mouth then dipped his head to kiss each breast and then he smiled at her wondrous expression. "There is more, Jemima. With you have a full portion?"

She did not hesitate. "Yes!"

He came into her slowly, whispering words she did not quite understand but did not need to. It was his voice, full of wonder and joy and passion of her making that made her

clutch at him and urgently return his thrusts. When she heard
his coarse cry and felt his release, she knew he had become
part of her as much as she was now part of him.

She awakened in the night and for one wild moment
thought she was alone. But when she tried to move, the
weight of a heavy arm lay across her waist.

"Sleep, my love," Beau murmured. "You have exhausted
me."

Jemima lay back and smiled into the night. The first time
had been too feverish and bright for her to recall in detail.
She had been all need and then joy and shock at the sur-
passing ecstasy of the moment.

But the second time, in full knowledge of her ignorance
and indecency, she had experienced a shamed dampening
of her joy. The more he tried the more she withdrew, until
he too withdrew and found brandy to extinguish his hopes.
He told her it did not matter, that she found fulfillment once
and that was enough.

Still, she had felt cheated as she readied for bed. And
when an hour had passed and sleep was no nearer than the
dawn, she had gone back downstairs and found him sitting
in a chair with his shirt still open and his breeches open and
his hand working in his lap.

He looked abashed to be found so. But she came down
to him anyway and knelt before him as much out of curiosity
as in seeking comfort. And after a moment he reached for
her hand and brought it to his arousal. He filled her hand
with heat and strength and trembling life. He murmured
deep in his throat as he pressed her hand to his flesh and
wrapped her fingers tightly about it. And then he showed
her how to please him.

He grew and thickened under the friction of her hand,
becoming ever more restless until he could stand no more

and bent and lifted her off the floor into his lap. She straddled him and then he arched up under her, finding and filling her so perfectly that she reached the peak before she could fully comprehend it. This time there was no tenderness, no slow feeding of himself to her. He moved quickly, almost frantically in and out of her, all control gone. And it was a revelation. He climaxed in a volcano of power, gripping her so tightly she could scarcely breathe.

And when the world was again steady, he tucked her head under his chin and laughed. She did not ask him what amused him. Finally she heard him say, "May I lose at cards to you every day for the rest of my life."

Chapter Thirty-Two

"She's gone? Are you sure?"

"I found this when I woke." Amelia held out the slip of paper. On it had been written in charcoal with a stick from the hearth. *TAK UR*.

Jemima sat down slowly. "What shall we do?"

"Nothing." Henrietta held the child who for a change was sleeping contently. Amelia had sent for Henrietta and Ianthe for counsel. Both had arrived before Jemima returned to Chapel Hill at midday. "Miss Amelia has found a wet nurse and 'tis clear as glass the mother doesn't want the child."

"That will do for now," Jemima said, thinking quickly of the practicalities, "but not forever."

Ianthe leaned over Henrietta's shoulder to peer down into the babe's face. "She's a sound child, for all she is small. But that's soon answered."

Jemima shook her head, wondering what this new responsibility would cost her. Though she would face up to it, a little part of her wished the child at the wind. She was still over the boughs in love and in awe of the power of that much-maligned emotion, lust.

Beau had brought her back to Chapel Hill over his better judgment. He left her behind only when she promised to return with the carriage that he would immediately send down from London to fetch her. It was all very high-handed of him, and possessive, and wonderful. But even a wonderful man had his limits.

Would Beau allow her to care for an illegitimate child she had once accused him of fathering? He had proven himself to be all that she ever hoped he might be. He was a good man, a just man, and generous. But to take on the upbringing of Pru's child seemed, even in her newly love-besotted mind, more than he should have to endure. Yet the common alternative, the workhouse, would not do. No, she would not abandon a helpless infant though it cost her more than she as willing to think on just yet. Some other way, there must be—

"About your young man."

Jemima blushed when she looked up and found three pairs of eyes watching her in speculation. She had not said a word to anyone about where she had spent the night and now it seemed unnecessary. "Lord Bellaire has asked me to marry him."

"And so he should!" Henrietta nodded her approval. "You did give him the proper answer?"

"I said I must have time."

"Oh, miss, don't do it." Ianthe sounded very distressed, her pretty face strained by thoughts she would never share with a soul. "If you love him, you must not allow anything to keep you apart."

"She's right." Henrietta began to rock into quiescence again the stirring bundle in her arms. "You must marry his lordship. The sooner the better."

Jemima lifted a brow, the Bluestocking rabble-rouser in her reasserting itself. "Because it is the proper thing to do?"

"Because you love him," Ianthe answered. "You do. 'Tis writ broadly on your face, Miss Jemima." She blushed herself. "I'd give anything to feel . . . Well, you must not allow anything to hold you back."

" 'Tis the proper thing," Henrietta, the vicar's daughter, stuck in a second time.

"What about the babe? Oh, we can't keep calling her the babe. She needs a name."

"What about Faith or Hope?" Henrietta suggested.

"Charity or Prudence," Amelia took up.

Ianthe frowned. "Justice?"

"Temperance!" Henrietta called with a chuckle. "Her mother was in sore need of it."

"Not Fortitude," Jemima said with a smile. "Though she will certainly have need of courage to go with the other virtues."

Henrietta looked down into the tiny red face and said, "What of Eve? The firstborn of a new breed. She shall be reared in the spirit of the LADIES."

"You all have a great deal to say about it, I see." Amelia marched up and scooped the child from Henrietta's arms and gathered her protectively close. "Pru left the babe with me. That makes Eve mine. I shall take care of her as I see fit."

"But you—" Jemima bit her lip. There were a dozen good reasons Amelia should not take on the burden of a by-blow, not the least of which was the practicality of finances. But there, at least, she could help. "I should be happy to support you in this."

"Thank you, but I am not without resources." Amelia held herself stiffly. "I have come into a small inheritance. I cannot think of a better use to put it to than the care of an unwanted child. In fact, I must insist."

"I too should like to take part in Eve's care," Henrietta said. "She will need a strong Christian upbringing if she is to overcome the liability of her birth."

"And her blood," Amelia added. "She has a slut for a mother!"

The vehemence of her cousin's condemnation surprised Jemima. Then she remembered what Amelia had endured to care for the ungrateful Pru while she was away in London. Perhaps she was in a better position to sit in judgment.

"I have no quarrel with the arrangement," Jemima said at last. "Eve will be the luckiest child in England to have you for her mother and Miss Henrietta as guardian of her soul."

Amelia at last permitted herself a small smile. "To have something in this world to love and who, God willing, will one day love one back. That is no small thing."

"No." Jemima agreed with all the gravity of her own new understanding of what it meant to love and be loved. "It is the greatest goodness in the world."

"So then, you will say yes to your young man." Henrietta regarded her with an arch expression.

"I am not certain it will serve. There is his future to think of. A gentleman may soon recover from nearly any infamy. But for him to be daily reminded of what the shortcomings of a notorious wife presents to his hopes? I do not know that even love could long prevail against the injury."

"Then it's no sort of love." Ianthe spoke again at last. "I have thought a great deal on the matter of men and women these last weeks," she declared in a voice grown strong at the back of her musings. "If a man loves a woman, he will make a way. If it is less than love, he will find an excuse."

The truth of her words echoed in the room. Each of them, in her way, had suffered from the lack of an enduring love.

"Miss Ianthe is correct," Henrietta said at length. "My

dear Tom loved adventure better than me. And then another.''

When her friends did not ask what she meant, she flushed up quickly. "So you've known all the while."

'' 'Twas not our business," Jemima said kindly. "Too often we make a meal of scraps that are not ours."

"Not you." Ianthe smiled. "You've shown us how it should be. I am proud to have been part of the LADIES.'' She smiled at Amelia and the babe in her arms. "Just look at what good we've done. Who knows what might have happened to little Eve without our intervention?"

The four of them gathered around the bundle Amelia held, in awe of their own audacity.

"We are like fairy godmothers," Henrietta said. "If a God-fearing body believed in such nonsense."

"I don't know that the evils of gossip is a lesson that can long endure," Amelia added a bit harshly, thinking of the hard road ahead for her foundling.

"Yet retribution is best handled by wiser heads than ours," Jemima agreed.

Henrietta nodded. '' 'Vengeance is mine,' sayeth the Lord."

"What of the villagers?" Jemima voiced, as the alarming thought struck her. "What will they have to say about Eve?"

"I shouldn't worry too much about them!" Henrietta's scathing tone carried the authority of certainty. "Papa is even now working on his Sunday sermon. "It concerns a fallen woman. 'Tis entitled 'Let He Who Is Without Sin . . .' ''

Chapter Thirty-Three

"Is it true that Papa will never marry again?"

Jemima cast a speculative glance on her first visitor since her return to Town two days before. "Who told you that?"

"Aunt Susanna." Emma dabbed at her mouth with her napkin then spread it out again carefully on her lap. "She says Mama was the most beautiful lady in the whole world and that Father loved her so much that he can never love anyone again."

"I see." Jemima had wondered at the wisdom of Beau sending his daughter to spend an afternoon in her company. He had said it was so that Emma might see Monsieur again. Now she wondered if there was a different purpose afoot.

Emma inspected a ginger cookie before popping it into her mouth. "I shall never love anyone."

"Certainly you shall. When you grow up, you will have many suitors and you shall choose one to marry."

"Why did you not marry? Did you not have suitors?"

The frankness of children was new to her, but Jemima

was learning. "I did. Alas, my choice did not end in a match."

"Did you love him very much, as much as Papa did Mama?"

"You are impertinent. But no, I did not love him so much as that."

"I think that is best. If I marry, it will not be for love."

"Why would you say such a thing?"

"Because I think it is unfair to love someone and then leave them. Aunt Susanna says it's a wretched disgrace the way Papa treats me. She says it's because he can't stand to be reminded of Mama and I remind him."

Jemima cast a faint disapproving glance out the window. "Your aunt has a great number of opinions."

Emma nodded solemnly as she very slowly lifted her teacup to her lips without spilling a drop. When she had accomplished a sip and set her cup down again without making a sound, she turned to her hostess with a smile. "I wish someone could make Papa forget Mama. Then perhaps, he would like me better." She cast a shy glance at Jemima. "I believe he likes you very well."

"I like you very well, too," Jemima responded to skirt the issue. "And your father most certainly loves you. Is he not purchasing Monsieur for you?"

"Yes. He is much nicer when you are about."

"Your father is a very important gentleman. Sometime busy gentlemen forget to show their feelings."

"Is that what is wrong between you? Papa forgets to show his feelings for you?"

This time Jemima blushed. Beau had made his feelings all too plain recently. She was the one reluctant to declare a wedding date. And then there was Emma. "The goings-on between adults are complicated, Emma."

Emma reached for her hand and squeezed it. "I am sorry."

The offer of solace from one so young quite touched her. But she was not about to confide her fears in a child.

"Did your father tell you the story of how I came to own Monsieur?"

Emma shook her head.

"Your father is responsible. He is a very brave gentleman, if you do not know it. He saved Monsieur from a crowd who had set their dogs on him."

Emma's eyes bucked wide. "Father did that?"

"That and more." If a bit reluctantly, she reminded herself. "He first saved me from a blacksmith who took—well, who had very bad manners."

"How did Father do that?" Emma demanded doubtfully.

"He punched the smithy in the—er, nose."

"Papa landed him a facer?" Emma cried in delight.

"Wherever did you hear such horrid cant?"

"Aunt Susanna's son Edward is a veritable dictionary of the Fancy," she answered unrepentantly. "He says all Cambridge men are."

"Perhaps so, but it is no language for a lady."

Deflated by Jemima's disapproving tone, Emma subsided. "Yes, ma'am."

Seeing the girl's expression droop, Jemima could not resist. "Now then, to answer your question. Your father did land him a one proper 'un!" She brought up her fist in demonstration. "Right in the breadbasket!"

Emma gave her a doubtful glance but seeing Jemima's smile began to giggle. "I like you."

"And I you. But we must keep this story a secret."

"Why?"

"Because your father is a very great man, but he is also quite modest and would not want this business to be known abroad. Some stories are best kept between friends."

Emma studied her seriously for a moment and Jemima saw in her young vulnerable expression a sense of herself at that age and for a very long time after. "You like Papa, don't you?"

Jemima reached out and took Emma's chin in her fingers. "You are a minx and minxes do not deserve answers to their impertinent questions."

But Emma would not be put off. "Do you like him?"

Jemima looked into that serious face and could not lie. "I like him, Emma. Very much."

Emma took another sip of her tea, her face still serious. "Papa does not like everyone."

"What a curious thing to say, Emma. I'm certain he likes most everyone."

"Papa had his pistols out last night. He was angry that I saw them."

Jemima set her teacup down with a clunk. "What sort of pistols?

"They were in a box. He shut the lid before I could see them properly."

Dueling pistols! Julien had a pair. He had once taken them out and showed them to her as proof of his proficiency in the art.

"Well, I would not bother my head about it. Gentlemen must have their secrets, too."

Yet when Emma had gone Jemima found that she was unable to shake off the touch of fear that had accompanied the girl's revelation. Beau with dueling pistols? Perhaps he had only taken them out to clean them so as to keep them in proper working order. But some sense of unease would not let her be. Finally she sat and wrote a note to her cousin.

She had sent Julien a letter informing him of the fire but received no response. Since arriving in town, she had sent round two more messages. The first was answered by the delivery of Monsieur, complete with a cage on wheels so that he might be conveyed about more easily. The second one, informing him that she was considering Beau's proposal of marriage, received no reply.

She knew he would be hurt, not so much because he had made her a similar offer but because she supposed he would not like being one-upped by anyone. But she owed him the truth. There would be no more hiding, no more shame and secrecy. She was much too happy, even if she had yet to say yes. Lord Bellaire still wanted her as his wife. That was quite enough excitement for one week.

Yet Julien had been acting strangely of late, strangely even for Julien. She was still furious with him for the way he had treated her the last time they were together. She would expect an apology the next time they met. Even so he was the closest family member in her life, and that part of their relationship made her eager to have things patched up.

He was angry, too, but not even Julien would call Beau out to heap his revenge on her.

"He wouldn't!" she whispered low, even though she was alone.

"I will apply for a special license in the morning. Then we may away to be married at our leisure in a place of our own choosing."

Jemima snuggled down next to Beau under the covers, still too much in awe of this new freedom of nakedness to be cavalier about it. She had begun to shiver in the night air. The heat of his body was warming her everywhere they touched.

The candle on the bedside revealed his passion-flushed face from their recent lovemaking. She thought she could not be happier, until he smiled. It was like the sun had suddenly appeared from behind a cloud. "So then all that there is left is for you to say yes, my love."

Jemima nuzzled his bare shoulder. "I am told that once a lady is betrothed, she cannot dispose of any property of her own without her fiancé's approval and consent."

"Have you so much business to attend to?"

"As a single lady I have had the same rights, but for the vote, as a gentleman. I shall not ever allow you to dress me to suit your tastes. Or even choose my gowns."

He ran a hand possessively over her shoulder and then cupped a breast. "I do not wish to choose your gowns, only when and where you wear them. And I will only be interested in undressing you, whenever I can."

Jemima flushed at his boldness. "So then I must think what best suits my interests."

He slid a hand up between her thighs to the apex. "Does this help clear your mind?"

"No." She could scarcely think at all when his hands were on her. Now, for instance, sensation rippled through her like cool fire.

"So then if I wished to sell off your jewels or lease your property I have only to do this"—he cupped her—"to gain your quiescence?"

The laughter in his tone made her want to argue but she had learned a lot about being a woman in a very short time and knew that he did not really want words. What was sauce for the Goose . . .

She leaned forward and licked his firm, warm mouth. Then she let her breasts flatten over his chest as she kissed him.

He released a deep sigh that ended on a groan when she lifted a leg over his hips as if she would straddle him. "I think two can play this game," he said in an unsteady breath between her kisses. "So then, a truce. I will be a merciful and generous master."

She lifted her head and looked at him. "Partners. No man will ever own me."

Beau was suddenly still, aware that while her actions were playful something at the back of her gaze was in absolute earnest.

His lifted his hands and framed her face. "What happened to you nine years ago?"

Jemima flinched. "I can't speak of it."

She tried to slip away, but he caught her by the waist and held her to him. He searched her face as if he thought he might read the answers in her eyes. "Have you never told anyone what really happened?"

"No."

He lifted his head and kissed her very softly. "You should."

Looking into his eyes Jemima felt a vulnerability that surpassed even nakedness. "He did not want me."

The story tumbled out of her, her gullibility, her trusting nature, and finally her fiancé's complicity in her betrayal. "He said Sir Jeremy found bedding virgins loathsome and messy. He set his friend to do the task for him. But in the end, it was about money, about my dowry. He meant to break the betrothal by casting me as an adulteress."

Beau could not speak directly to the matter, worried his reaction would frighten her with its murderous design. Instead her pulled her close until they met from head to toe in a full body embrace. "What happened to this manly paragon?" he asked lightly.

"He died of the influenza a year later."

"Good. It saves me the trouble of calling him out. Though I regret that he shall never know the thrashing he deserved for what he did to you. Yes, I should have enjoyed that very much."

Jemima remembered Beau in the moment before he struck the smithy, strong, resolute, in full command of his power, and felt a sudden rush of gratitude for his sentiment in the matter. Still . . . "One should not speak ill of the dead."

"Some of the dead deserve to be spoke ill of. He was not a man, Jemima, but a sick and weak fellow."

She buried her face in his neck. "Perhaps I was not womanly enough for his tastes."

"You were too womanly, I shouldn't doubt. What sort of man could look at you and not want you?"

"Evidently the whole of London's male society. Mister Holton's was the only offer of marriage I received."

He did not correct her. But to his own knowledge she had received two others, both recent. "An offer of marriage is not a test of a man's feelings, only his intentions. My feelings where you are concerned are often not strictly honorable. I am having that feeling at the moment."

"You are incorrigible!" She protested as he rolled her over and under him.

"I devoutly hope so."

"Wait." She was not done with serious matters. "There is something I must tell you. If we are to be partners, there must be no secrets between us."

"St. Ives asked you to marry him."

"How did you— He told you! *Wretch.*"

Beau was suddenly as serious as she. "When did he propose?"

Jemima shrugged. "You will not believe it. 'Twas the same day you did. He came to see me shortly after."

"Did you tell him I had proposed?"

"I don't think I did. I told him that you had lied about knowing Pru. I thought then it was proof of your guilt."

"And that is why you refused my proposal." Beau tenderly smoothed the hair back from her face. "Why then did you refuse him?"

"I did not believe him serious."

Beau cocked a brow. "And if you had?"

Jemima shook her head. She did not want to think of

Julien as he had been that day. Certainly she would say nothing to Beau to provoke his enmity toward her cousin.

"He isn't the sort of man a lady marries," she said airily. "He is a creature of the senses; he would soon have tired of me."

"Don't believe it." Beau touched her face as if it were the most fragile of things. "I think in his own way, he loves you."

Jemima was silent.

Beau touched her eyes closed with his fingertips. "I think he would not hesitate to kill me if he thought it would eventually bring you back to him."

Jemima smiled behind the blind of his fingers. "Now who is being fanciful?"

Beau was glad she could not see his expression. He bent his head and kissed her quickly. "I wonder. If I had not come to you when I did . . ."

"But you did," Jemima answered and hugged him close.

It was not quite the answer he sought.

Sensing a new uneasiness in him, Jemima reached up and pried his fingers from her eyes so that she could look up into his face. "You would not do anything reckless?"

"Do I strike you as an imprudent man?"

"Not in the main, but—"

He stopped her speech with his mouth and then his tongue and then he was very busy showing her how very reckless he could be with her in his arms.

Much later when each was reassured and just a little more certain of the feelings of the other he said, "Now I have a story to tell you. About a very proud young man who mistook infatuation for love and learned a very hard lesson . . ."

Chapter Thirty-Four

Something awakened Jemima. She sat up in the dark. "Beau?"

He had promised always to leave her before the light of day, to save her honor with her servants, but this was different. He had not awakened her with a kiss to say good-bye.

And then she heard it. From deep in the house came the distinct *click* of a door closing.

She threw back the sheet and hurried to the front windows of her bedroom to look out. The dawn was dove gray and in the mists hanging low on the street she saw a shadow move. He crossed the street and hurried to the corner where a carriage was waiting. The door opened before he reached it and two gentlemen in top hats stepped down to greet him.

Though she had no experience of it, she could think of only one reason gentlemen would gather, fully dressed, before dawn. "A duel!"

She dressed as quickly as she could, feeling hot and cold and a little sick. She did not know what she would do or where to go or how to find them.

She rang her maid's bell and sent poor Mary out into the early morning to find a Bow Street Runner. For a price he might reveal the preferable spots for a duel. She had to prevent Beau from facing Julien.

In some things Julien did not exaggerate. He had killed one man in a duel many years ago and severely wounded another the year of her first and only Season.

With an icy dread, she knew it would be Julien who goaded Beau into it. Who knew what Julien might have said? Had he lied about their encounter in Haversham House? Or had he told the truth and used his own nefarious behavior to bring Beau to a supposed defense of her honor?

"Oh Beau, you dear sweet fool! You should never listen to my cousin."

She had thought she was frightened when Julien had shown his true feelings to her. Yet she had never been in fear of losing more than her dignity. Beau stood to lose his life.

Beneath the canopy of ancient oaks in the heart of the City of London proper lay a dirty white fog thick as wool. One might pass within a few yards of a party of twelve and, but for the strangely carrying quality of voices in the air, not know any other person was about. This morning there were whispers, male and low. The talk was of pistols and paces and when the damned physician would arrive.

When a carriage finally approached, its creaking and clomps of hooves heard long before it appeared out of the mists, a general cry of relief went up. But the figure to emerge was no sawbones. It was distinctly female.

Jemima tumbled out of the hired carriage without a clear idea of what she would do. She need not have worried. Beau saw her and recognized at once who it must be.

"I should have locked you in," he said without preamble when he had walked up to her.

"You have not fought him?" she cried, taking in the fact that he was in his shirtsleeves.

Beau's expression went blank. "Go home, Jemima. There are some affairs of honor that a gentleman cannot explain to a lady."

She grabbed his arm when he would have turned away from her. "You are right," she whispered frantically, aware that even his friends would consider it bad *ton* for her to be here. "I do not understand it. If you love me you would not be preparing to fire upon the only other person in this world I—"

"Love?"

She fell back before the stare he turned on her. "Don't look at me like that. I love you. You know that."

"I do." Beau also knew what it meant to love her. And, like Julien, he was ready to commit murder to keep her. "I cannot explain to you what is to happen here. But if you love me, you will climb back in that carriage and leave this place. I will come to you when I am done."

"If you can," she answered indignantly, and saw her words reflected as reproach for her doubt of his abilities. Yet she could not get out of her mind Julien's victory over two other men. "If you will not listen to reason, perhaps Julien will."

"Do not depend upon it," Beau answered, and went back to checking his weapon.

She turned and ran across the open ground toward the place where she heard other phantom voices.

Julien seemed no more surprised than Beau to see her emerge from the mists. He stood in shirtsleeves holding a pistol negligently in his right hand.

"Puss! I should have known you could not resist the opportunity to witness a duel in your honor."

"It is no honor to me, or either of you!" she answered hotly. "You owe me an apology."

"Doubtless I owe you many. You may have them all, as freely given as the dawn. Is there anything else?"

Jemima tried to speak but her voice caught on a sob.

For the first time Julien looked at her. "You are not crying? No tears for me are needed, Puss."

"Don't kill him, Julien. I love him."

She thought then he would strike her. His gaze turned icy, his face a study in granite. She braced for ugly words, but they did not come. "You think I do not know that?" He looked down at the pistol he held. "Go home, Puss. He is safe."

"You mean you will not fight him?"

The ice began to melt, the granite in his expression softening into strangely tender emotion as he looked back at her. "It is not loaded."

It took several seconds for his words to penetrate her fear and become sensible. Even then they made no sense. "I don't understand."

Julien reached out and ran a finger down her cheek to the corner of her mouth where a muscle trembled. "Soft," he said, watching the horror in her gaze fade. "I know that if I kill your paragon you will never forgive me."

Jemima tried to smile but she did not have the courage. "So then you are prepared to die? With no thought of how I should feel about it?"

He removed his hand from her face, his expression receding back behind a cool and unreadable facade as vague as the mist. His voice held a faint note of contempt. "Have you ever known me to show an ounce of true sentiment for another? I was thinking of myself."

Jemima's mind would not come to order. "I don't— Julien, I do not need you to die for me."

"Perhaps I need it." He watched her now with the disin-

terested gaze of a hawk, curious but remote. "I could not
live with your dislike, Puss. Ah, but if he kills me, I know
you care enough that you will never quite forgive *him*. That
way, even in death, I will know that a part of your heart
belongs to me."

Jemima shook her head slowly. "That is too devious for
me to believe it of even you."

Julien watched her for a moment, more in tune with her
confused feelings than she would ever know. Then he
shrugged. "I would not for love of this world deprive you
of the man you love."

"I—" Jemima could not finish the sentence, and she saw
in Julien's face a longing she could not ever adequately
answer.

"But not enough." The bleak look in his eyes was for
once naked truth. And then it was gone. "So go to him and
take him away before I think better of it and reload."

She turned away, but he caught her from behind when
she would have moved away. "Be nauseatingly happy,
Puss!" he said against her ear. "Make the one and only
noble gesture of an unrepentant rake worth it."

Jemima nodded, unable to soften the truth with a lie. "I
will. Thank you, Julien."

She sat tucked in the curve of Beau's arm as the carriage
carried them home. Once she told him what Julien said,
Beau agreed to simply walk away and come with her.

But she was brooding about it and could no longer hold
her thoughts in silence. "Does it not seem strange that Julien
should only profess his love for me now, after so many
years?"

"No." Beau pulled her closer, as if he held her tight
enough she might be absorbed into him. "He had no need
to risk anything as long as you were tucked away out of

reach of any life other than that he brought to your door. You were his possession, untouched. He might take you out and play with you, but he did not want to share you.''

"I wonder." Tears gathered in her throat, but she swallowed them. She must not cry. That was a silly female thing to do and Lord Beau Bellaire did not seem at the moment to be in the mood for foolishness. The anger that had braced him for a battle to the death still ran like lava beneath his exterior. "Beau, I think you had better kiss me."

Beau did not have to be asked twice. He took her face very gently in his hands and kissed her. But the gentleness would not hold. And, in truth, she did not want gentleness. She wanted that wild hunger that had brought her to him in the first place. That had made her risk reputation and her heart for a chance to experience it. To have come too close to losing it—

"You are crying," he said against her mouth.

"I am not!" she sobbed, and kissed him harder and more frantically until his face was smeared with her tears.

And then she forgot to be afraid for him and for herself because his hands were moving over her, touching her and making her weep with desire.

"I love you," she said finally, holding his head in her hands. "And I know you love me."

He smiled at her. "I have seen men risk their very lives to prove they are not cowards. More afraid of fear than of dying. I have been afraid of love. I am no more. I love you, Jemima."

She did not know that people could make love in a moving carriage. But with an economy of grace and action, he unfastened his breeches, lifted her skirts and entered her in one powerful thrust. Bodies humming in mutual need and affirmation of life, he made love to her with long, slow, deep thrusts that sent the fear scattering and the coach to trembling.

Later, when they were stretched out on her bed behind locked doors, Jemima sank back into reflection. "I know so little of men."

Beau chuckled. "You know enough. Today you have had two men willing to risk life and limb to possess you. Does that not puff up your consequence?"

"No! I feel sick when I think of what might have occurred."

Beau chuckled and shook his head. "You can never then aspire to be part of the *haute ton,* my love. Ladies of great repute are ever at discovering a cause that would make gentlemen fight for their honor."

"Is that what you were doing? Fighting for my honor?"

"I would do anything to keep you. My gun was loaded."

And so Jemima turned into him with that piece of news to keep her in abashed silence on the subject for the rest of her life.

The wedding was a quiet one; the ceremony performed in the chapel of Bellaire Estate, far from the prying eyes of the *ton* and the commoner alike. On Jemima's side were Henrietta and Amelia, with Eve bawling lustily throughout. Mrs. Strickland "could not spare" Ianthe. On Beau's side were Emma, looking as delighted as a bride herself, his stepmother, and his brother, Guy, looking quite splendid in his regimentals. If the brothers were not precisely on loving terms, they did shake hands and Guy signed the register as groomsman.

Julien did not send his regards. She heard he had sailed for Italy. It was said he had become a particular friend of the poet Byron and was thoroughly enjoying the debauched life of a continental.

But Jemima's mind and heart were not with any of her

family and friends as she stepped up into the carriage that would bear her and her new husband toward their new life.

At the end of the ceremony, he had whispered the most shocking suggestion in her ear. She was not certain it was possible. But if it was, she was very much afraid she would never outlive the impression of audacity that had first made her seem in his eyes notorious!